D1550489

Stephen McCranie's

SPACE

BOY

VOLUME 15

Written and illustrated by
STEPHEN McCRANIE

DARK HORSE BOOKS

President and Publisher **Mike Richardson**

Editors **Brett Israel** and **Shantel LaRocque**

Assistant Editors **Sanjay Dharawat**

Designer **Anita Magaña**

Digital Art Technician **Allyson Haller**

STEPHEN MCCRANIE'S SPACE BOY VOLUME 15

Space Boy™ © 2020, 2023 Stephen McCranie. All rights reserved. Dark Horse Books® and the Dark Horse logo are registered trademarks of Dark Horse Comics LLC. All rights reserved. Dark Horse is part of Embracer Group. No portion of this publication may be reproduced or transmitted, in any form or by any means, without the express written permission of Dark Horse Comics LLC. Names, characters, places, and incidents featured in this publication either are the product of the author's imagination or are used fictitiously. Any resemblance to actual persons (living or dead), events, institutions, or locales, without satiric intent, is coincidental.

This book collects *Space Boy* episodes 227–240, previously published online at WebToons.com.

Published by Dark Horse Books
A division of Dark Horse Comics LLC, 10956 SE Main Street,
Milwaukie, OR 97222
StephenMcCranie.com I DarkHorse.com

To find a comics shop in your area, visit comicshoplocator.com

MIX
Paper from
responsible sources
FSC
www.fsc.org   FSC® C016973

First edition: March 2023
ISBN 978-1-50672-878-0
10 9 8 7 6 5 4 3 2 1
Printed in China

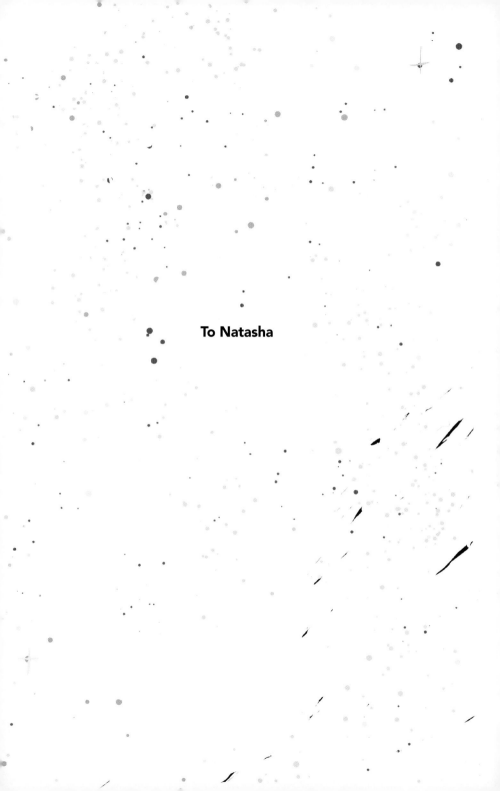

To Natasha

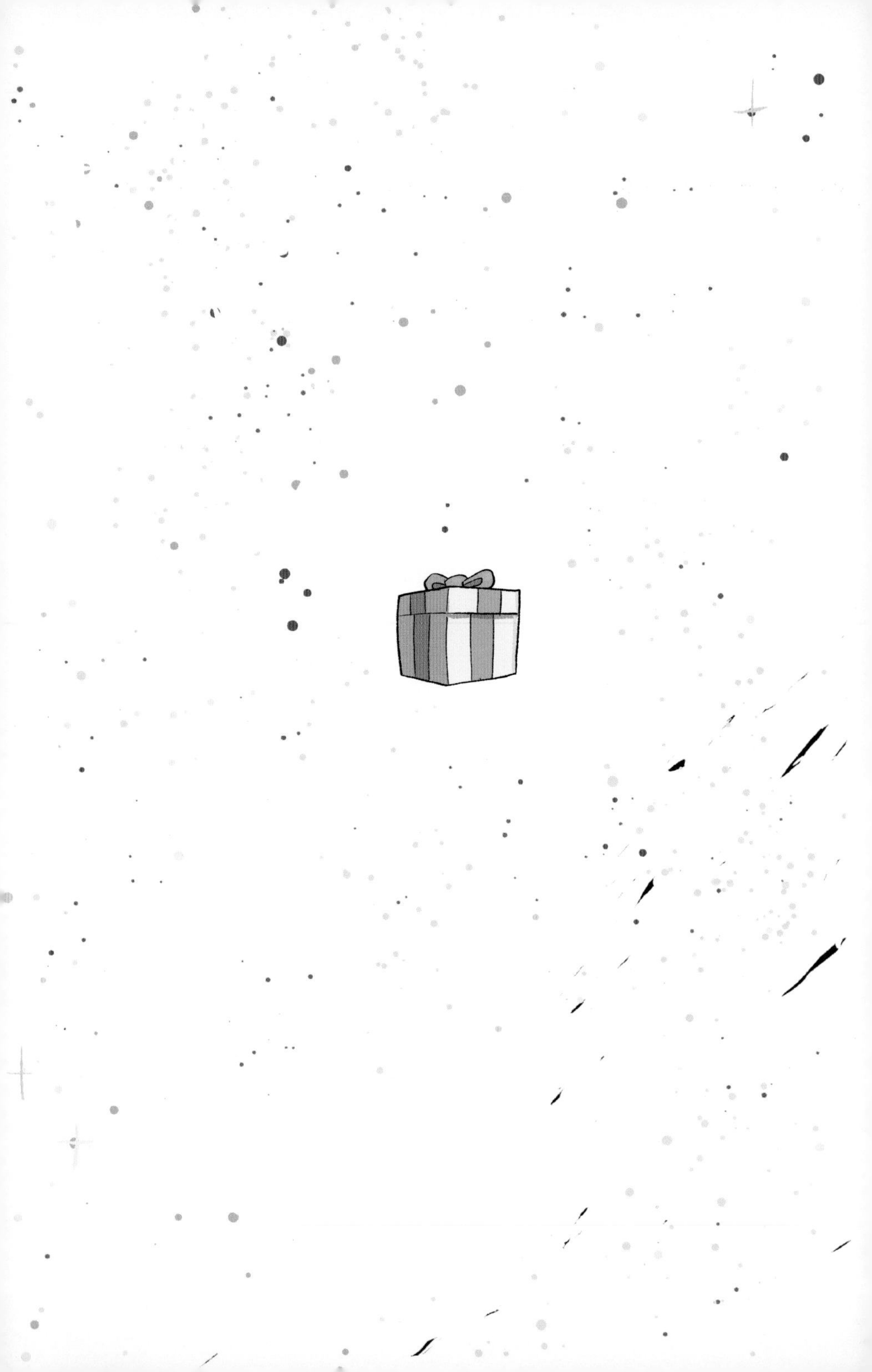

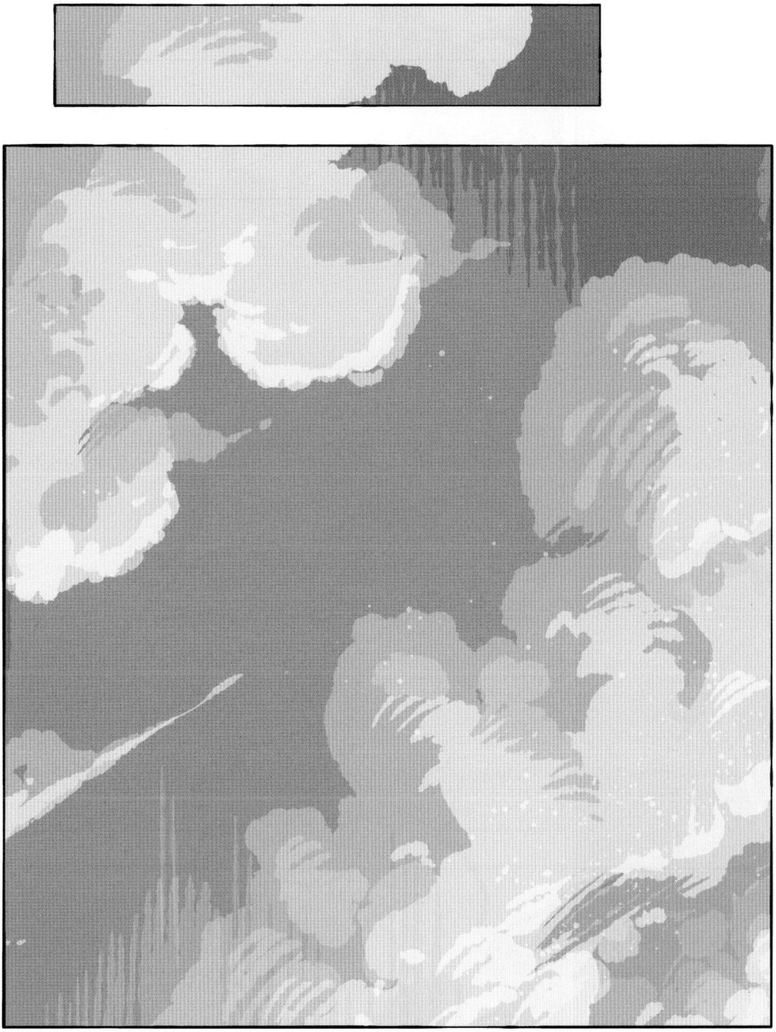

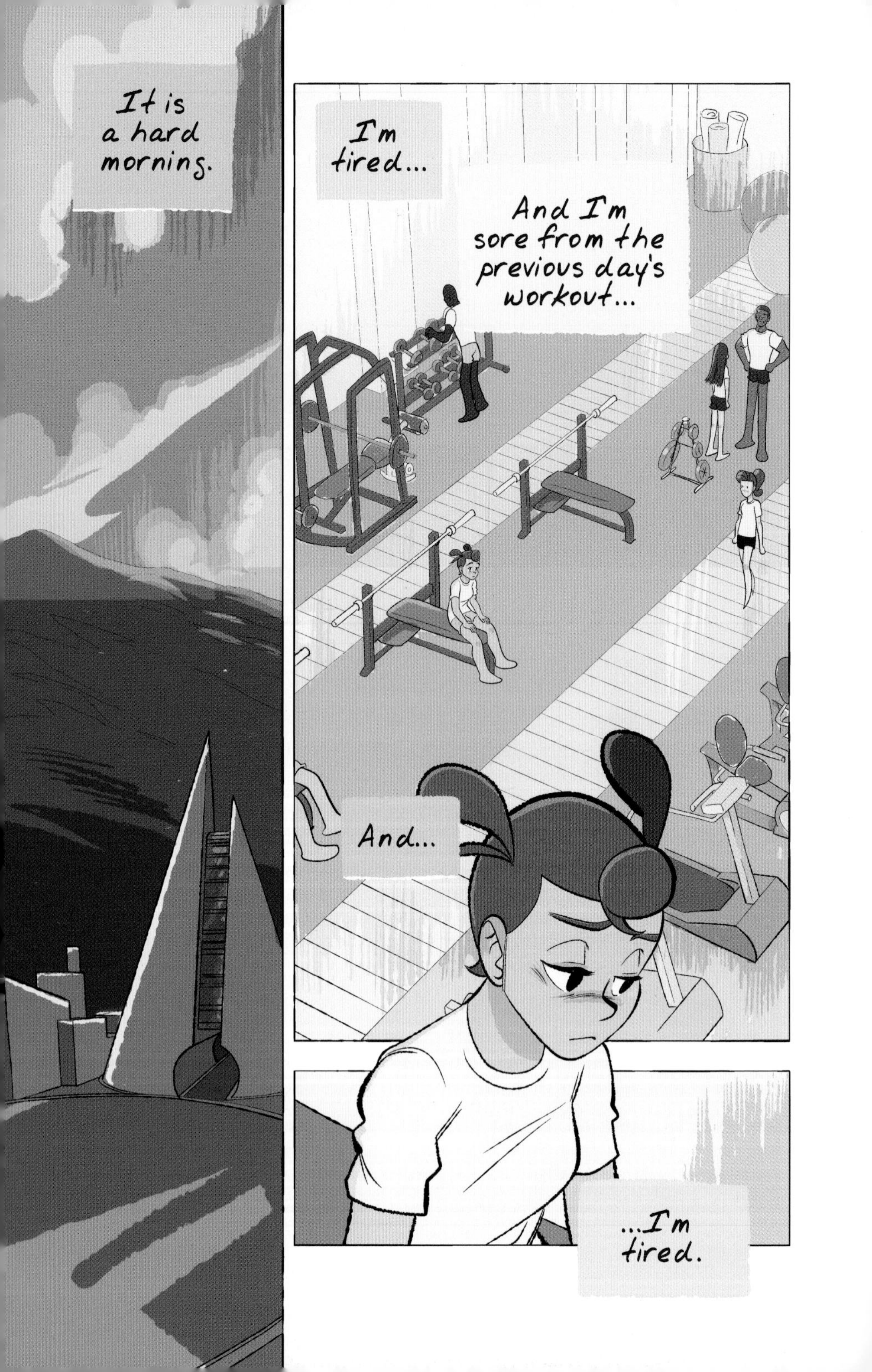
It is a hard morning.
I'm tired...
And I'm sore from the previous day's workout...
And...
...I'm tired.

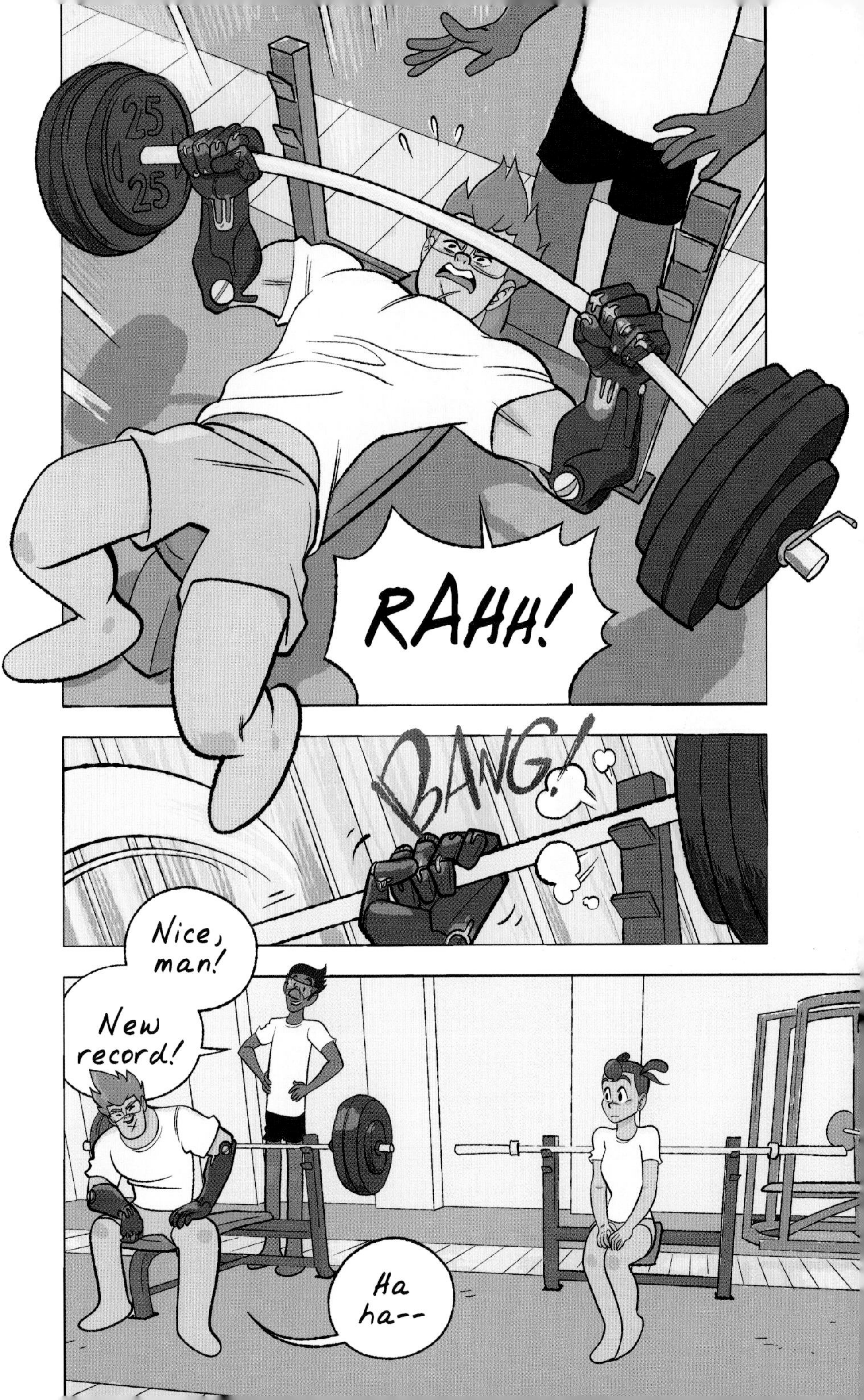
25
25
25
RAHH!
BANG!
Nice, man!
New record!
Ha ha--

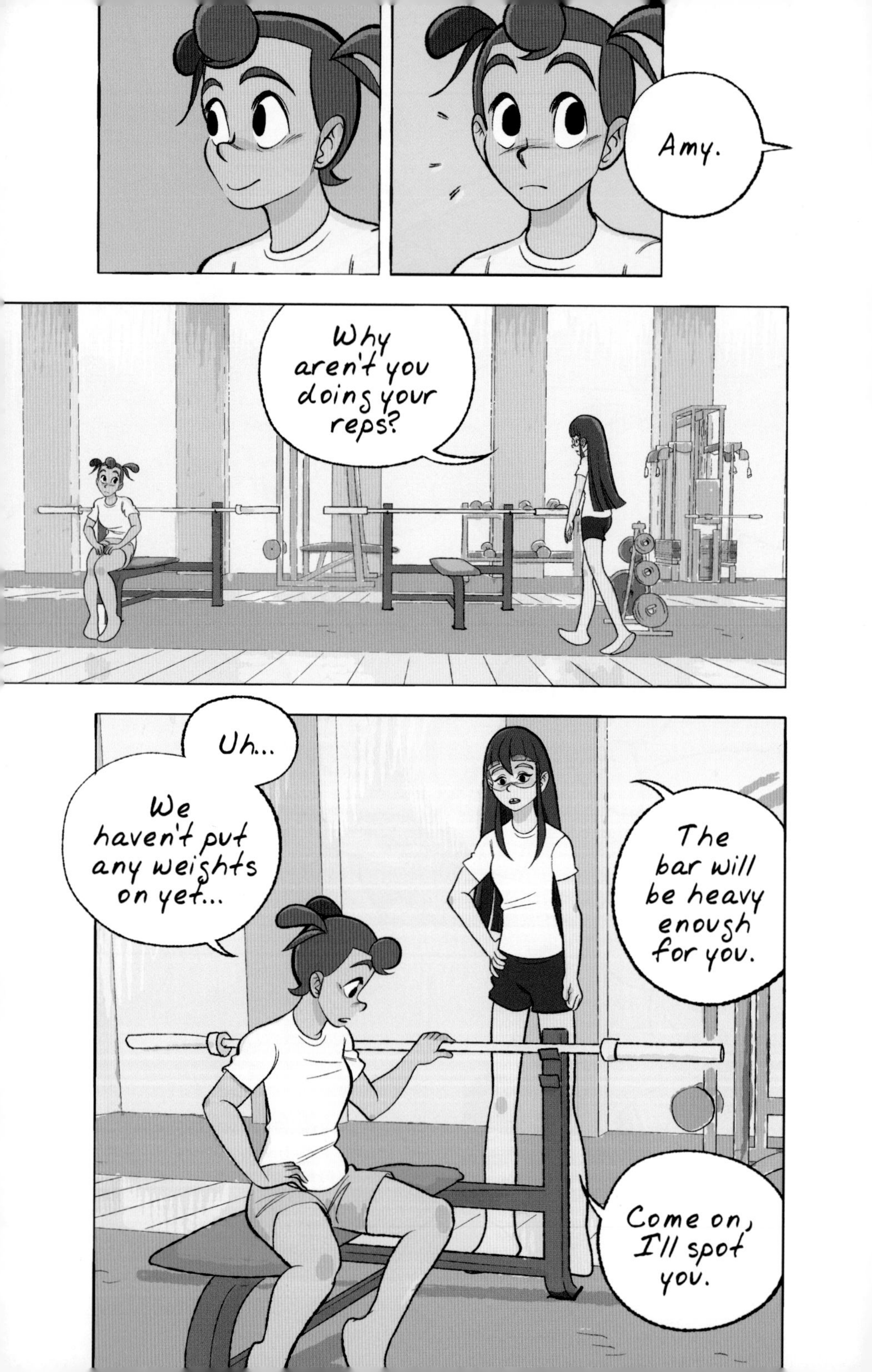
Amy.
Why aren't you doing your reps?
Uh...
We haven't put any weights on yet...
The bar will be heavy enough for you.
Come on, I'll spot you.

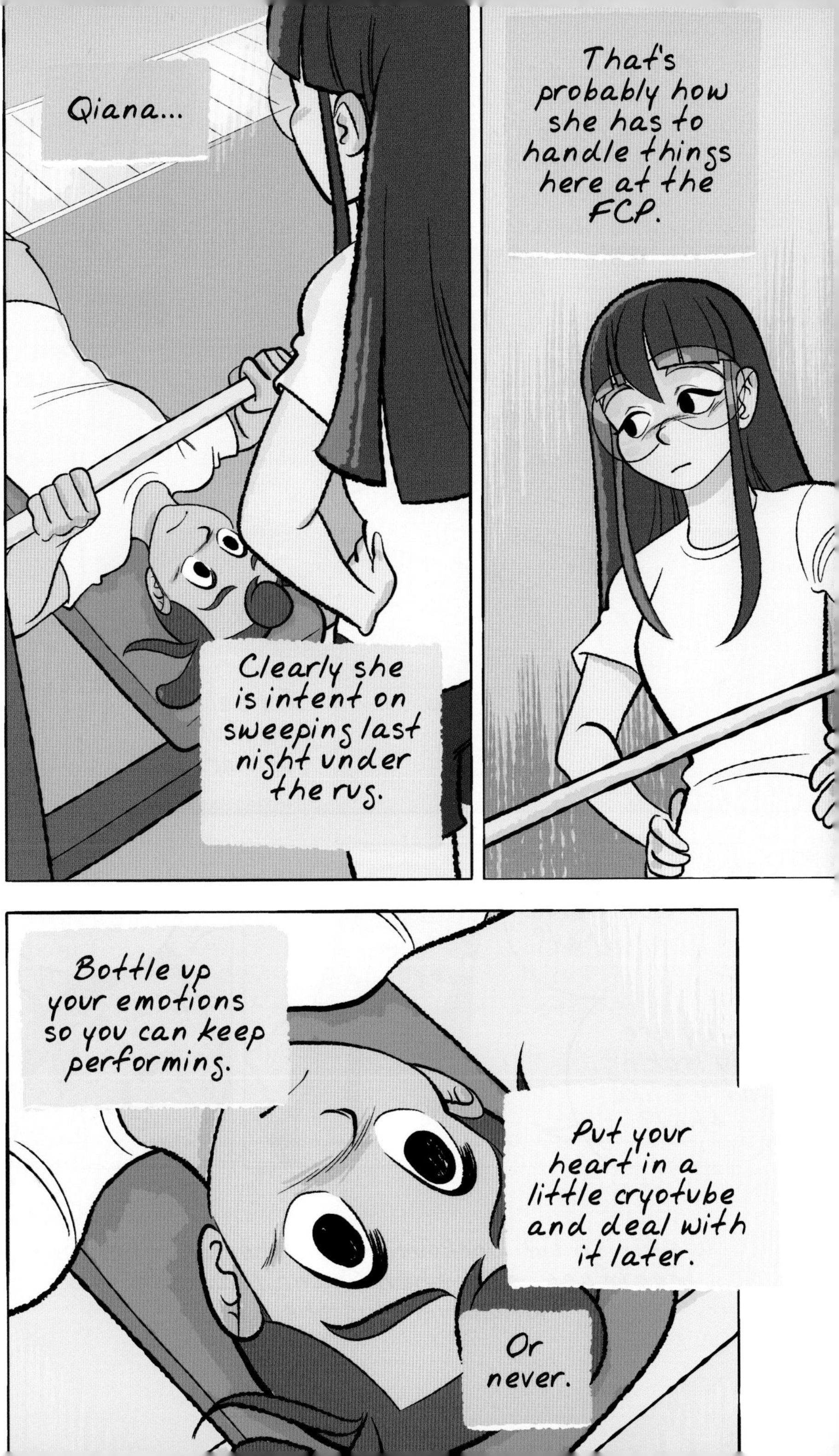
Qiana...
Clearly she is intent on sweeping last night under the rug.
That's probably how she has to handle things here at the FCP.
Bottle up your emotions so you can keep performing.
Put your heart in a little cryotube and deal with it later.
Or never.

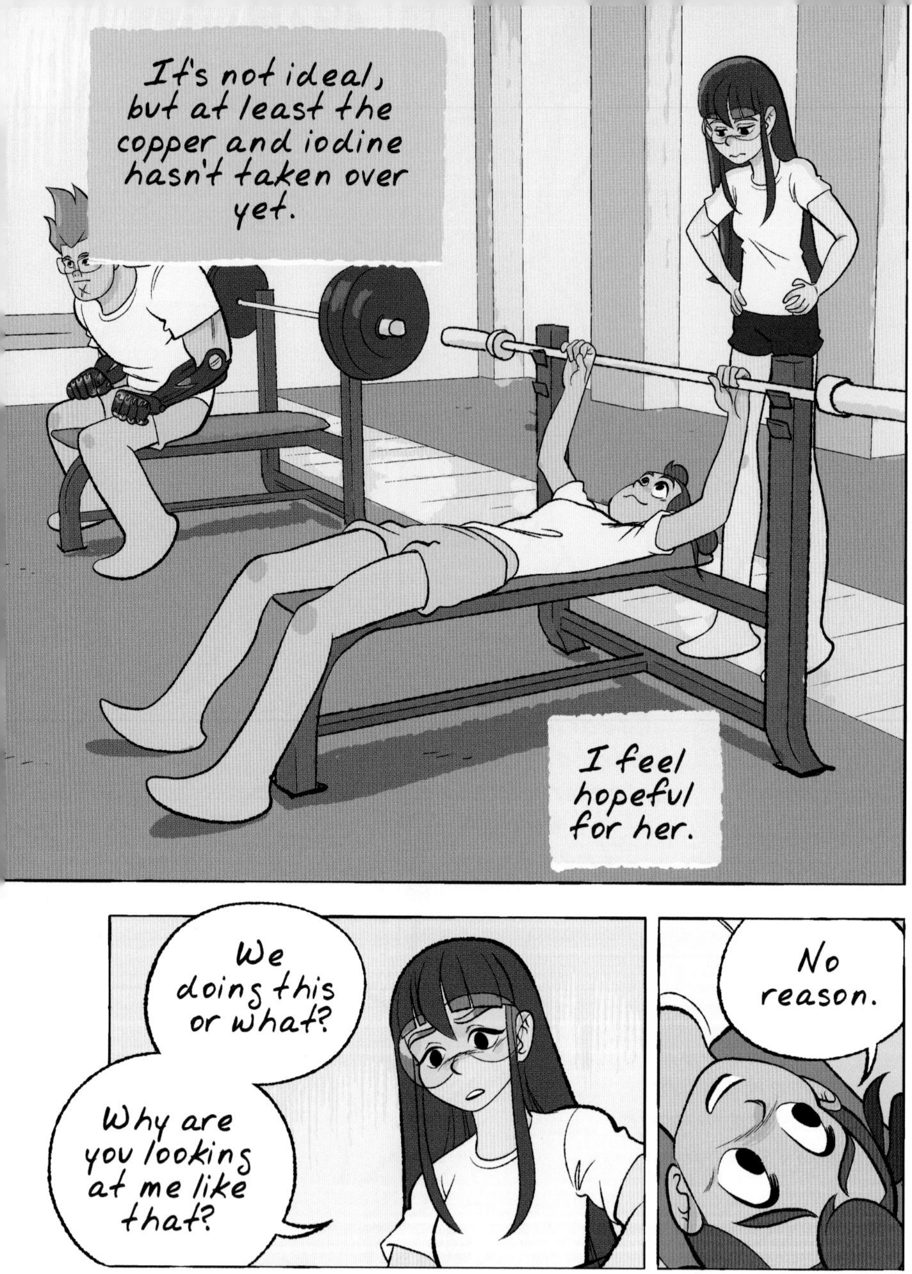
It's not ideal, but at least the copper and iodine hasn't taken over yet.
I feel hopeful for her.
We doing this or what?
Why are you looking at me like that?
No reason.

We finish our workout, then shower, then eat breakfast, and then Qiana leaves to go do whatever it is she does.

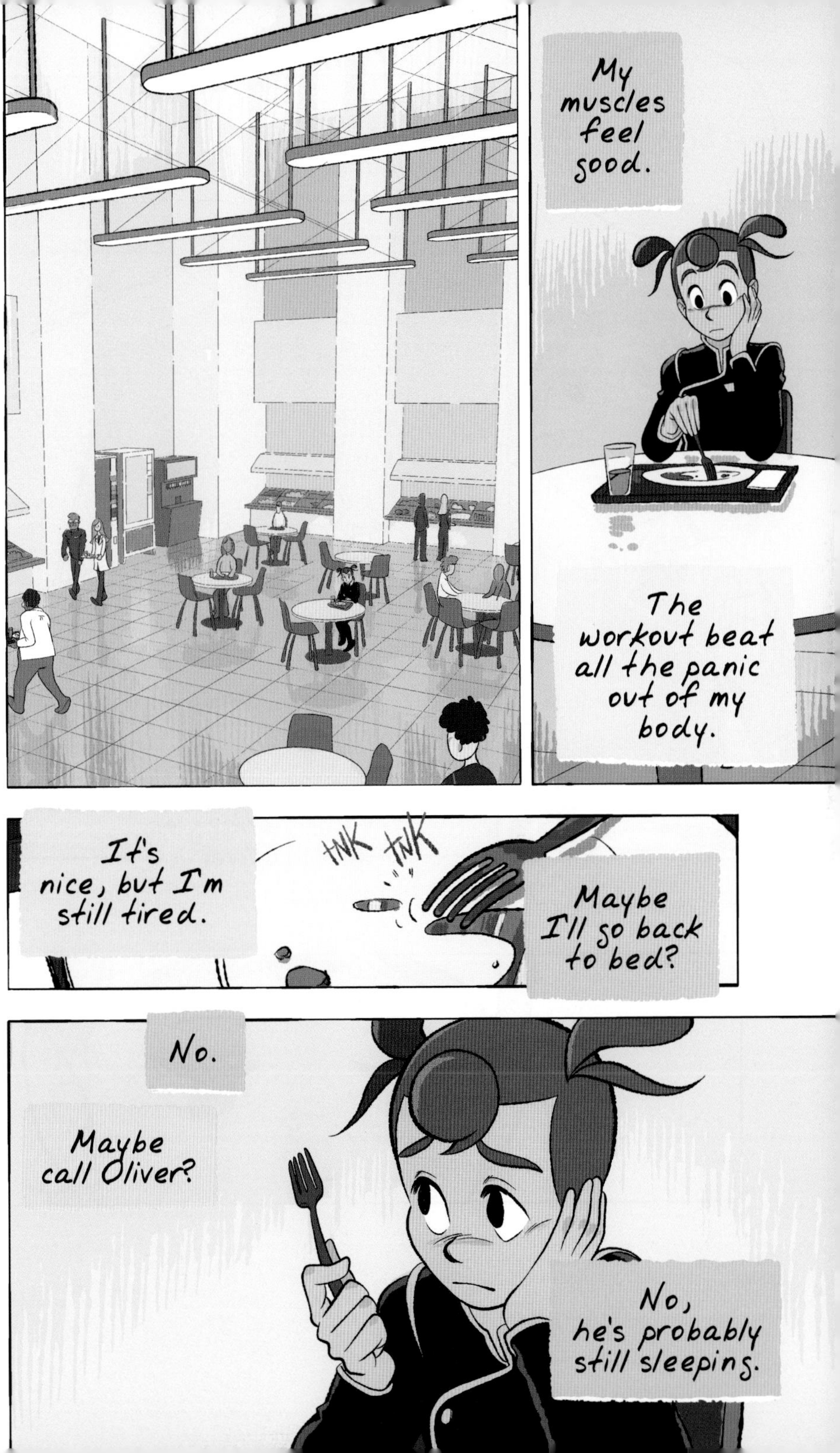
My muscles feel good.
The workout beat all the panic out of my body.
It's nice, but I'm still tired.
TNK TNK
Maybe I'll go back to bed?
No.
Maybe call Oliver?
No, he's probably still sleeping.

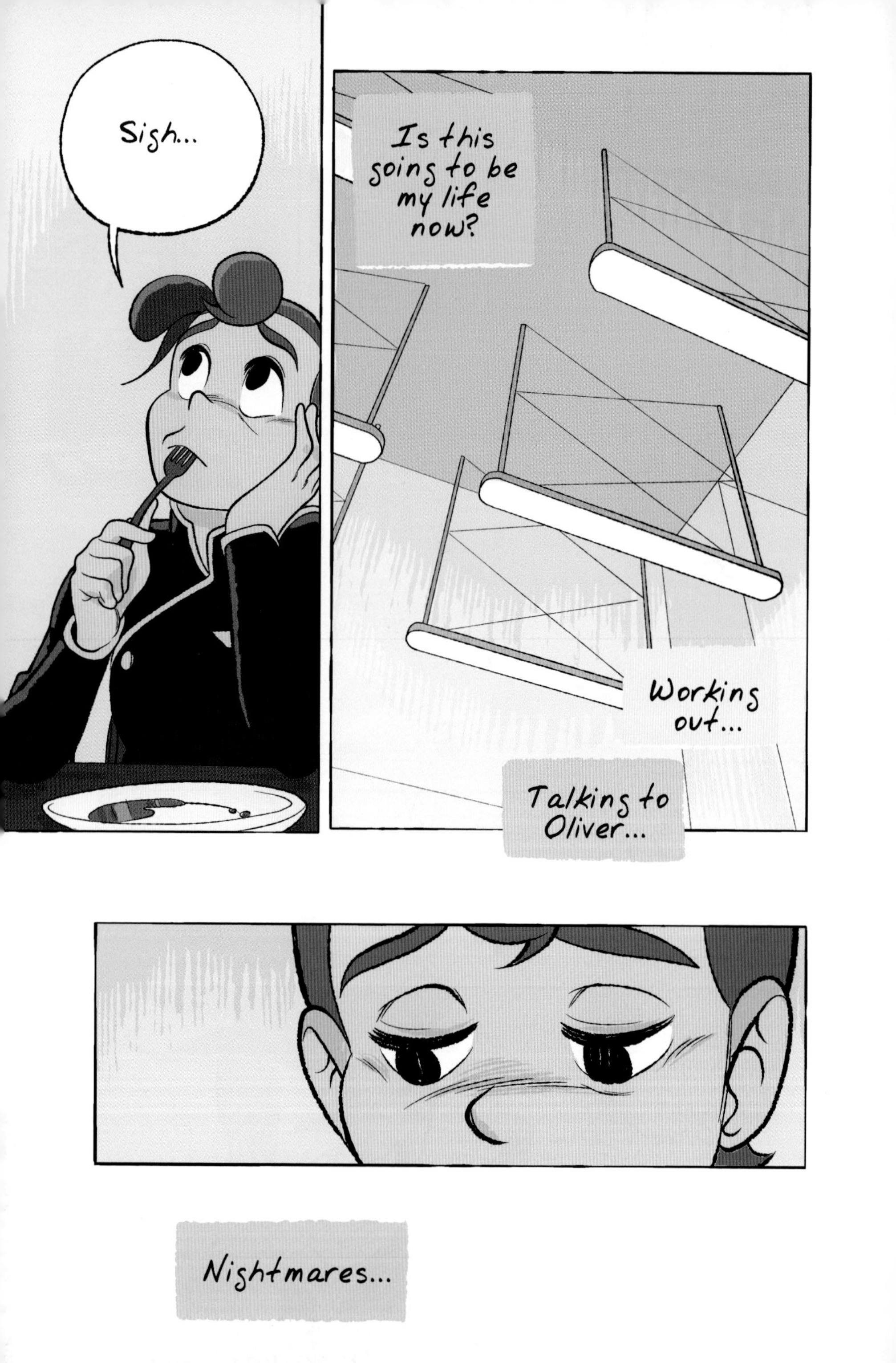
Sigh...
Is this going to be my life now?
Working out...
Talking to Oliver...
Nightmares...

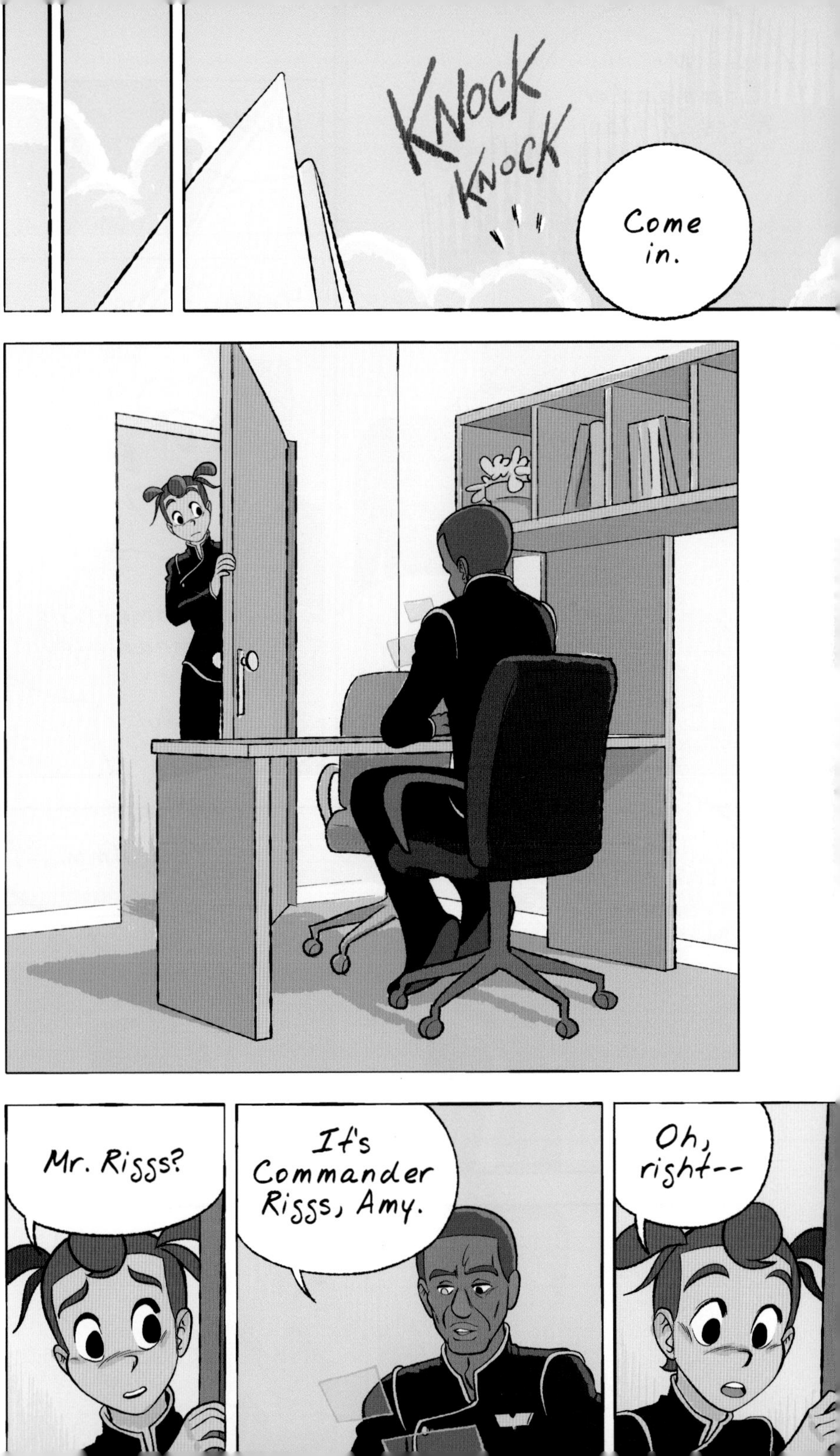
KNOCK KNOCK
Come in.
Mr. Risss?
It's Commander Risss, Amy.
Oh, right--

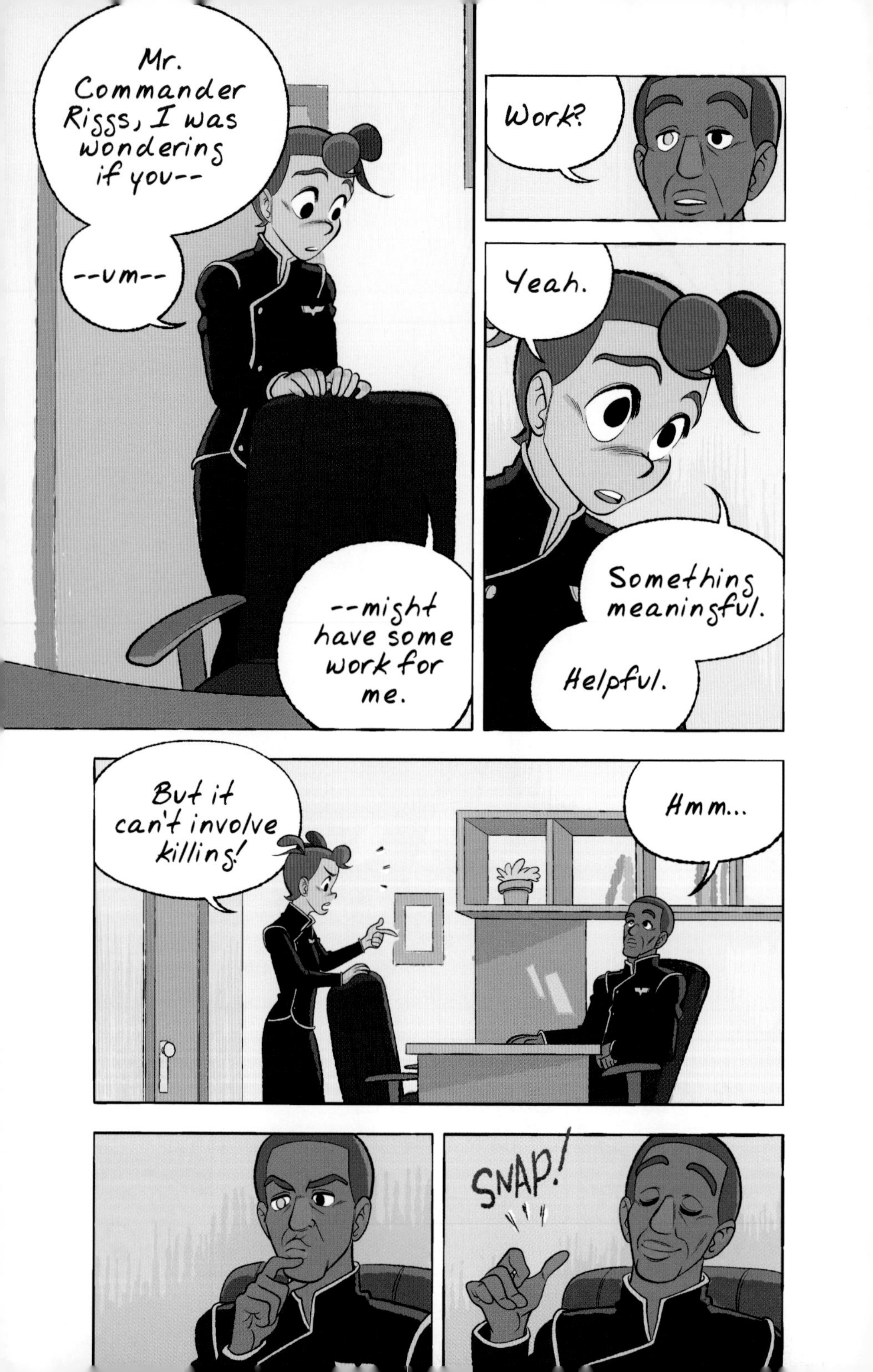
Mr. Commander Risgs, I was wonderins if you--
--um--
--might have some work for me.
Work?
Yeah.
Somethins meaninsful.
Helpful.
But it can't involve killins!
Hmm...
SNAP!

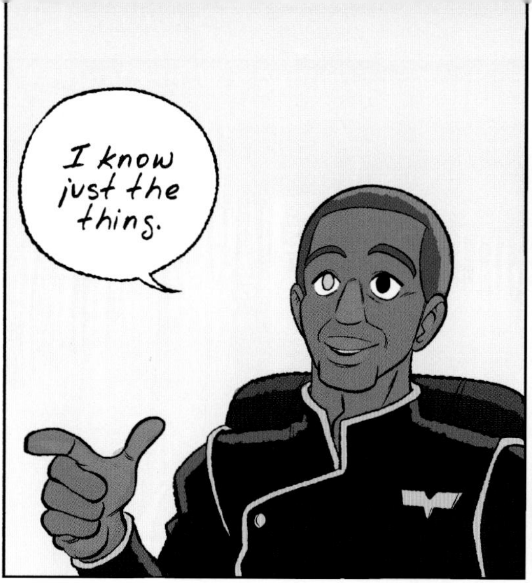
I know just the thing.
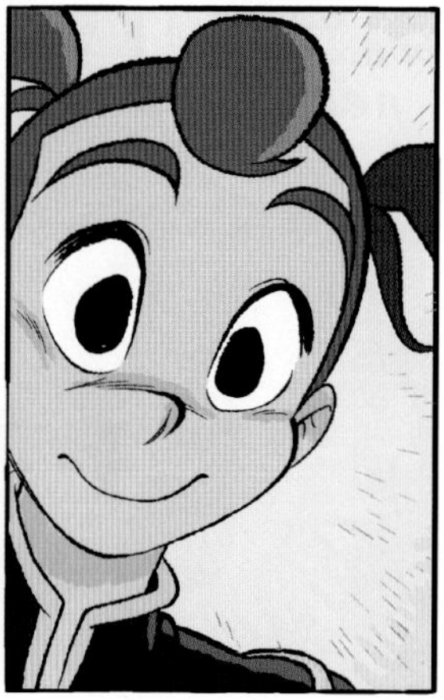
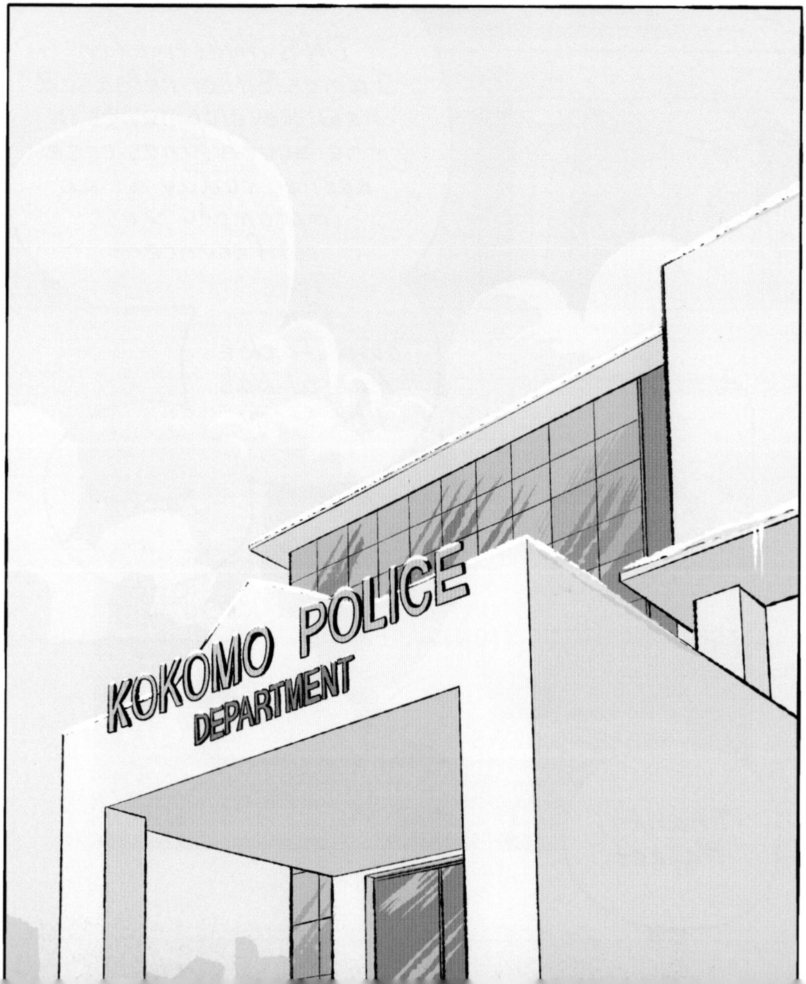
KOKOMO POLICE
DEPARTMENT

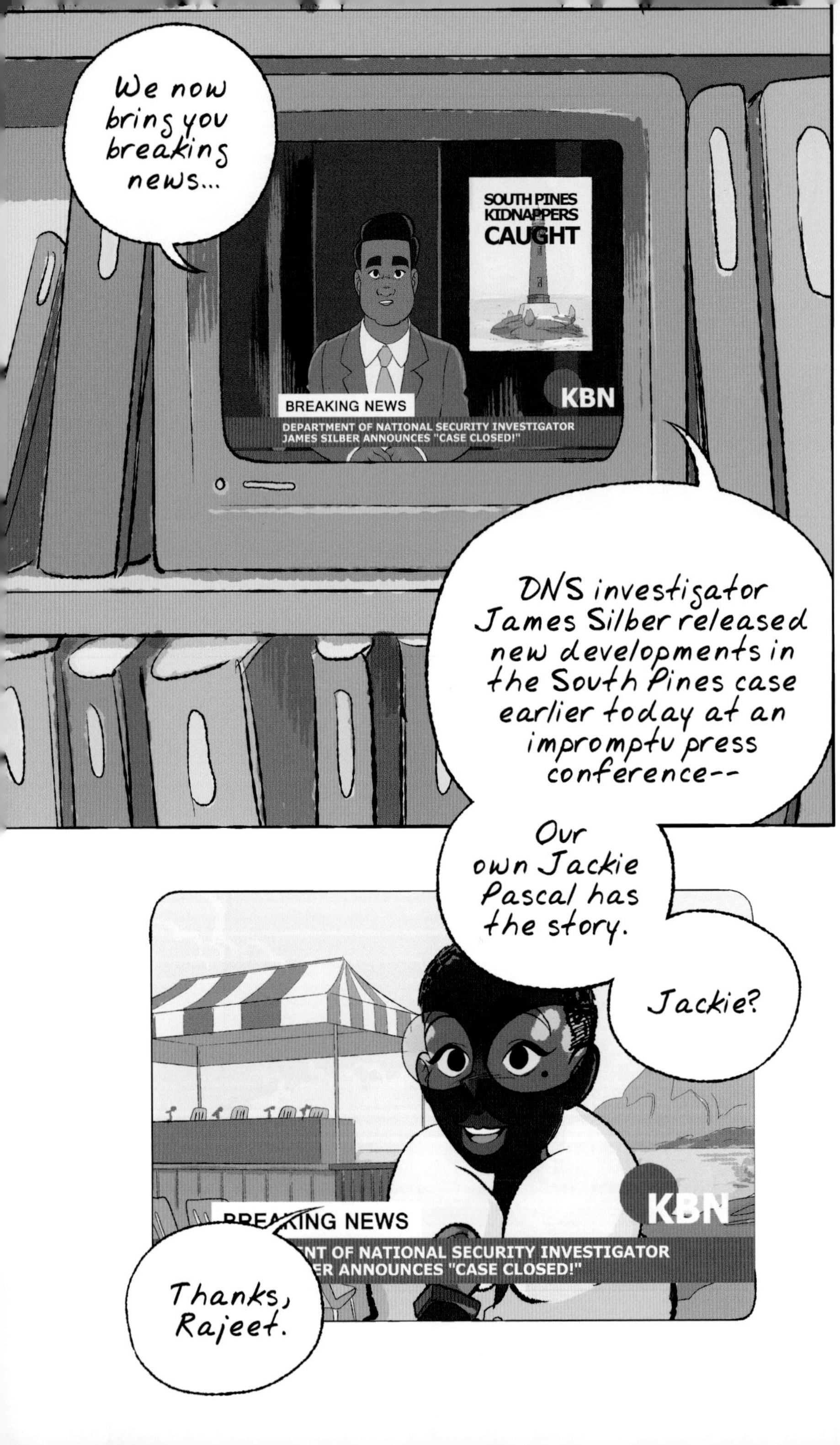
We now brings you breakings news...
SOUTH PINES KIDNAPPERS CAUGHT
KBN
BREAKING NEWS
DEPARTMENT OF NATIONAL SECURITY INVESTIGATOR JAMES SILBER ANNOUNCES "CASE CLOSED!"
DNS investigator James Silber released new developments in the South Pines case earlier today at an impromptu press conference--
Our own Jackie Pascal has the story.
Jackie?
KBN
Thanks, Rajeet.

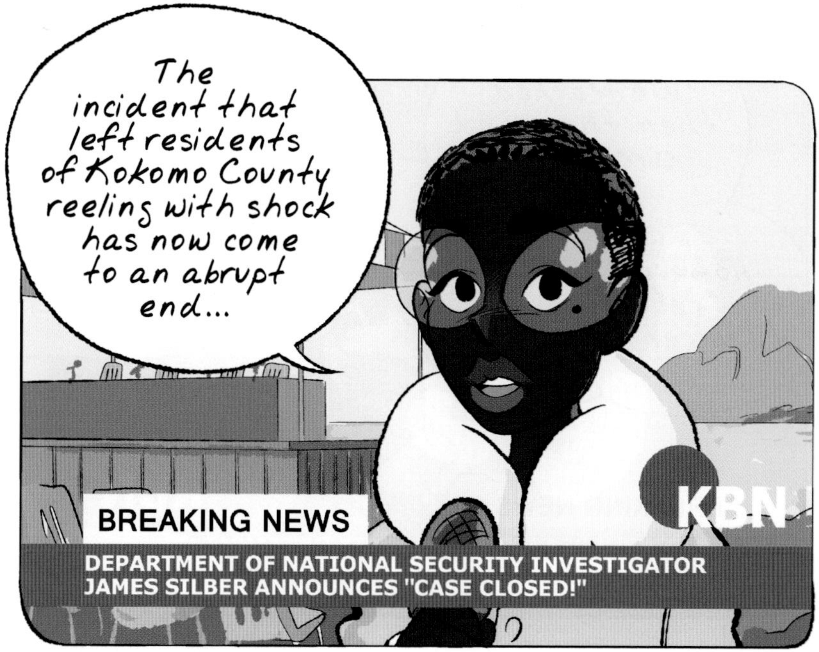
The incident that left residents of Kokomo County reeling with shock has now come to an abrupt end...
KBN
BREAKING NEWS
DEPARTMENT OF NATIONAL SECURITY INVESTIGATOR JAMES SILBER ANNOUNCES "CASE CLOSED!"

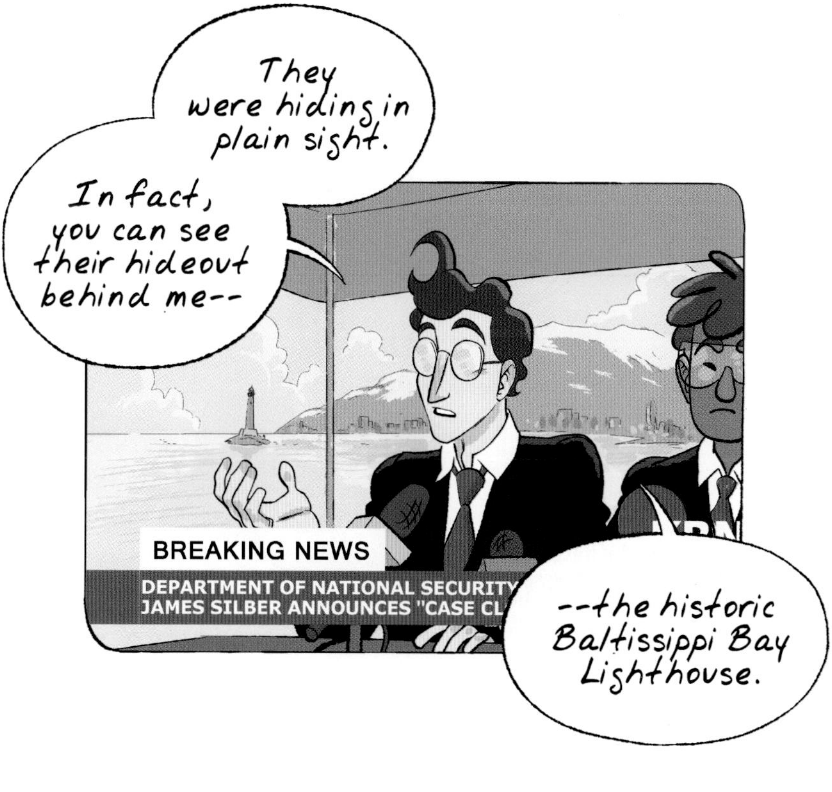
They were hiding in plain sight.
In fact, you can see their hideout behind me--
BREAKING NEWS
DEPARTMENT OF NATIONAL SECURITY
JAMES SILBER ANNOUNCES "CASE CL
--the historic Baltissippi Bay Lighthouse.

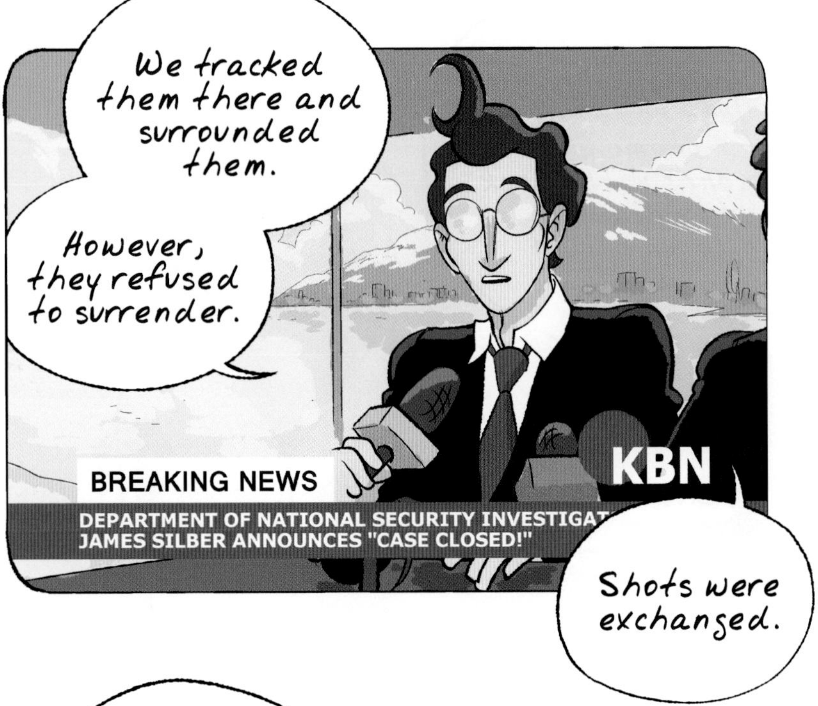
We tracked them there and surrounded them.
However, they refused to surrender.
BREAKING NEWS
KBN
DEPARTMENT OF NATIONAL SECURITY INVESTIGAT
JAMES SILBER ANNOUNCES "CASE CLOSED!"
Shots were exchanged.

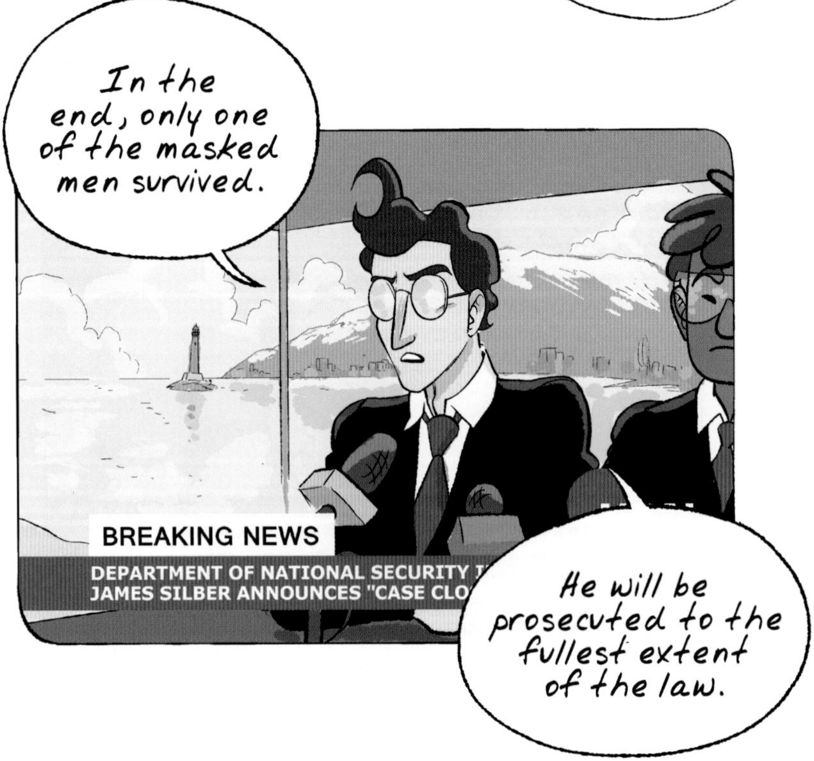
In the end, only one of the masked men survived.
BREAKING NEWS
DEPARTMENT OF NATIONAL SECURITY I
JAMES SILBER ANNOUNCES "CASE CLO
He will be prosecuted to the fullest extent of the law.

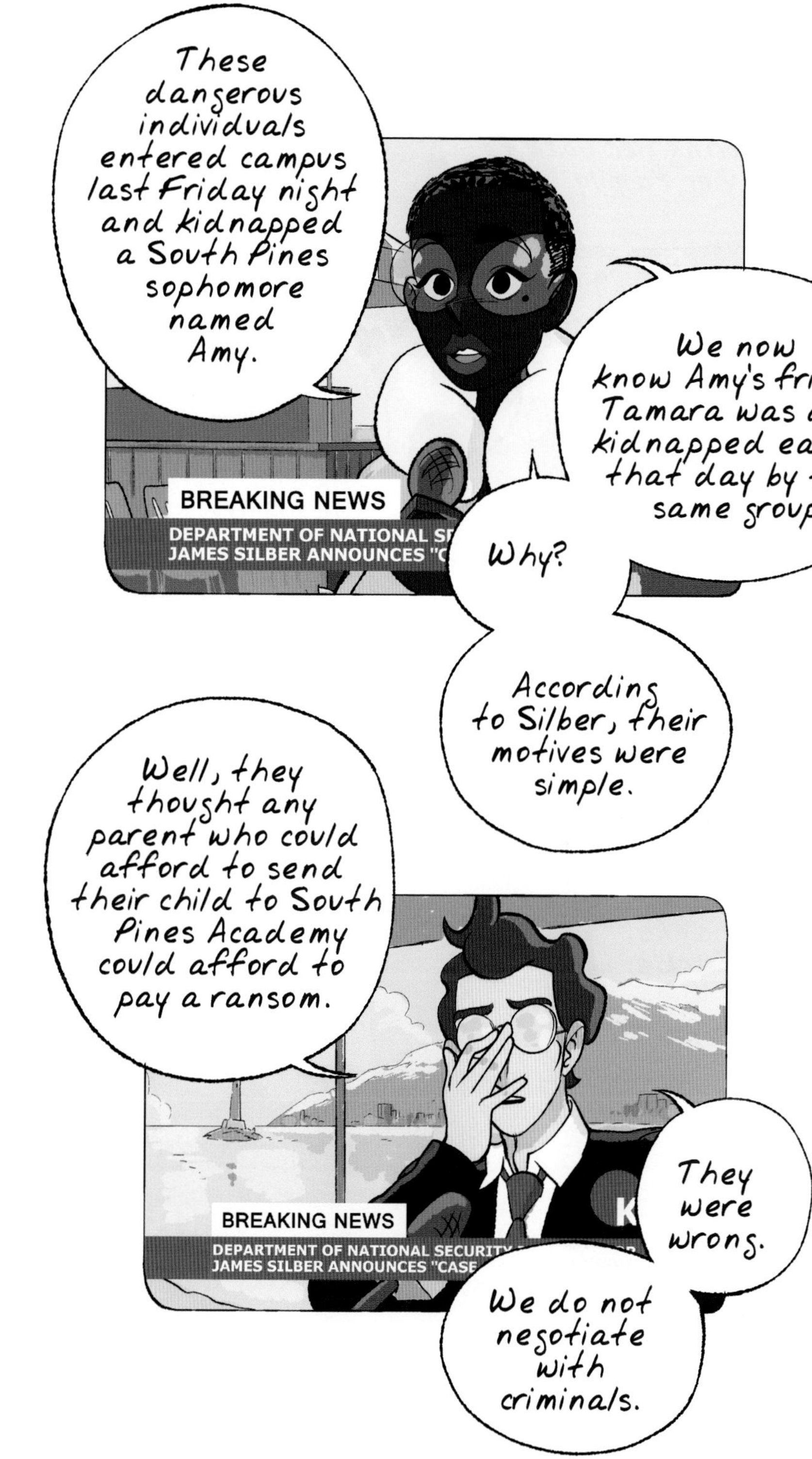
These dangerous individuals entered campus last Friday night and kidnapped a South Pines sophomore named Amy.
BREAKING NEWS
DEPARTMENT OF NATIONAL
JAMES SILBER ANNOUNCES
We now know Amy's friend Tamara was also kidnapped earlier that day by the same group.
Why?
According to Silber, their motives were simple.
Well, they thought any parent who could afford to send their child to South Pines Academy could afford to pay a ransom.
BREAKING NEWS
DEPARTMENT OF NATIONAL
JAMES SILBER ANNOUNCES "CASE
They were wrong.
We do not negotiate with criminals.

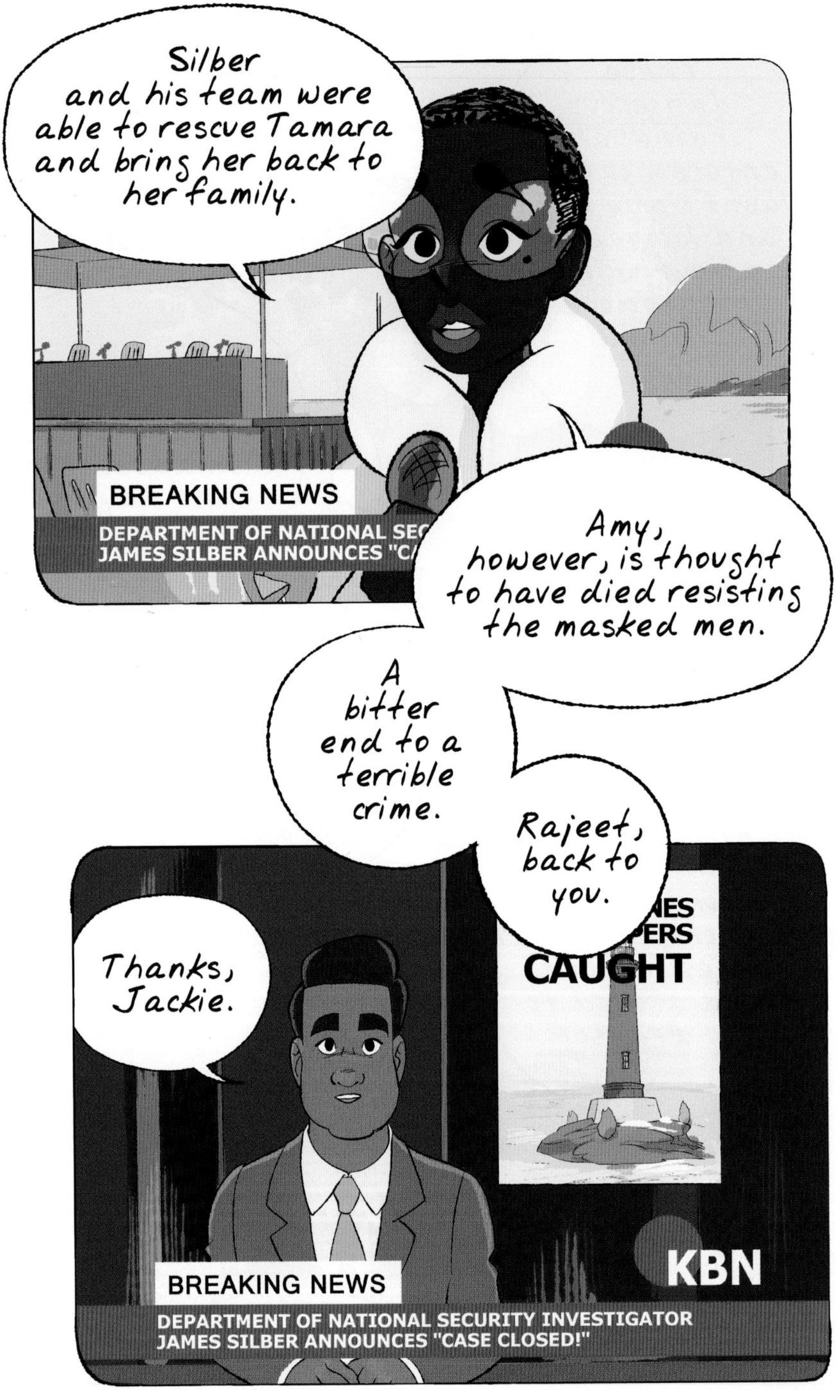
Silber and his team were able to rescue Tamara and bring her back to her family.
BREAKING NEWS
DEPARTMENT OF NATIONAL SEC
JAMES SILBER ANNOUNCES "CA
Amy, however, is thought to have died resisting the masked men.
A bitter end to a terrible crime.
Rajeet, back to you.
CAUGHT
Thanks, Jackie.
KBN
BREAKING NEWS
DEPARTMENT OF NATIONAL SECURITY INVESTIGATOR
JAMES SILBER ANNOUNCES "CASE CLOSED!"

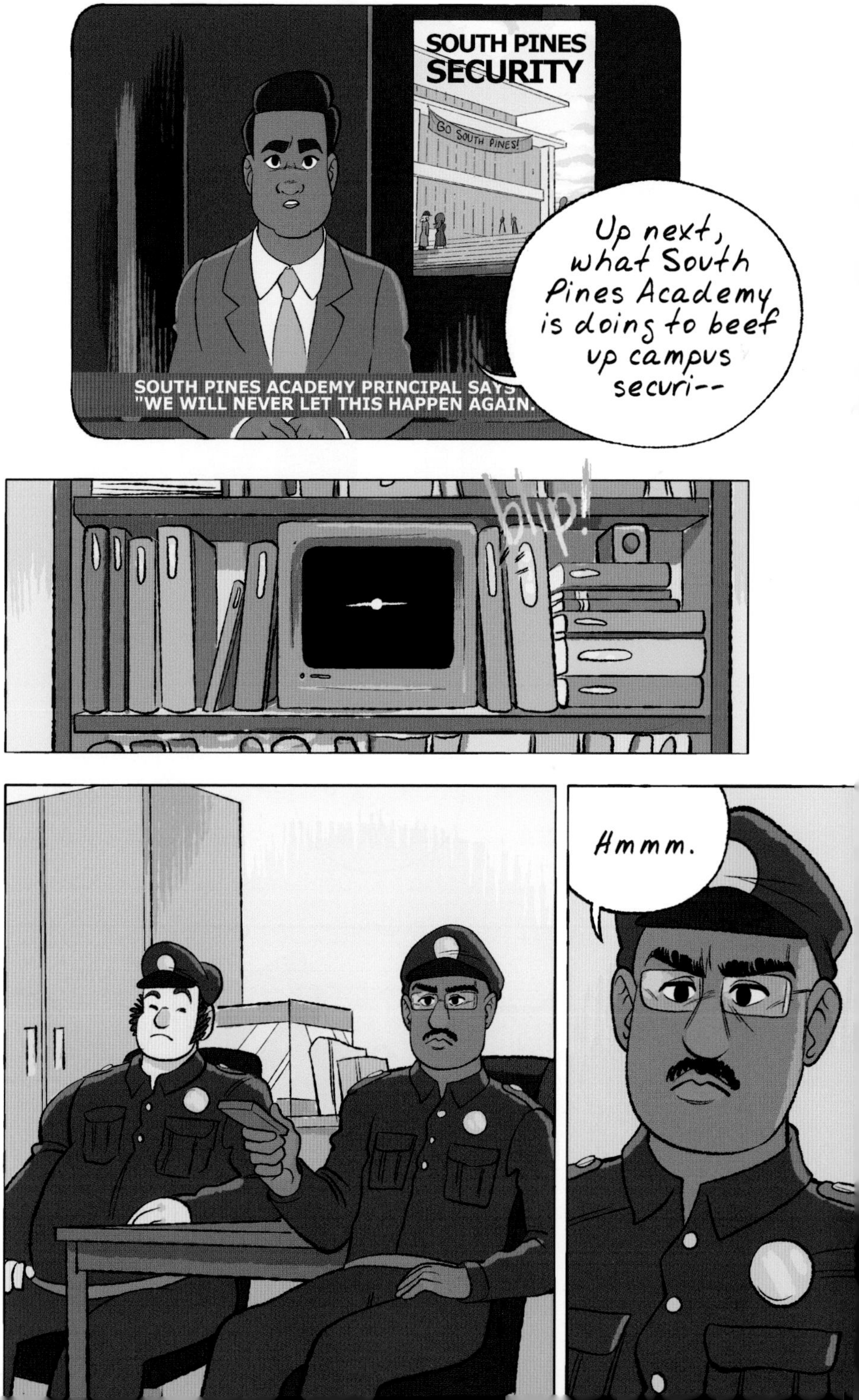
SOUTH PINES SECURITY
GO SOUTH PINES!
SOUTH PINES ACADEMY PRINCIPAL SAYS
"WE WILL NEVER LET THIS HAPPEN AGAIN."
Up next, what South Pines Academy is doing to beef up campus securi--
blip!
Hmmm.

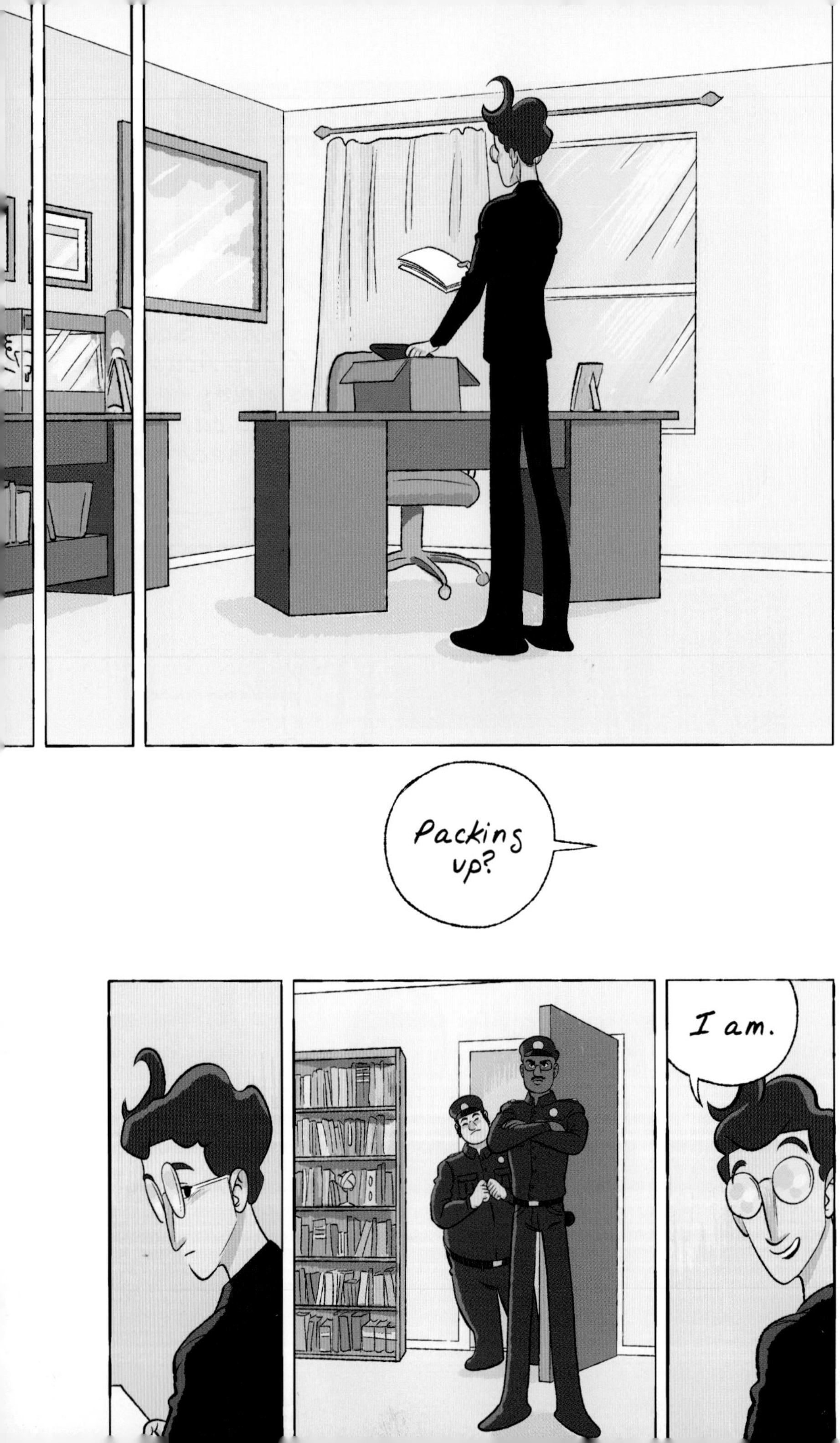

Packing up?
I am.

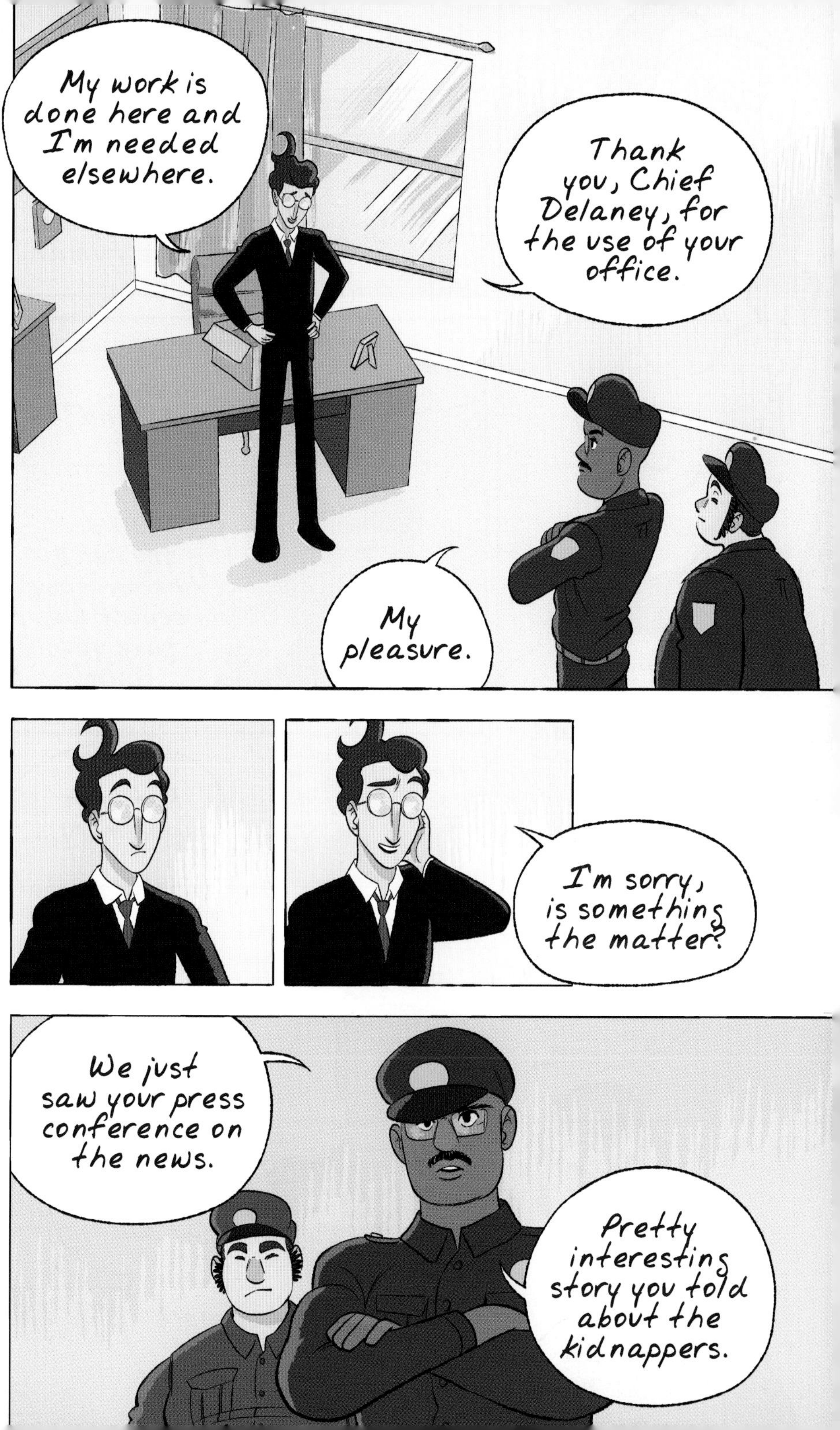
My work is done here and I'm needed elsewhere.
Thank you, Chief Delaney, for the use of your office.
My pleasure.
I'm sorry, is something the matter?
We just saw your press conference on the news.
Pretty interesting story you told about the kidnappers.

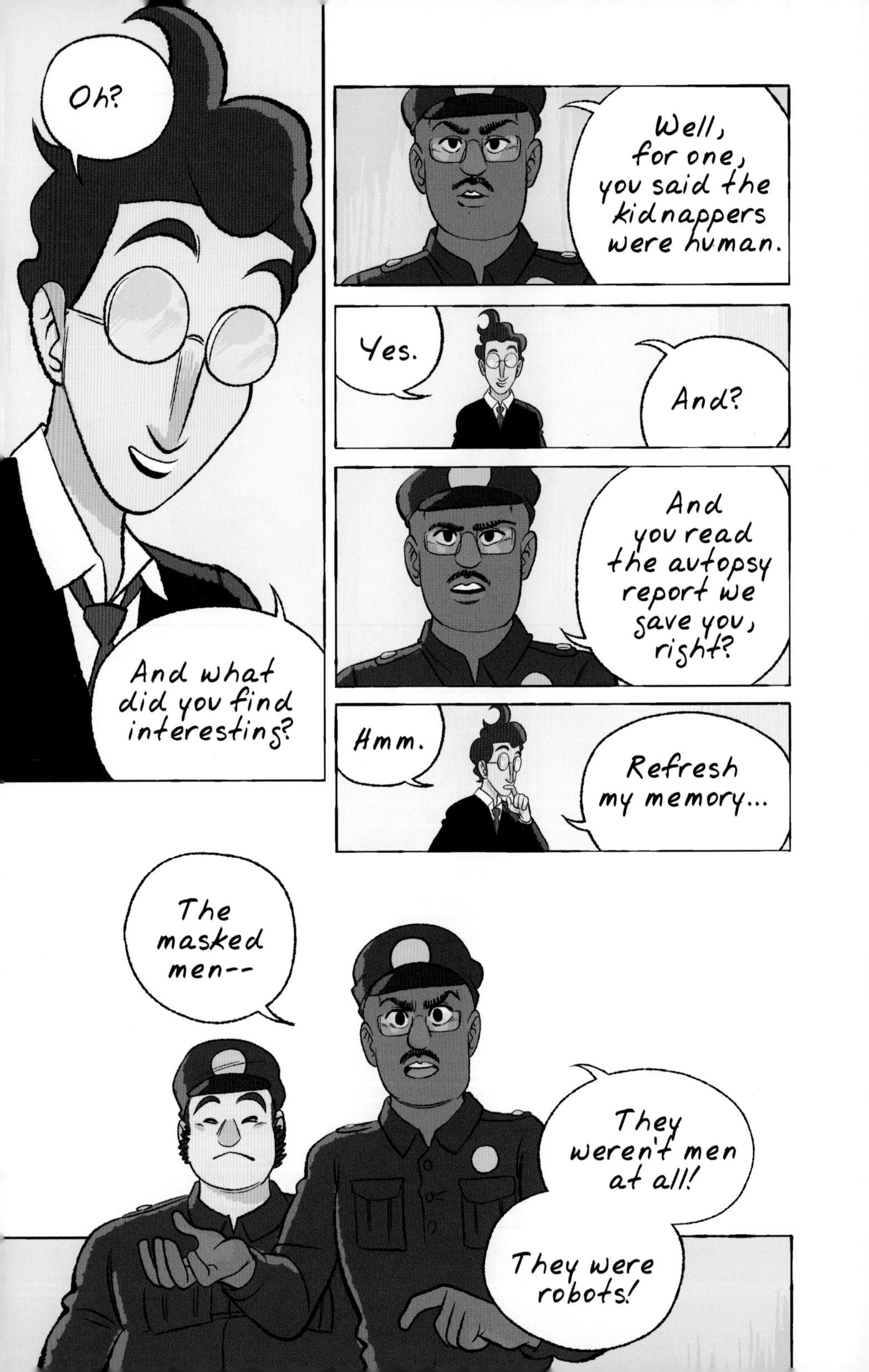
Oh?
And what did you find interesting?
Well, for one, you said the kidnappers were human.
Yes.
And?
And you read the autopsy report we gave you, right?
Hmm.
Refresh my memory...
The masked men--
They weren't men at all!
They were robots!

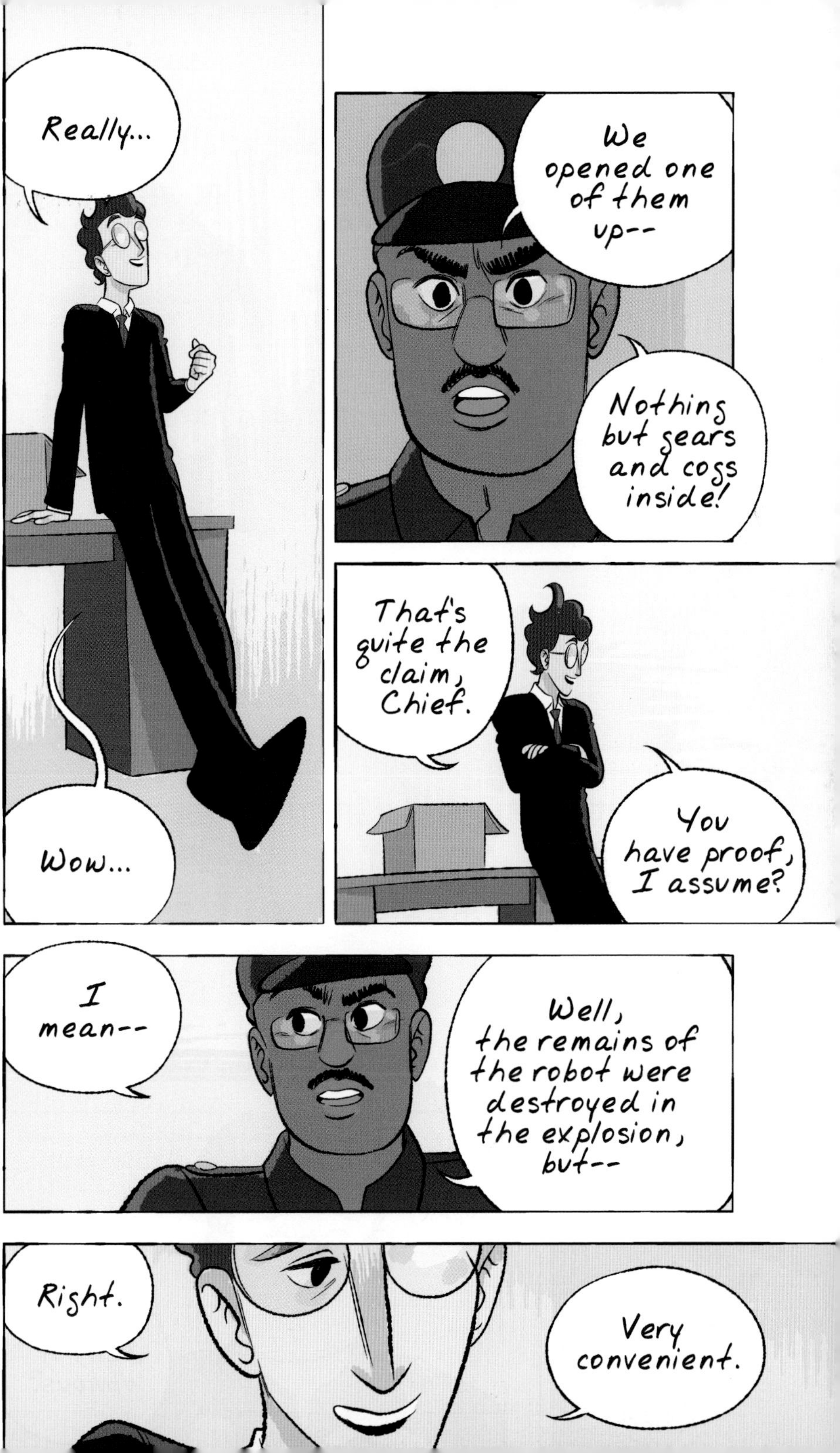
Really...
We opened one of them up--
Nothing but gears and cogs inside!
That's quite the claim, Chief.
Wow...
You have proof, I assume?
I mean--
Well, the remains of the robot were destroyed in the explosion, but--
Right.
Very convenient.

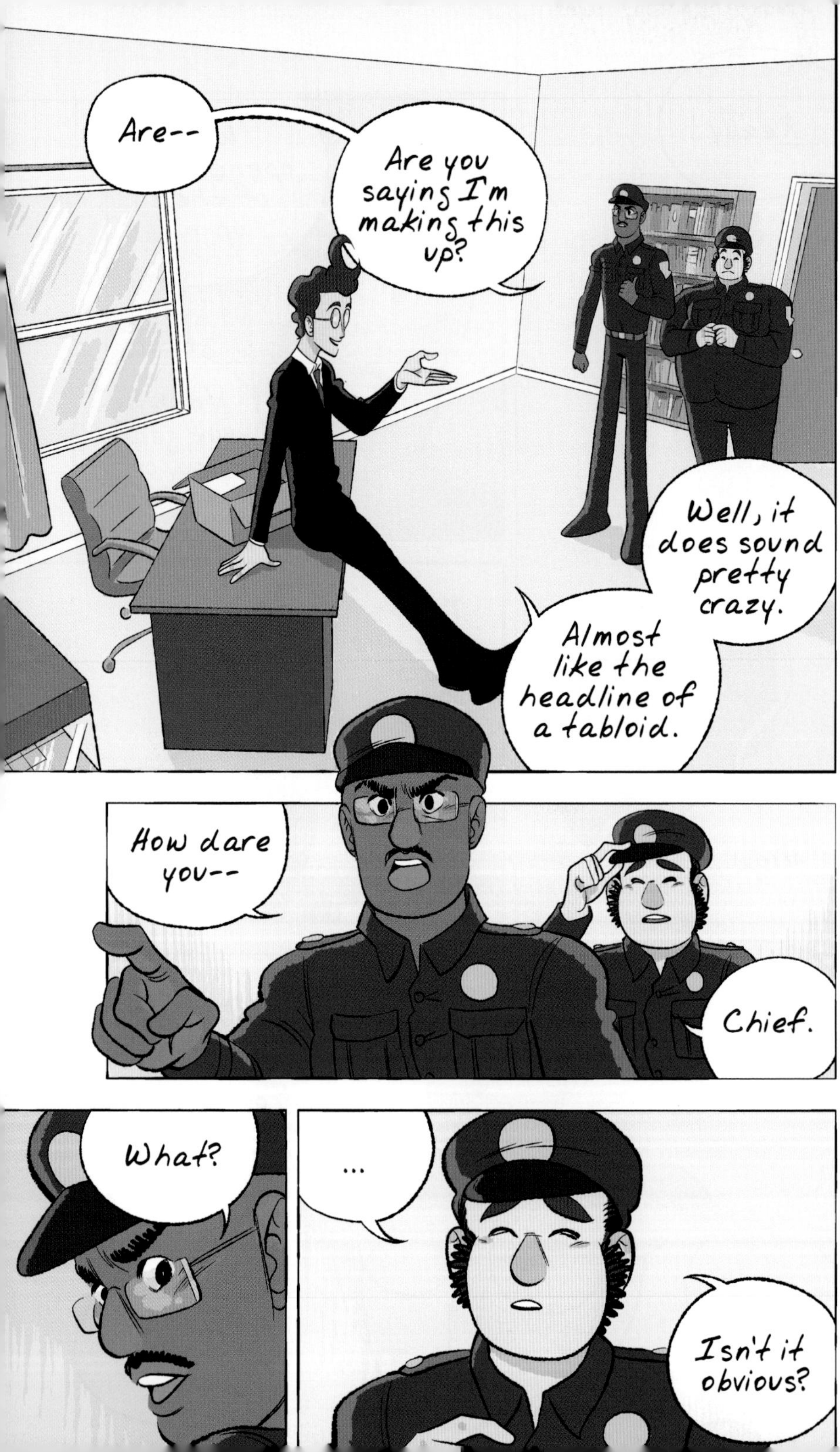
Are--
Are you saying I'm making this up?
Well, it does sound pretty crazy.
Almost like the headline of a tabloid.
How dare you--
Chief.
What?
...
Isn't it obvious?

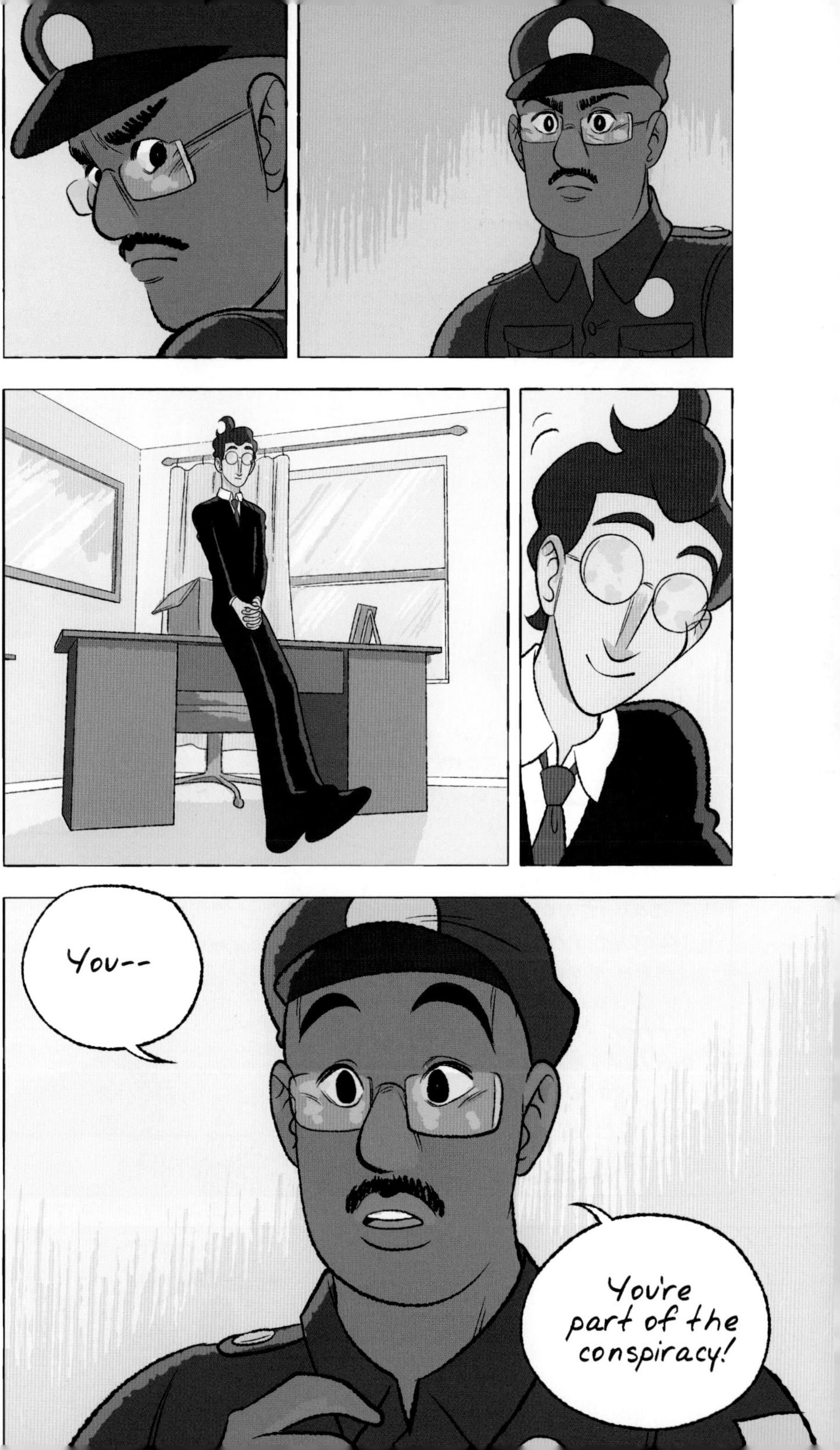
You--
You're part of the conspiracy!

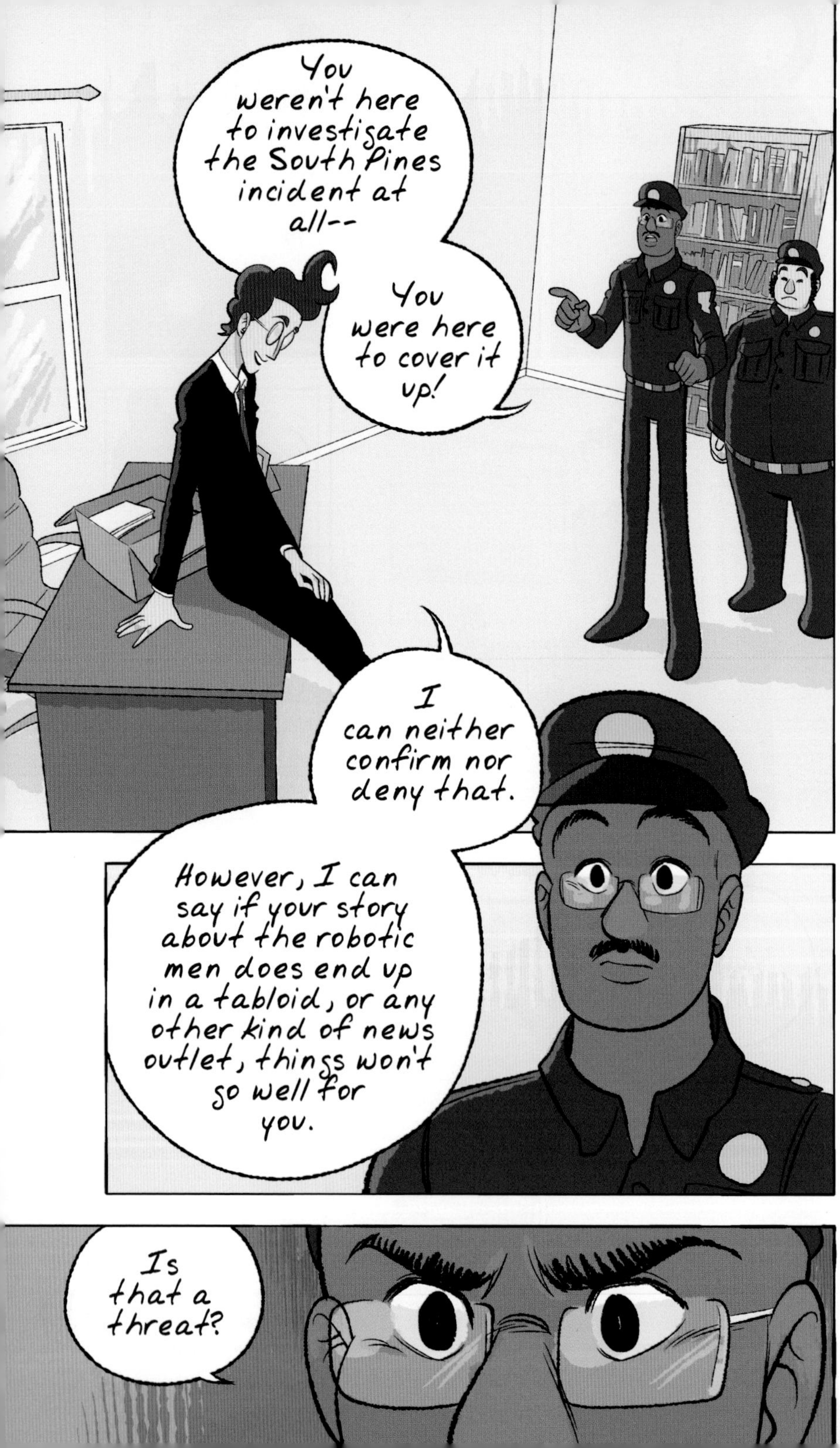
You weren't here to investigate the South Pines incident at all--
You were here to cover it up!
I can neither confirm nor deny that.
However, I can say if your story about the robotic men does end up in a tabloid, or any other kind of news outlet, things won't go so well for you.
Is that a threat?

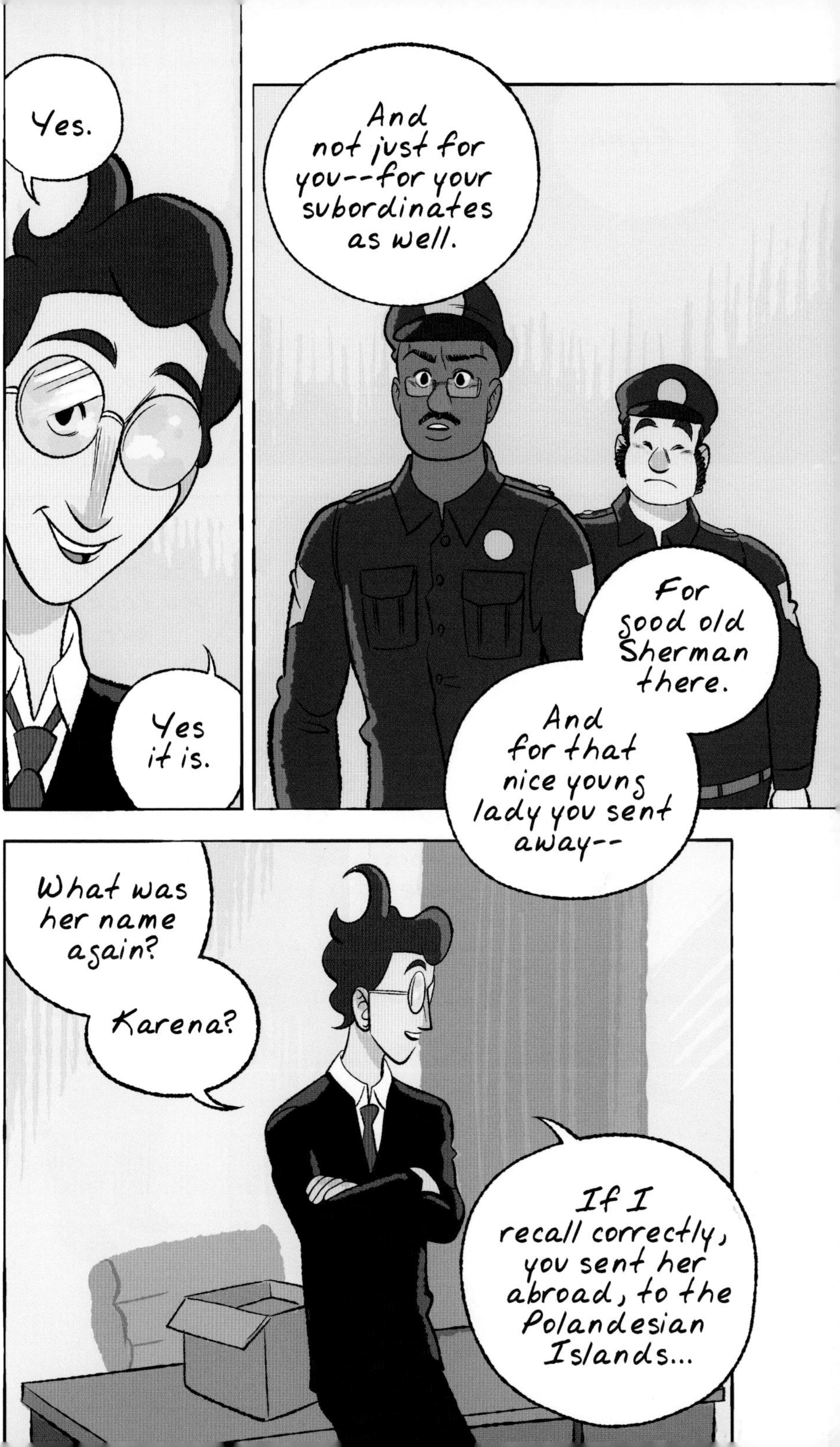
Yes.
Yes it is.
And not just for you--for your subordinates as well.
For good old Sherman there.
And for that nice young lady you sent away--
What was her name again?
Karena?
If I recall correctly, you sent her abroad, to the Polandesian Islands...

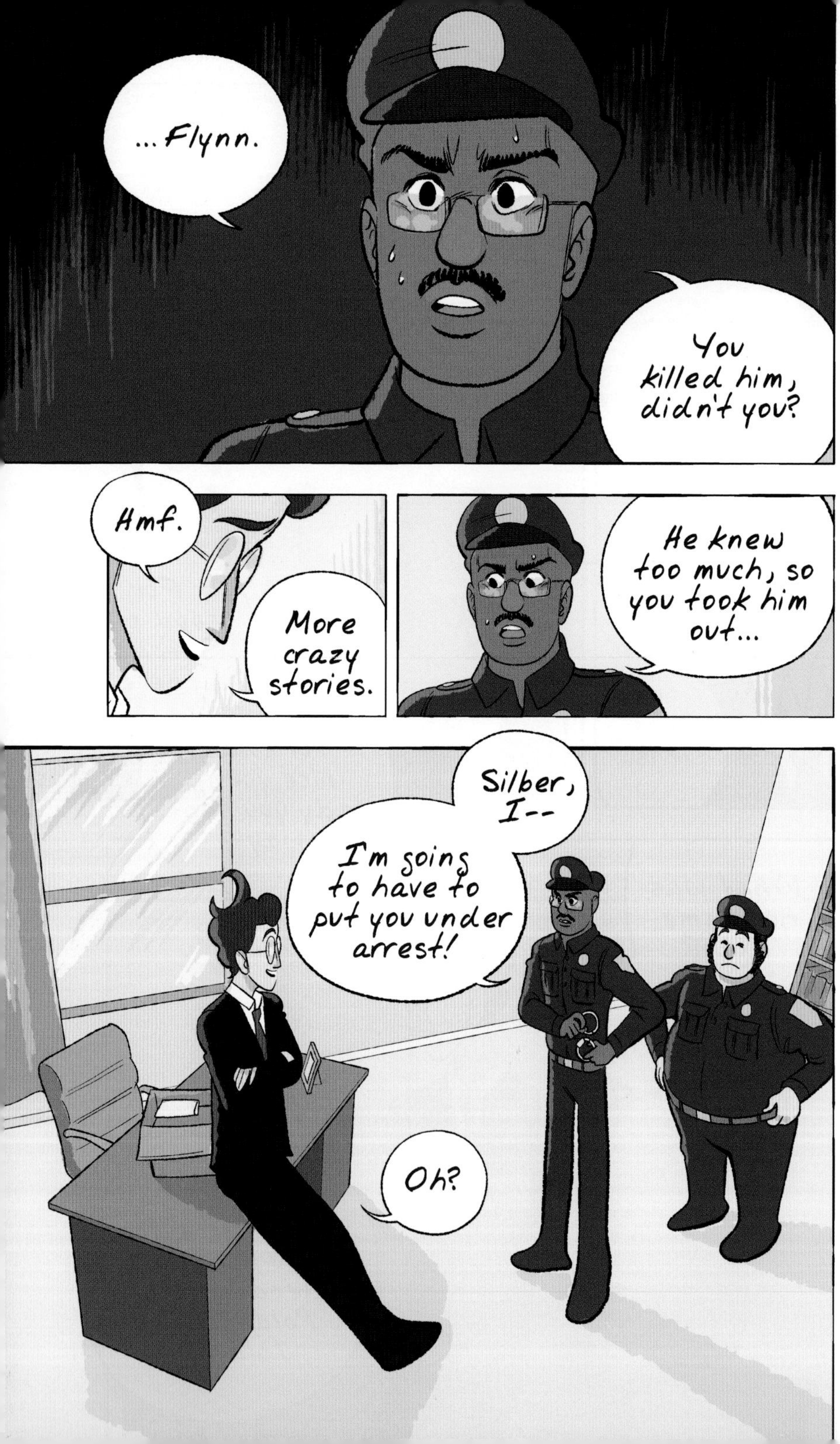
...Flynn.
You killed him, didn't you?
Hmf.
More crazy stories.
He knew too much, so you took him out...
Silber, I--
I'm going to have to put you under arrest!
Oh?

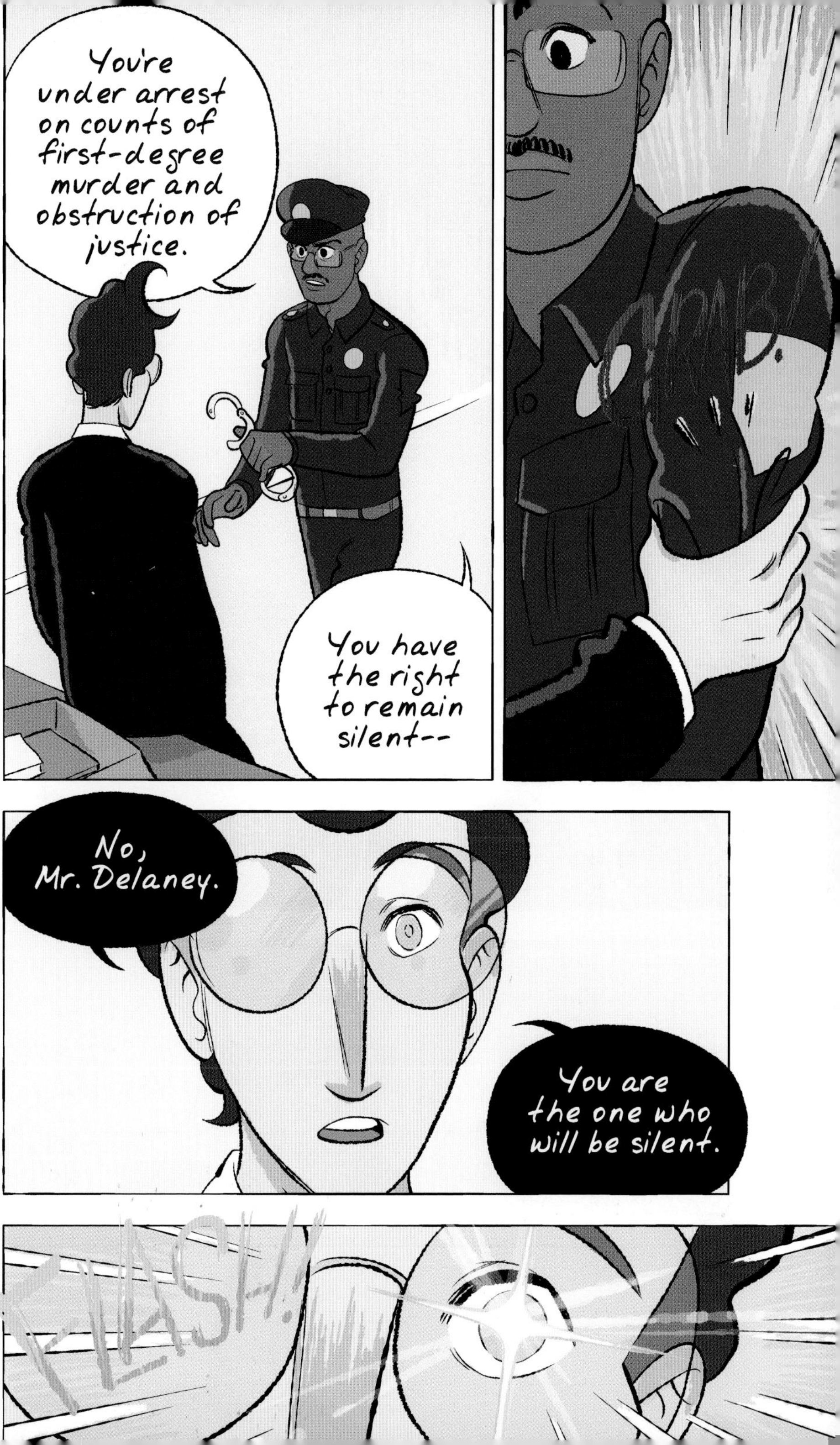
You're under arrest on counts of first-degree murder and obstruction of justice.
You have the right to remain silent--
GRAB!
No, Mr. Delaney.
You are the one who will be silent.
FLASH!!

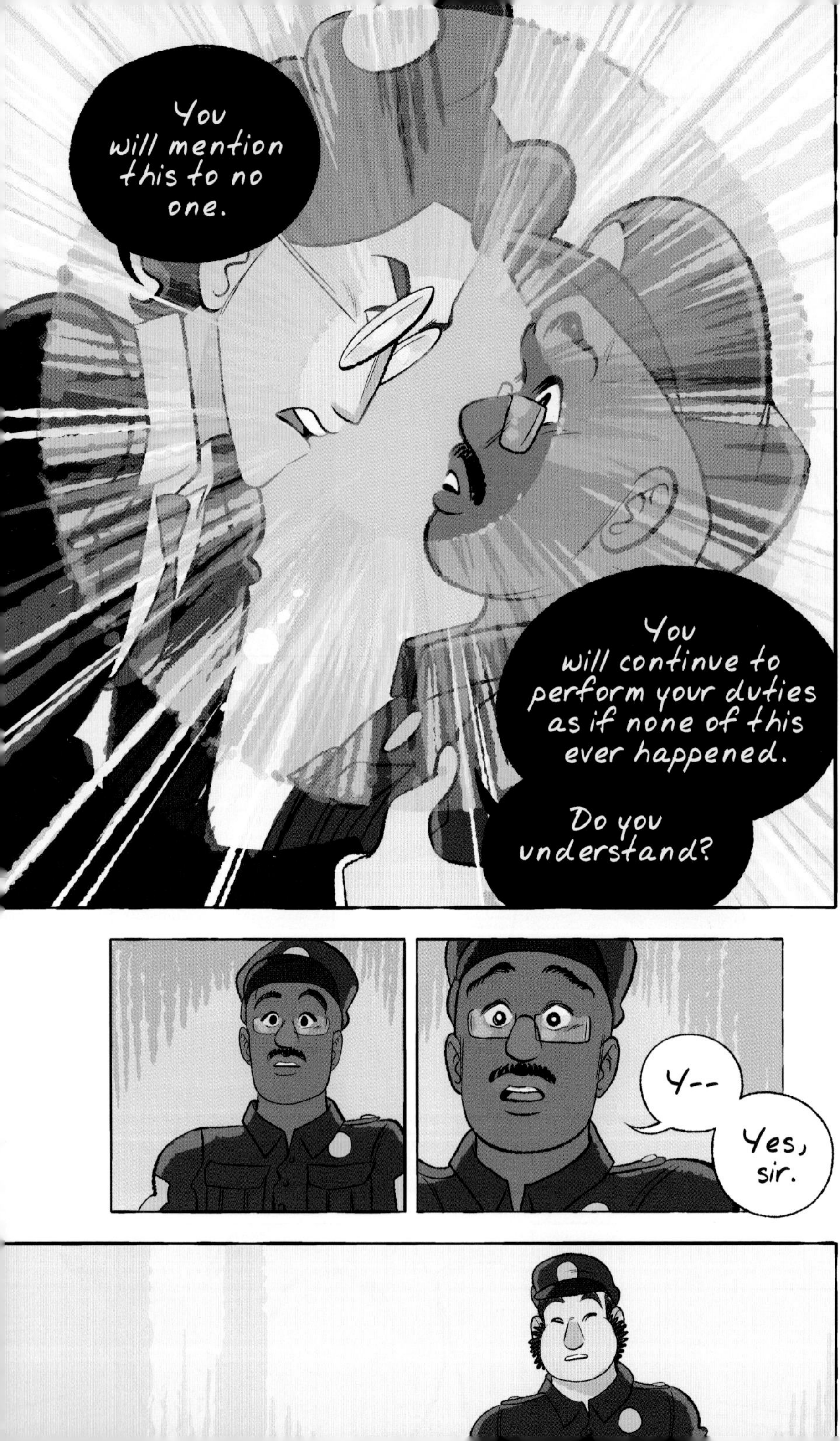
You will mention this to no one.
You will continue to perform your duties as if none of this ever happened.
Do you understand?
Y--
Yes, sir.

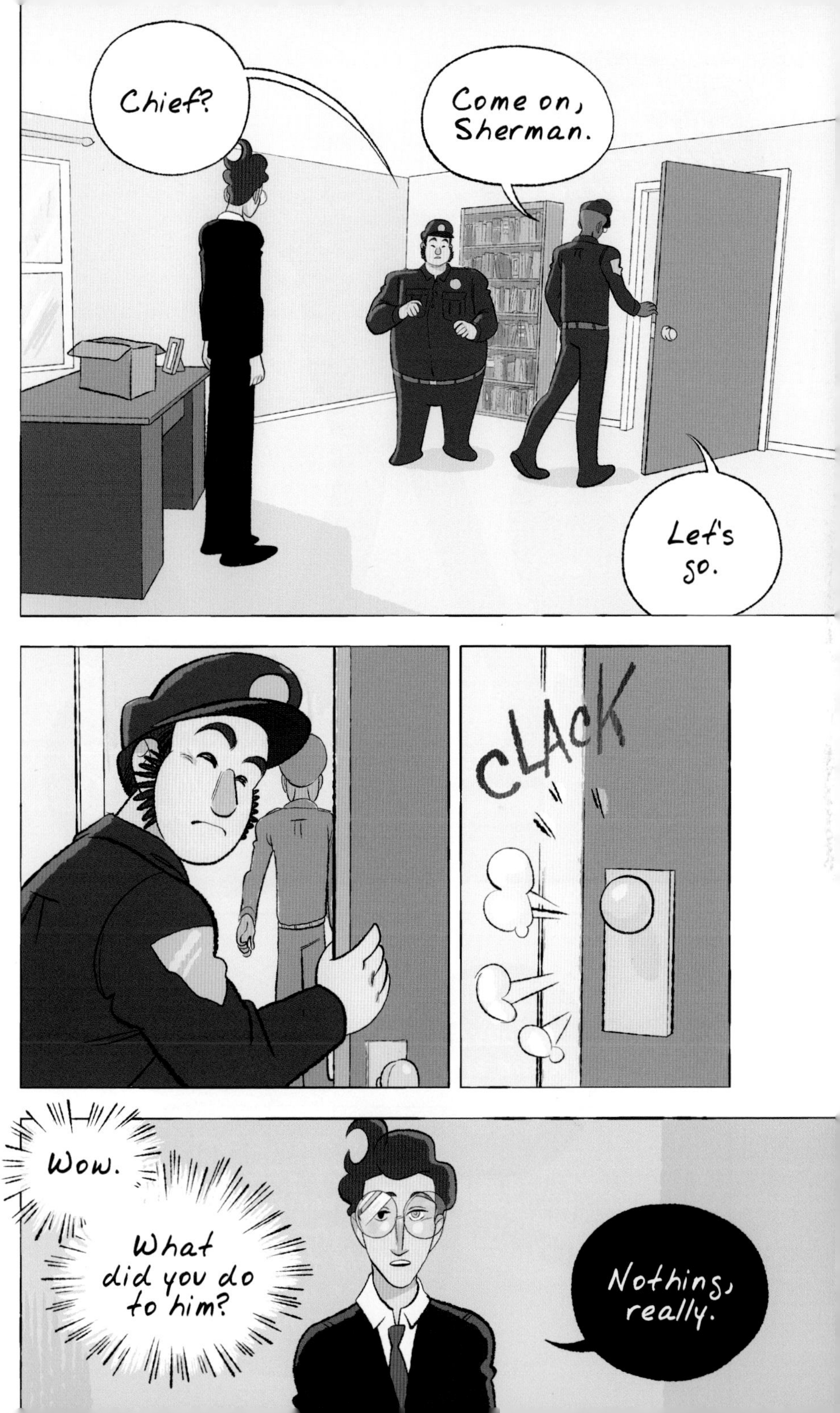

Chief?
Come on, Sherman.
Let's go.
CLACK
Wow.
What did you do to him?
Nothing, really.

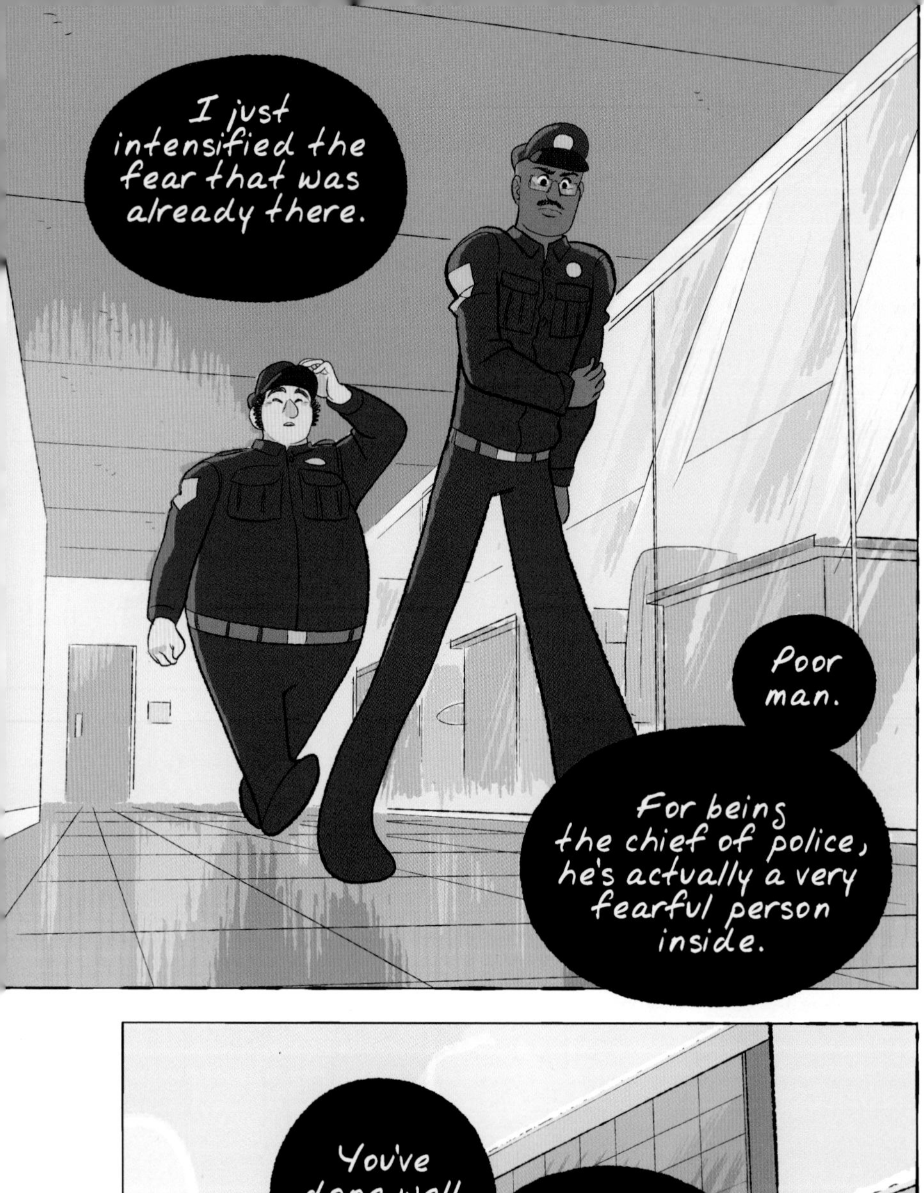
I just intensified the fear that was already there.
Poor man.
For being the chief of police, he's actually a very fearful person inside.

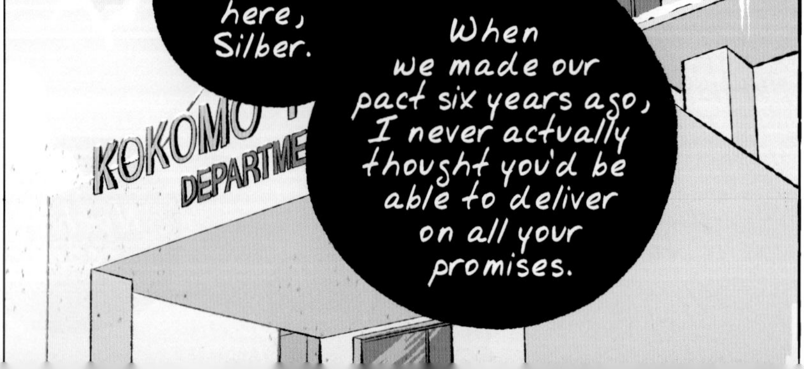
KOKOMO
DEPARTME
You've done well here, Silber.
When we made our pact six years ago, I never actually thought you'd be able to deliver on all your promises.

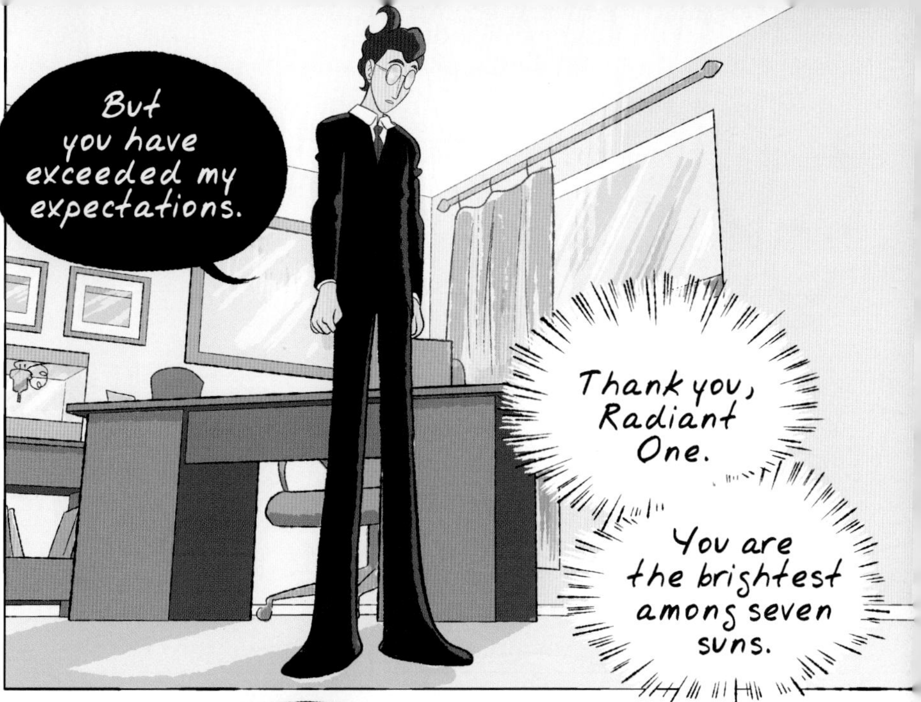
But you have exceeded my expectations.
Thank you, Radiant One.
You are the brightest among seven suns.

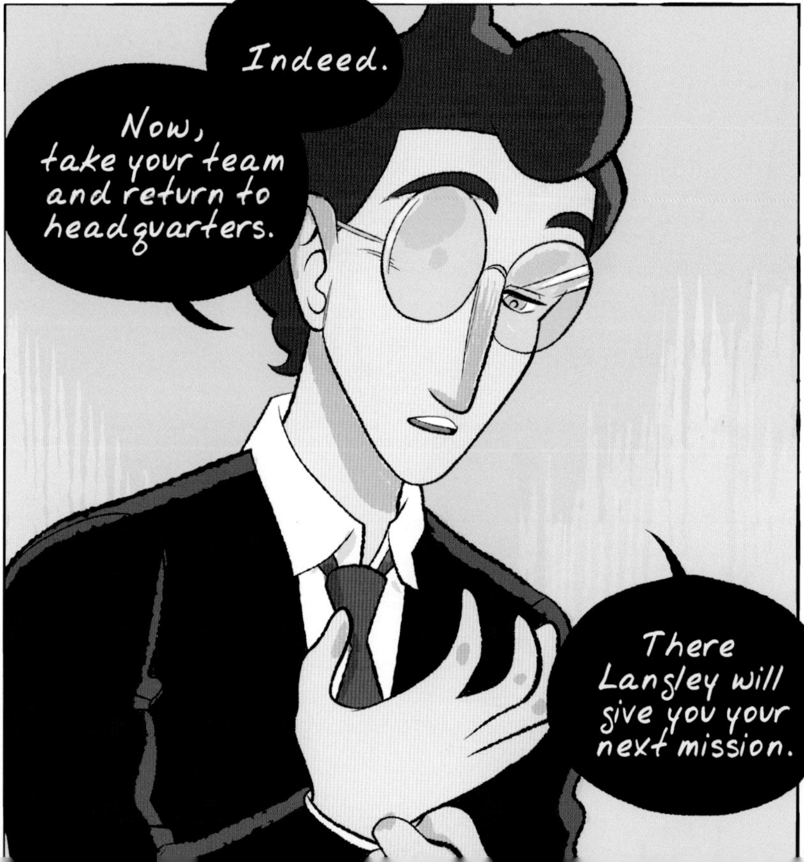
Indeed.
Now, take your team and return to headquarters.
There Langley will give you your next mission.

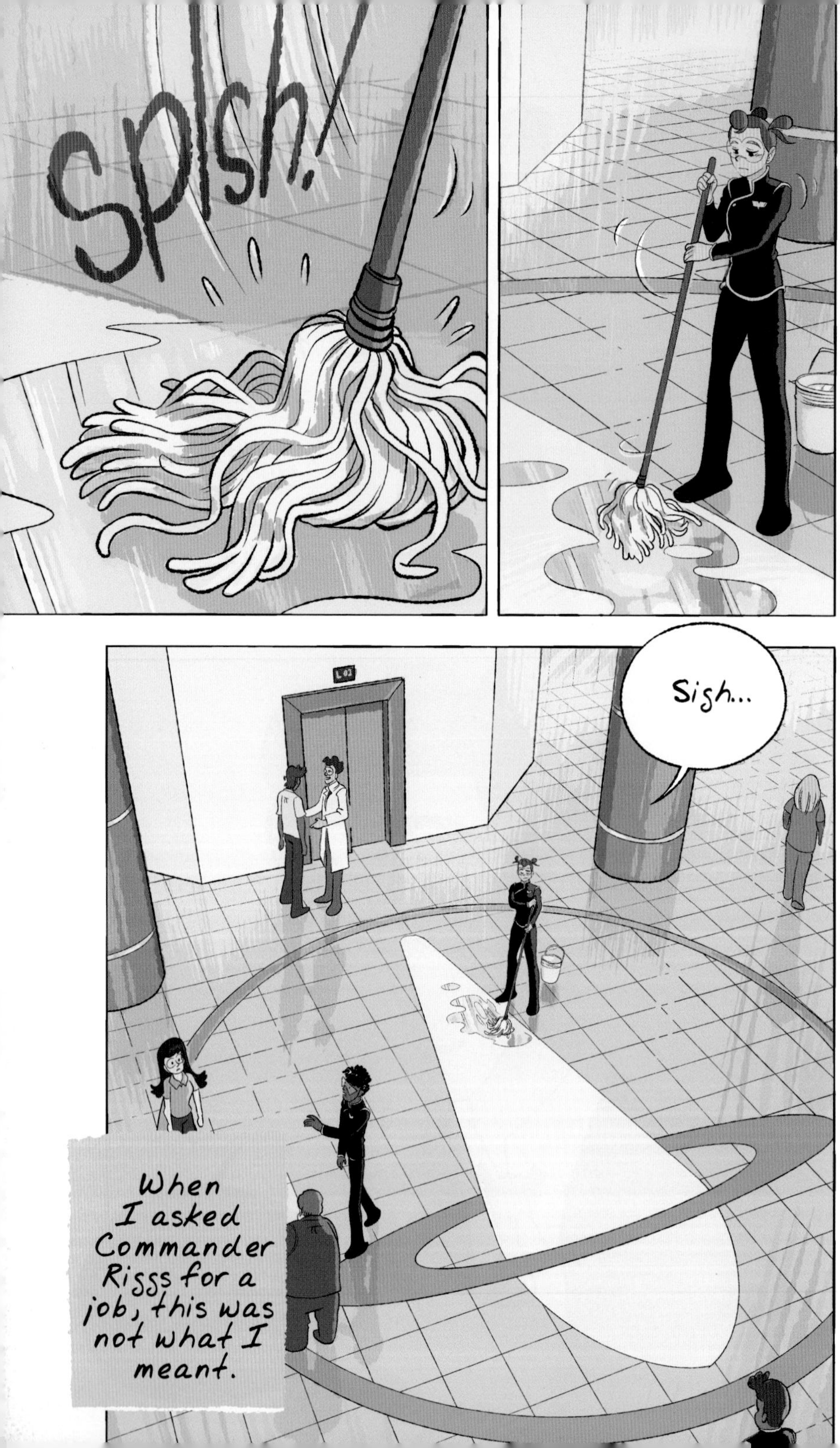
SPLSH!
Sigh...
When I asked Commander Risss for a job, this was not what I meant.

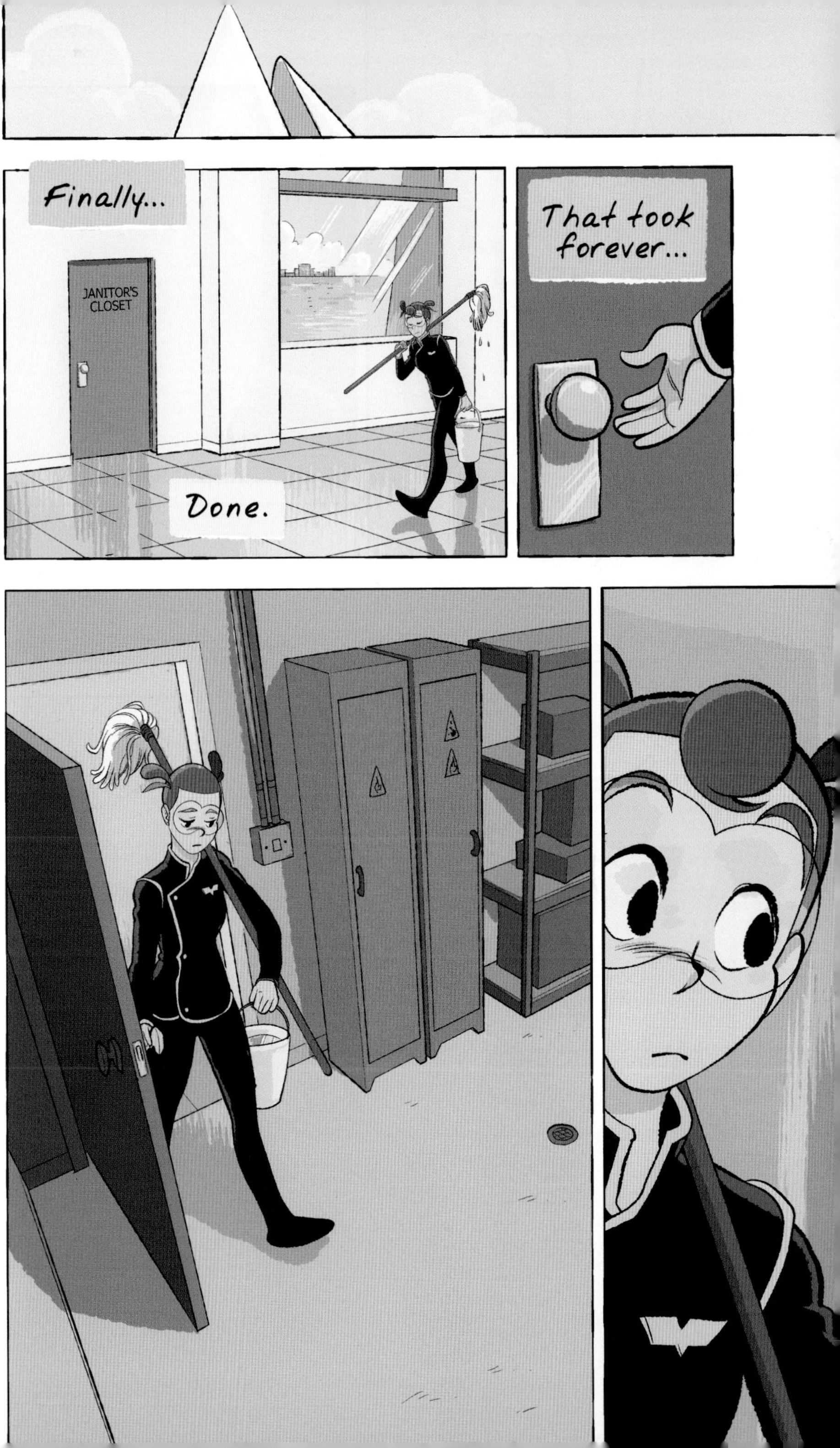

Finally...
JANITOR'S CLOSET
Done.
That took forever...

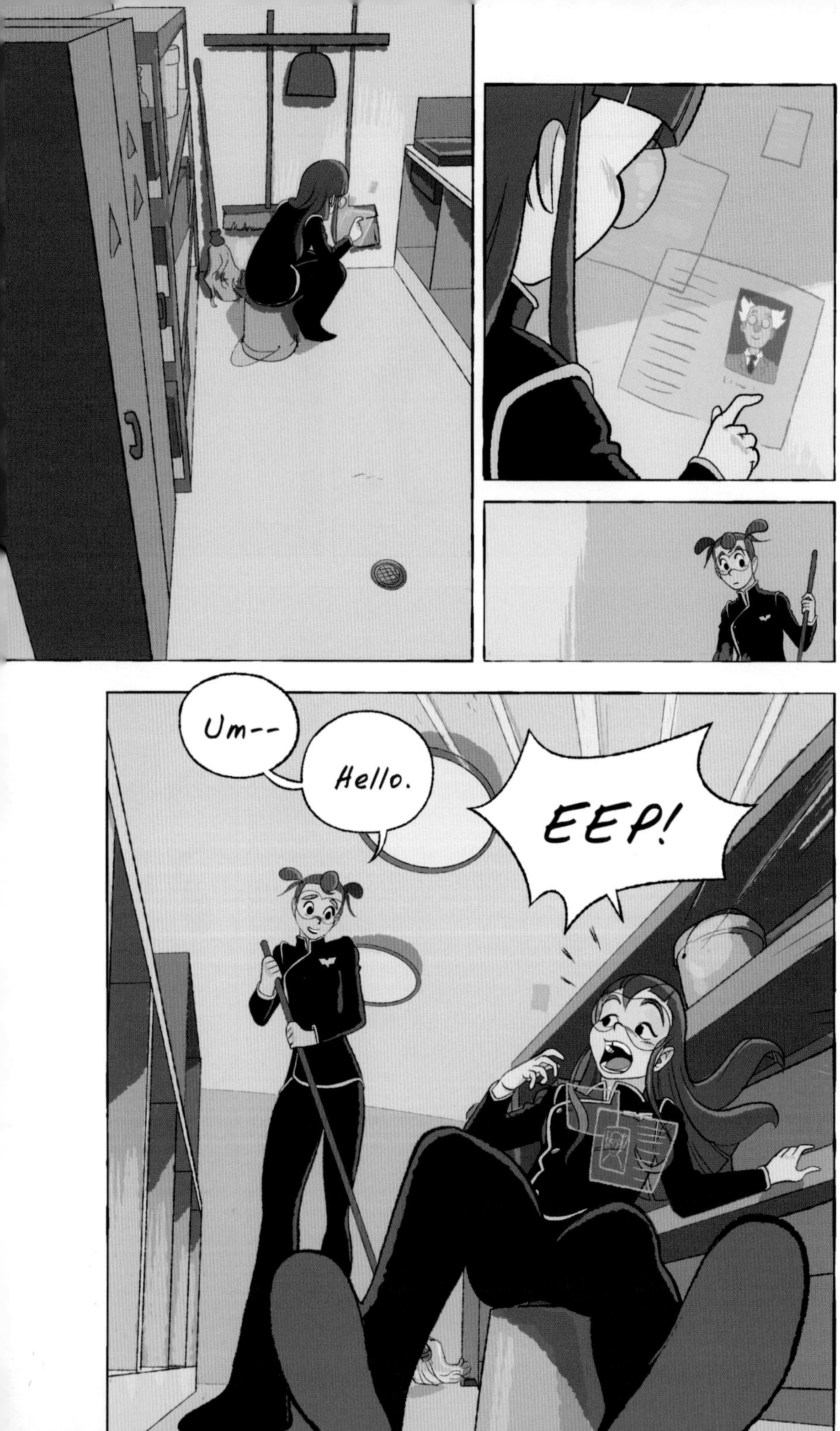
Um--
Hello.
EEP!

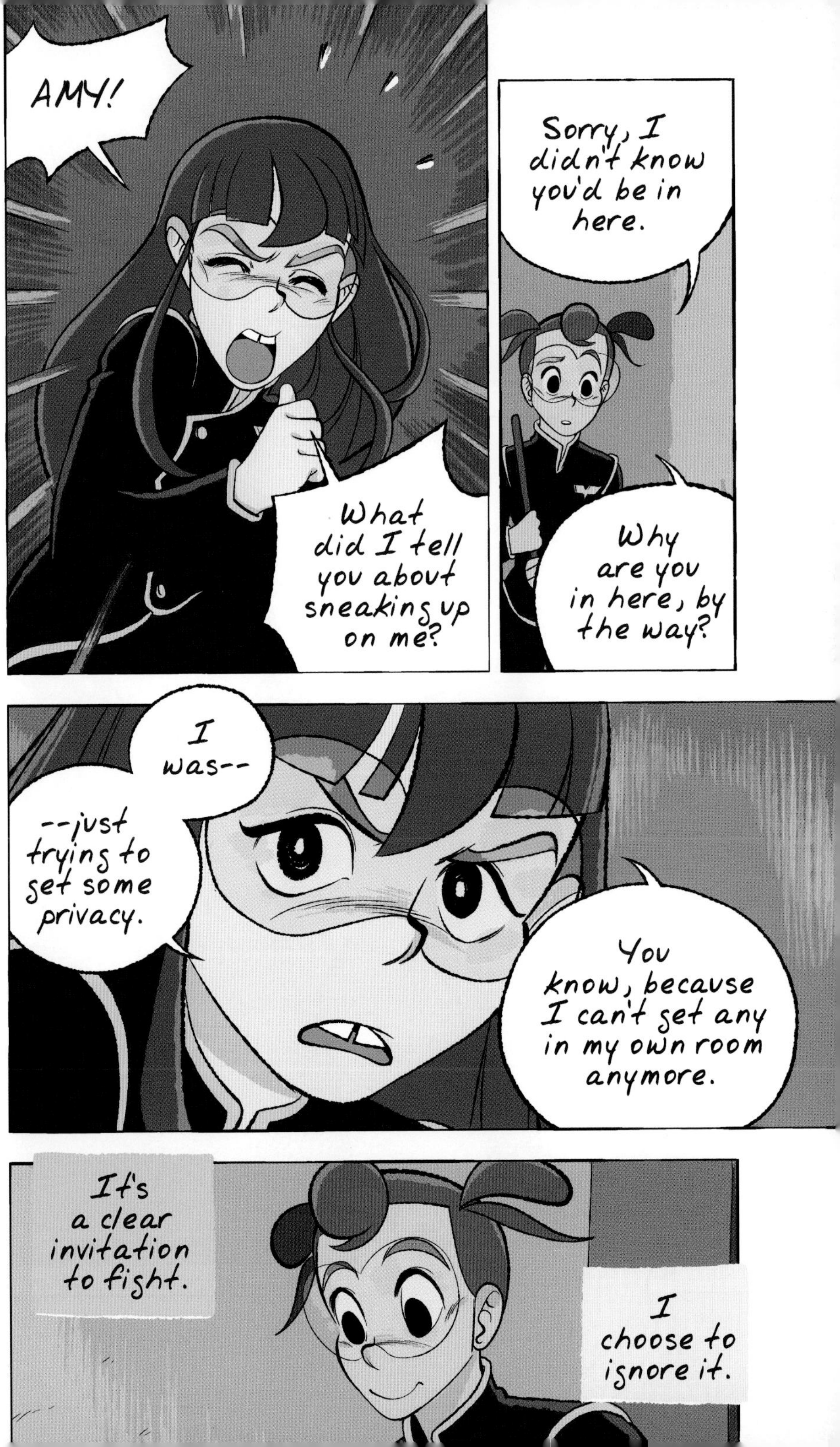
AMY!
Sorry, I didn't know you'd be in here.
What did I tell you about sneaking up on me?
Why are you in here, by the way?
I was--
--just trying to get some privacy.
You know, because I can't get any in my own room anymore.
It's a clear invitation to fight.
I choose to ignore it.

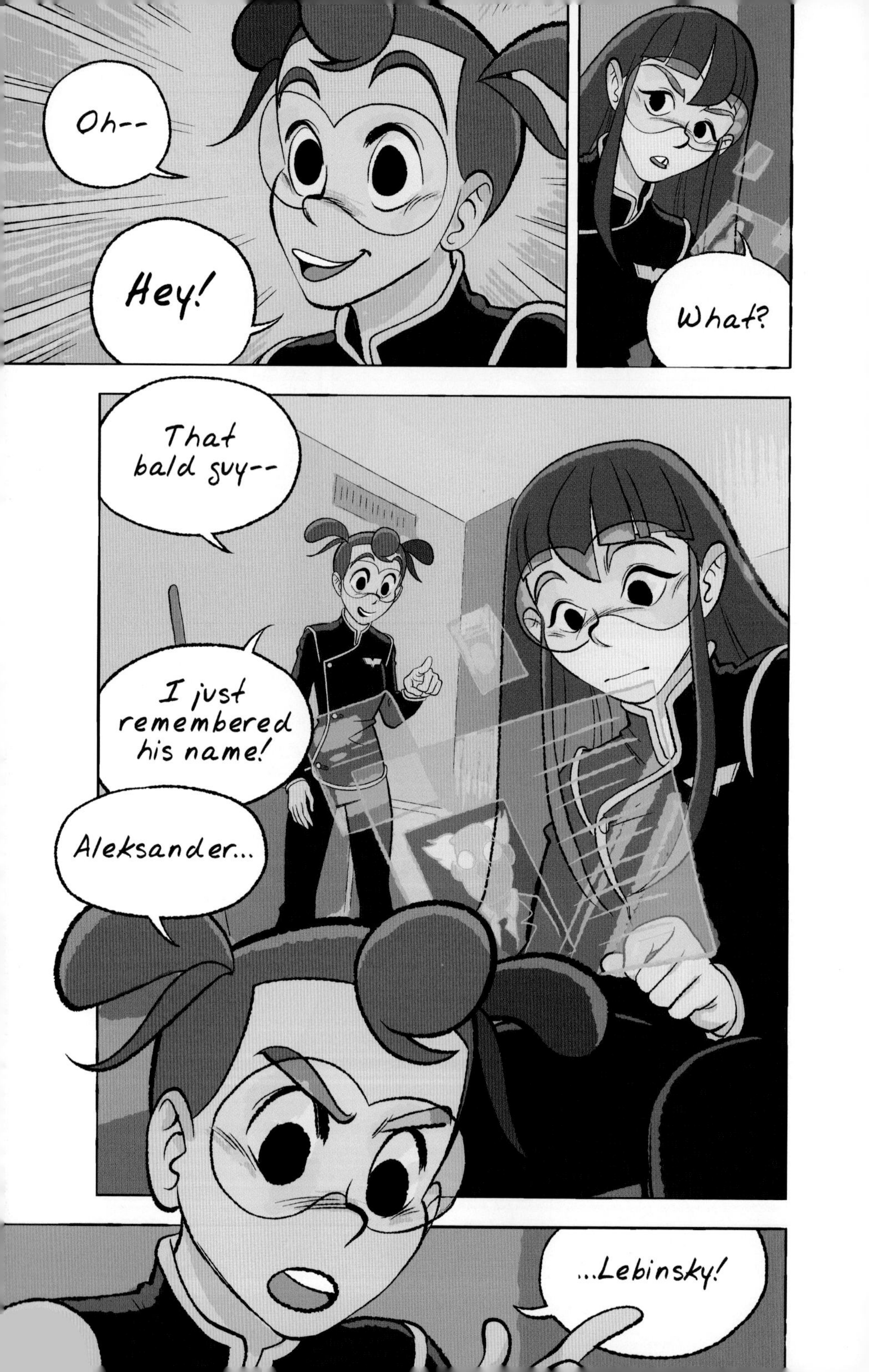
Oh--
Hey!
What?
That bald guy--
I just remembered his name!
Aleksander...
...Lebinsky!

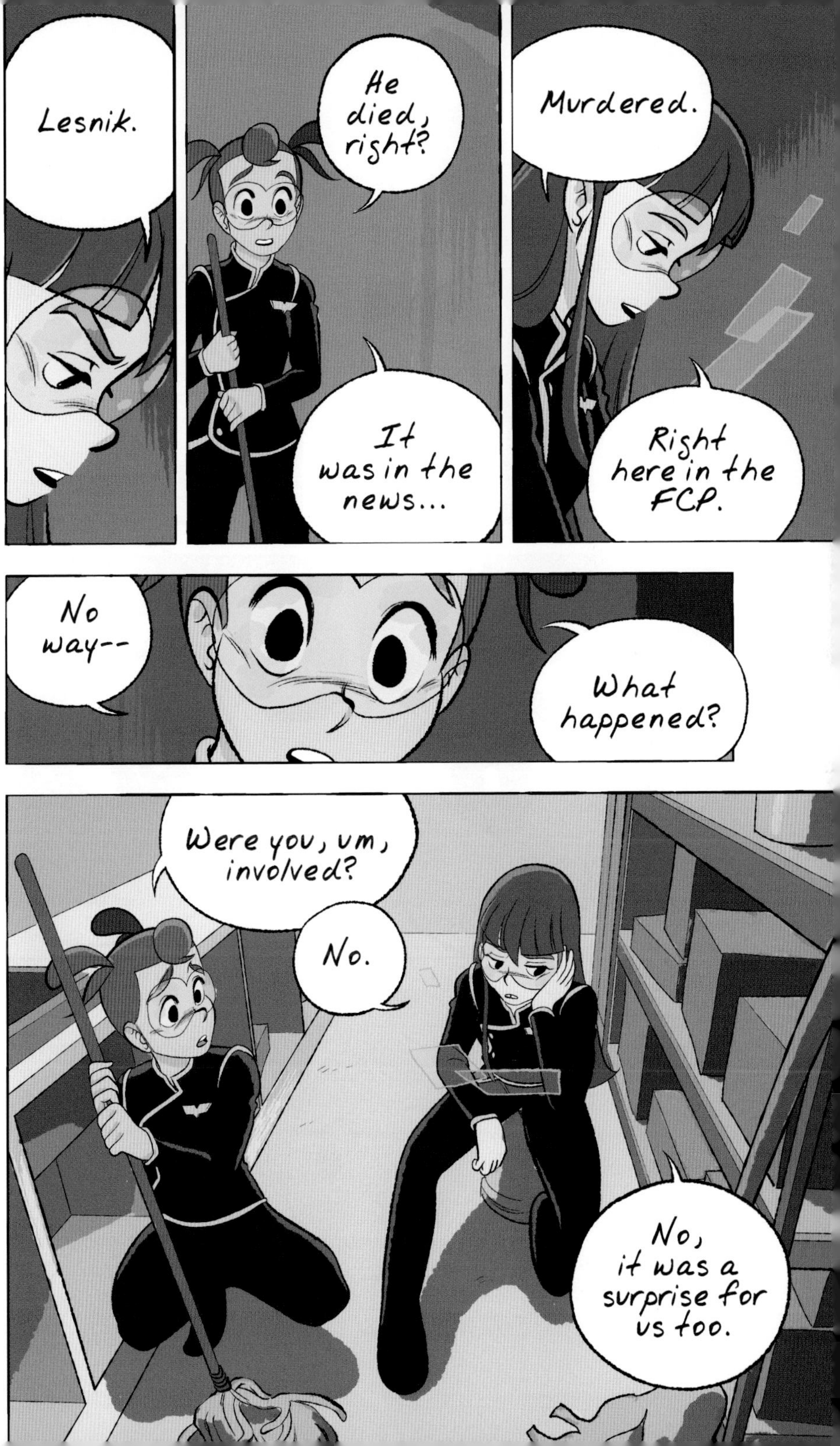
Lesnik.
He died, right?
It was in the news...
Murdered.
Right here in the FCP.
No way--
What happened?
Were you, um, involved?
No.
No, it was a surprise for us too.

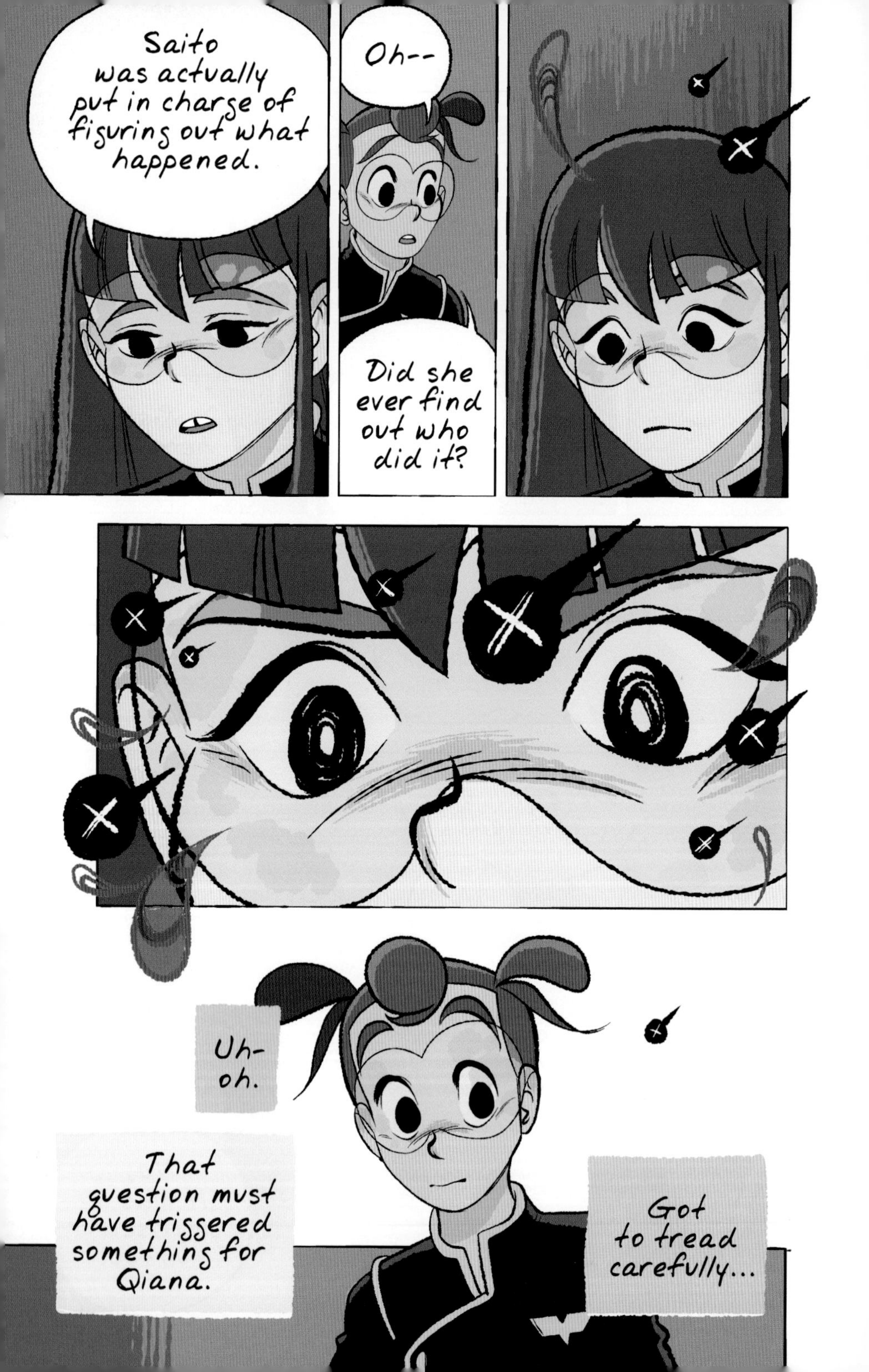
Saito was actually put in charge of figuring out what happened.
Oh--
Did she ever find out who did it?
Uh-oh.
That question must have triggered something for Qiana.
Got to tread carefully...

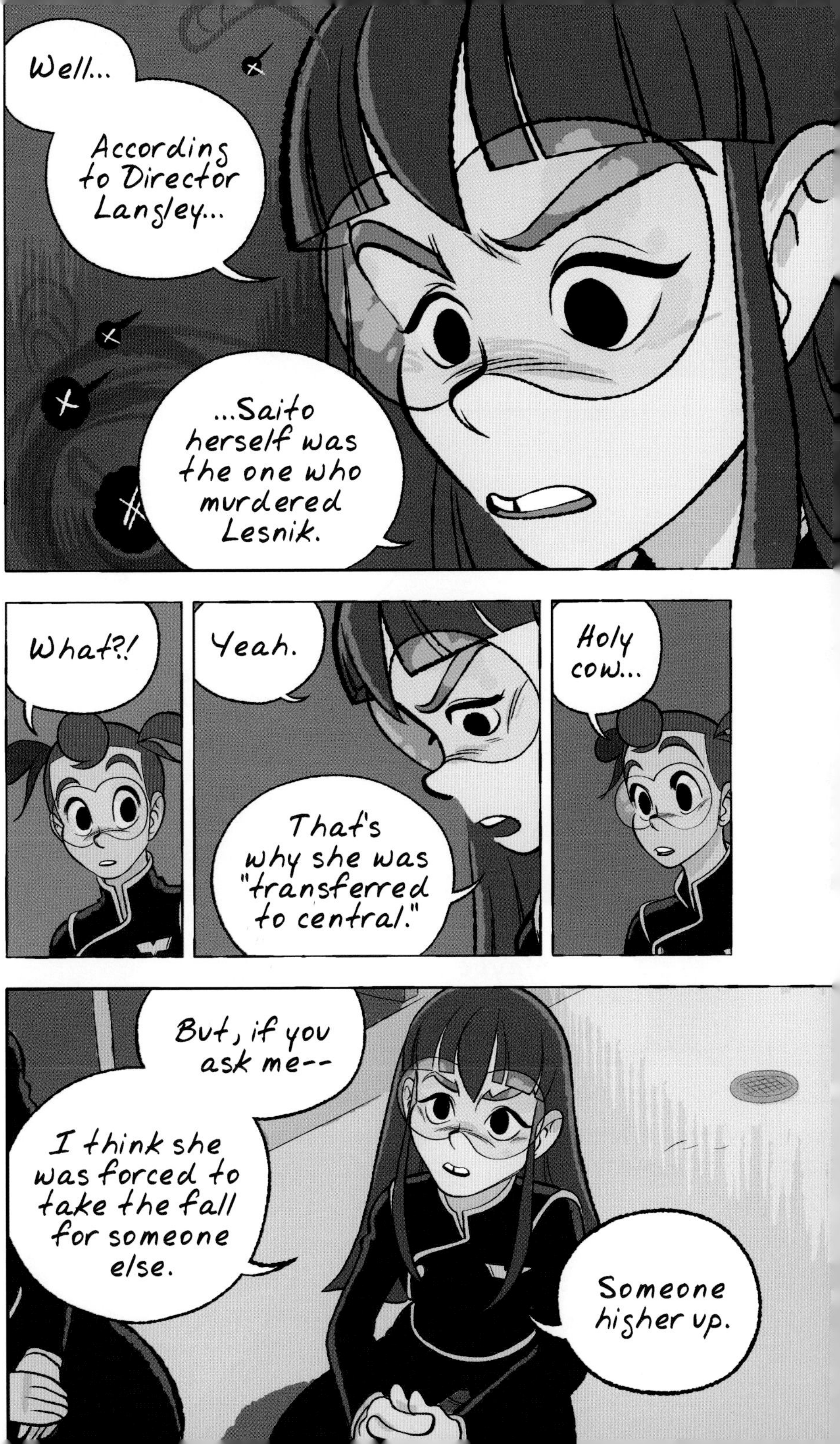
Well...
According to Director Langley...
...Saito herself was the one who murdered Lesnik.
What?!
Yeah.
That's why she was "transferred to central."
Holy cow...
But, if you ask me--
I think she was forced to take the fall for someone else.
Someone higher up.

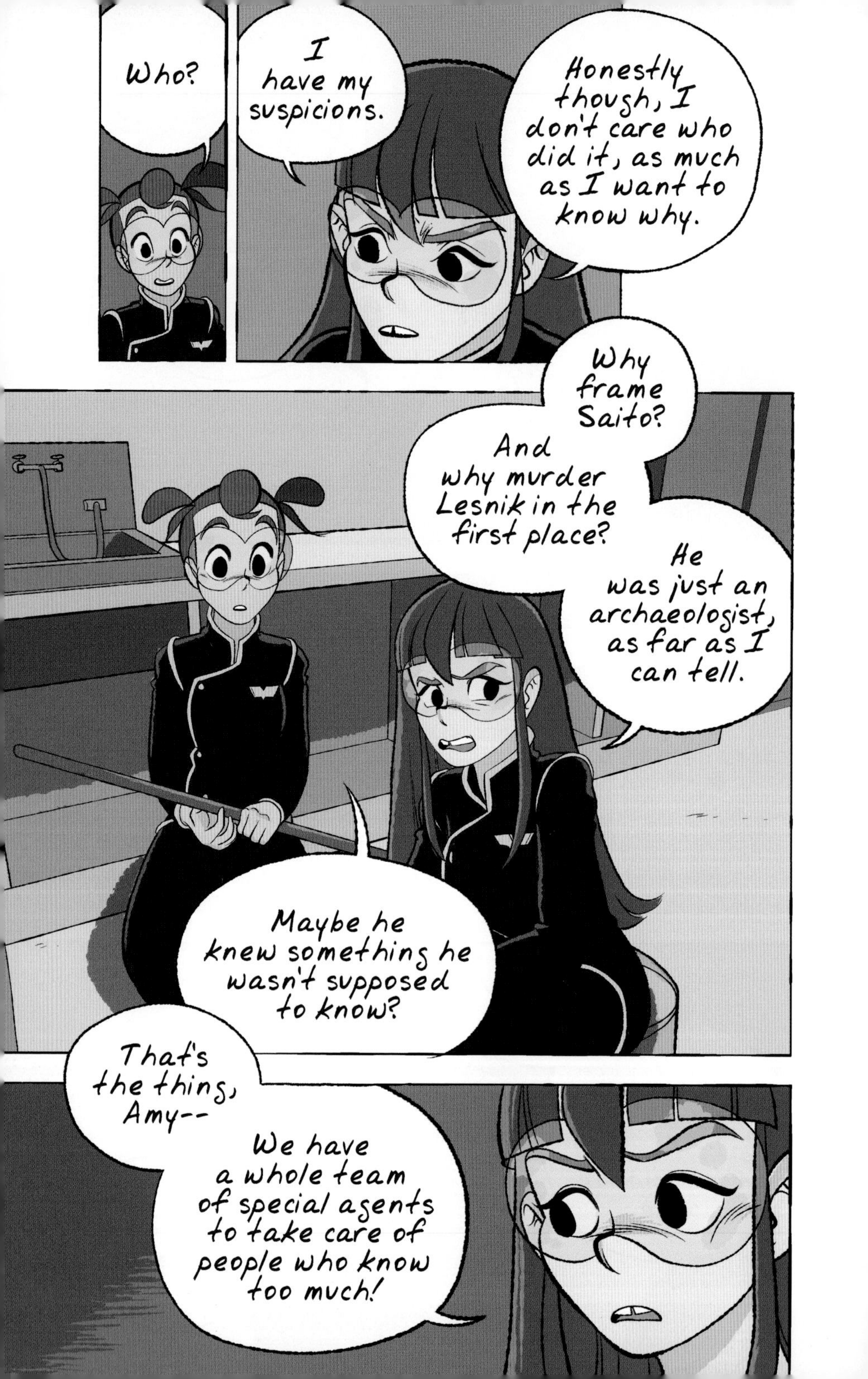
Who?
I have my suspicions.
Honestly though, I don't care who did it, as much as I want to know why.
Why frame Saito?
And why murder Lesnik in the first place?
He was just an archaeologist, as far as I can tell.
Maybe he knew something he wasn't supposed to know?
That's the thing, Amy--
We have a whole team of special agents to take care of people who know too much!

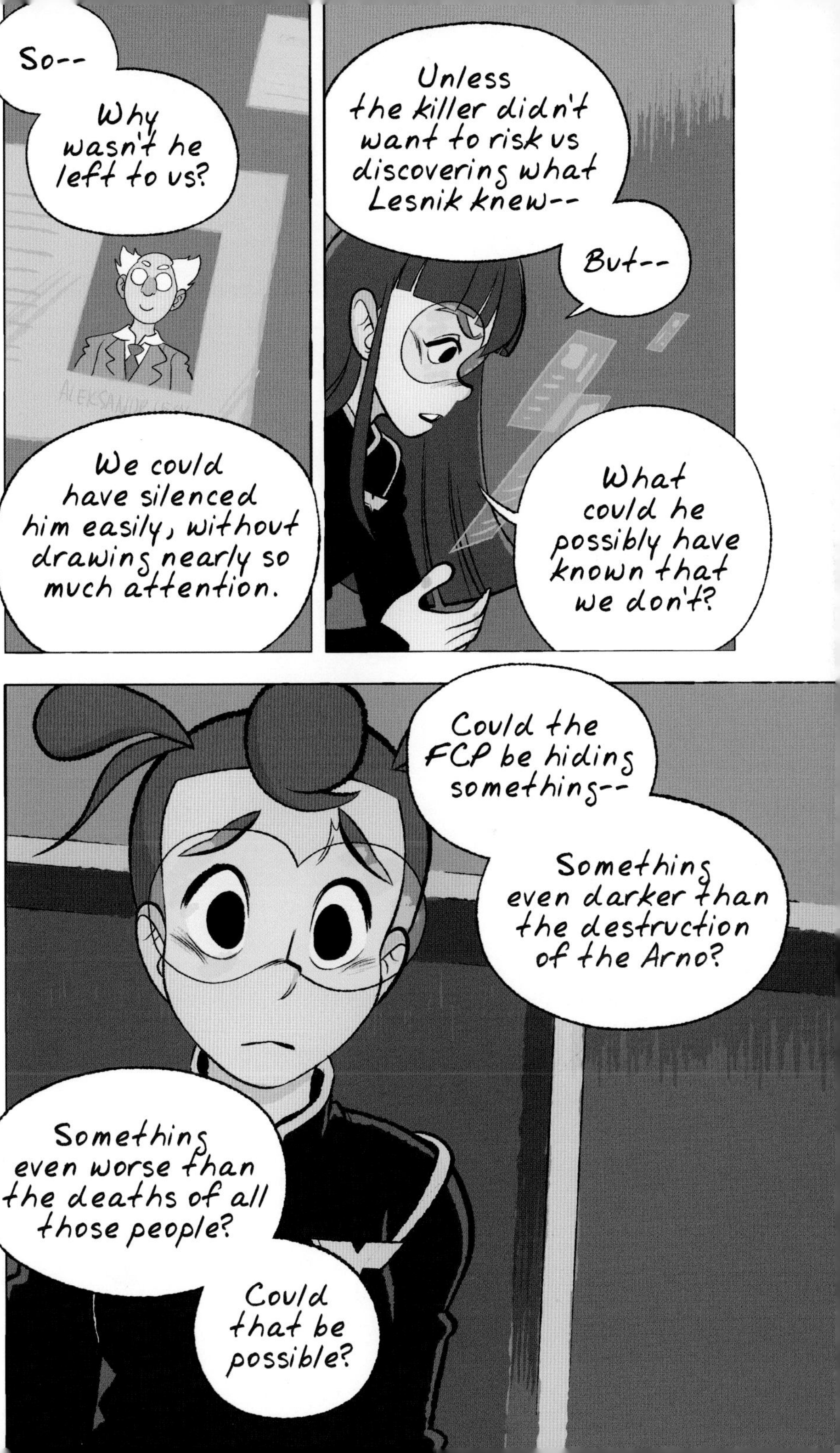
So--
Why wasn't he left to us?
Unless the killer didn't want to risk us discovering what Lesnik knew--
But--
We could have silenced him easily, without drawing nearly so much attention.
What could he possibly have known that we don't?
Could the FCP be hiding something--
Something even darker than the destruction of the Arno?
Something even worse than the deaths of all those people?
Could that be possible?

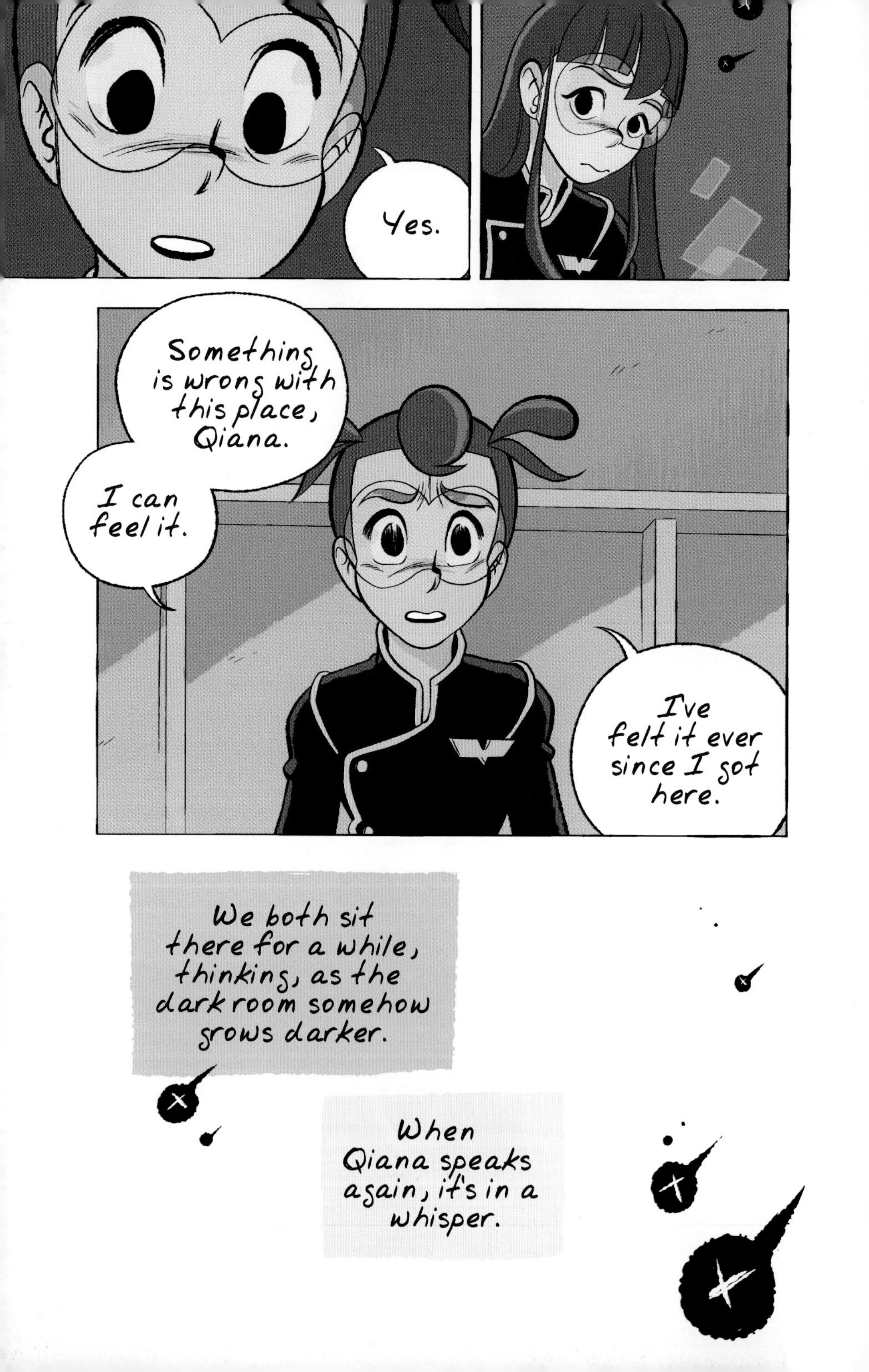
Yes.
Something is wrong with this place, Qiana.
I can feel it.
I've felt it ever since I got here.
We both sit there for a while, thinking, as the darkroom somehow grows darker.
When Qiana speaks again, it's in a whisper.

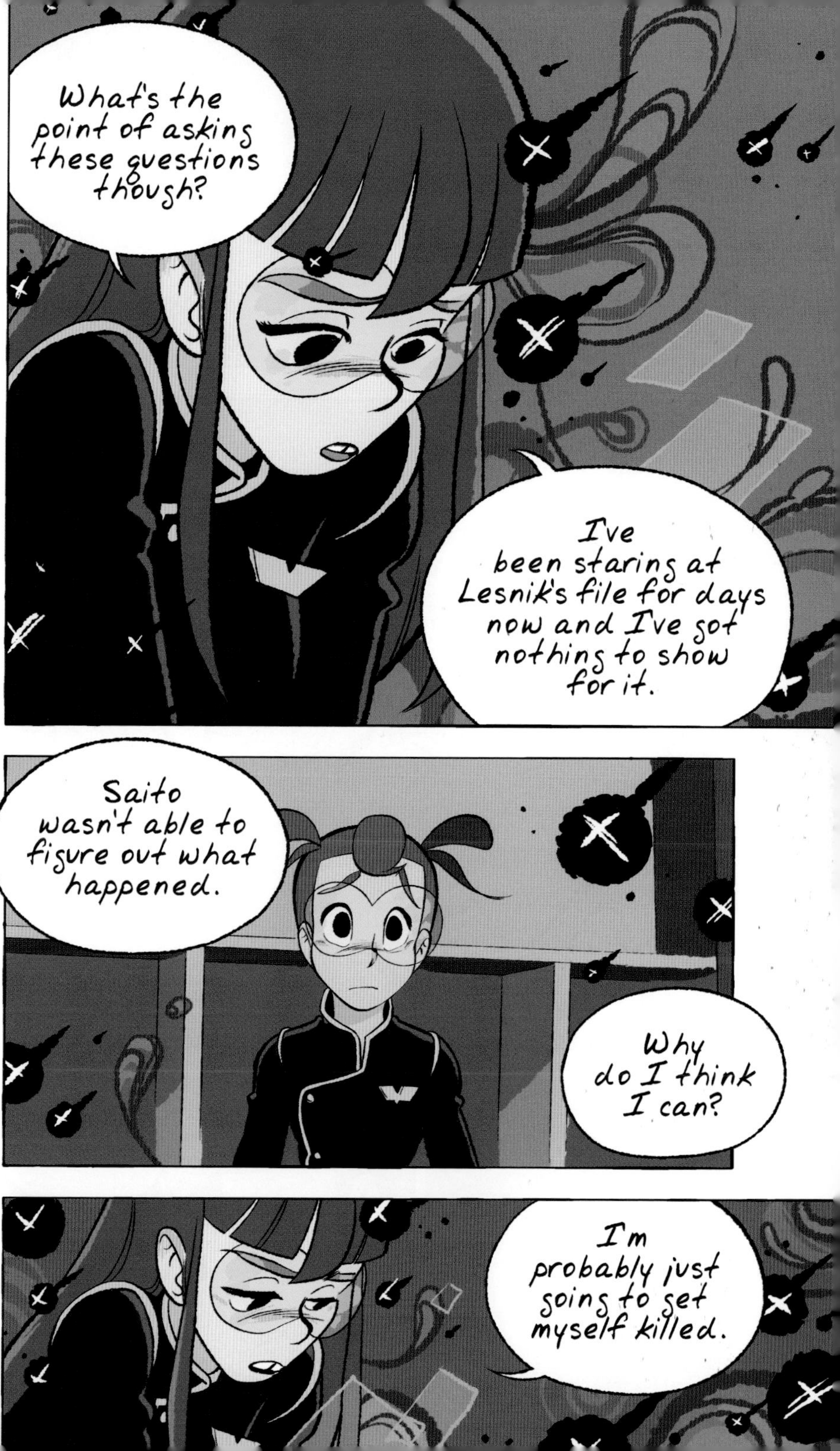
What's the point of asking these questions though?
I've been staring at Lesnik's file for days now and I've got nothing to show for it.
Saito wasn't able to figure out what happened.
Why do I think I can?
I'm probably just going to get myself killed.

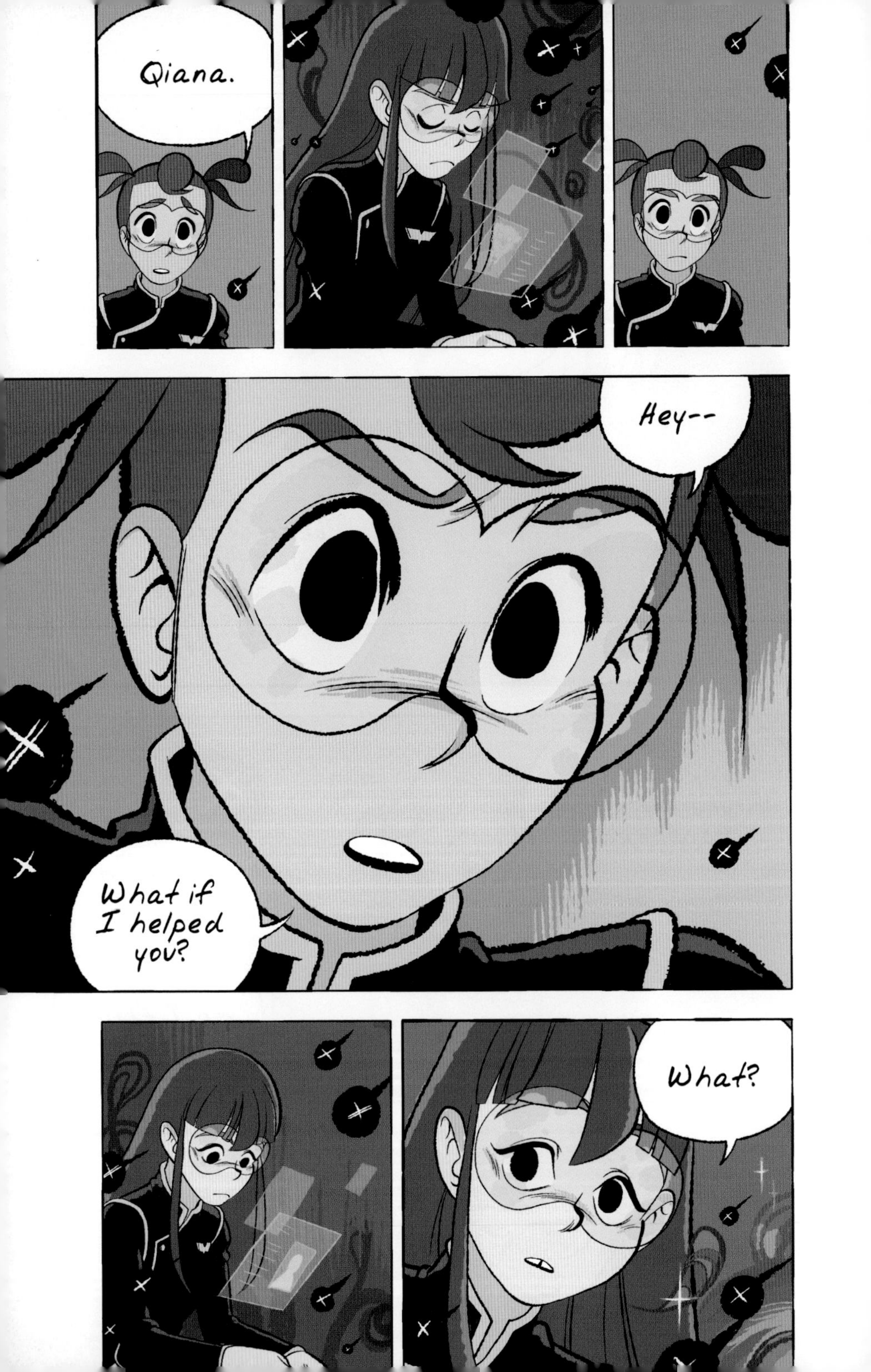
Qiana.
Hey--
What if I helped you?
What?

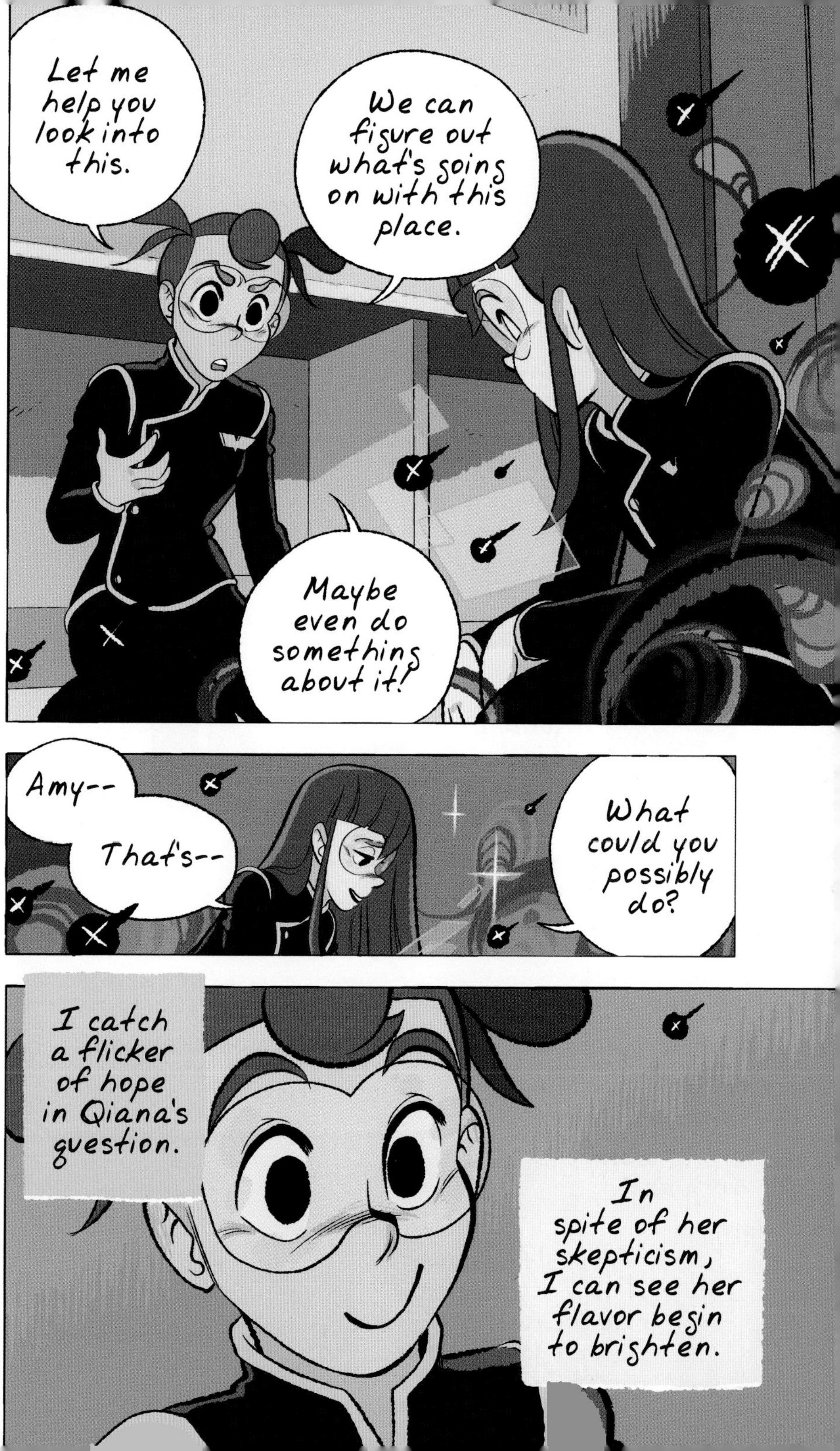
Let me help you look into this.
We can figure out what's going on with this place.
Maybe even do something about it!
Amy--
That's--
What could you possibly do?
I catch a flicker of hope in Qiana's question.
In spite of her skepticism, I can see her flavor begin to brighten.

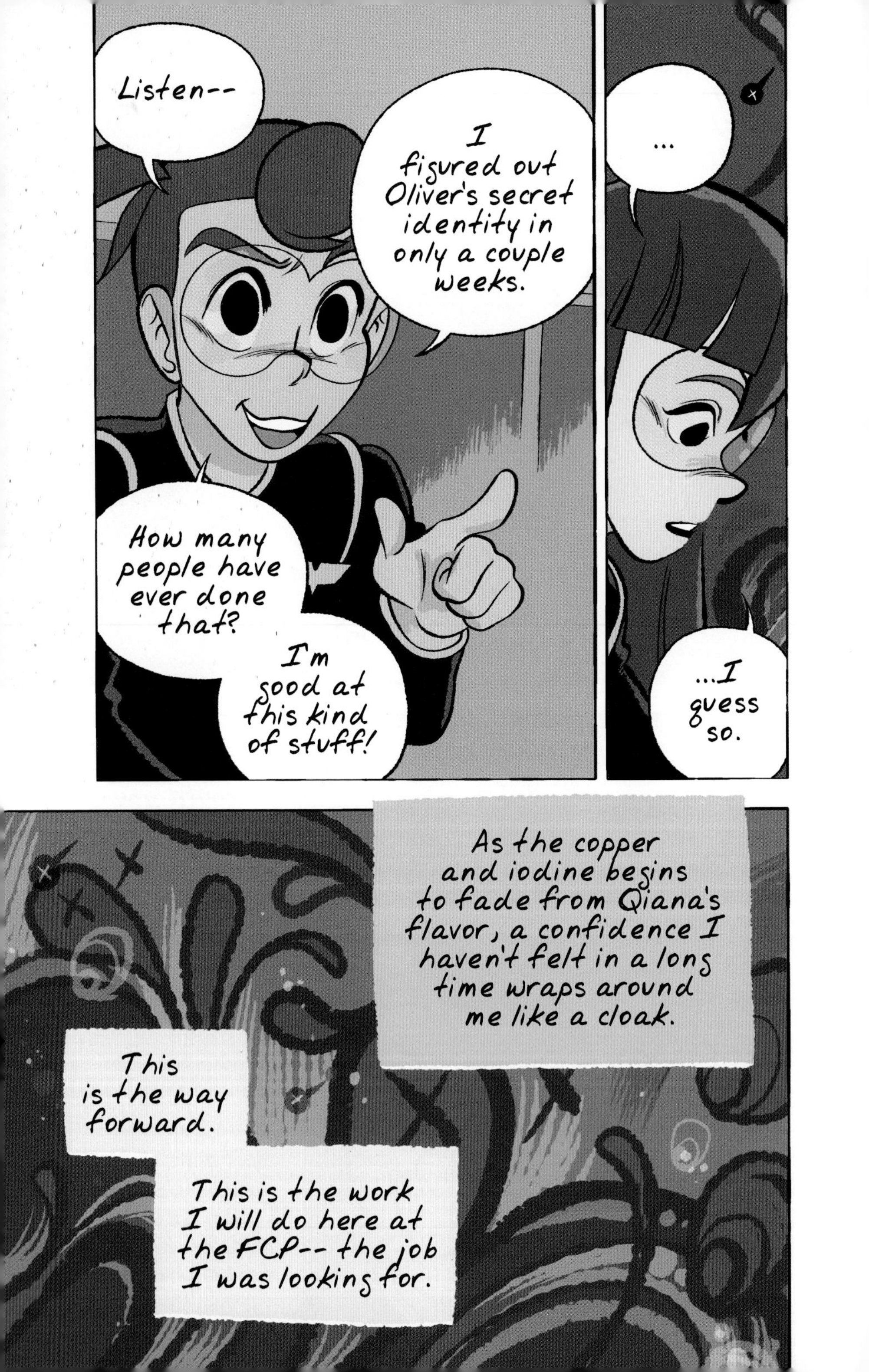

Listen--
I figured out Oliver's secret identity in only a couple weeks.
...
How many people have ever done that?
I'm good at this kind of stuff!
...I guess so.
As the copper and iodine begins to fade from Qiana's flavor, a confidence I haven't felt in a long time wraps around me like a cloak.
This is the way forward.
This is the work I will do here at the FCP-- the job I was looking for.

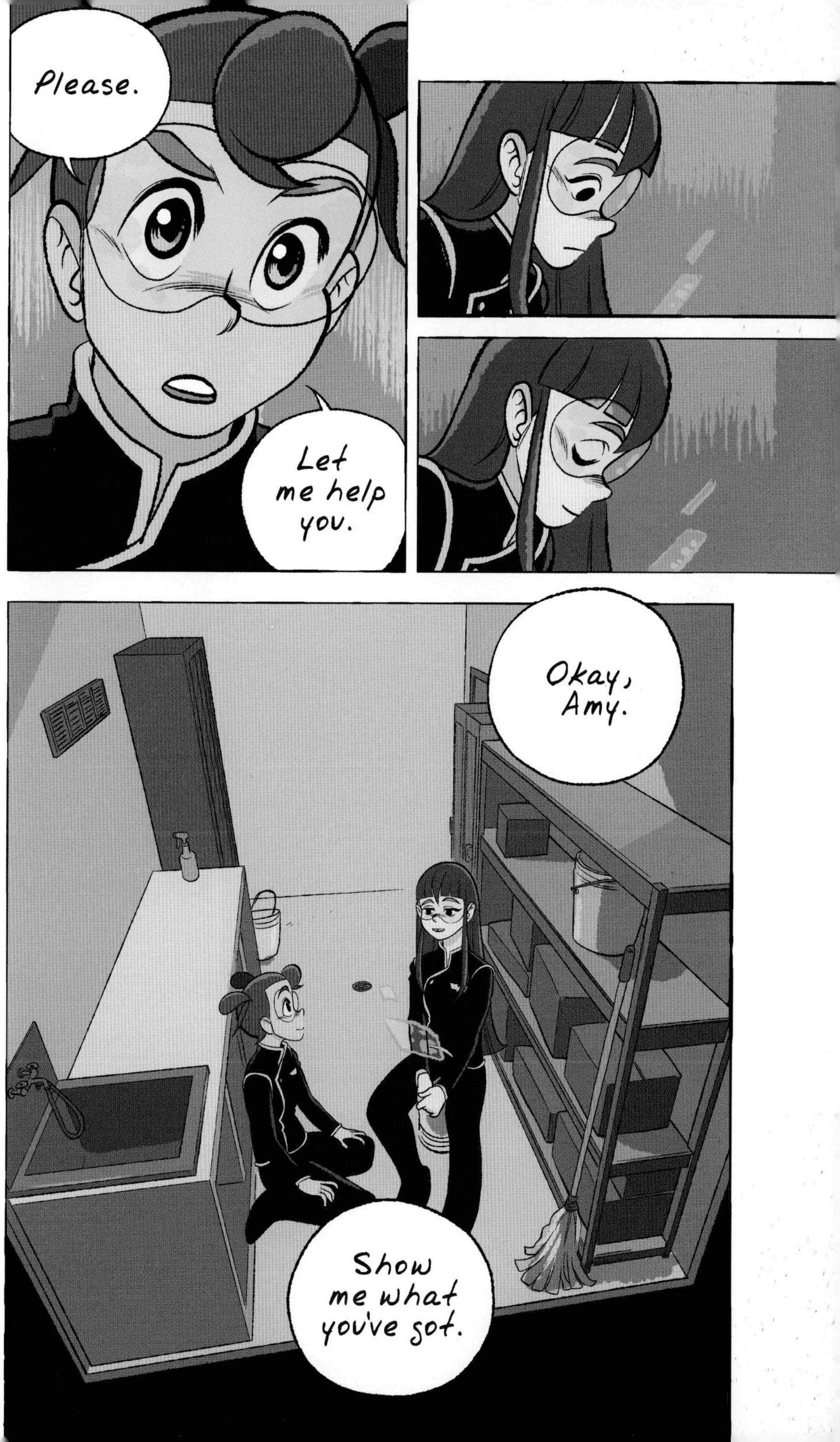
Please.
Let me help you.
Okay, Amy.
Show me what you've got.

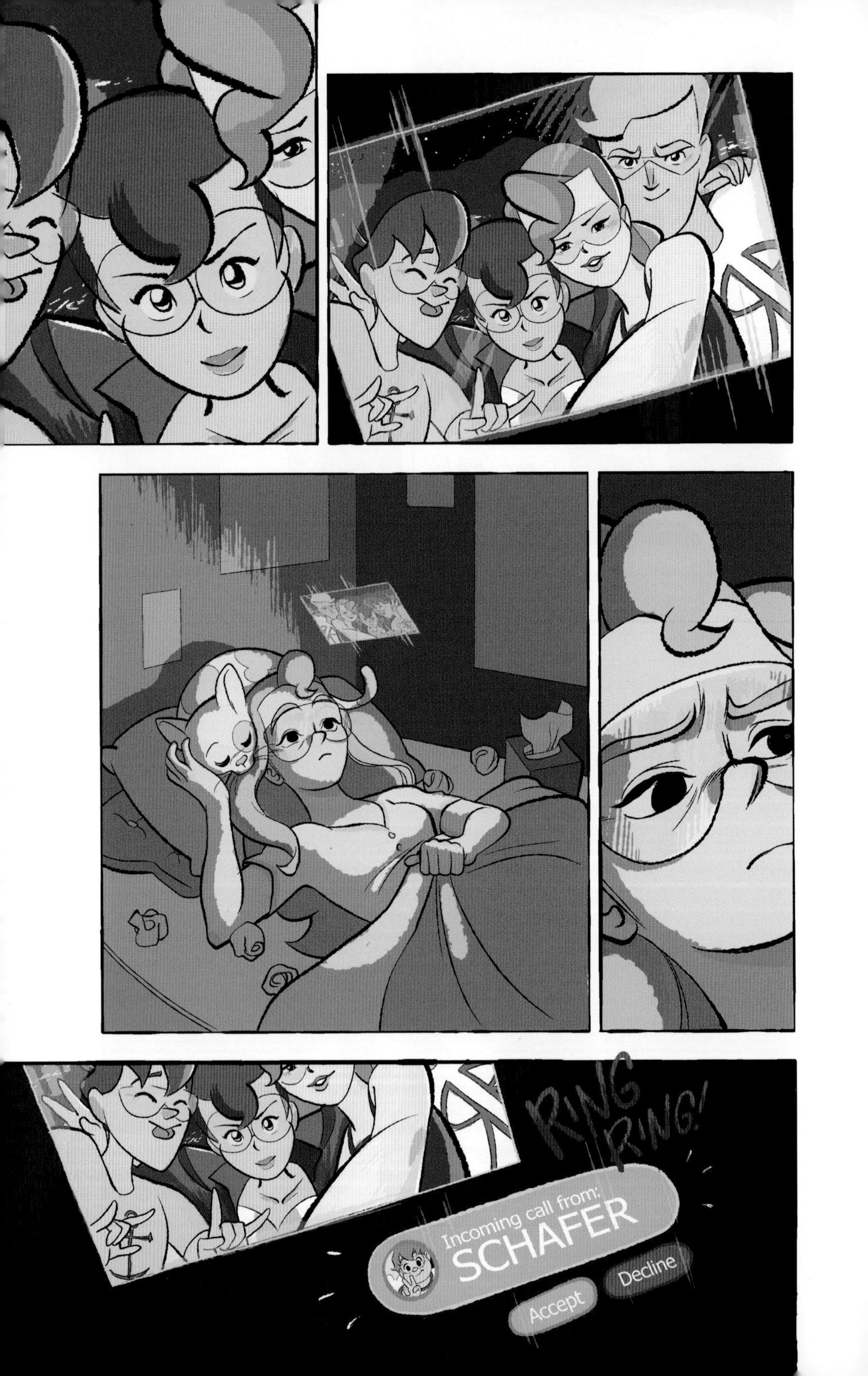
RING RING!
Incoming call from:
SCHAFER
Decline
Accept

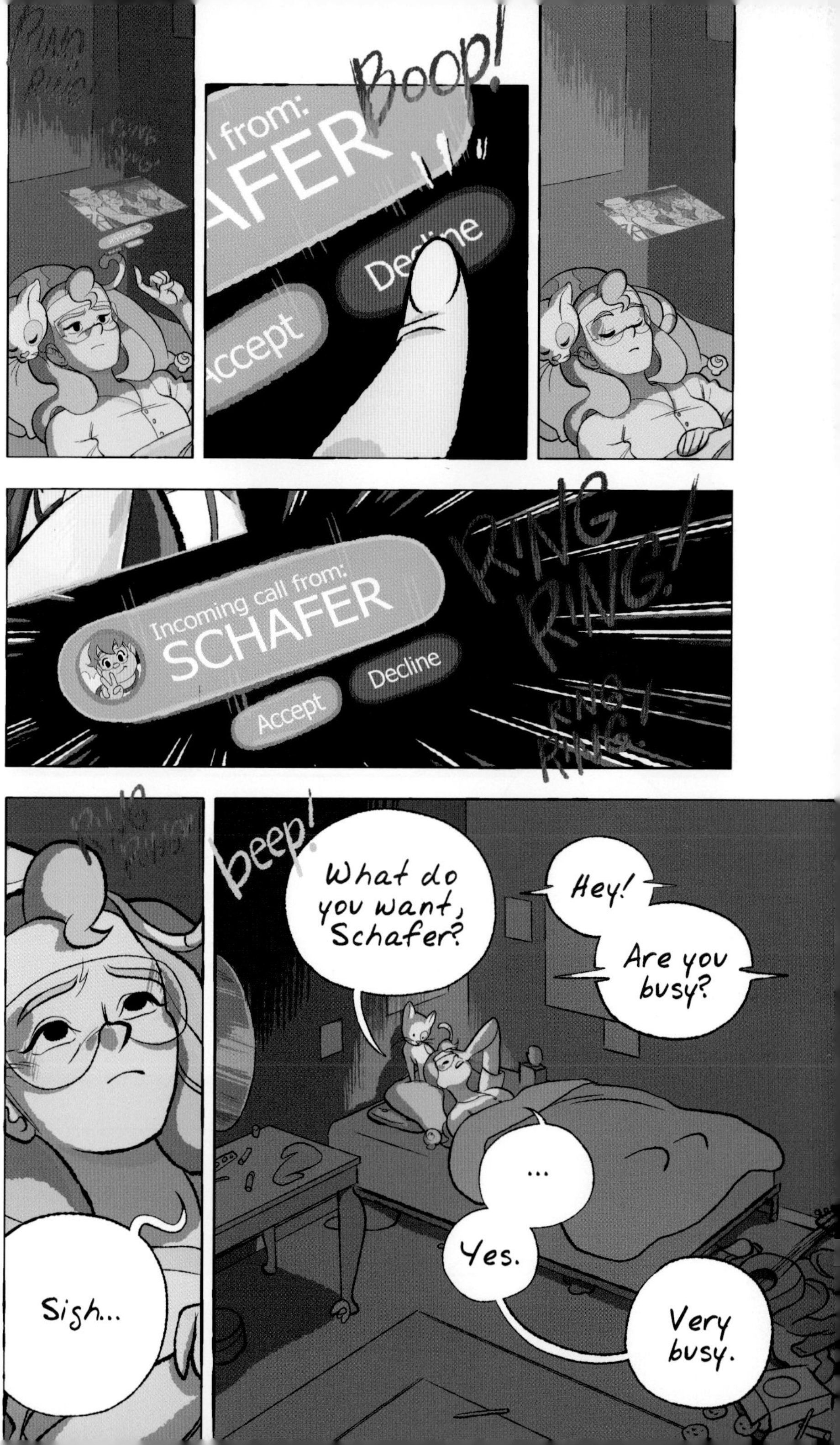
Ring ring!
Ring ring!
call from:
SCHAFER
Boop!
Accept
Decline
Incoming call from:
SCHAFER
Accept
Decline
RING RING!
RING RING!
beep!
What do you want, Schafer?
Hey!
Are you busy?
Sigh...
...
Yes.
Very busy.

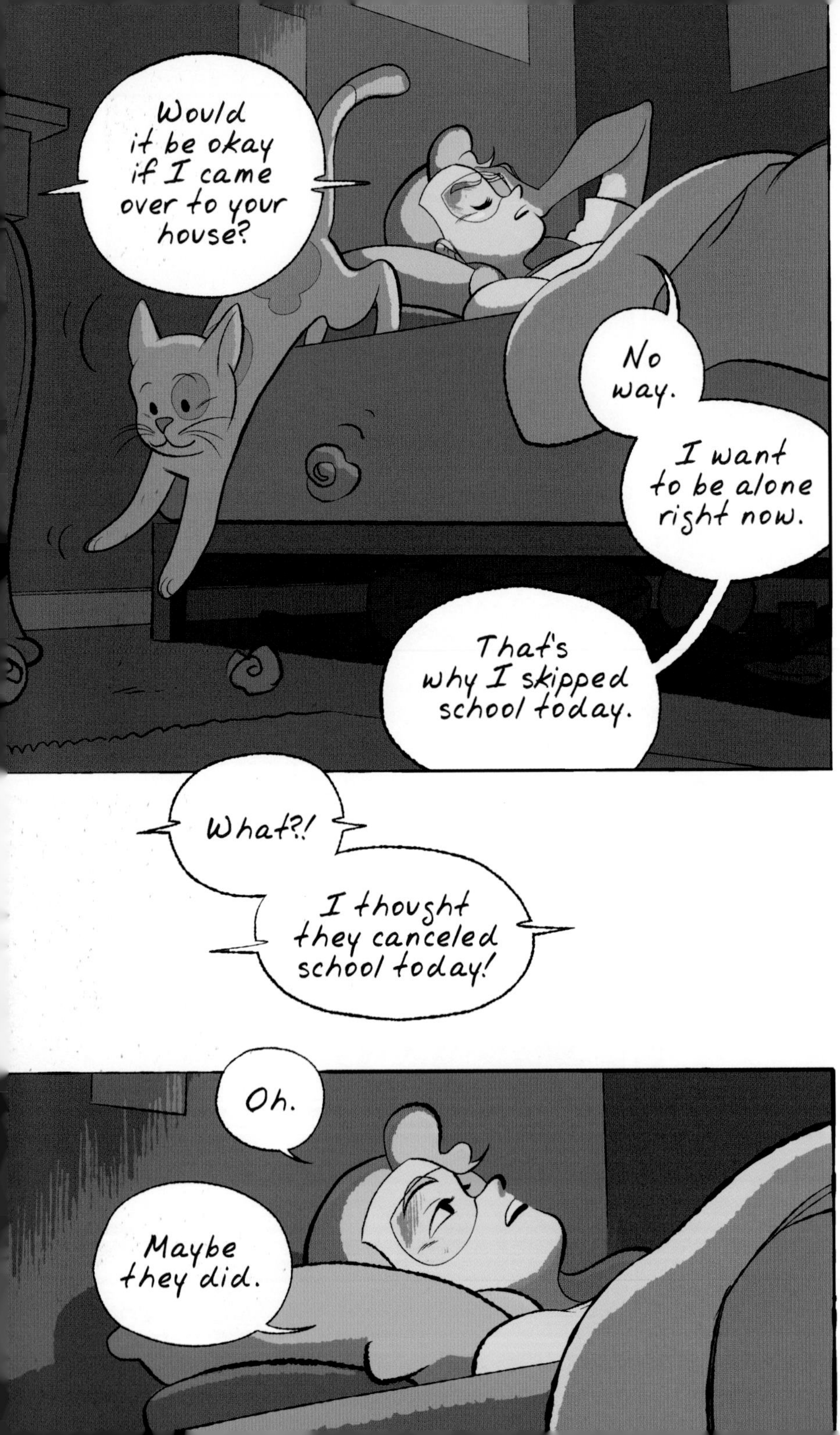
Would it be okay if I came over to your house?
No way.
I want to be alone right now.
That's why I skipped school today.
What?!
I thought they canceled school today!
Oh.
Maybe they did.

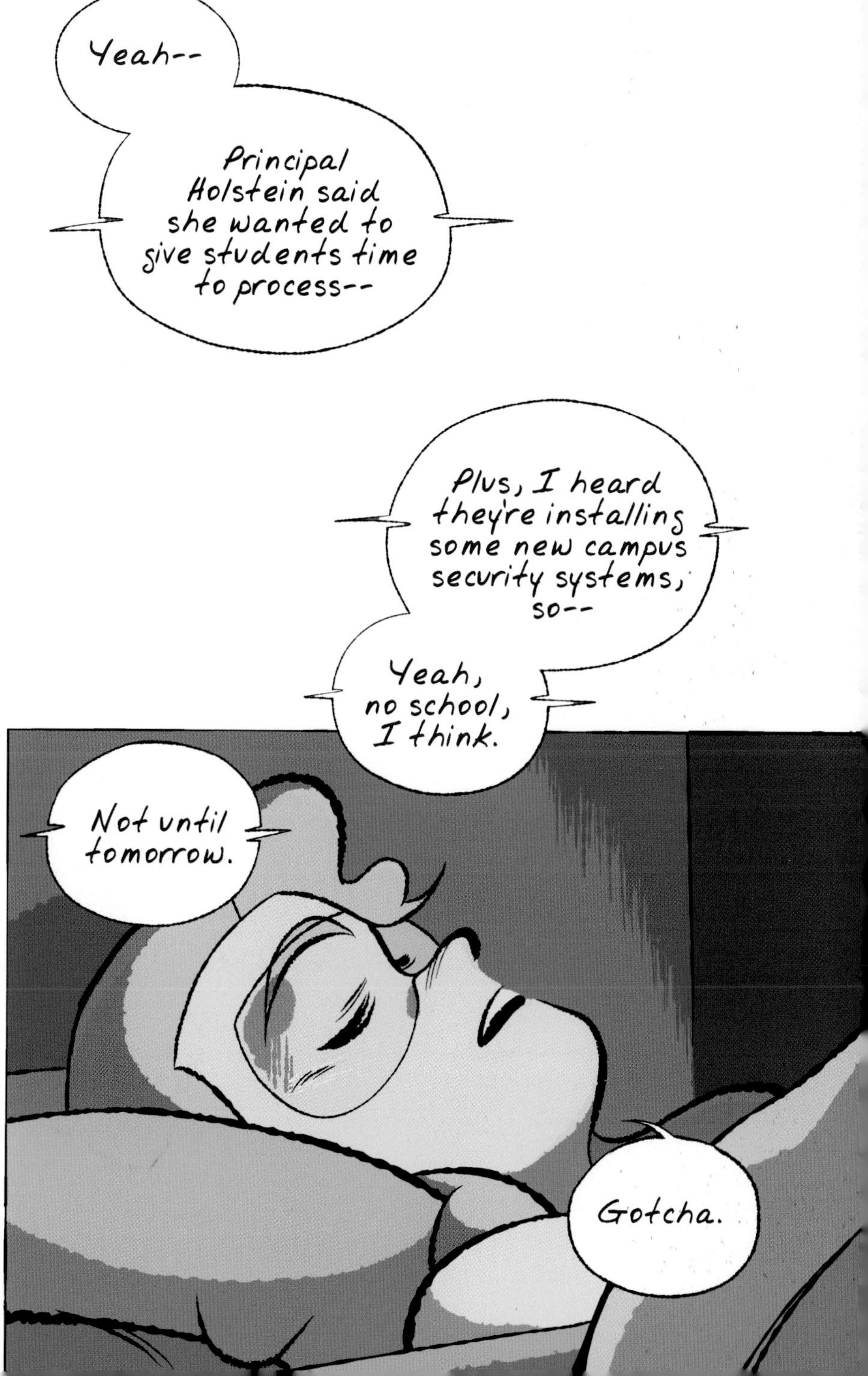
Yeah--
Principal Holstein said she wanted to give students time to process--
Plus, I heard they're installing some new campus security systems, so--
Yeah, no school, I think.
Not until tomorrow.
Gotcha.

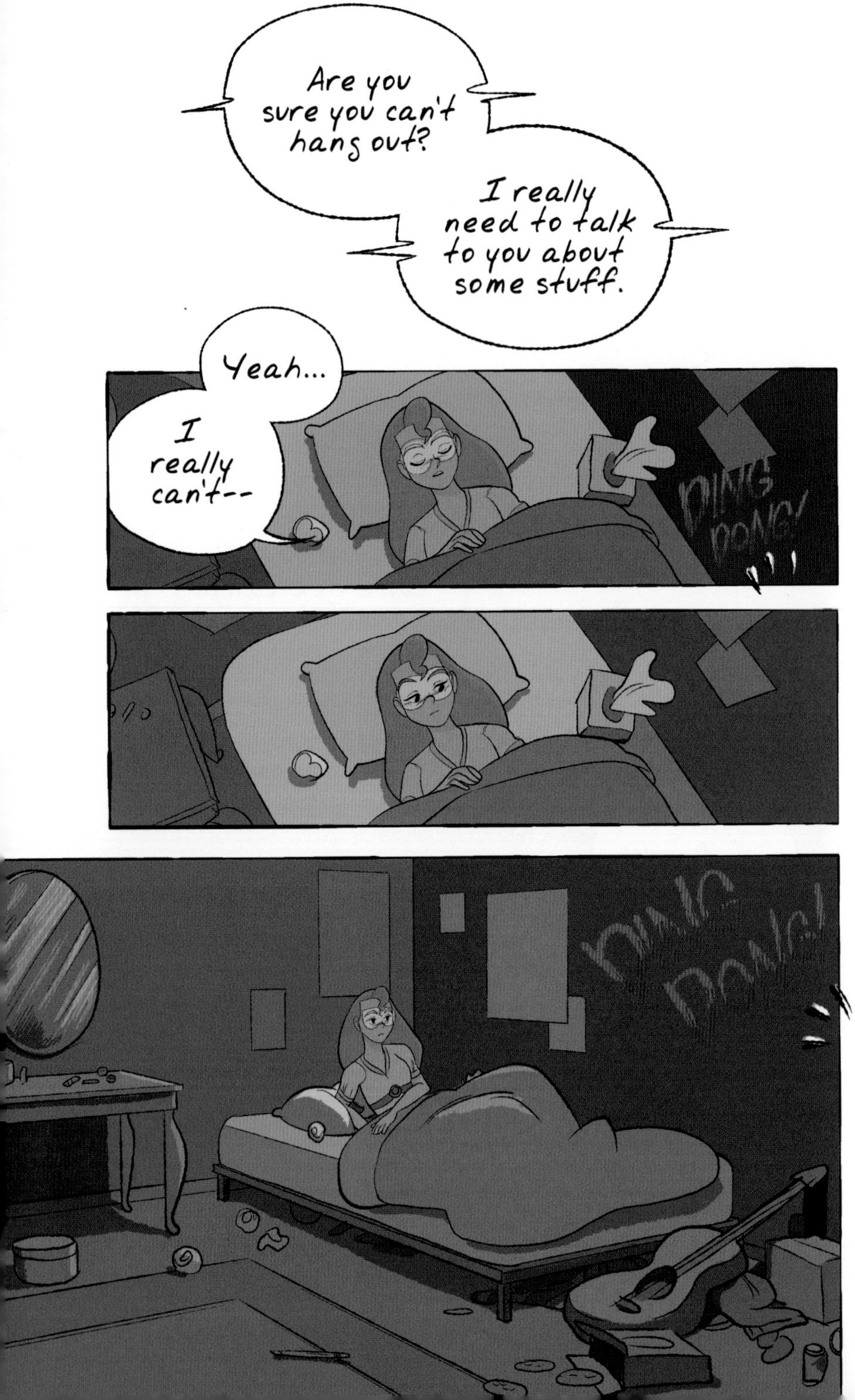
Are you sure you can't hang out?
I really need to talk to you about some stuff.
Yeah...
I really can't--
DING DONG!
DING DONG!

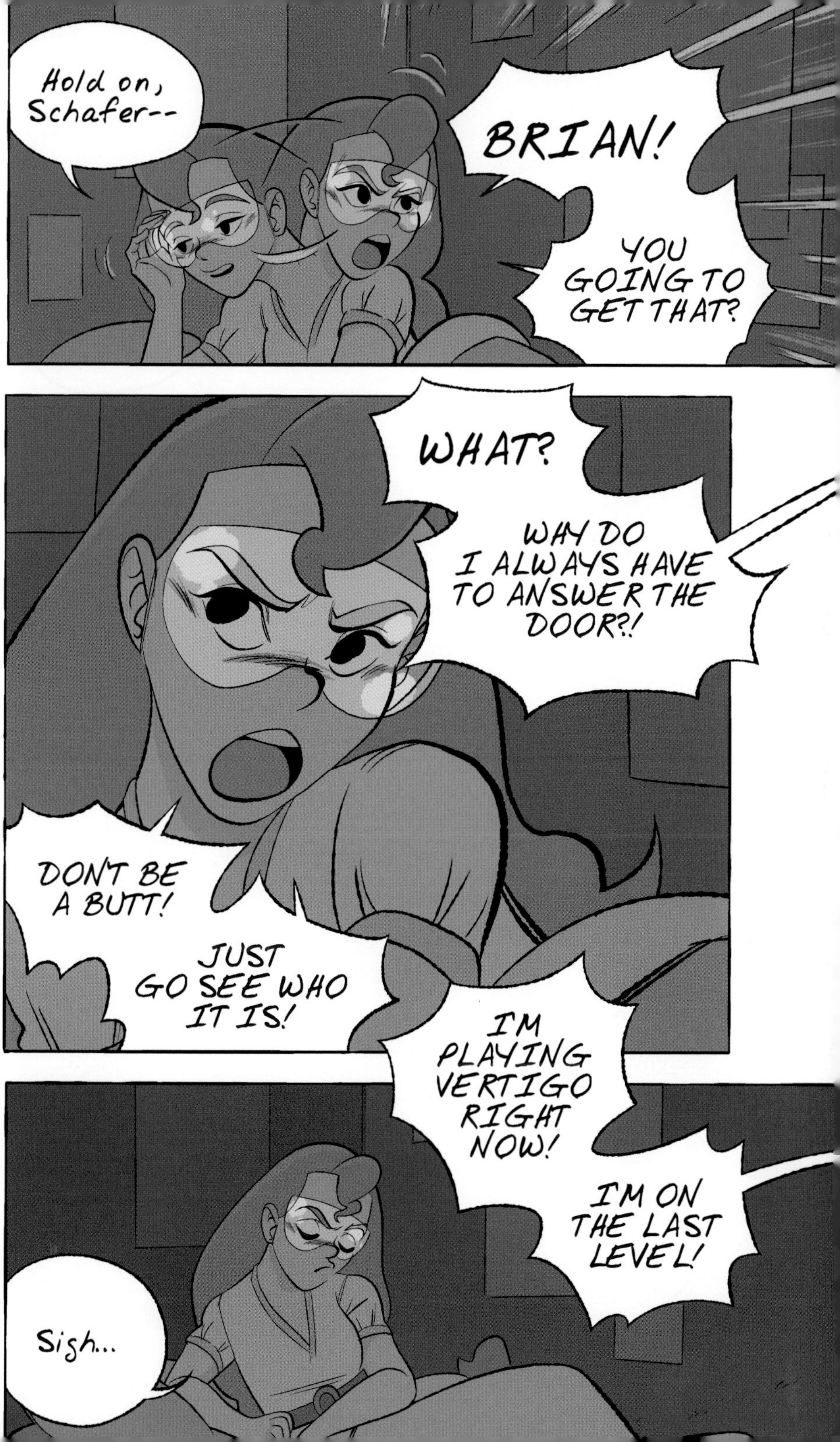
Hold on, Schafer--
BRIAN!
YOU GOING TO GET THAT?
WHAT?
WHY DO I ALWAYS HAVE TO ANSWER THE DOOR?!
DON'T BE A BUTT!
JUST GO SEE WHO IT IS!
I'M PLAYING VERTIGO RIGHT NOW!
I'M ON THE LAST LEVEL!
Sigh...

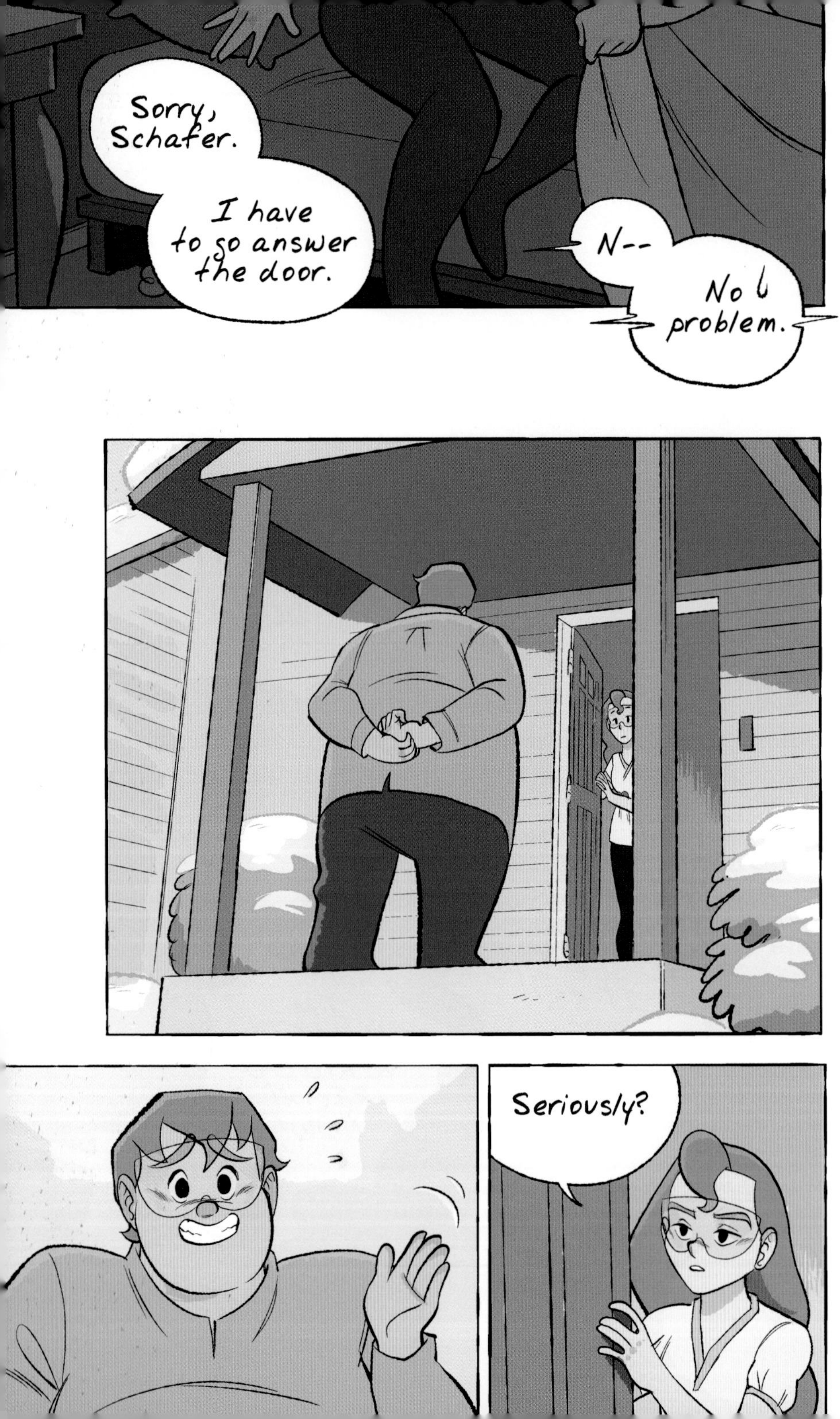
Sorry, Schafer.
I have to go answer the door.
N--
No problem.
Seriously?

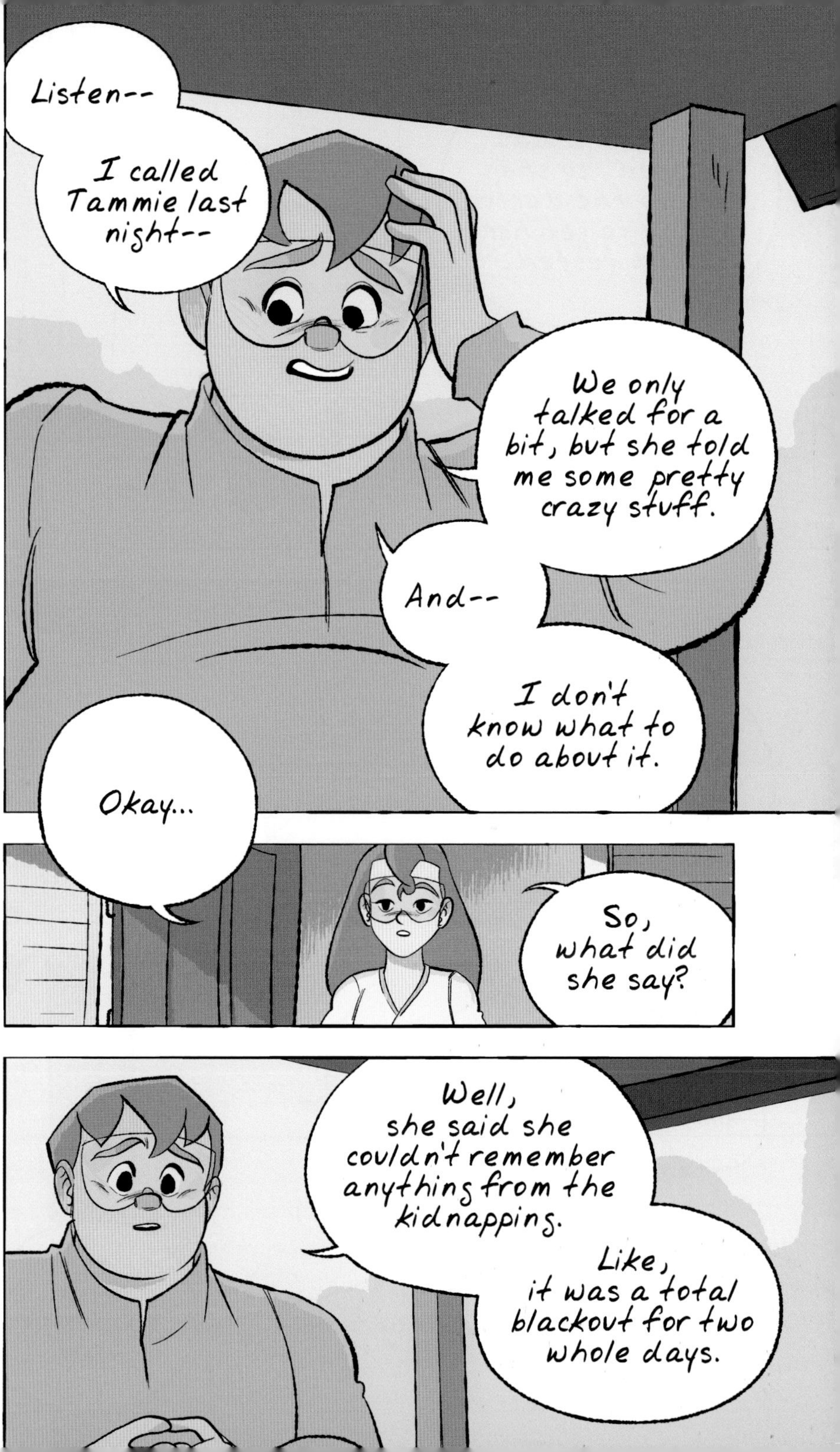
Listen--
I called Tammie last night--
We only talked for a bit, but she told me some pretty crazy stuff.
And--
I don't know what to do about it.
Okay...
So, what did she say?
Well, she said she couldn't remember anything from the kidnapping.
Like, it was a total blackout for two whole days.

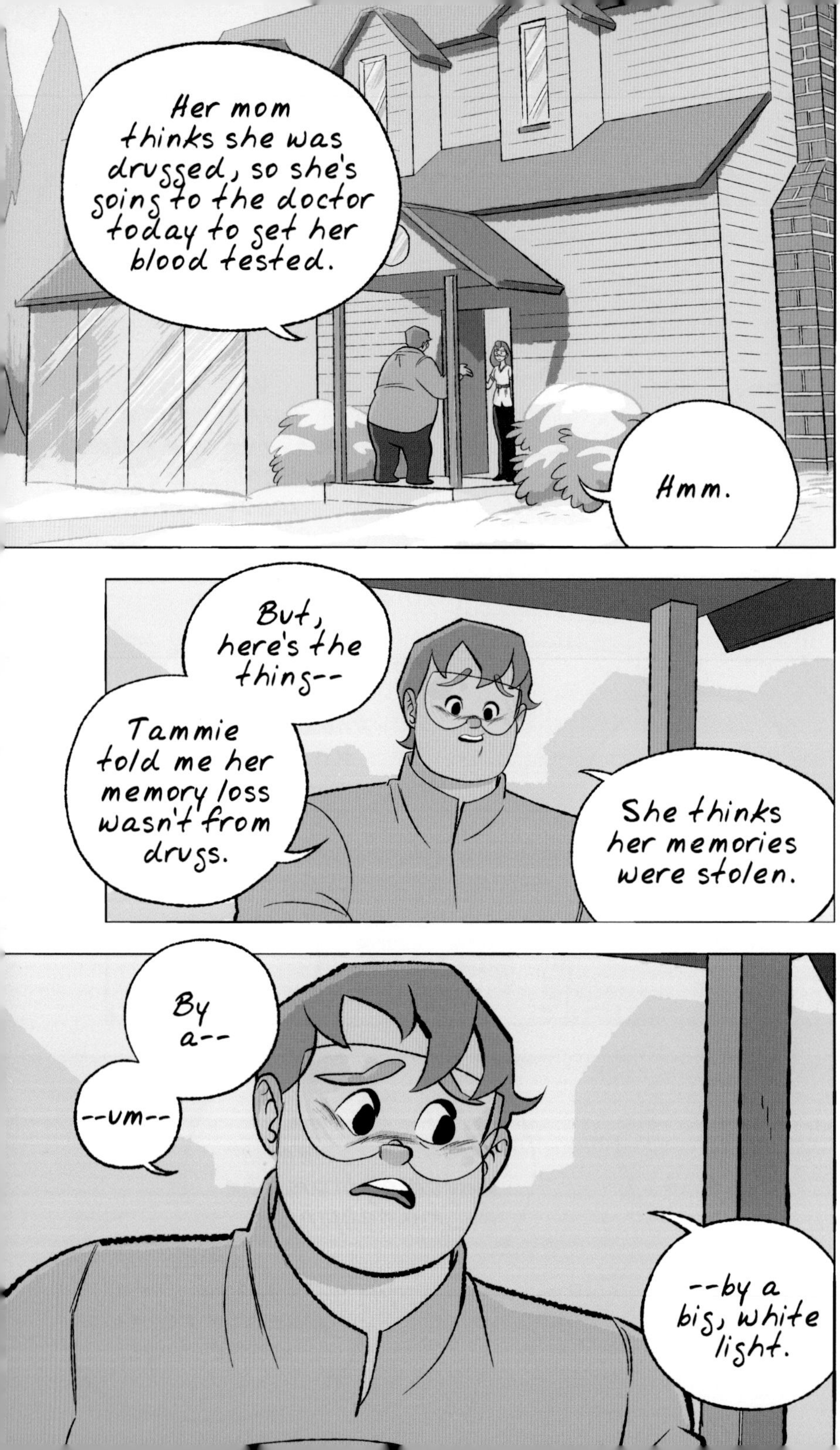
Her mom thinks she was drugged, so she's going to the doctor today to get her blood tested.
Hmm.
But, here's the thing--
Tammie told me her memory loss wasn't from drugs.
She thinks her memories were stolen.
By a--
--um--
--by a big, white light.

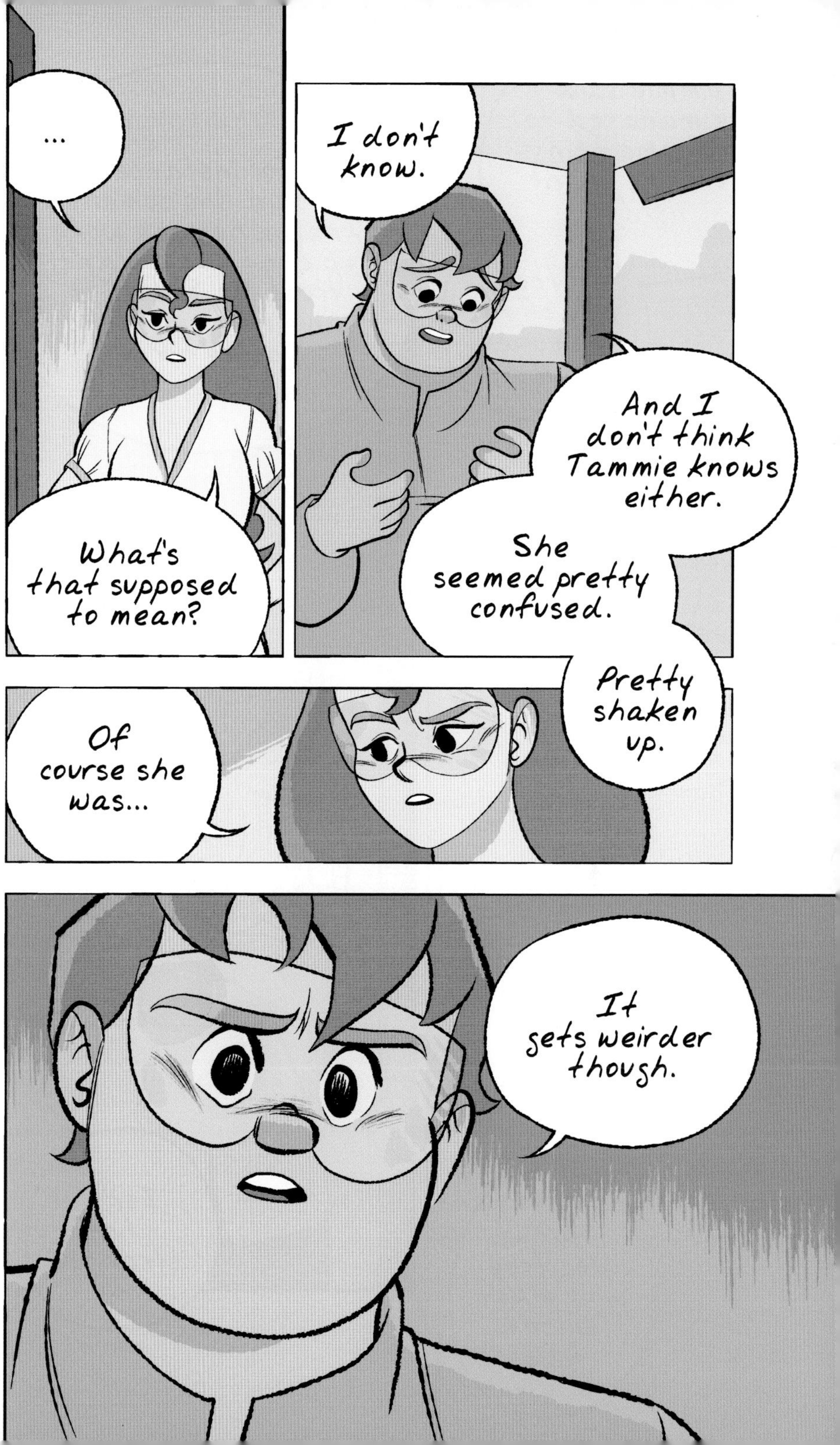
...
I don't know.
What's that supposed to mean?
And I don't think Tammie knows either.
She seemed pretty confused.
Pretty shaken up.
Of course she was...
It gets weirder though.

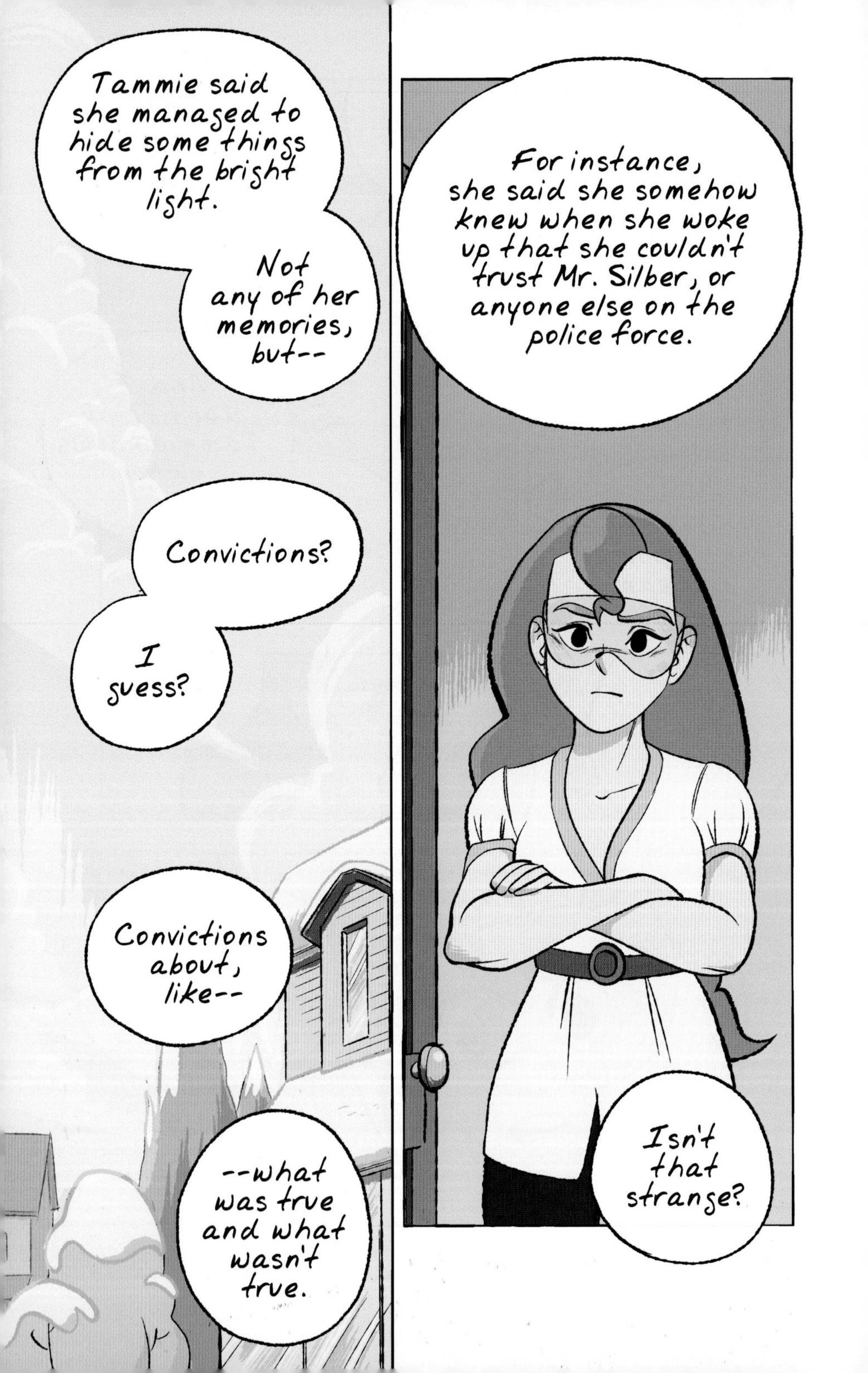
Tammie said she managed to hide some things from the bright light.
Not any of her memories, but--
Convictions?
I guess?
Convictions about, like--
--what was true and what wasn't true.
For instance, she said she somehow knew when she woke up that she couldn't trust Mr. Silber, or anyone else on the police force.
Isn't that strange?

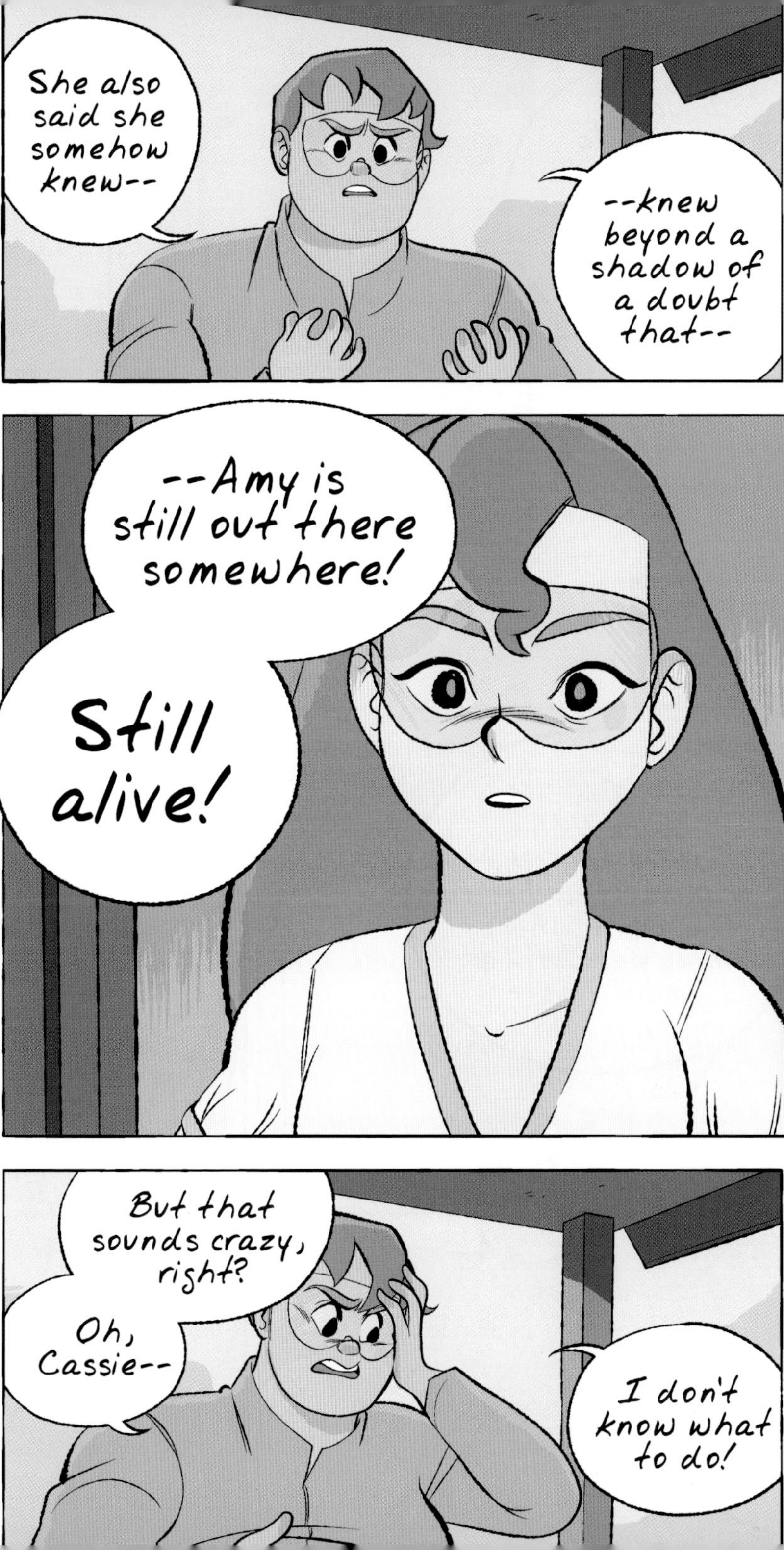
She also said she somehow knew--
--knew beyond a shadow of a doubt that--
--Amy is still out there somewhere!
Still alive!
But that sounds crazy, right?
Oh, Cassie--
I don't know what to do!

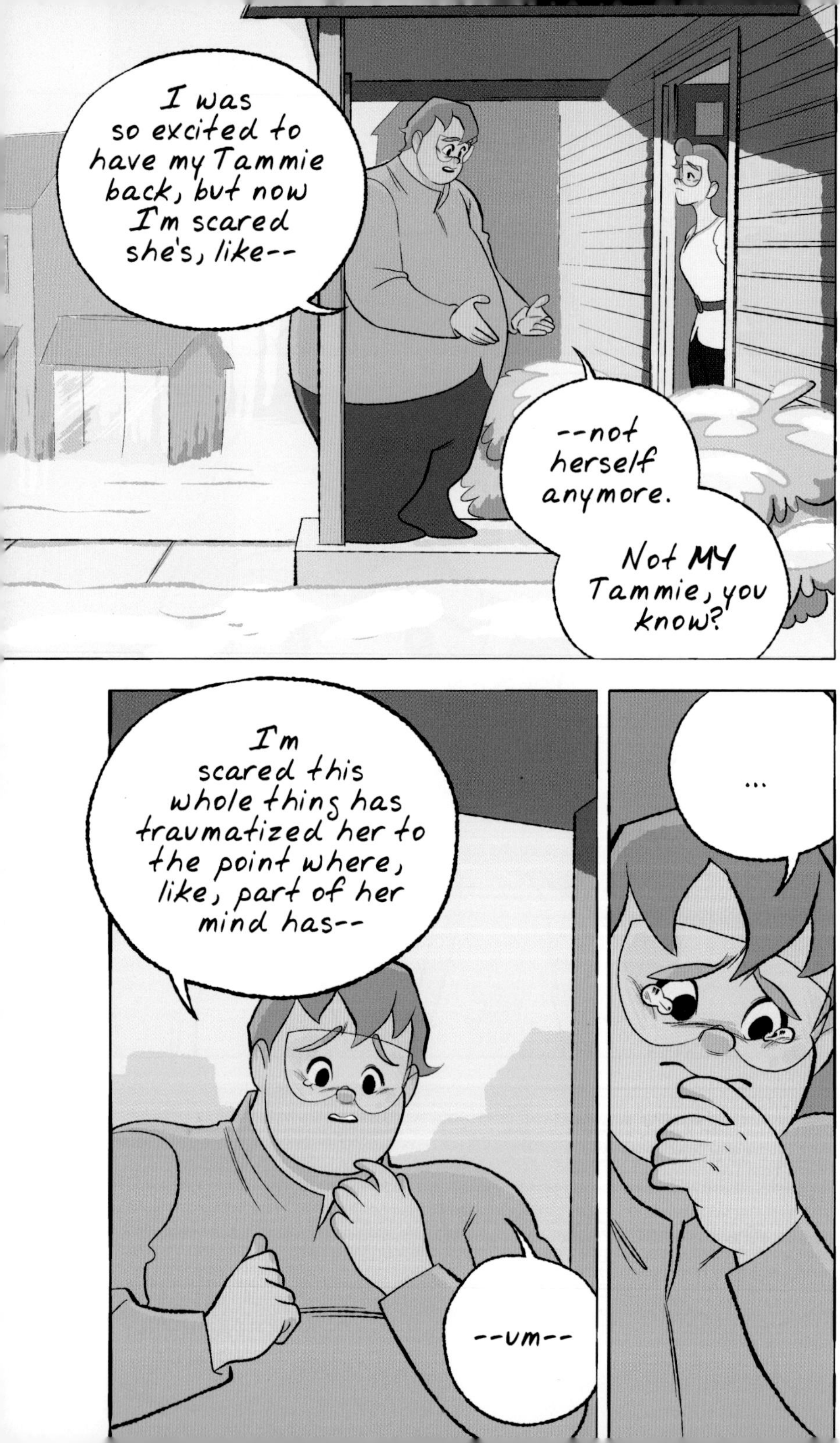
I was so excited to have my Tammie back, but now I'm scared she's, like--
--not herself anymore.
Not MY Tammie, you know?
I'm scared this whole thing has traumatized her to the point where, like, part of her mind has--
...
--um--

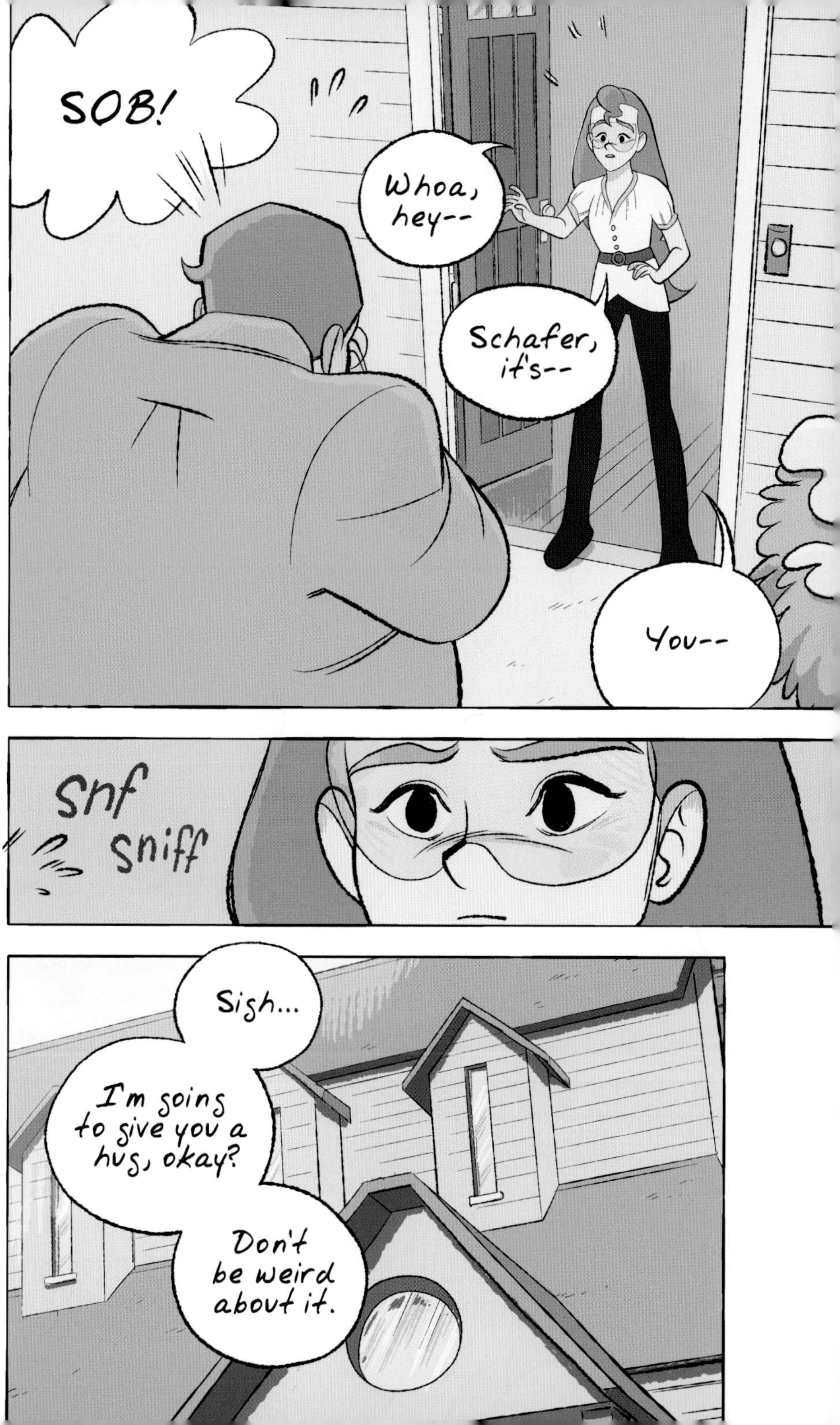
SOB!
Whoa, hey--
Schafer, it's--
You--
snf
sniff
Sigh...
I'm going to give you a hug, okay?
Don't be weird about it.

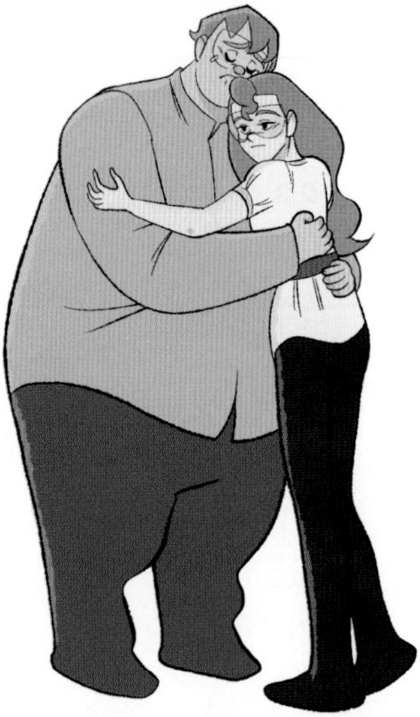

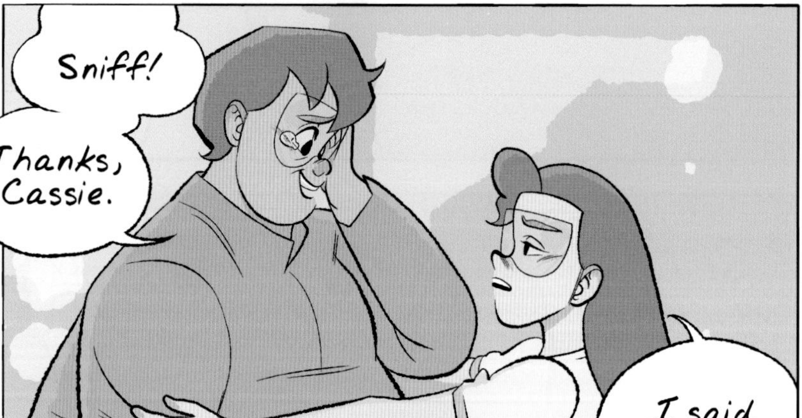
Sniff!
Thanks, Cassie.
I said don't be weird.

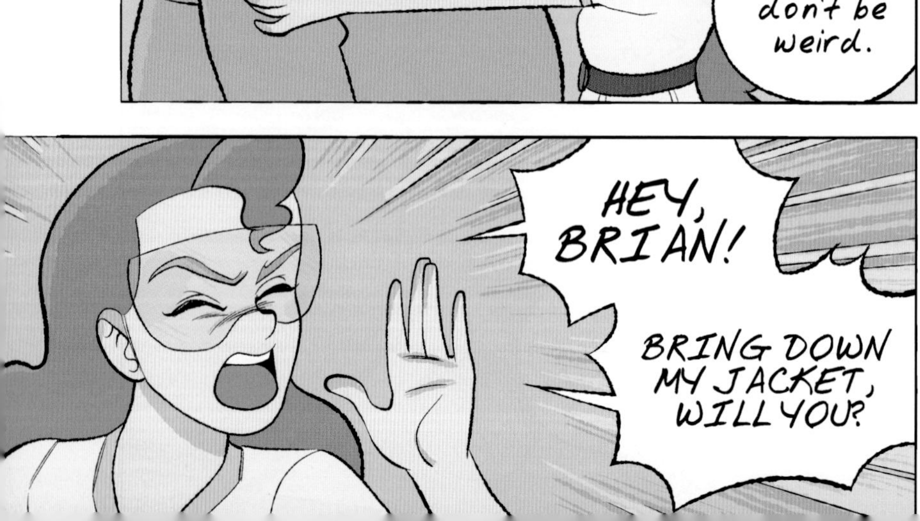
HEY, BRIAN!
BRING DOWN MY JACKET, WILL YOU?

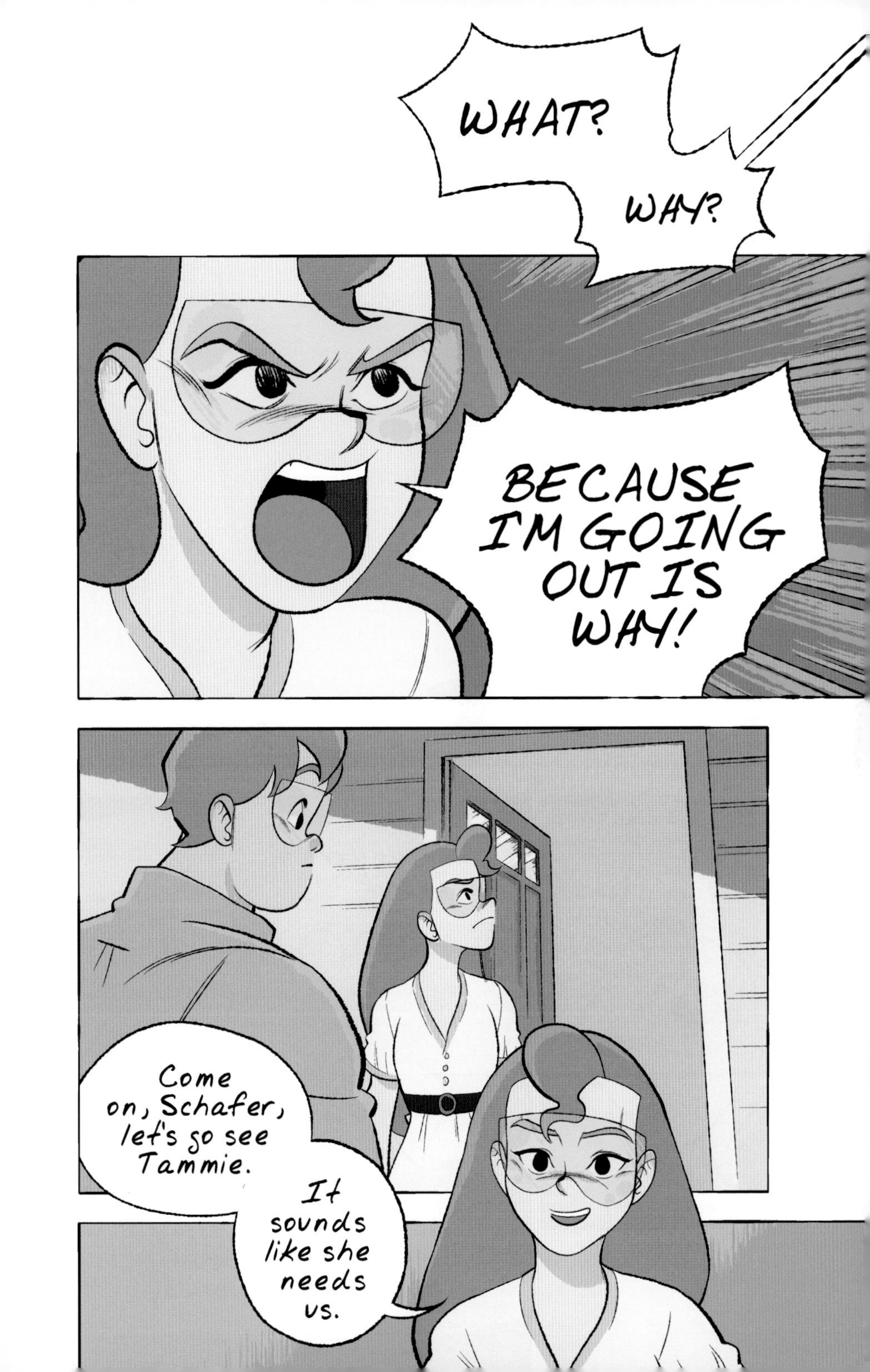
WHAT? WAY?
BECAUSE I'M GOING OUT IS WAY!
Come on, Schafer, let's go see Tammie.
It sounds like she needs us.

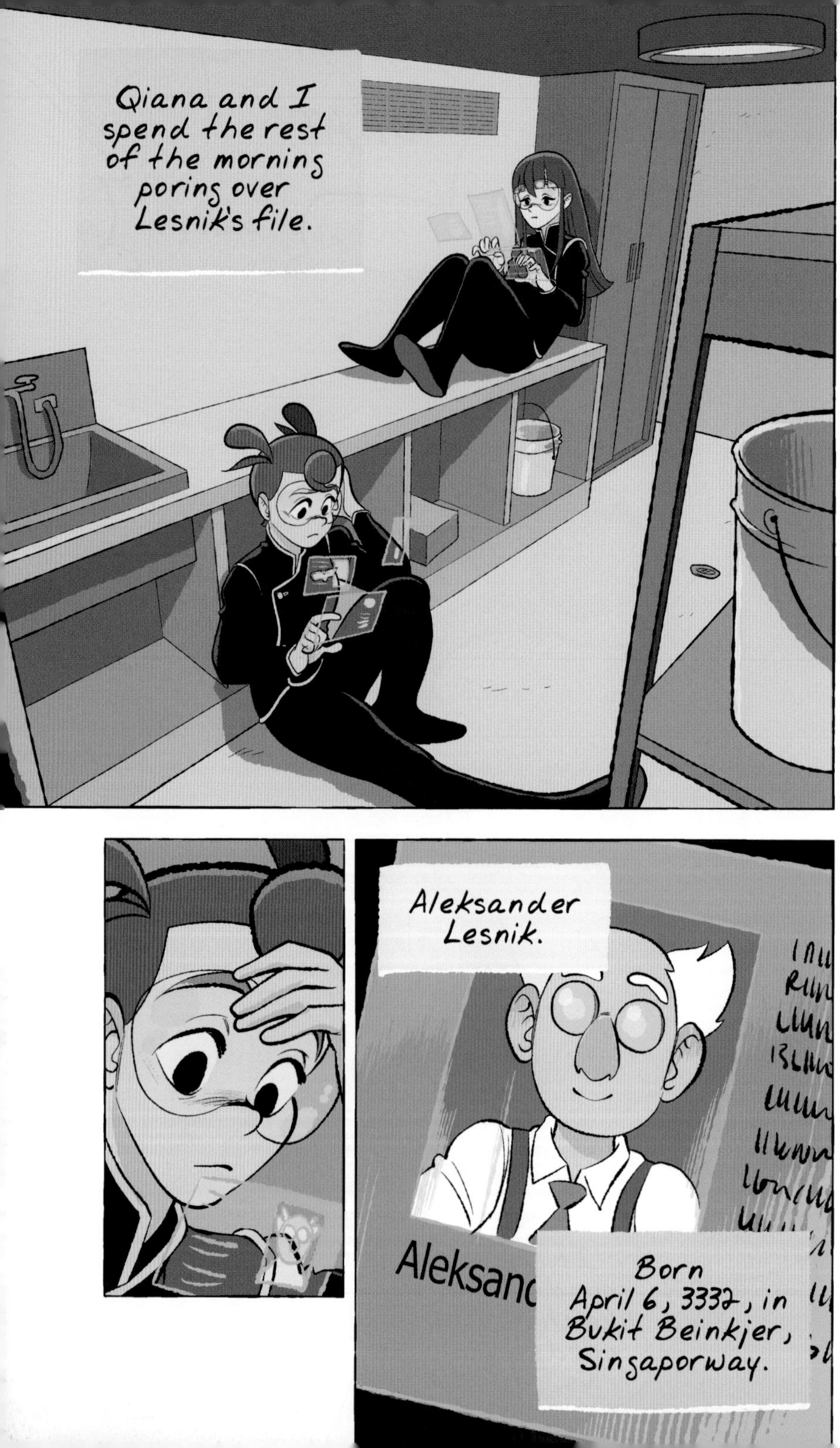
Qiana and I spend the rest of the morning poring over Lesnik's file.
Aleksander Lesnik.
Aleksand
Born April 6, 3332, in Bukit Beinkjer, Singaporway.

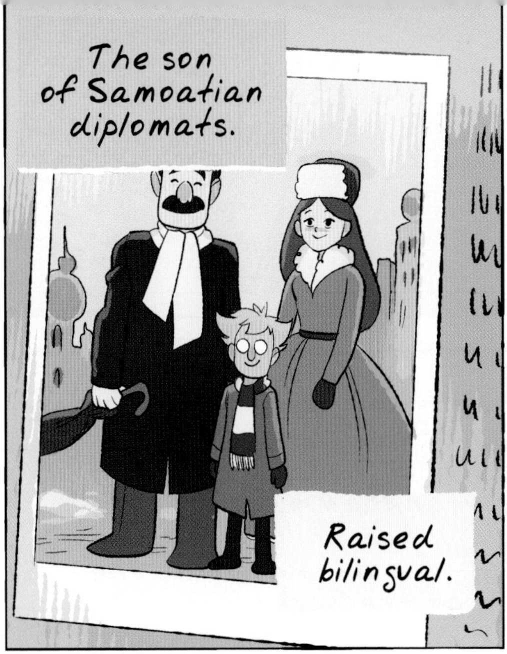
The son of Samoatian diplomats.
Raised bilingual.

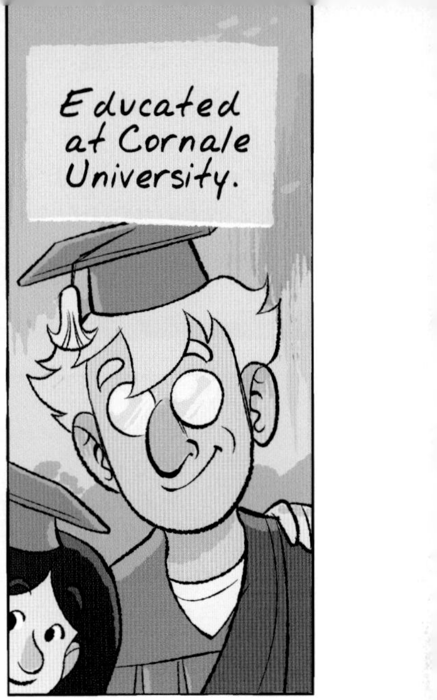
Educated at Cornale University.

Was poised for a promising career in politics, but decided to become an archaeologist, much to his parents' dismay.

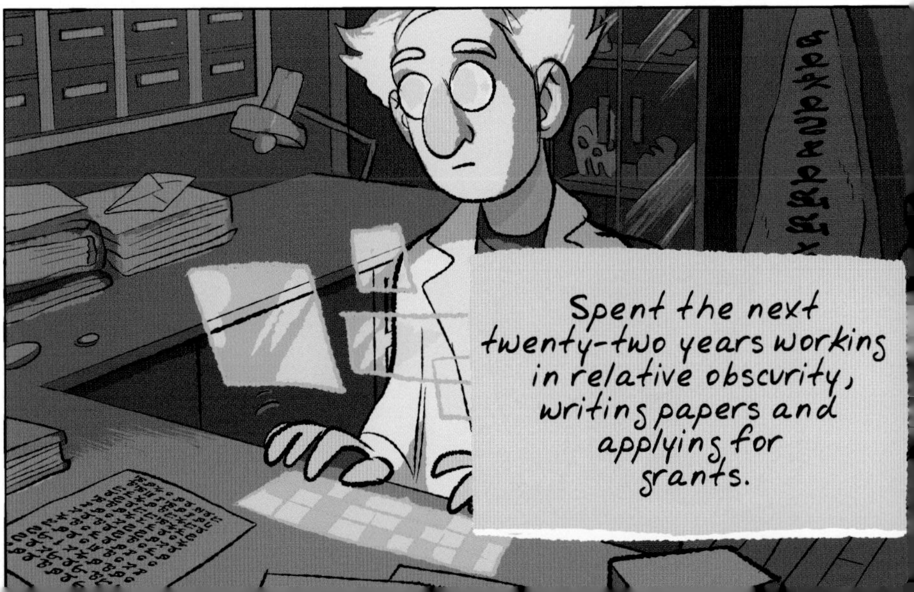
Spent the next twenty-two years working in relative obscurity, writing papers and applying for grants.

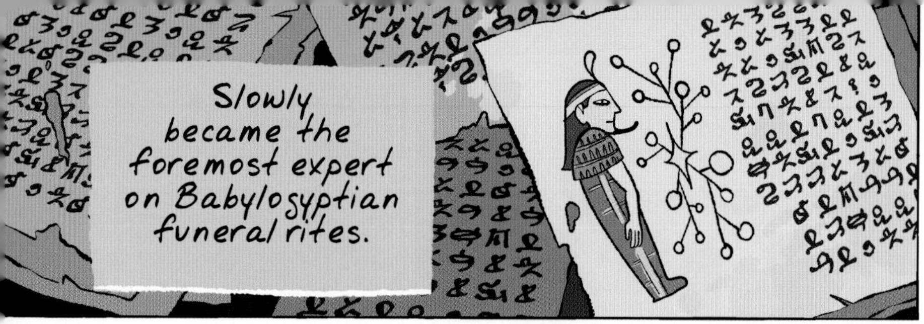
Slowly became the foremost expert on Babylosyptian funeral rites.

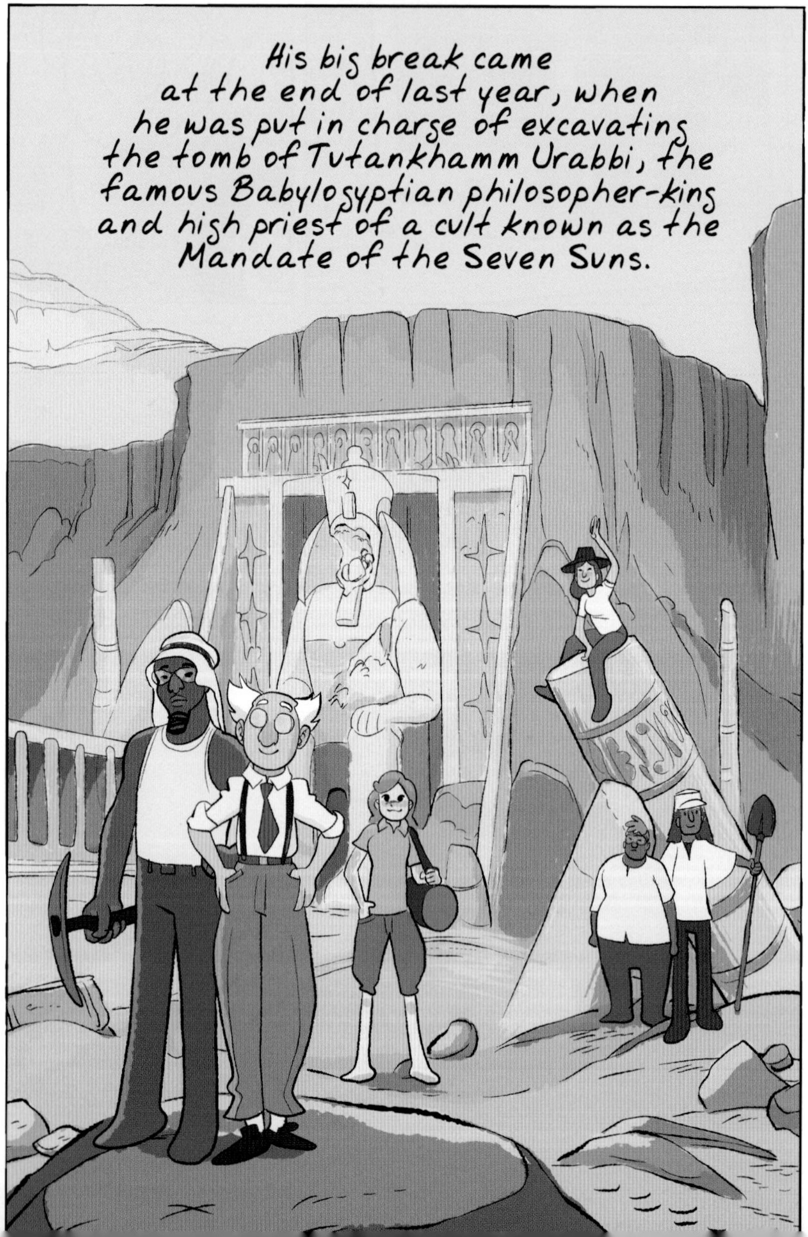
His big break came at the end of last year, when he was put in charge of excavating the tomb of Tutankhamm Urabbi, the famous Babylosyptian philosopher-king and high priest of a cult known as the Mandate of the Seven Suns.

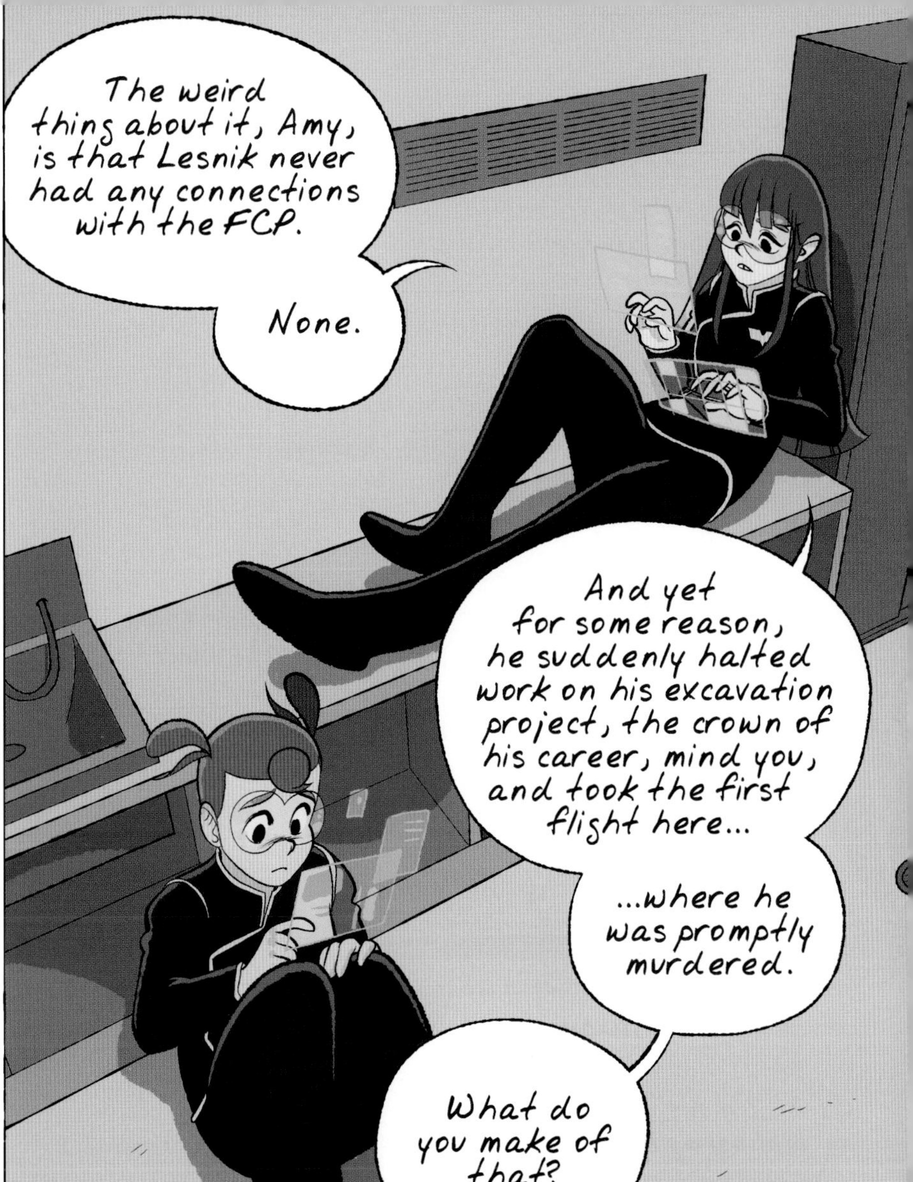
The weird things about it, Amy, is that Lesnik never had any connections with the FCP.
None.
And yet for some reason, he suddenly halted work on his excavation project, the crown of his career, mind you, and took the first flight here...
...where he was promptly murdered.
What do you make of that?

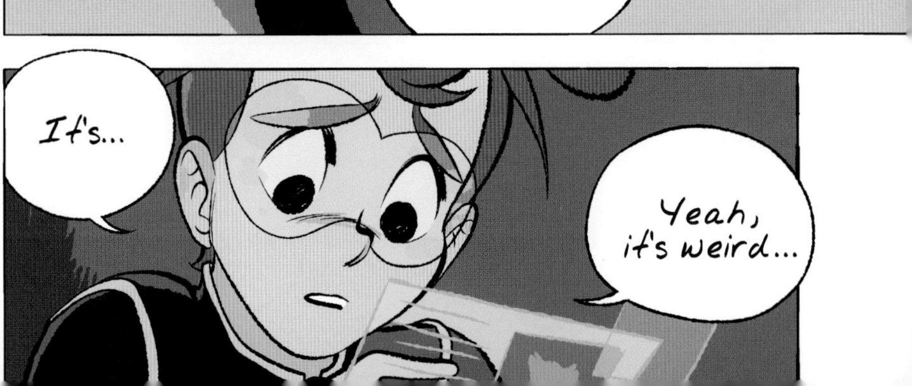
It's...
Yeah, it's weird...

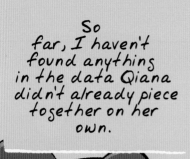

So far, I haven't found anything in the data Qiana didn't already piece together on her own.

Bibliograp[...]
Treasures from t[...]
Tombs and Mummie[...]
King Tutankhamm[...]
The Prince and the Croc[...]
Ancient [...]

I feel a lot of pressure to make good on my promise to help her solve this case, but--

It really does look like a dead end.

Wait, what's this?

In his bibliography--

The Prince and the Crocodile?

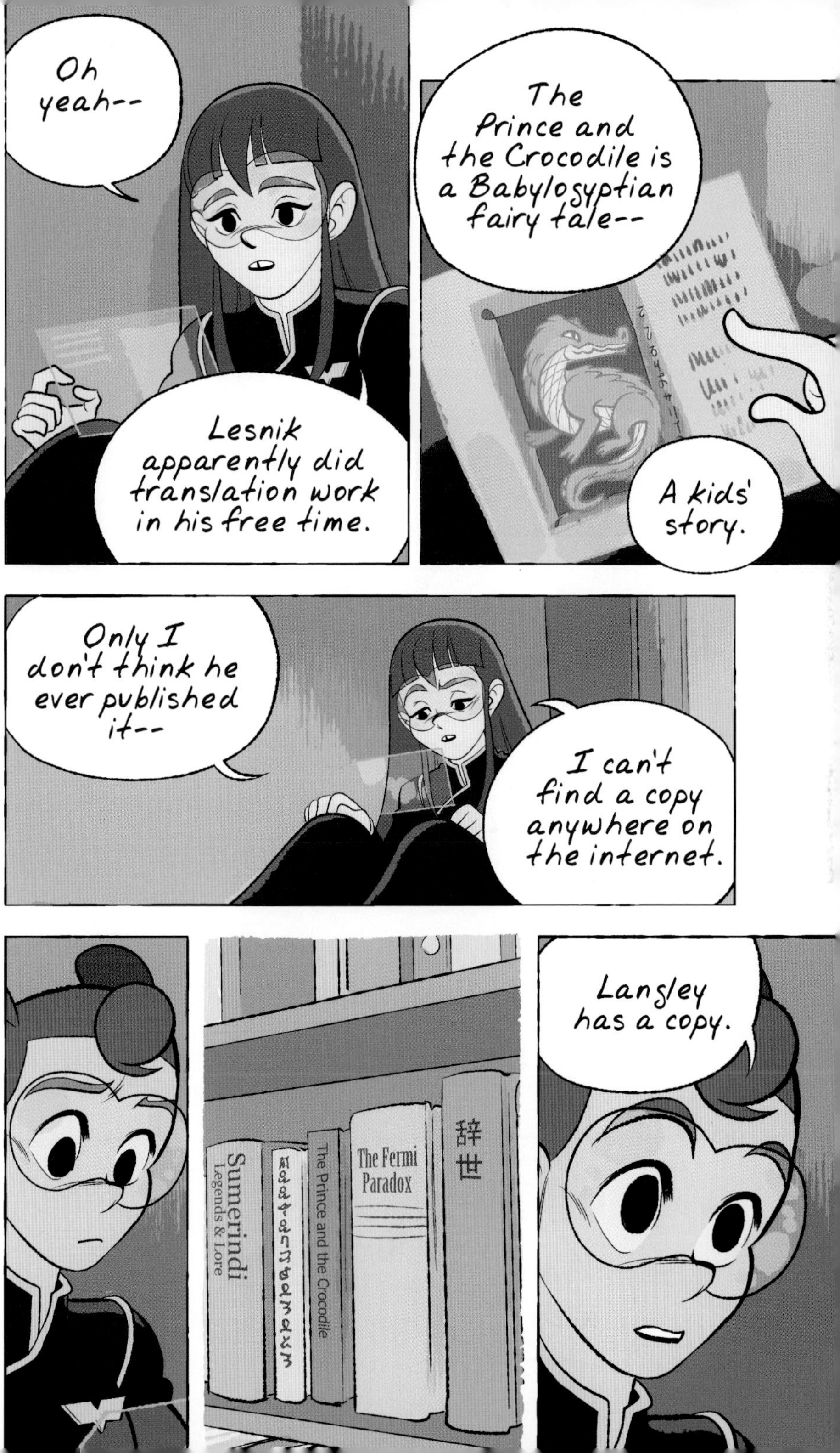
Oh yeah--
The Prince and the Crocodile is a Babylosyptian fairy tale--
Lesnik apparently did translation work in his free time.
A kids' story.
Only I don't think he ever published it--
I can't find a copy anywhere on the internet.
Sumerindi Legends & Lore
The Prince and the Crocodile
The Fermi Paradox
辞世
Langley has a copy.

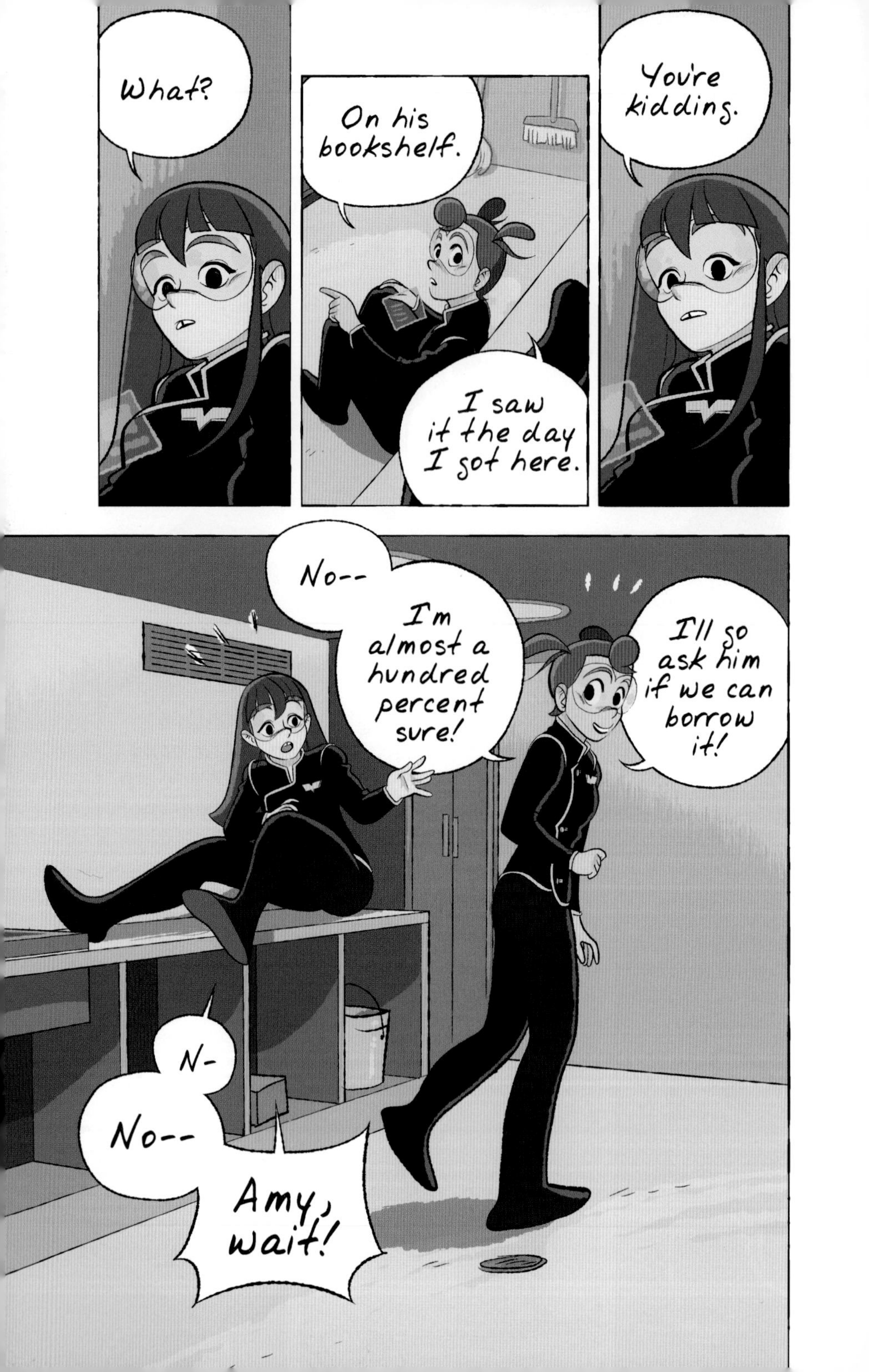
What?
On his bookshelf.
I saw it the day I got here.
You're kidding.
No--
I'm almost a hundred percent sure!
I'll go ask him if we can borrow it!
N-
No--
Amy, wait!

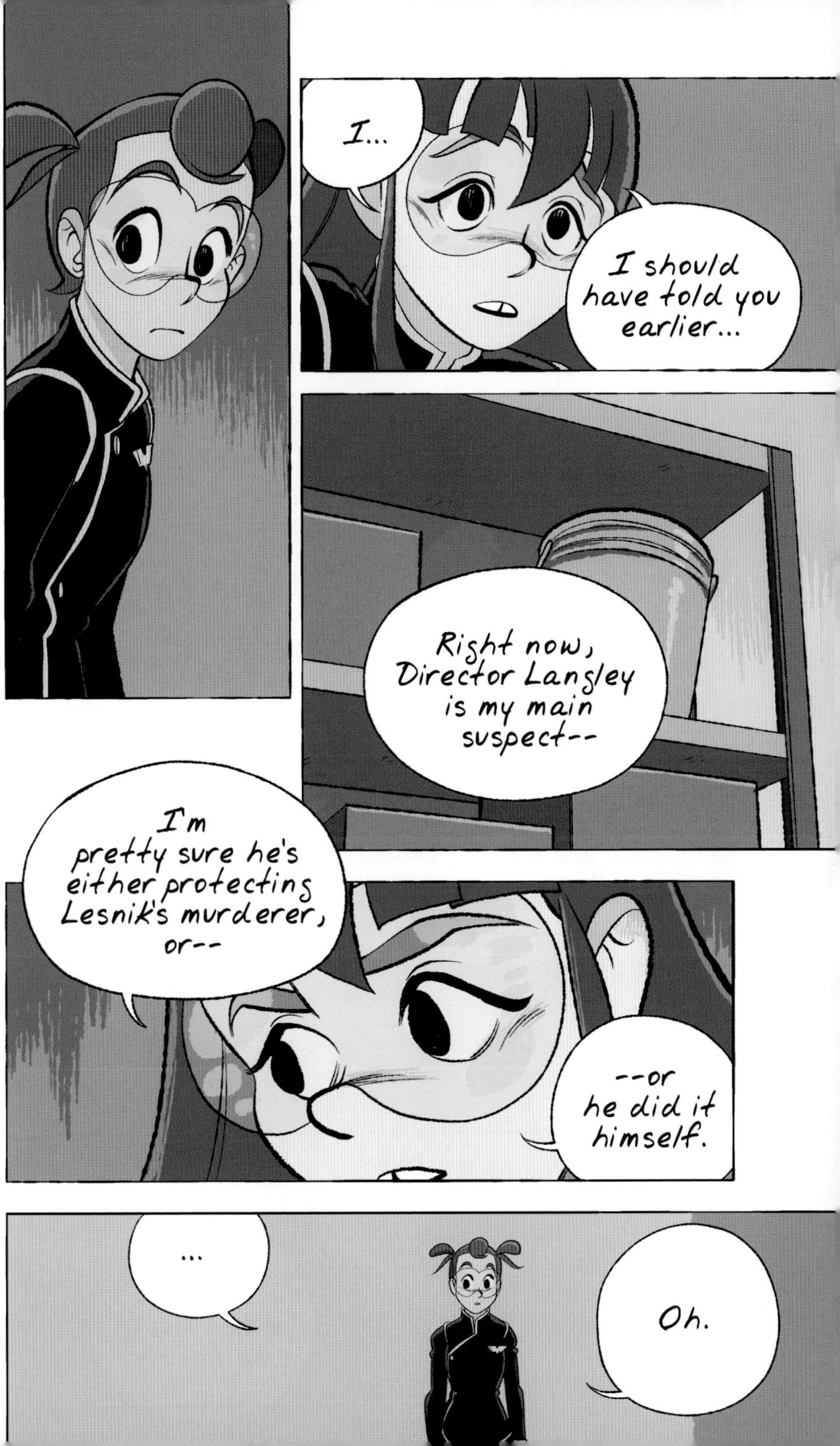
I...
I should have told you earlier...
Right now, Director Langley is my main suspect--
I'm pretty sure he's either protecting Lesnik's murderer, or--
--or he did it himself.
...
Oh.

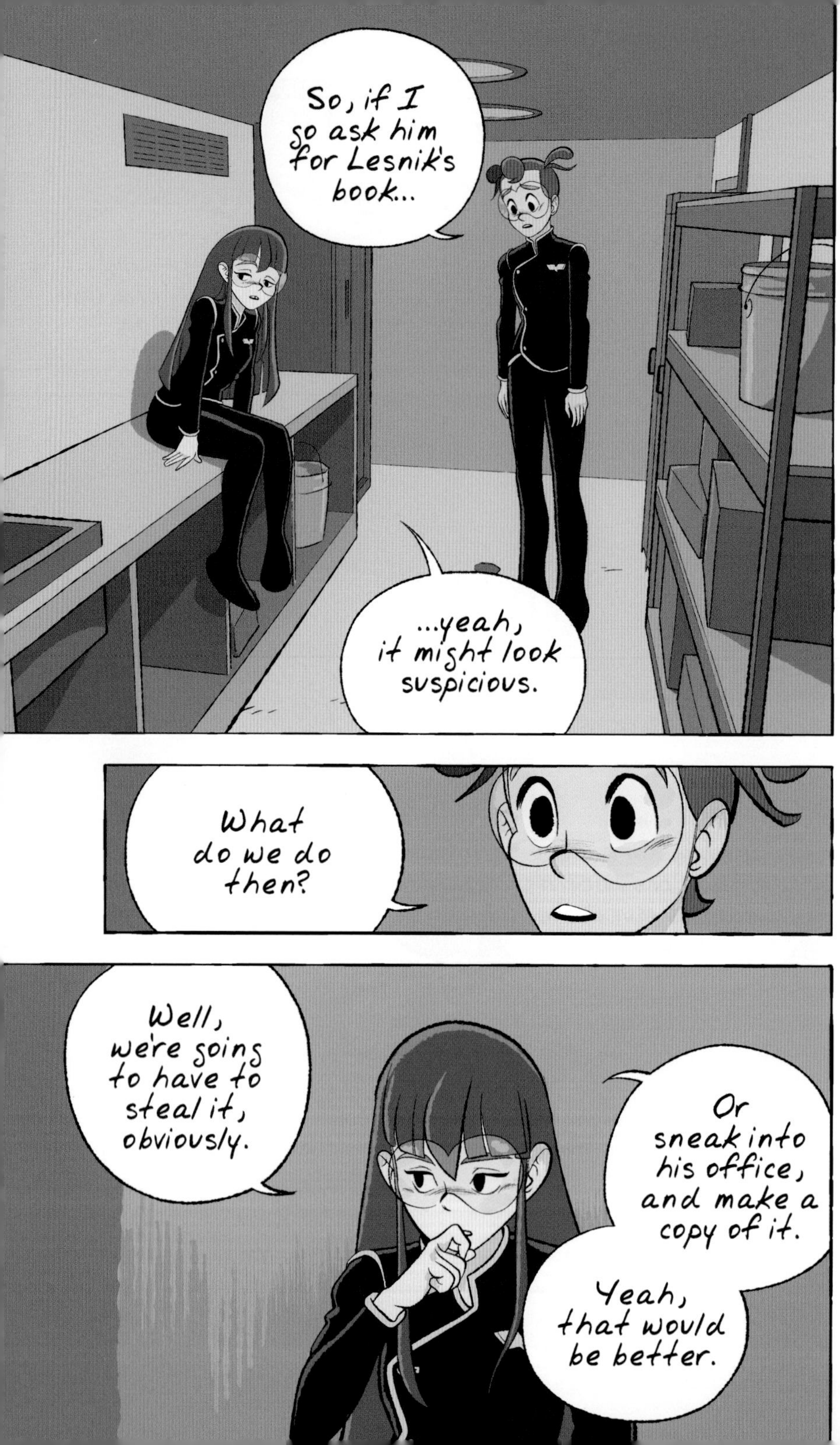
So, if I go ask him for Lesnik's book...
...yeah, it might look suspicious.
What do we do then?
Well, we're going to have to steal it, obviously.
Or sneak into his office, and make a copy of it.
Yeah, that would be better.

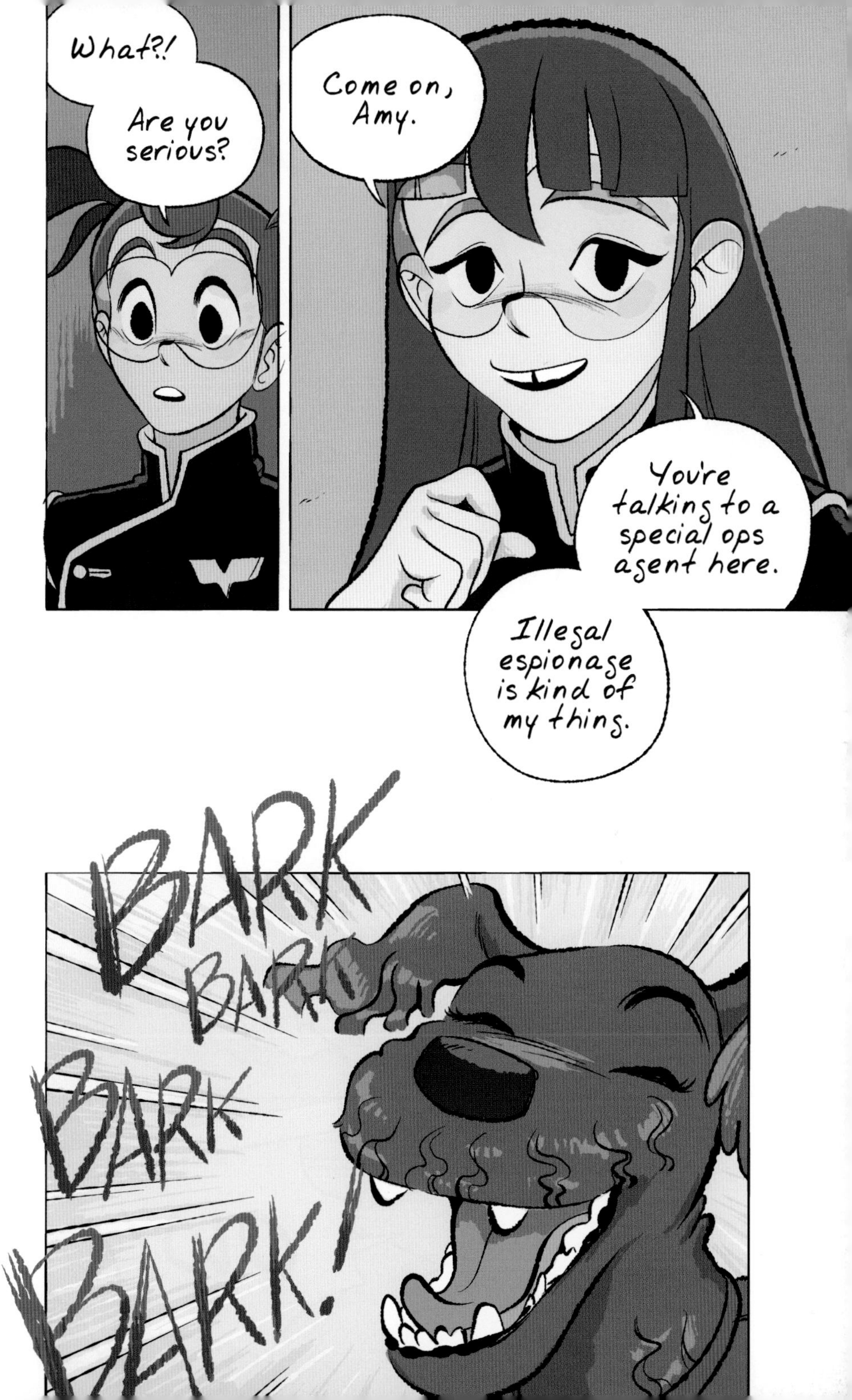
What?!
Are you serious?
Come on, Amy.
You're talking to a special ops agent here.
Illegal espionage is kind of my thing.
BARK
BARK
BARK
BARK!

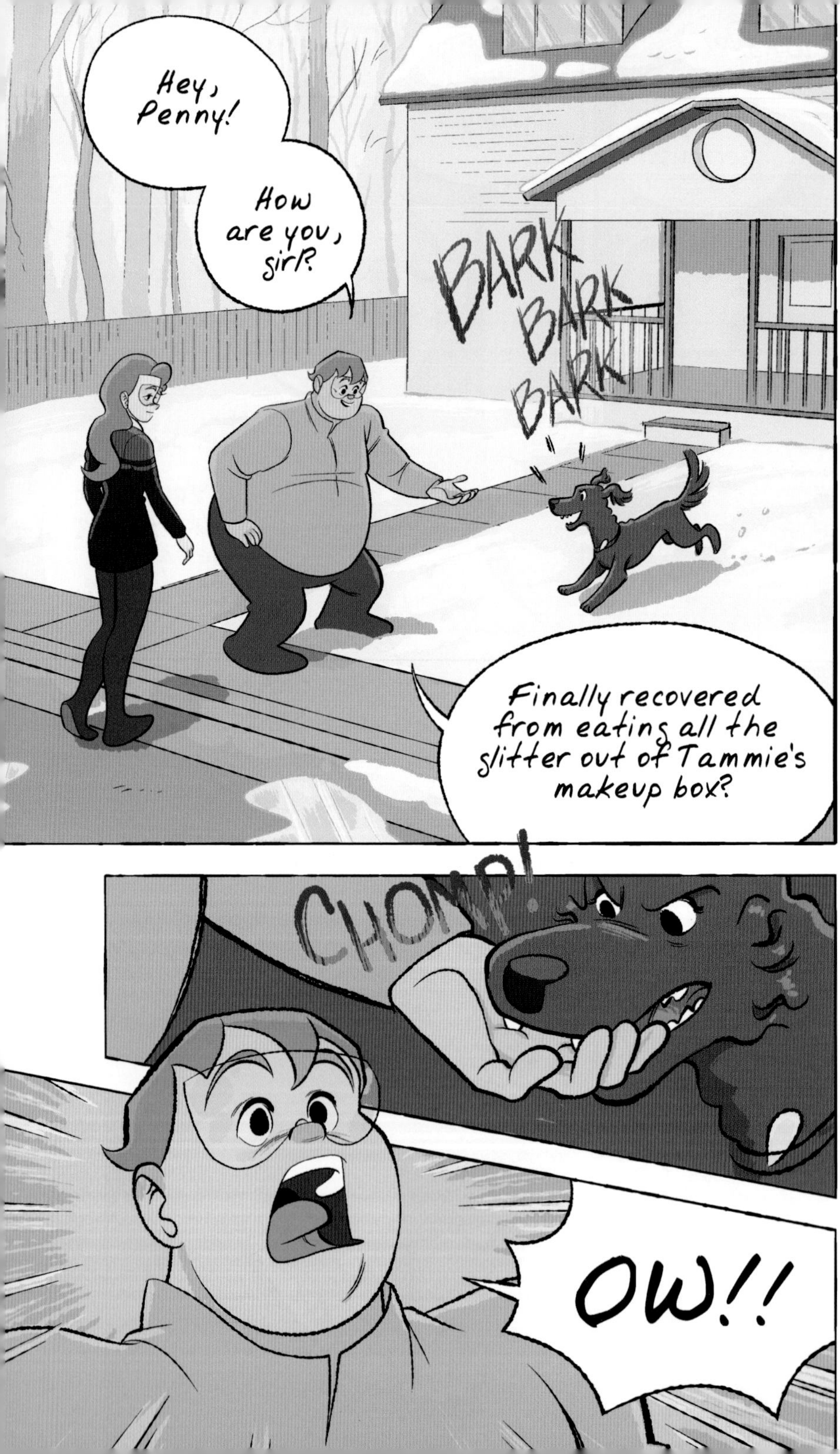
Hey, Penny!
How are you, sir?
BARK BARK BARK
Finally recovered from eating all the glitter out of Tammie's makeup box?
CHOMP!
OW!!

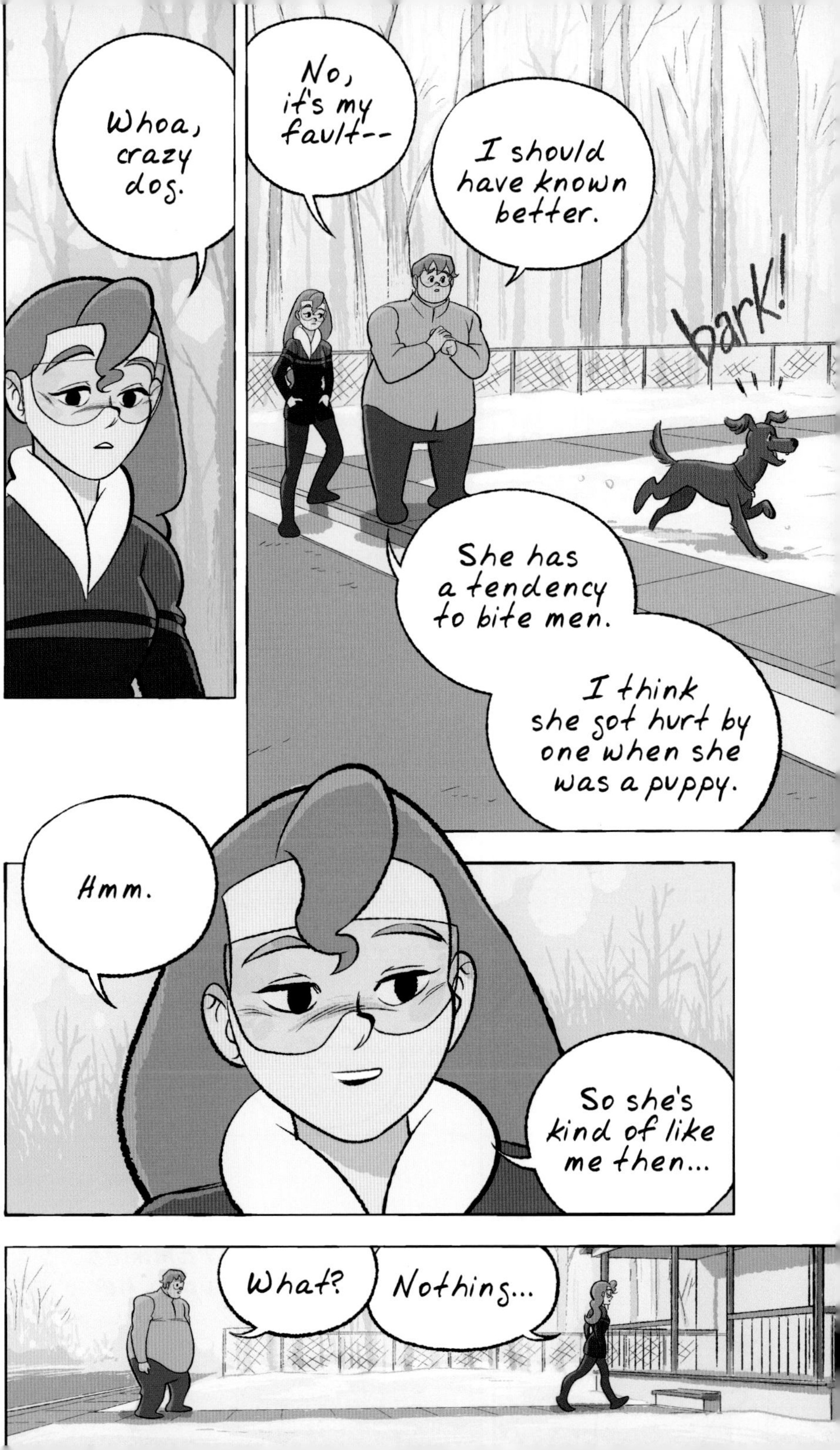
Whoa, crazy dog.
No, it's my fault--
I should have known better.
bark!
She has a tendency to bite men.
I think she got hurt by one when she was a puppy.
Hmm.
So she's kind of like me then...
What?
Nothing...

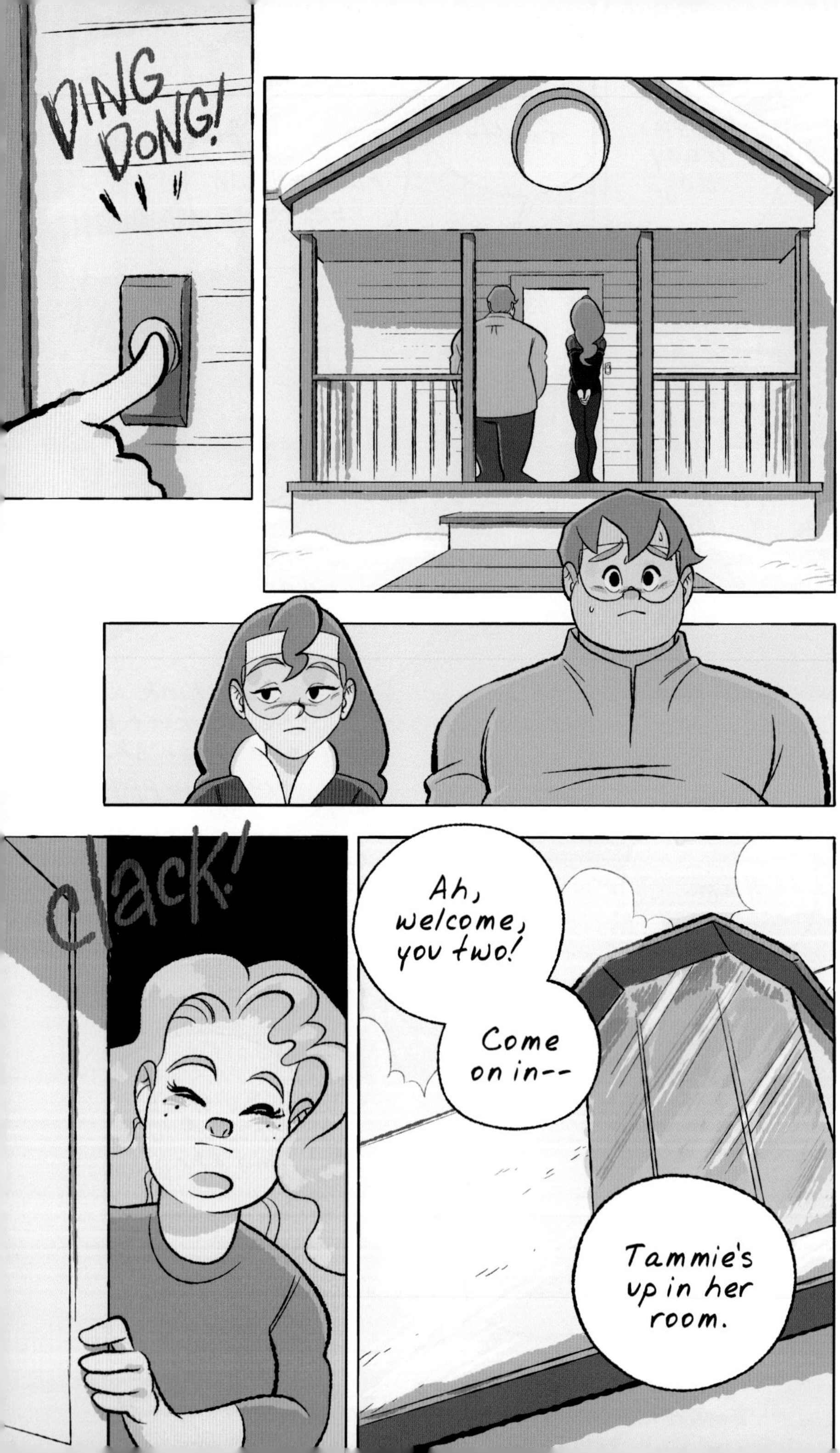
DING DONG!
clack!
Ah, welcome, you two!
Come on in--
Tammie's up in her room.

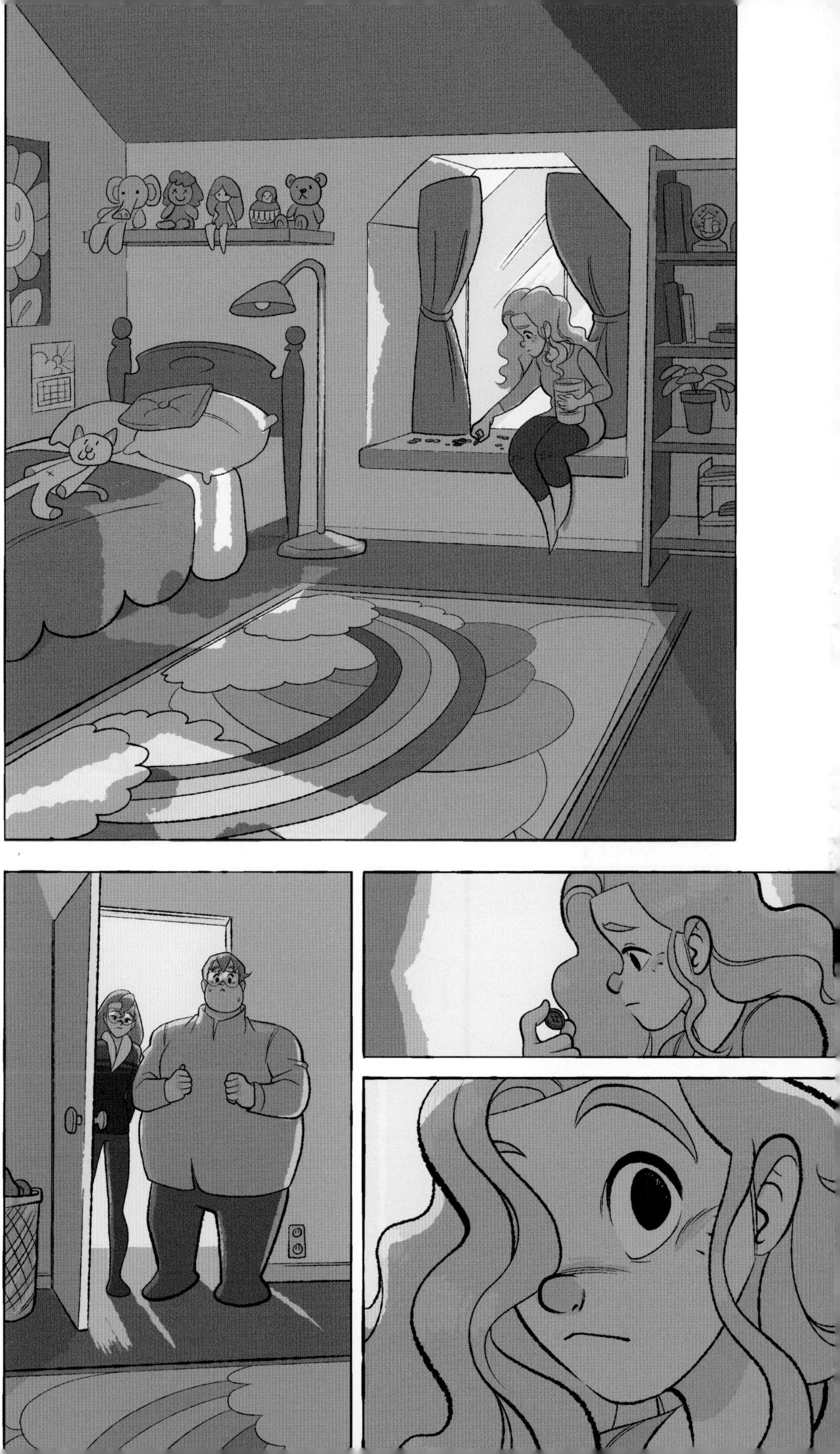

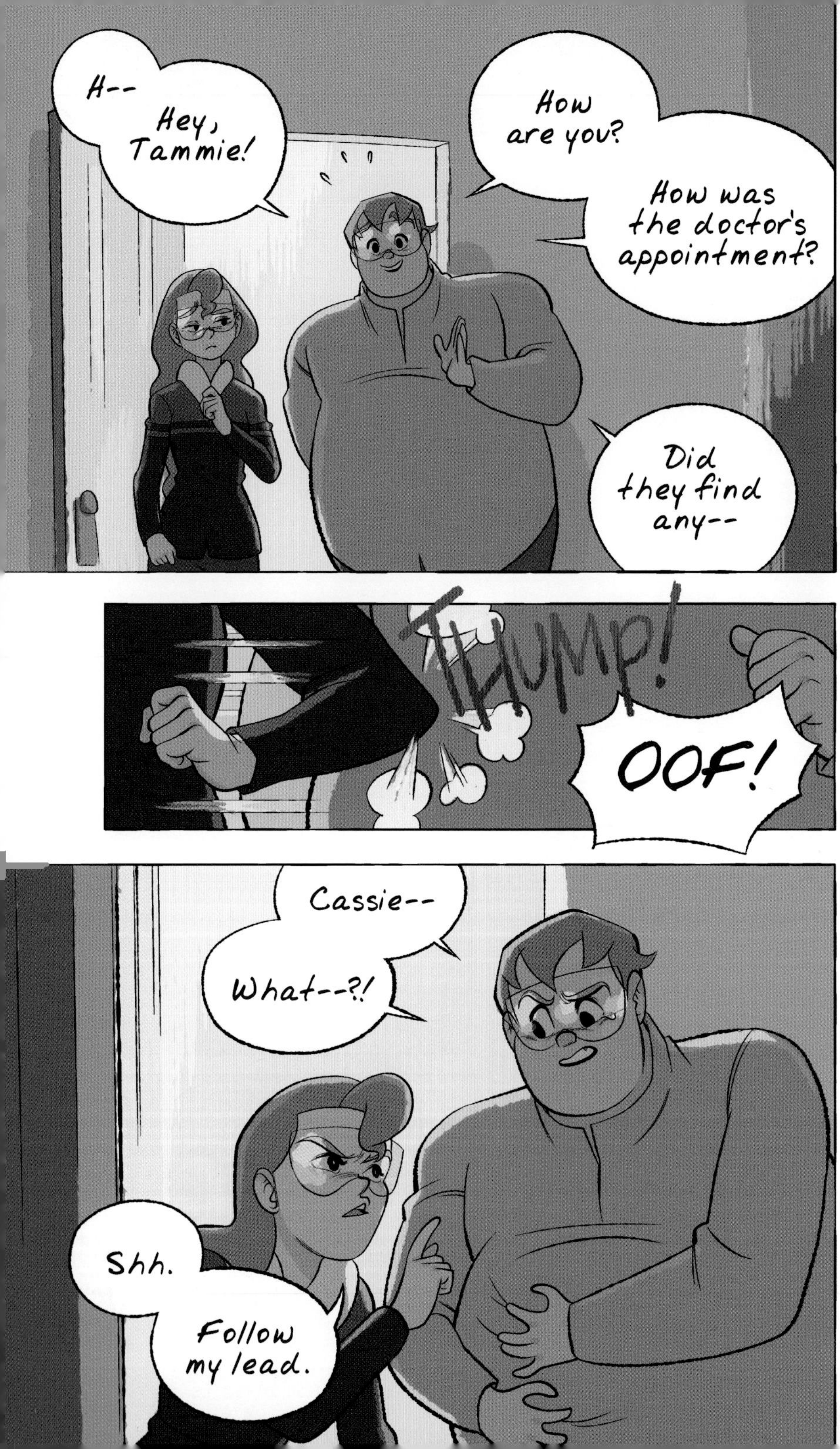
H--
Hey, Tammie!
How are you?
How was the doctor's appointment?
Did they find any--
THUMP!
OOF!
Cassie--
What--?!
Shh.
Follow my lead.

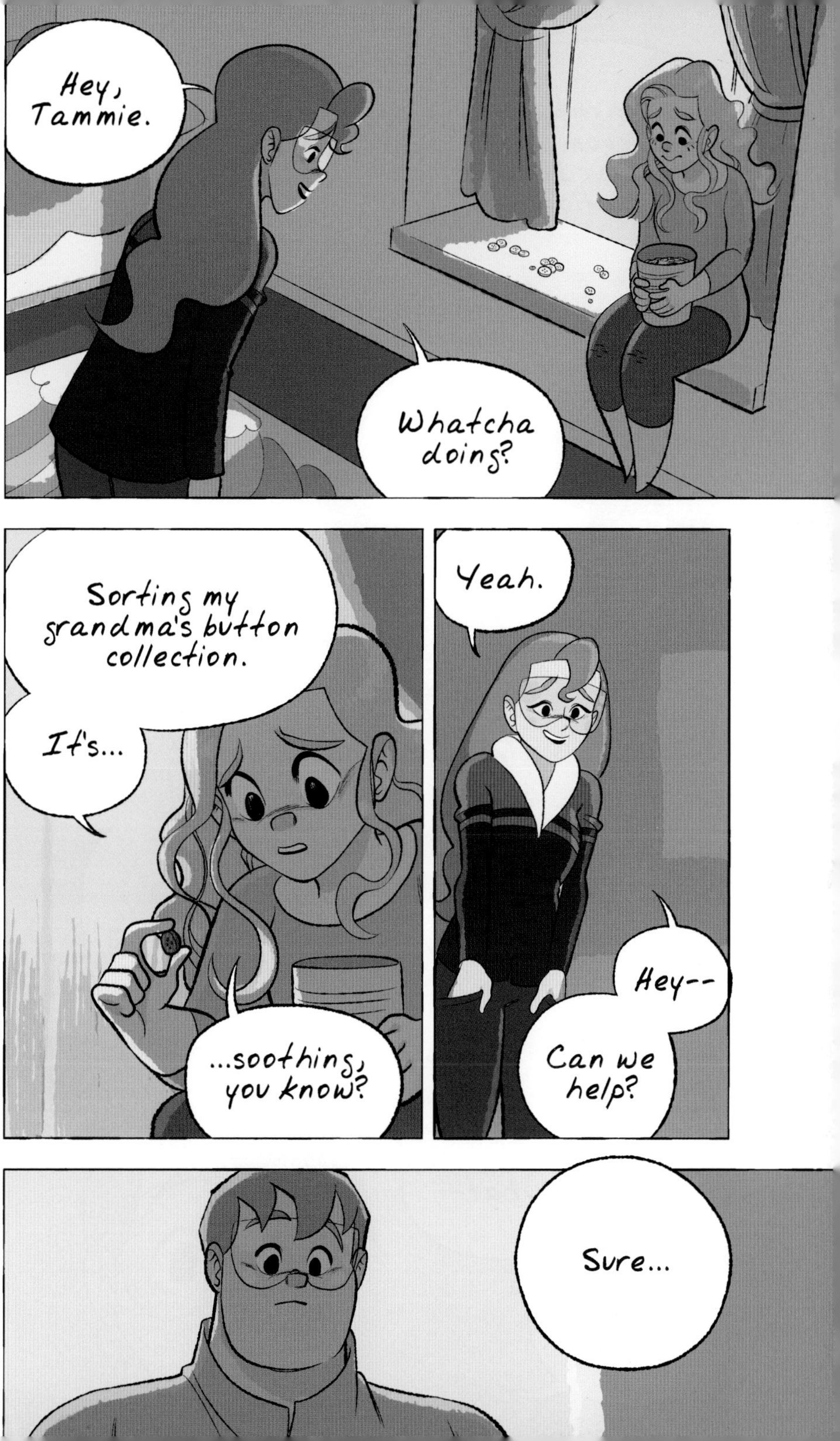
Hey, Tammie.
Whatcha doing?
Sorting my grandma's button collection.
It's...
...soothing, you know?
Yeah.
Hey--
Can we help?
Sure...

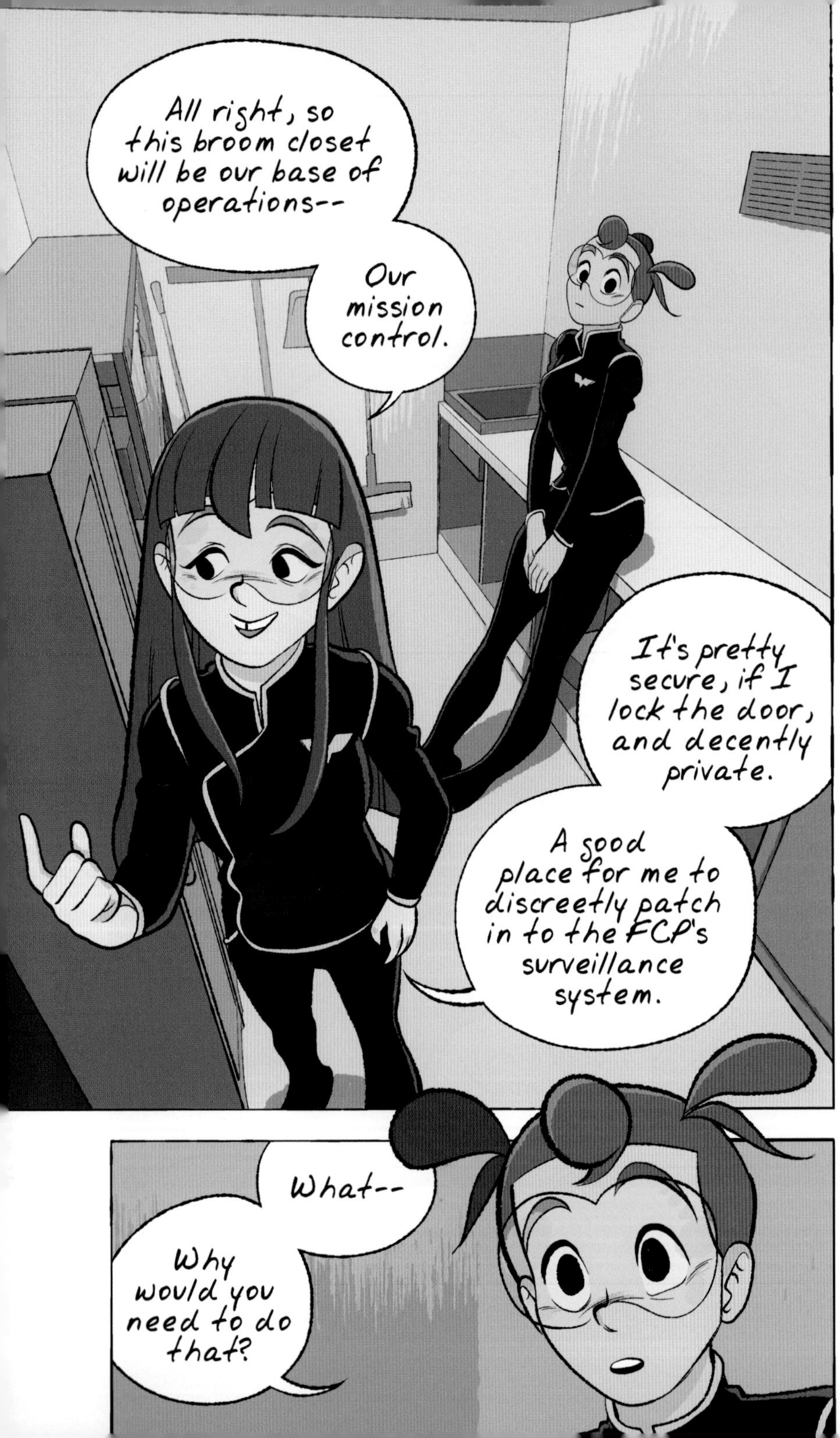
All right, so this broom closet will be our base of operations--
Our mission control.
It's pretty secure, if I lock the door, and decently private.
A good place for me to discreetly patch in to the FCP's surveillance system.
What--
Why would you need to do that?

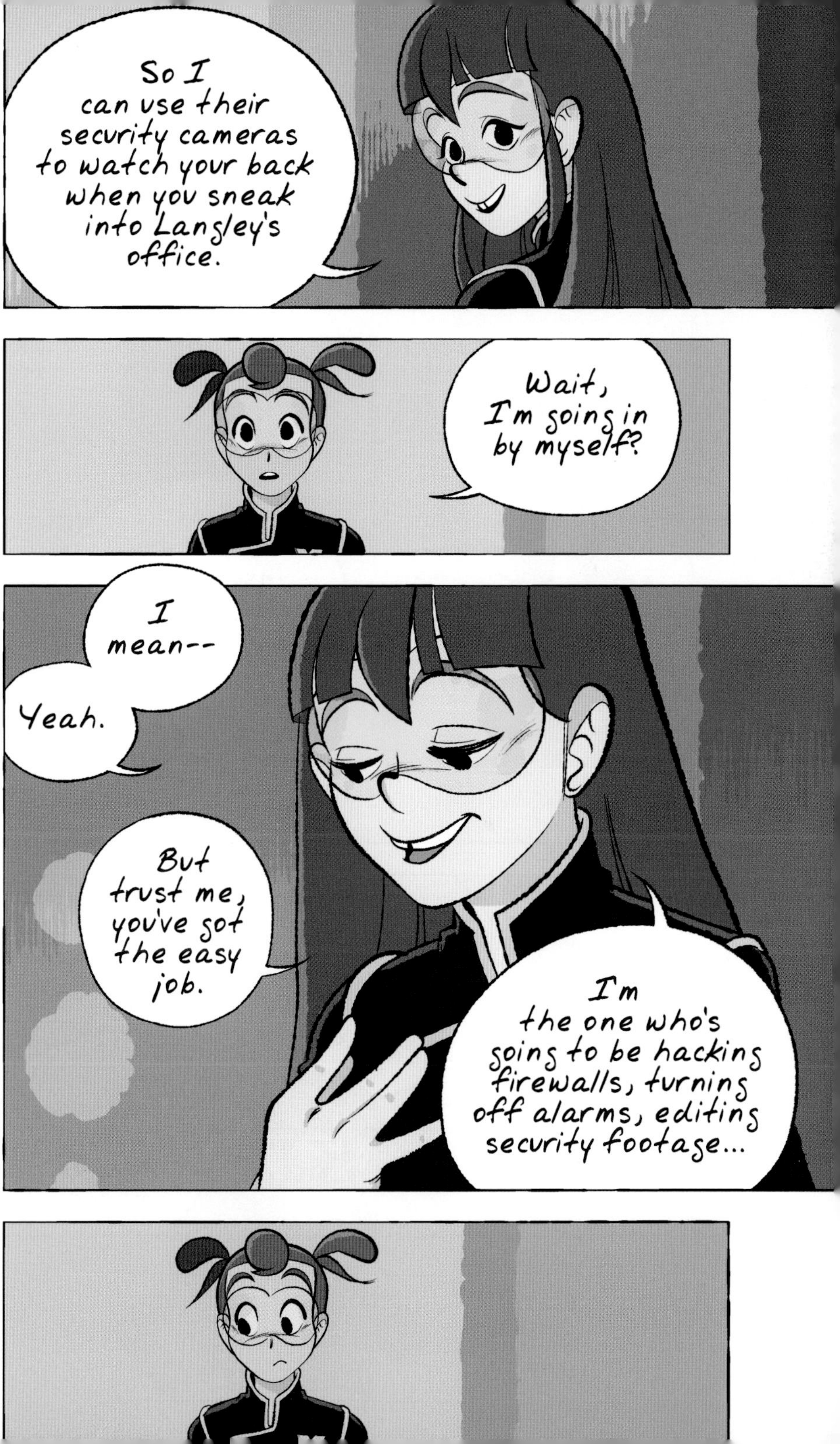
So I can use their security cameras to watch your back when you sneak into Langley's office.
Wait, I'm going in by myself?
I mean--
Yeah.
But trust me, you've got the easy job.
I'm the one who's going to be hacking firewalls, turning off alarms, editing security footage...

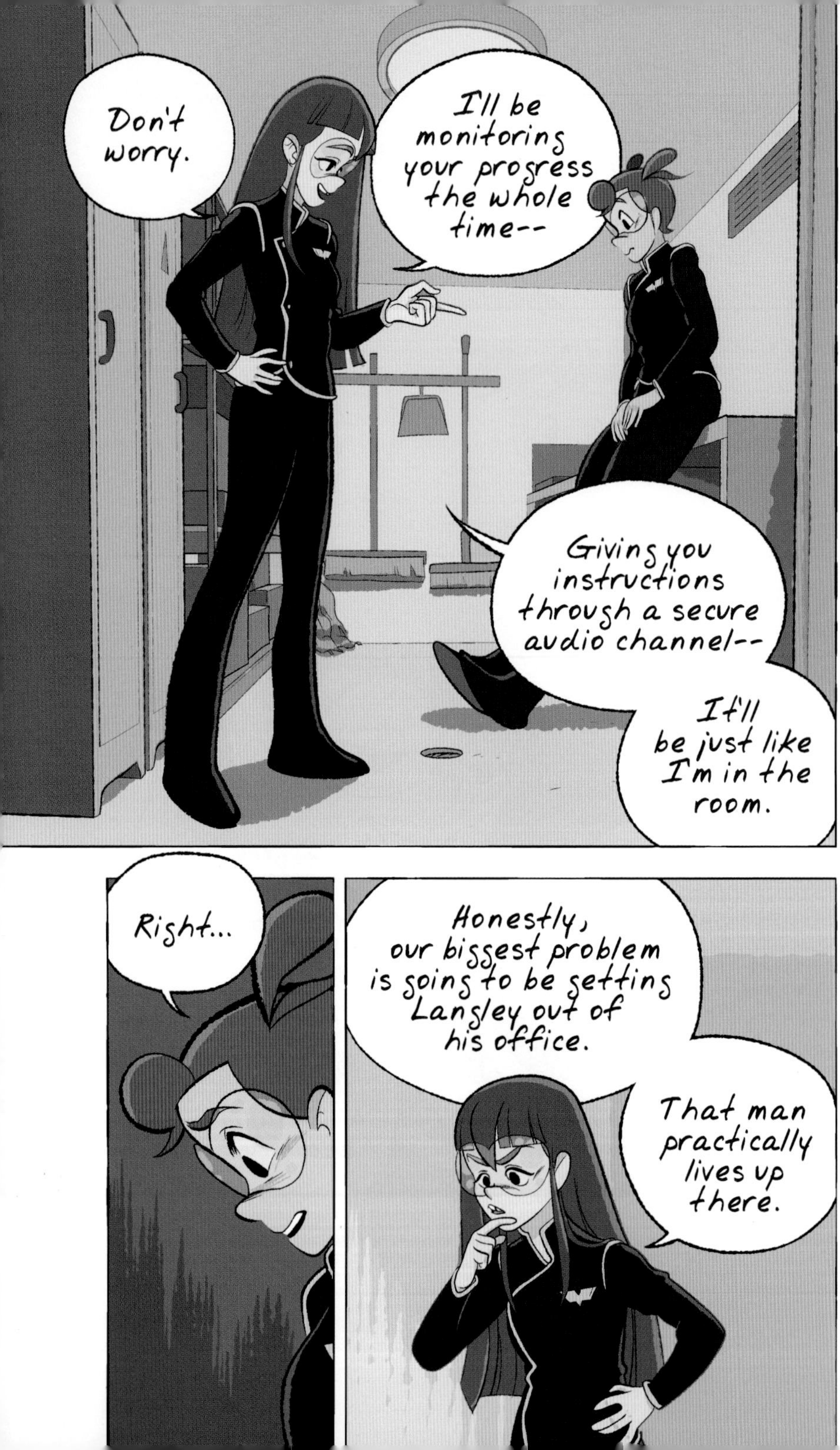

Don't worry.
I'll be monitoring your progress the whole time--
Giving you instructions through a secure audio channel--
It'll be just like I'm in the room.
Right...
Honestly, our biggest problem is going to be getting Langley out of his office.
That man practically lives up there.

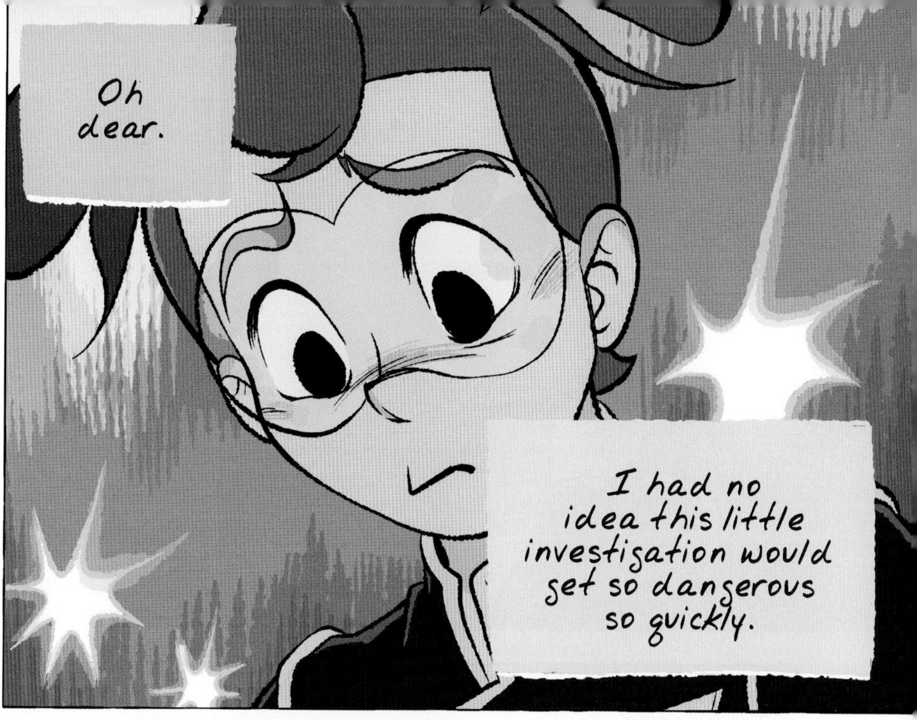
Oh dear.
I had no idea this little investigation would get so dangerous so quickly.

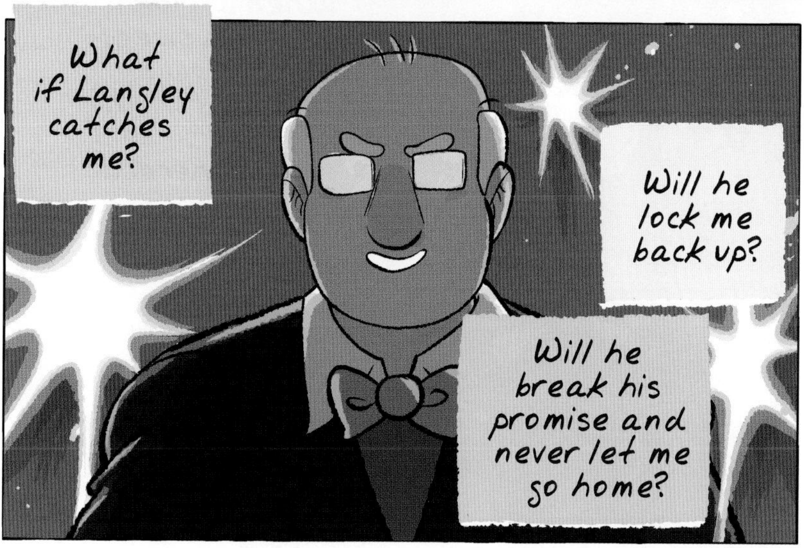
What if Langley catches me?
Will he lock me back up?
Will he break his promise and never let me go home?

I didn't know I'd be risking so much here.

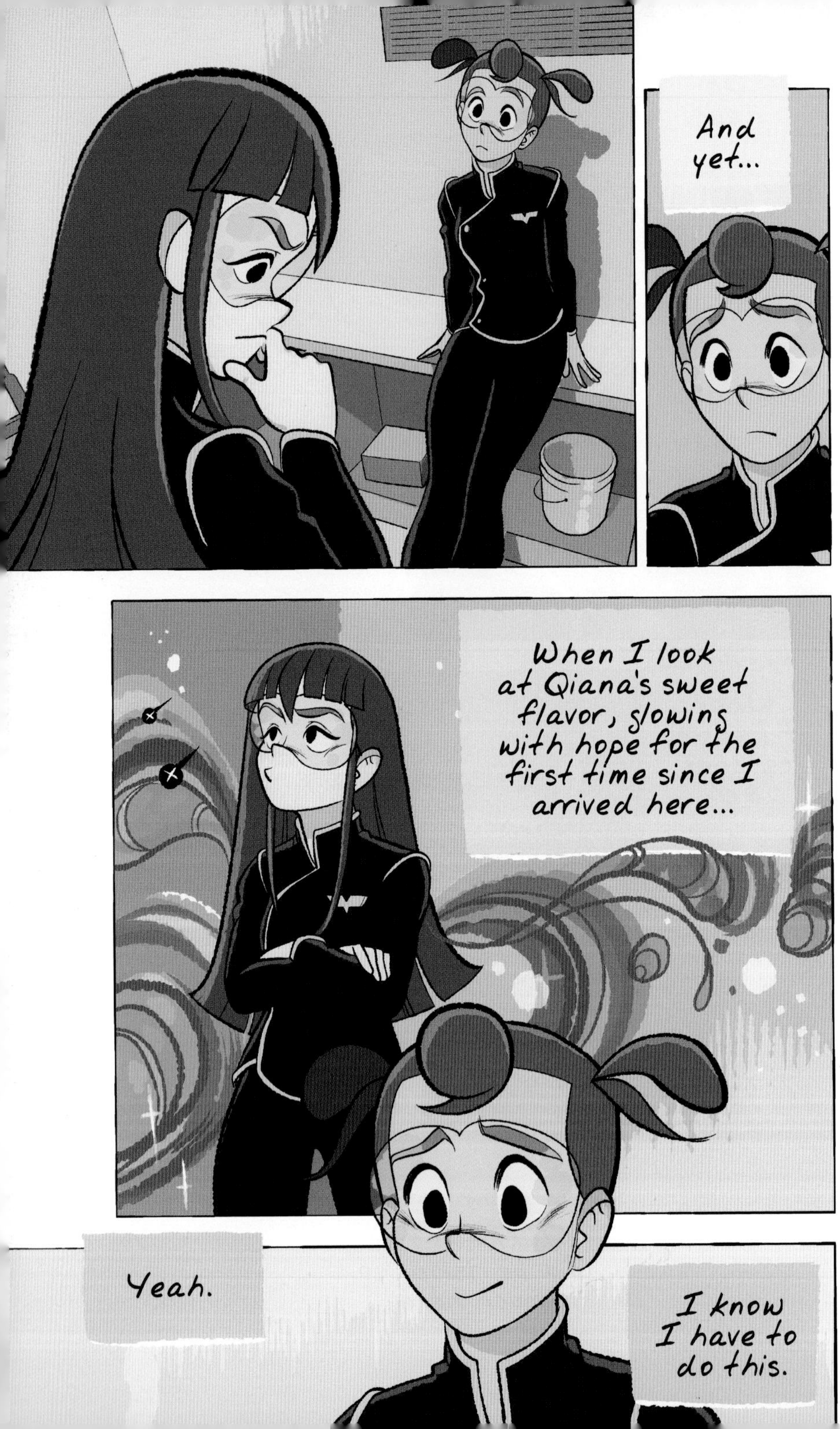
And yet...
When I look at Qiana's sweet flavor, glowing with hope for the first time since I arrived here...
Yeah.
I know I have to do this.

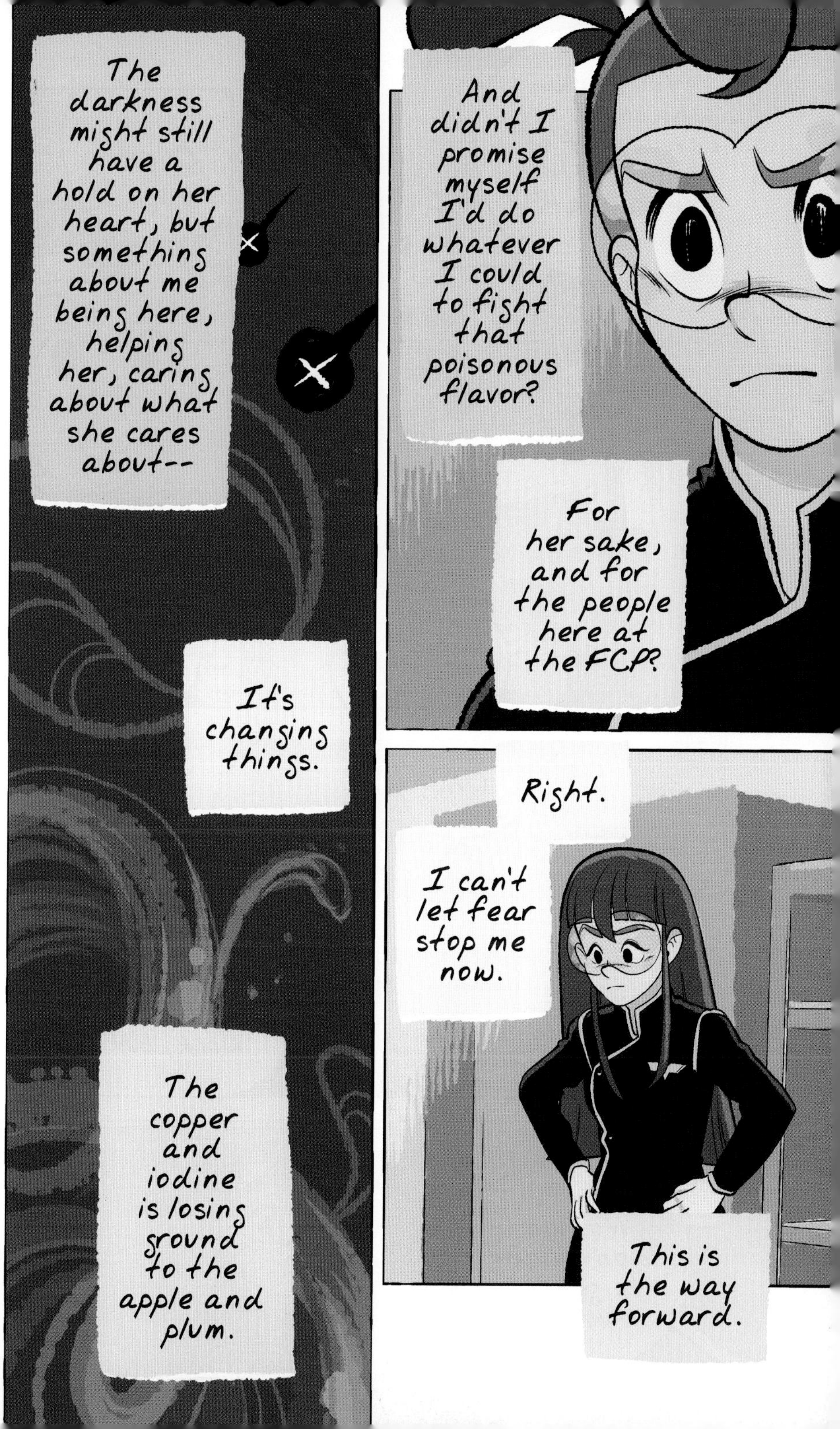
The darkness might still have a hold on her heart, but something about me being here, helping her, caring about what she cares about--
It's changing things.
The copper and iodine is losing ground to the apple and plum.
And didn't I promise myself I'd do whatever I could to fight that poisonous flavor?
For her sake, and for the people here at the FCP?
Right.
I can't let fear stop me now.
This is the way forward.

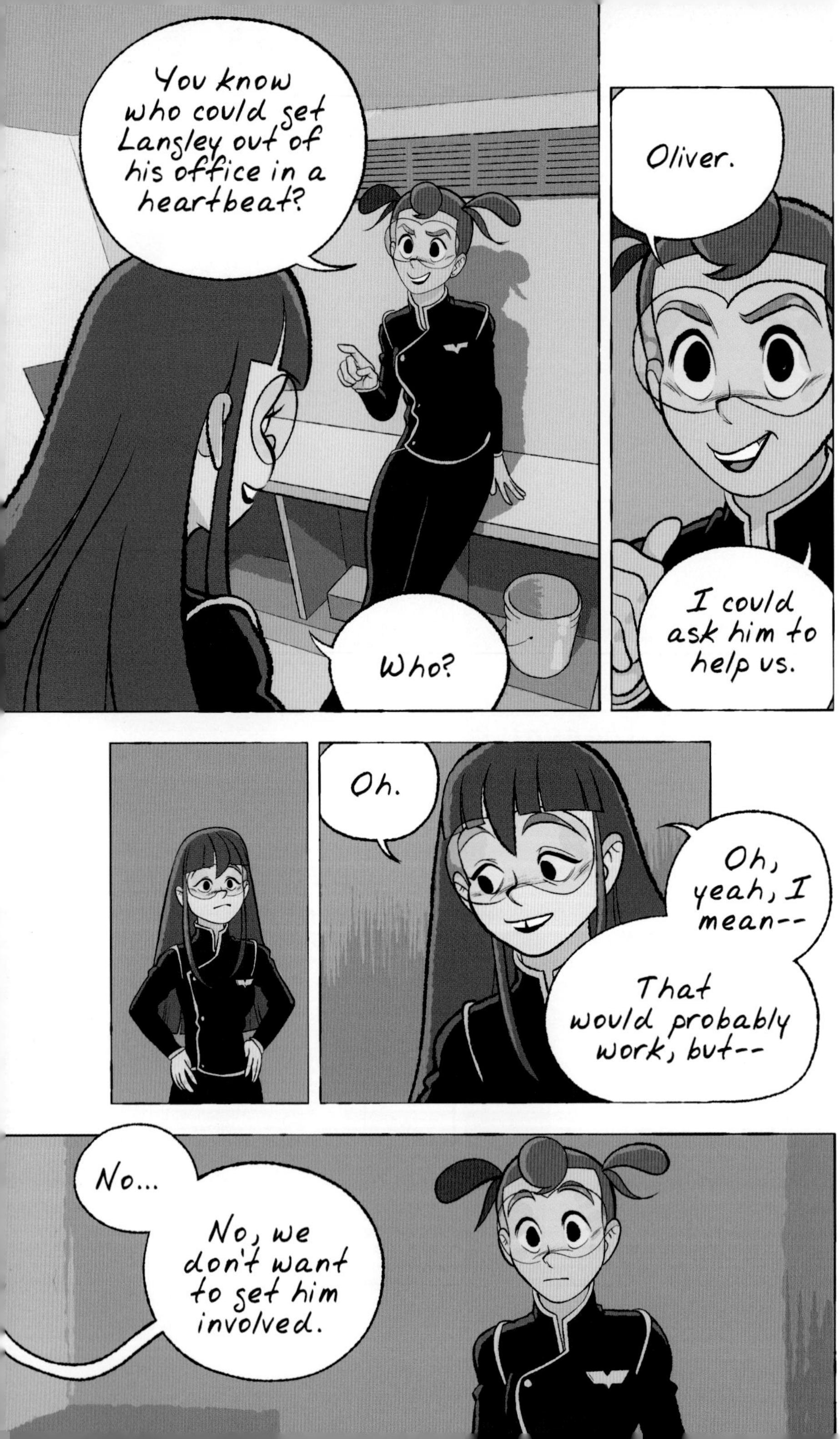
You know who could get Langley out of his office in a heartbeat?
Who?
Oliver.
I could ask him to help us.
Oh.
Oh, yeah, I mean--
That would probably work, but--
No...
No, we don't want to get him involved.

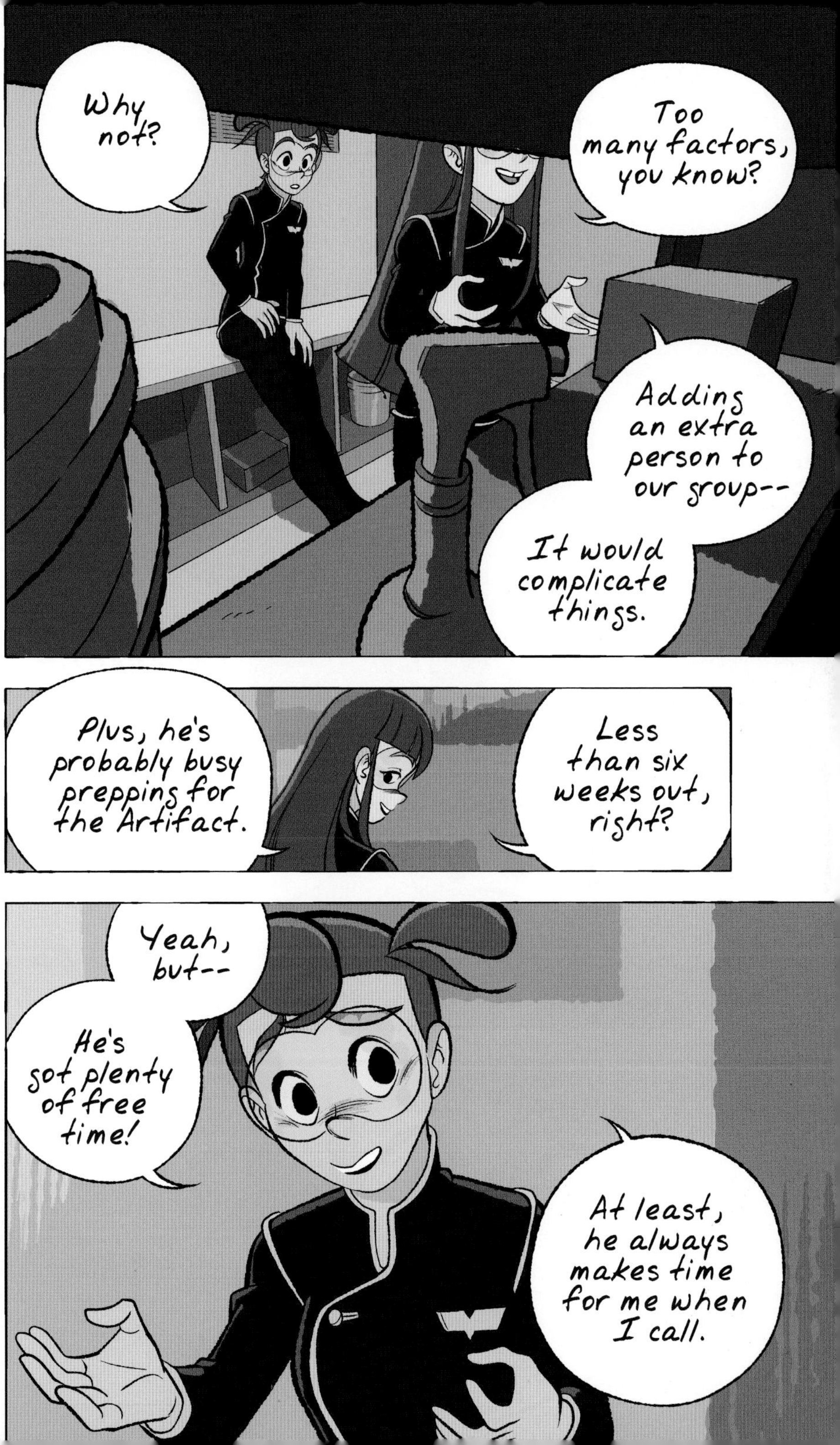
Why not?
Too many factors, you know?
Adding an extra person to our group--
It would complicate things.
Plus, he's probably busy prepping for the Artifact.
Less than six weeks out, right?
Yeah, but--
He's got plenty of free time!
At least, he always makes time for me when I call.

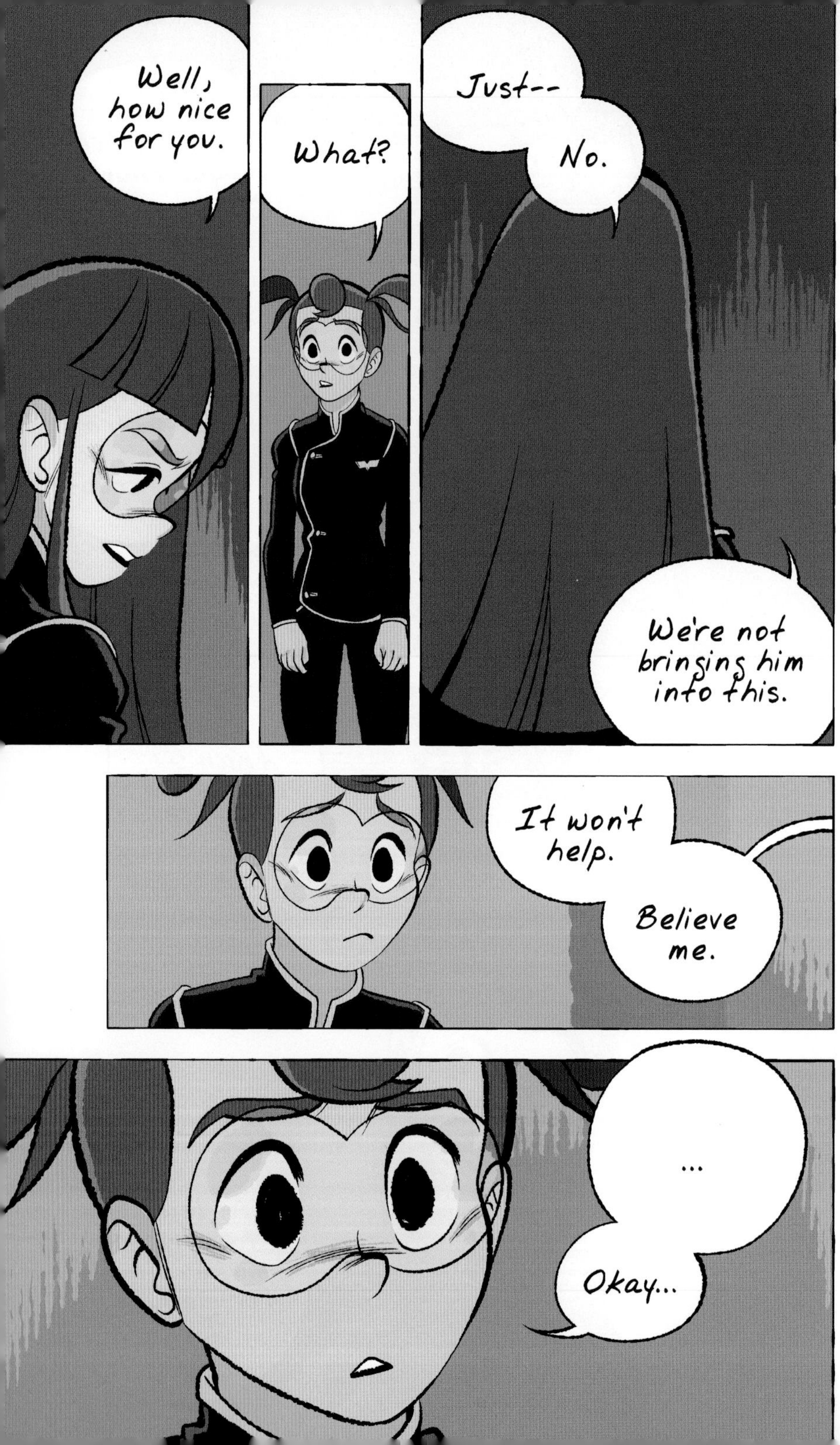
Well, how nice for you.
What?
Just--
No.
We're not bringing him into this.
It won't help.
Believe me.
...
Okay...

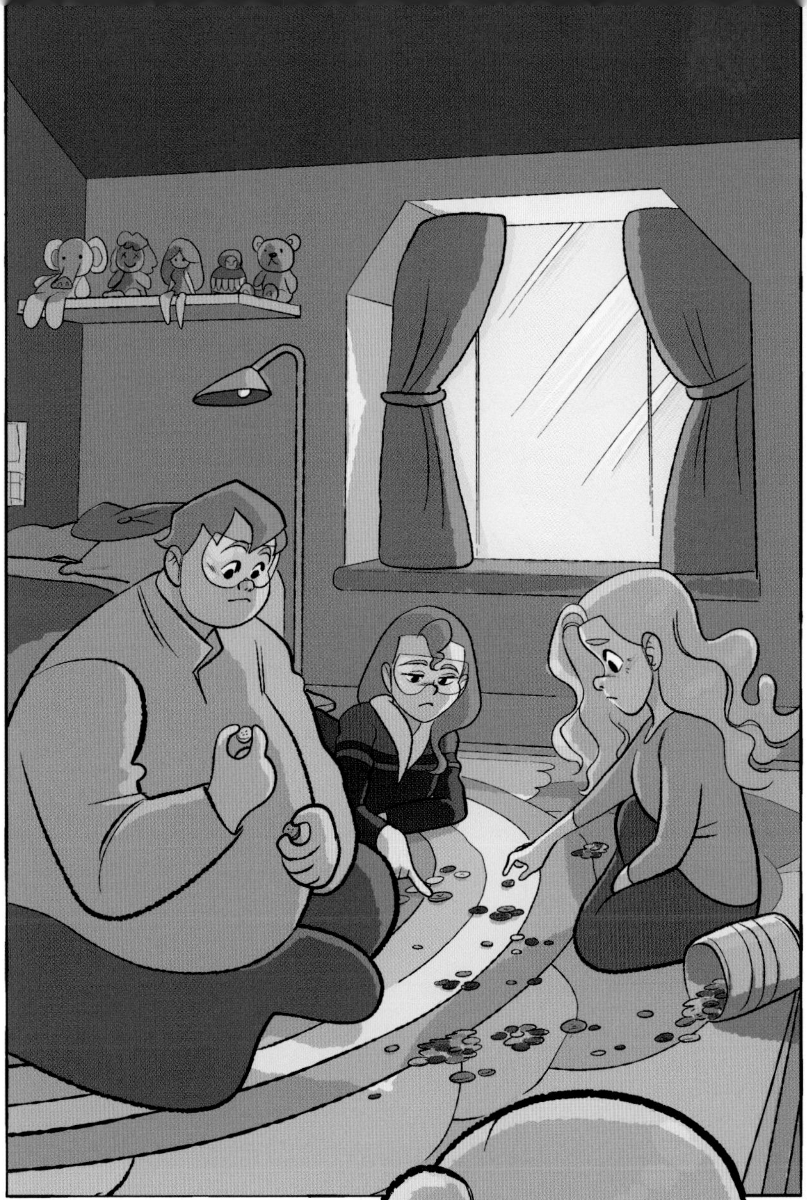

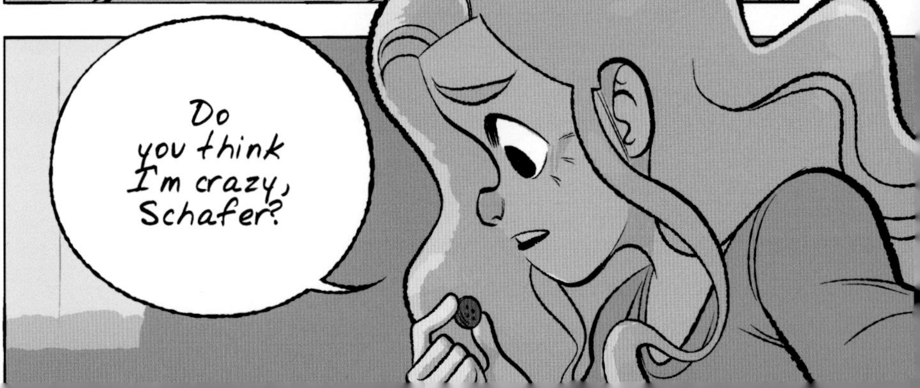
Do you think I'm crazy, Schafer?

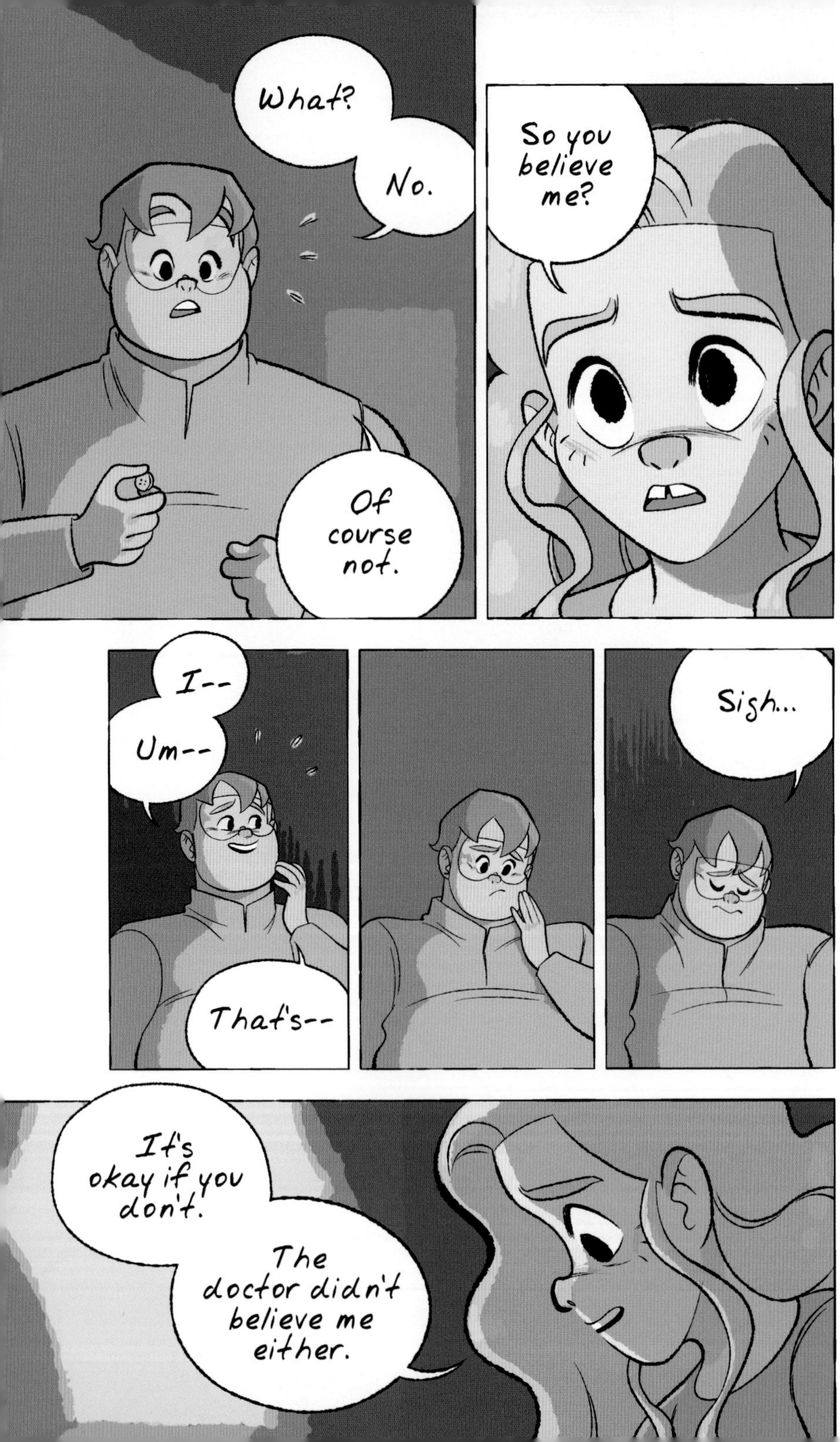
What?
No.
Of course not.
So you believe me?
I--
Um--
That's--
Sigh...
It's okay if you don't.
The doctor didn't believe me either.

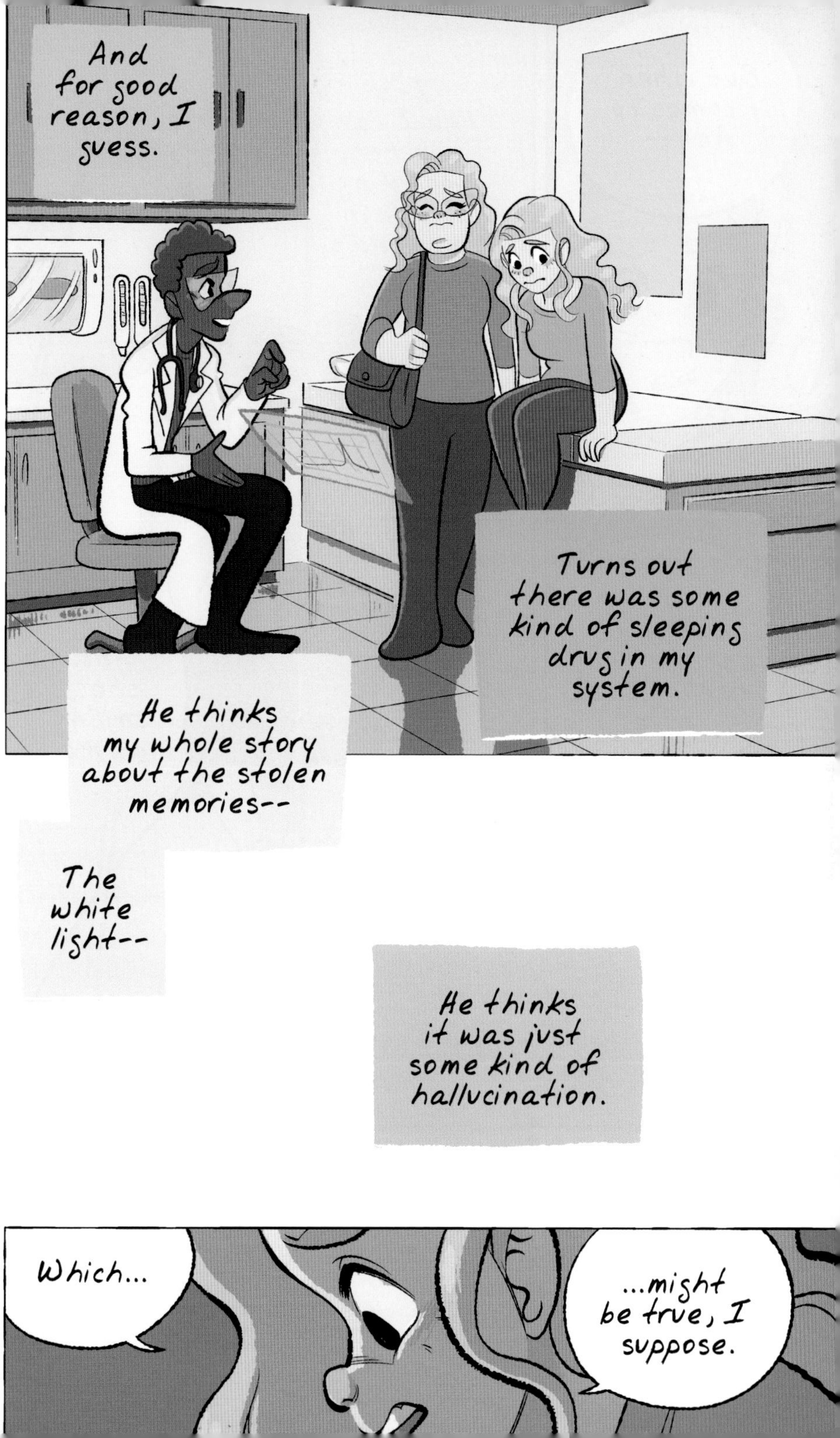
And for good reason, I guess.
Turns out there was some kind of sleeping drug in my system.
He thinks my whole story about the stolen memories--
The white light--
He thinks it was just some kind of hallucination.
Which...
...might be true, I suppose.

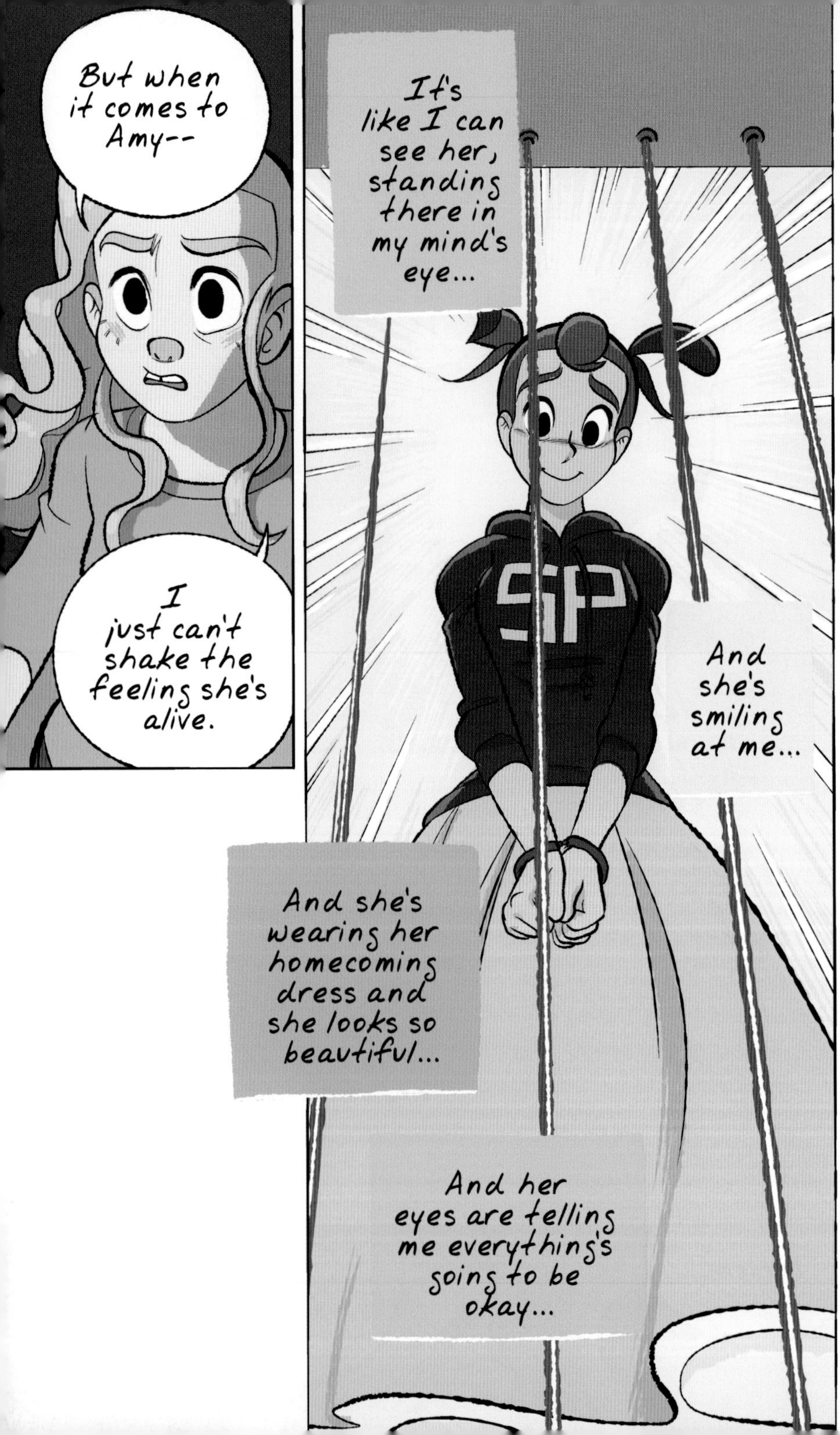
But when it comes to Amy--
I just can't shake the feeling she's alive.
It's like I can see her, standing there in my mind's eye...
And she's smiling at me...
And she's wearing her homecoming dress and she looks so beautiful...
And her eyes are telling me everything's going to be okay...
SP

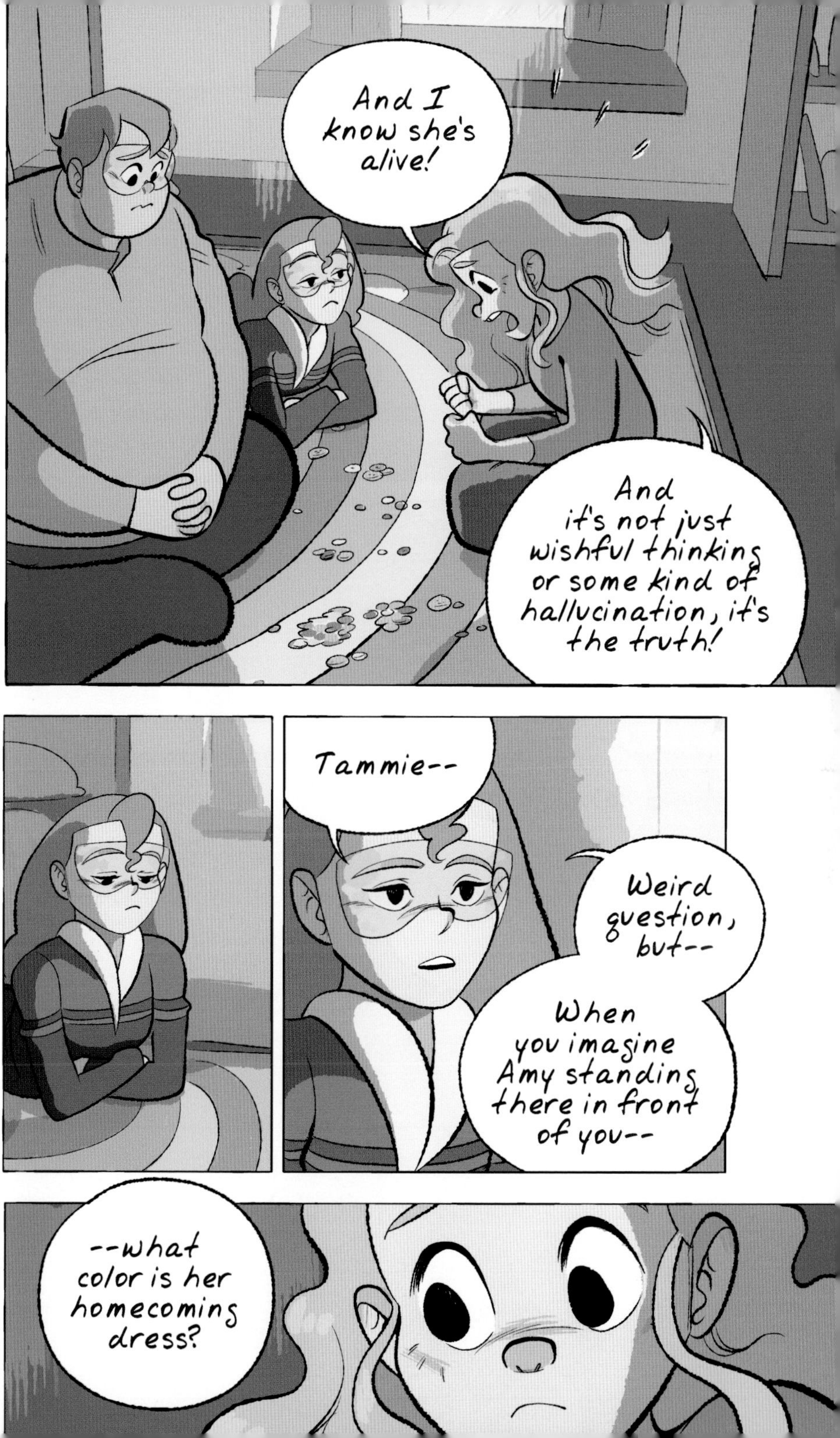
And I know she's alive!
And it's not just wishful thinking or some kind of hallucination, it's the truth!
Tammie--
Weird question, but--
When you imagine Amy standing there in front of you--
--what color is her homecoming dress?

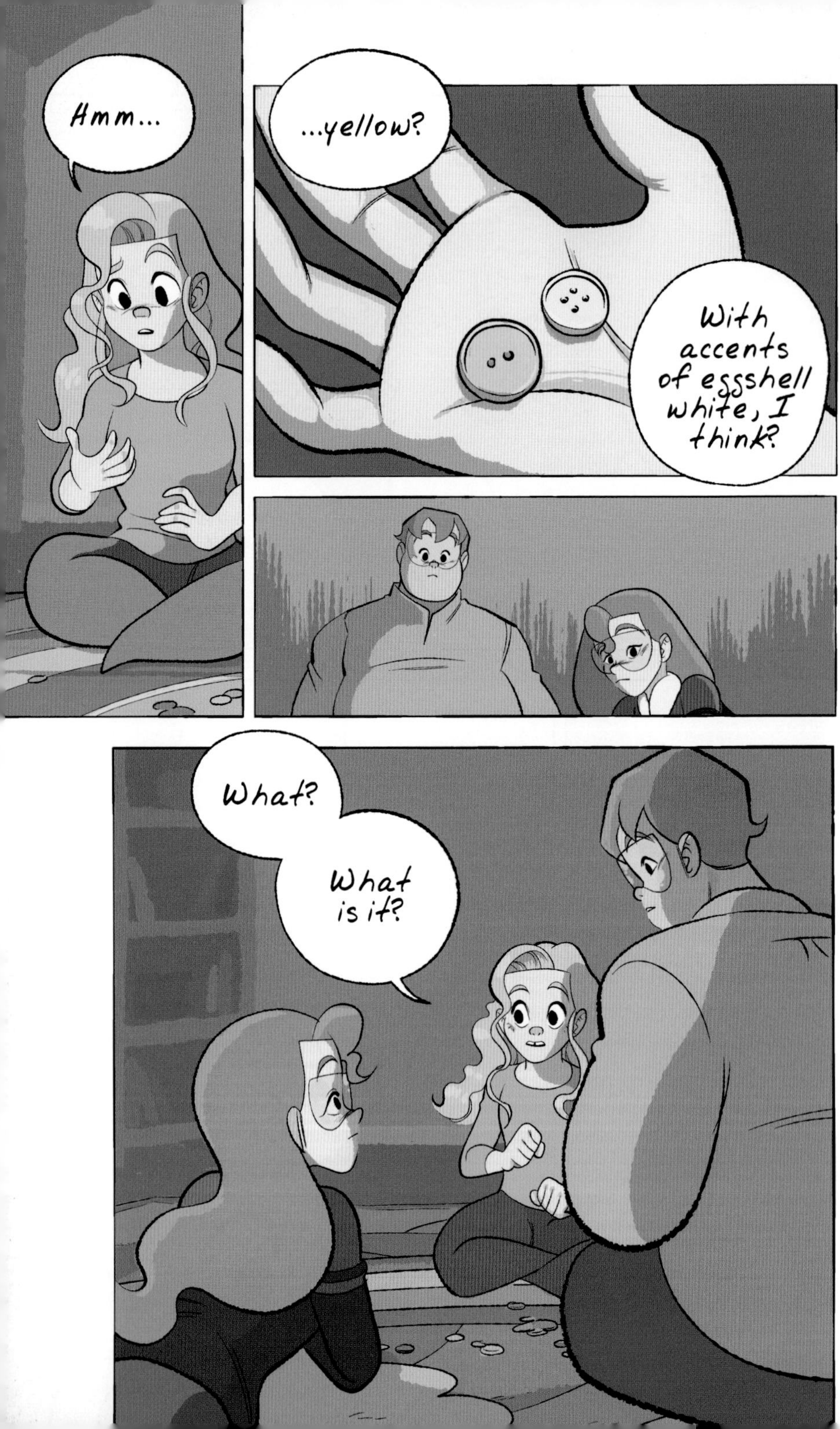
Hmm...
...yellow?
With accents of eggshell white, I think?
What?
What is it?

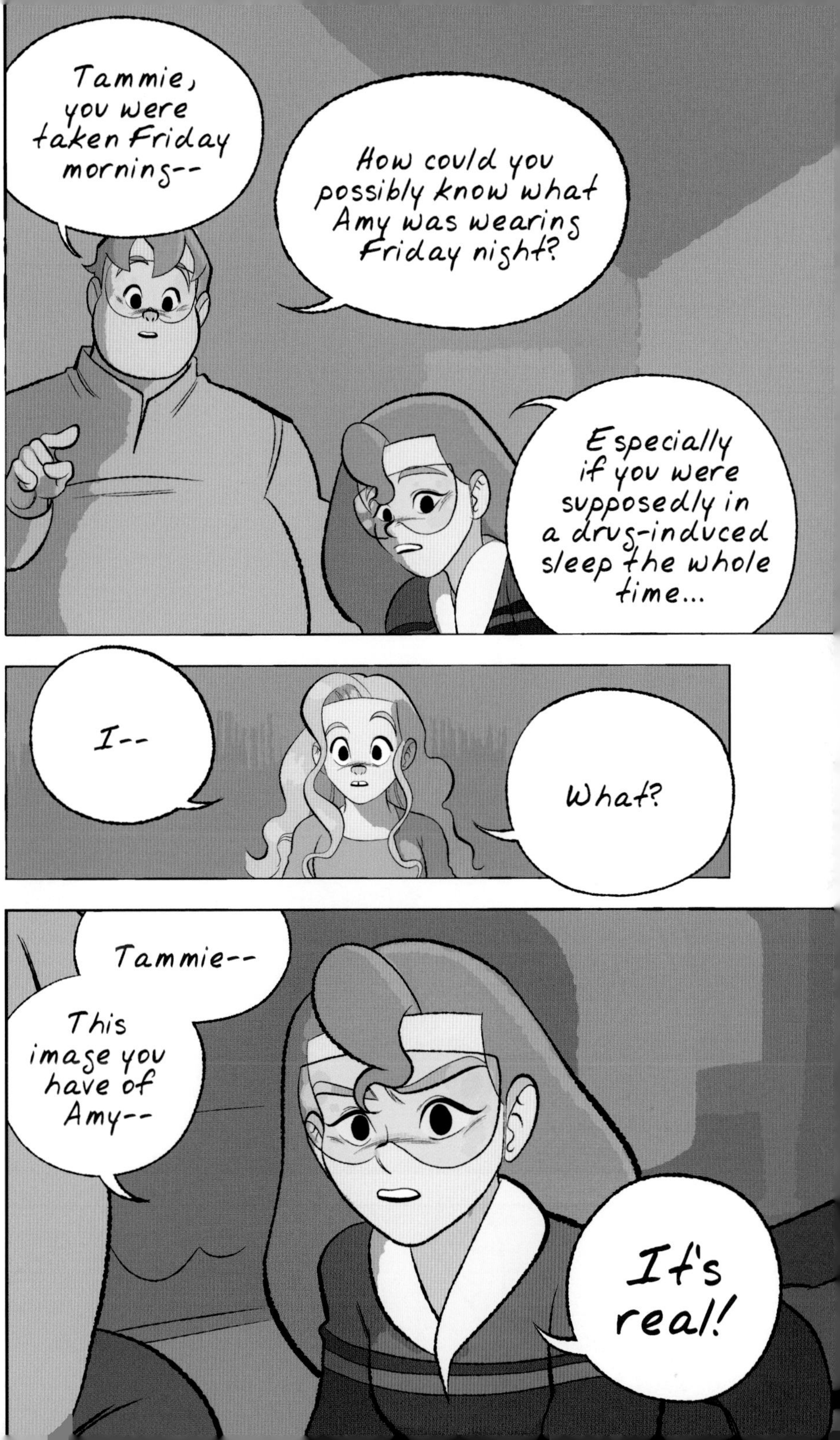
Tammie, you were taken Friday morning--
How could you possibly know what Amy was wearing Friday night?
Especially if you were supposedly in a drug-induced sleep the whole time...
I--
What?
Tammie--
This image you have of Amy--
It's real!

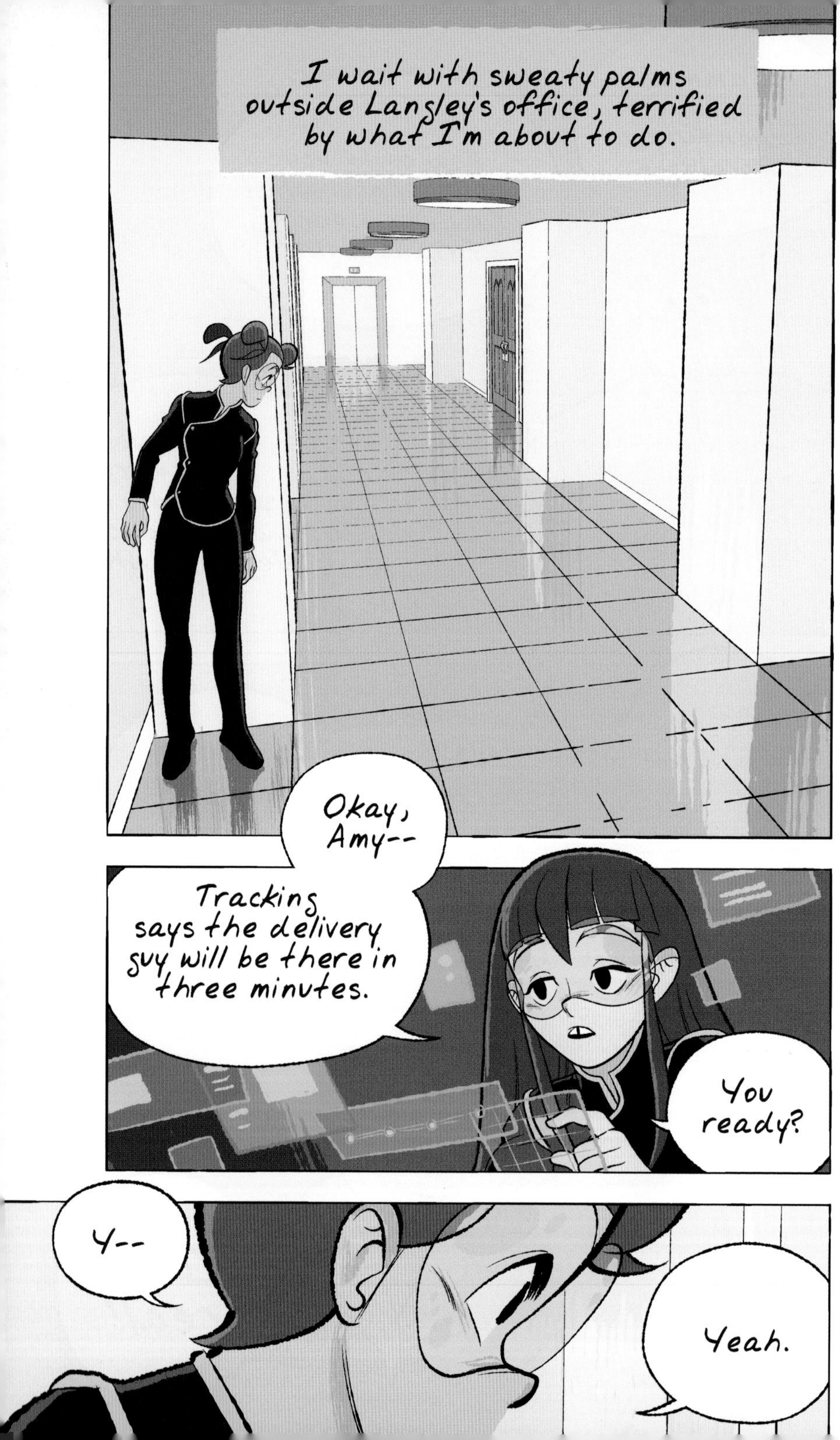
I wait with sweaty palms outside Langley's office, terrified by what I'm about to do.
Okay, Amy--
Tracking says the delivery guy will be there in three minutes.
You ready?
Y--
Yeah.

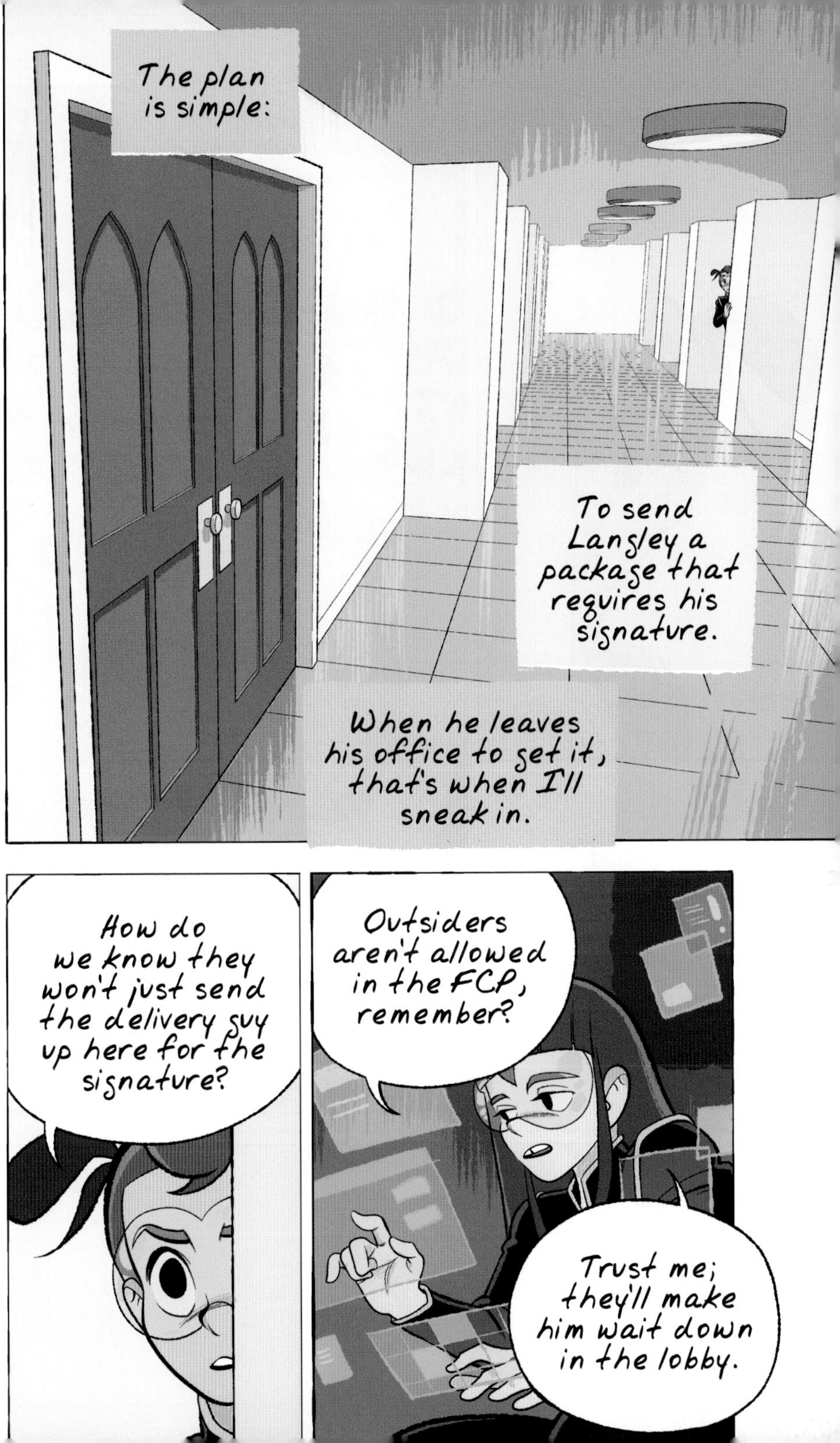
The plan is simple:
To send Langley a package that requires his signature.
When he leaves his office to get it, that's when I'll sneak in.
How do we know they won't just send the delivery guy up here for the signature?
Outsiders aren't allowed in the FCP, remember?
Trust me; they'll make him wait down in the lobby.

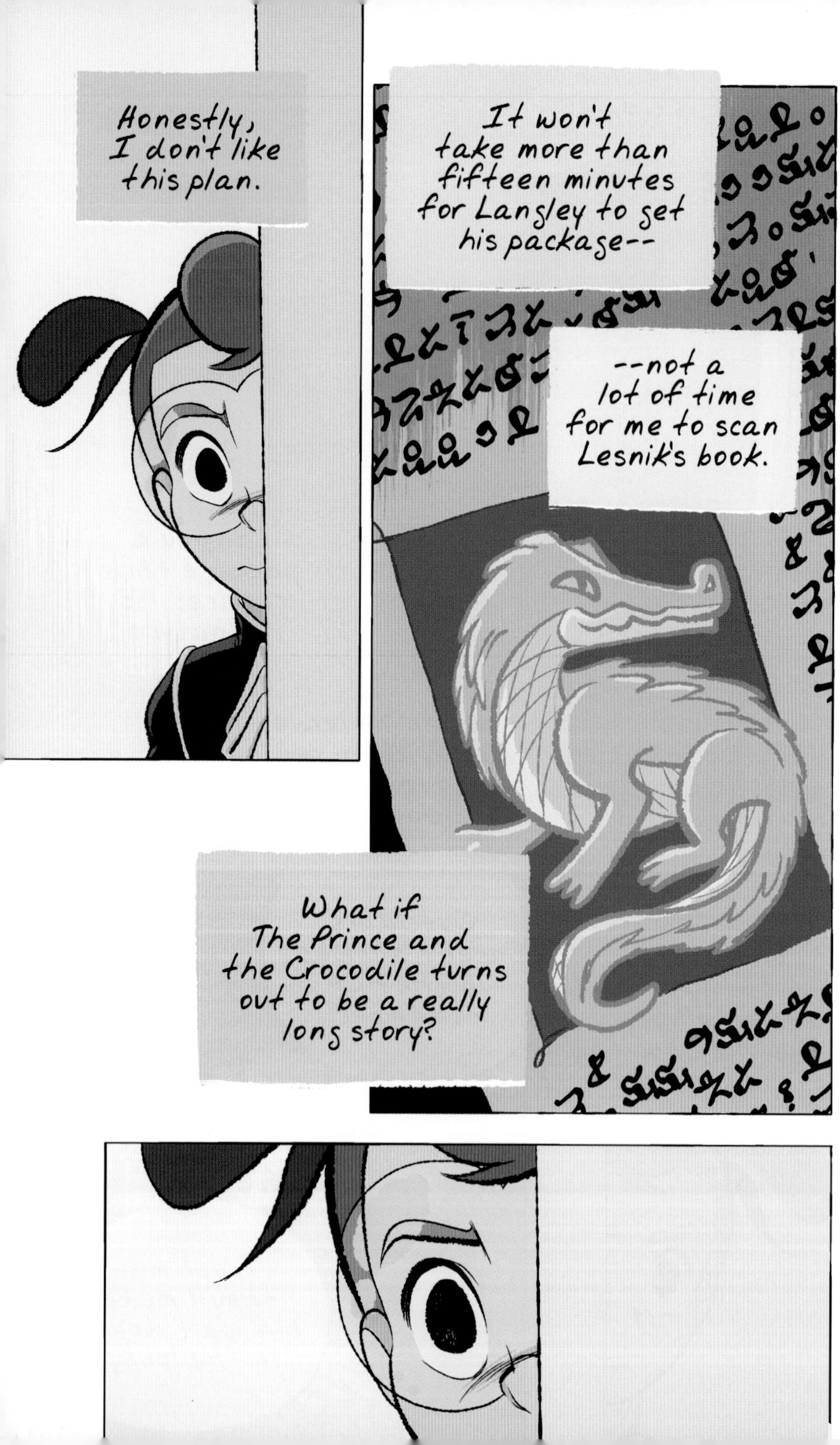
Honestly, I don't like this plan.
It won't take more than fifteen minutes for Langley to get his package--
--not a lot of time for me to scan Lesnik's book.
What if The Prince and the Crocodile turns out to be a really long story?

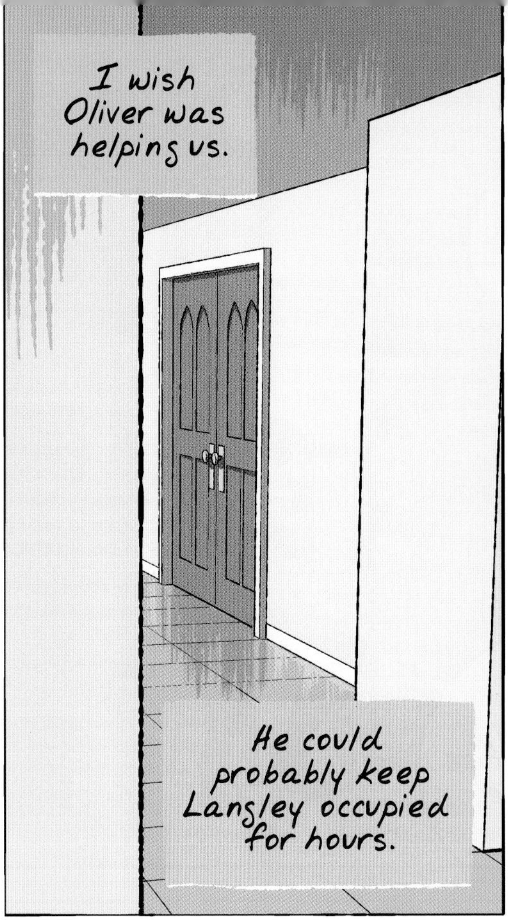
I wish Oliver was helping us.
He could probably keep Langley occupied for hours.

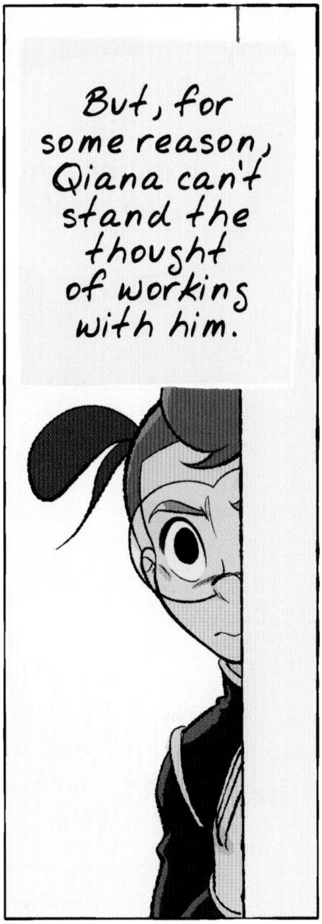
But, for some reason, Qiana can't stand the thought of working with him.

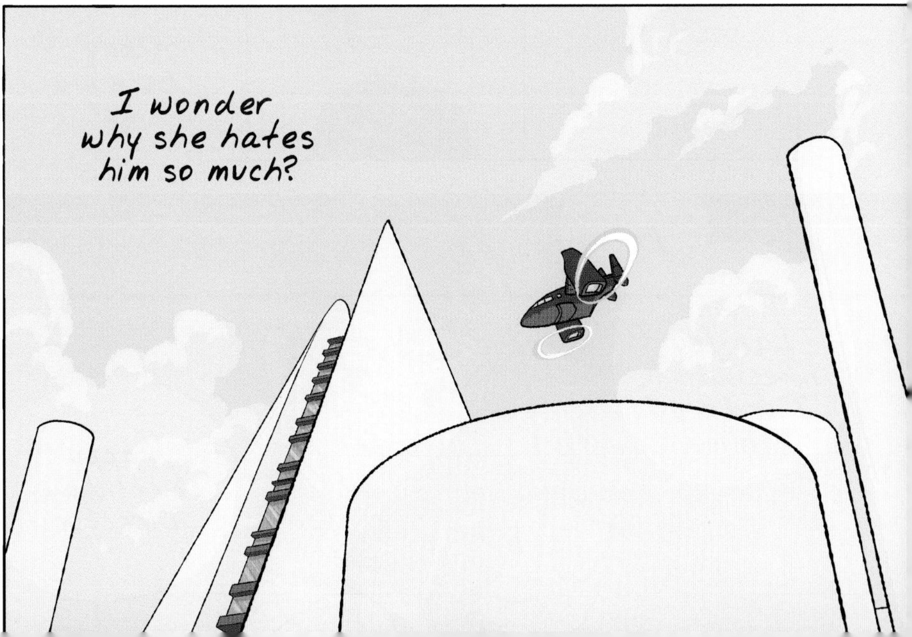
I wonder why she hates him so much?

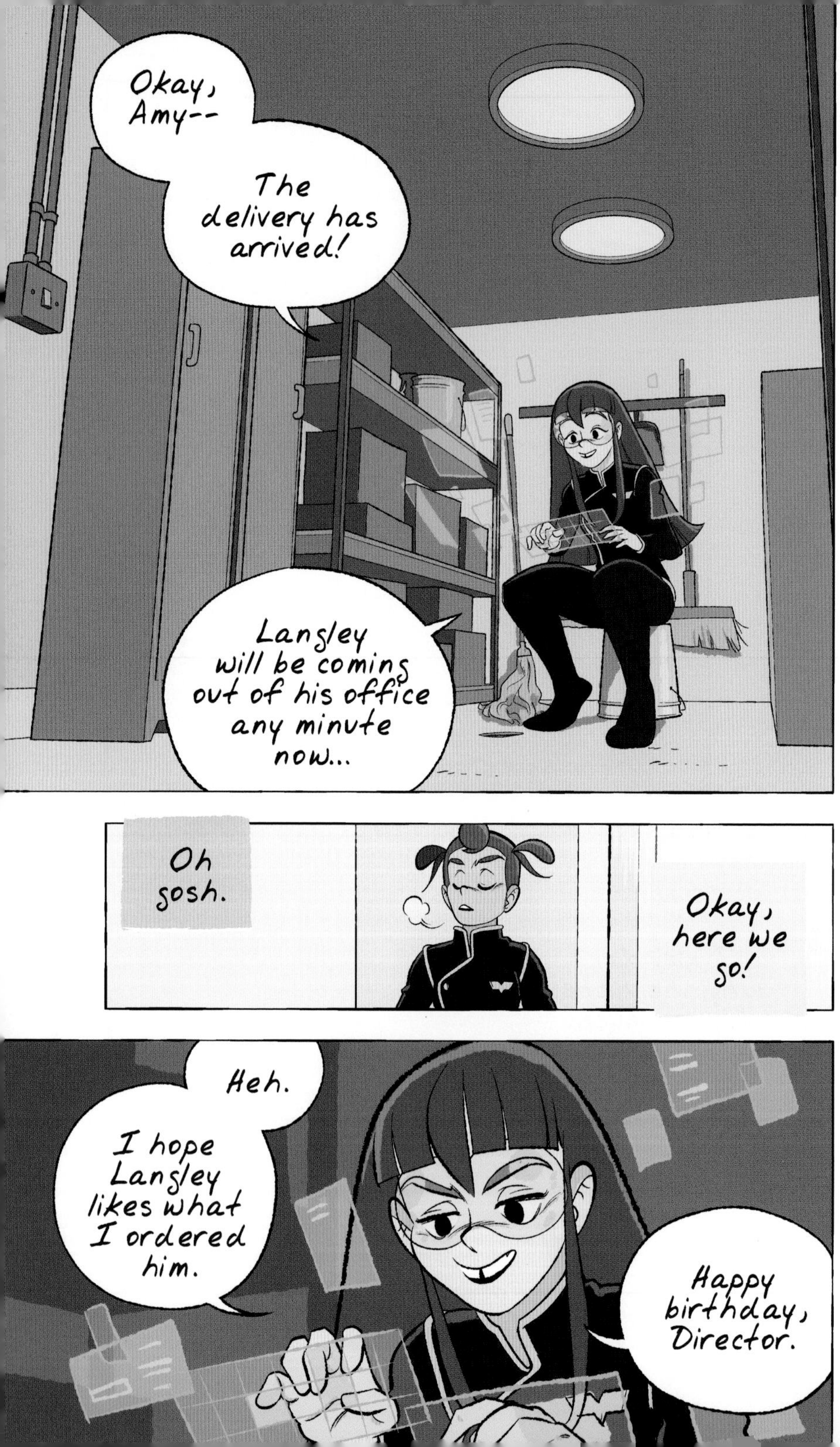
Okay, Amy--
The delivery has arrived!
Langley will be coming out of his office any minute now...
Oh gosh.
Okay, here we go!
Heh.
I hope Langley likes what I ordered him.
Happy birthday, Director.

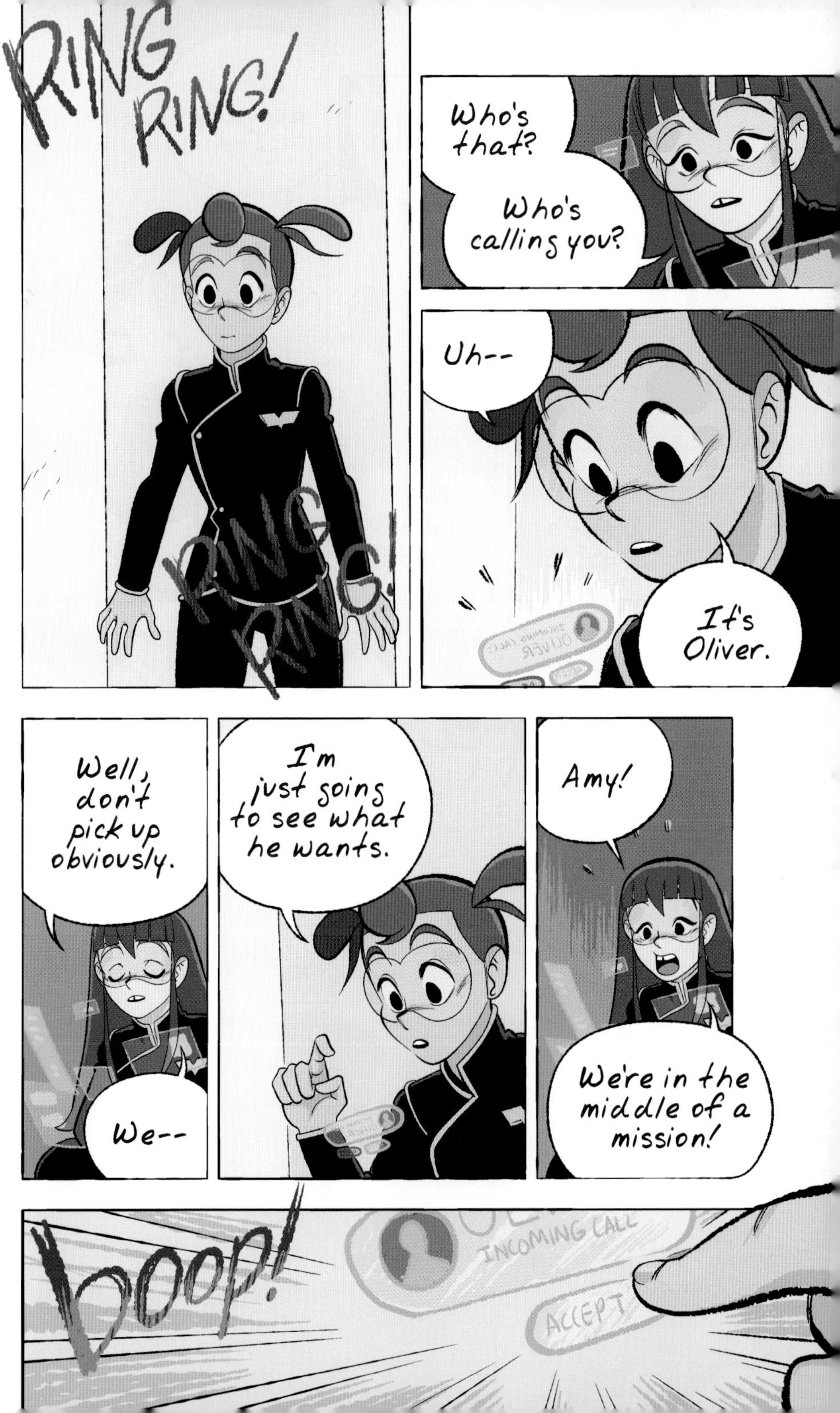
RING RING!
Who's that?
Who's calling you?
RING RING!
Uh--
It's Oliver.
INCOMING CALL:
OLIVER
Well, don't pick up obviously.
We--
I'm just going to see what he wants.
Amy!
We're in the middle of a mission!
boop!
INCOMING CALL
ACCEPT

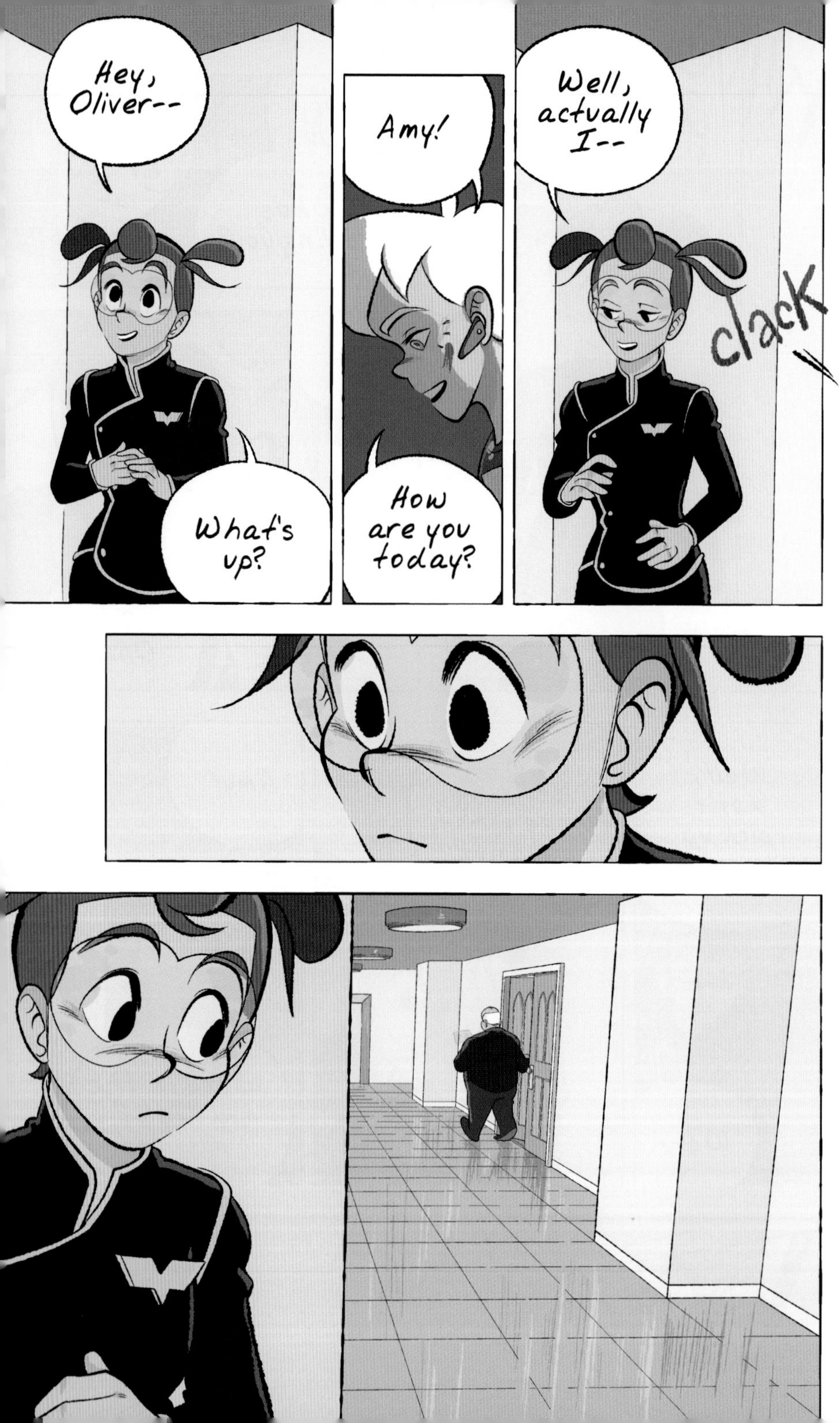

Hey, Oliver--
What's up?
Amy!
How are you today?
Well, actually I--
clack

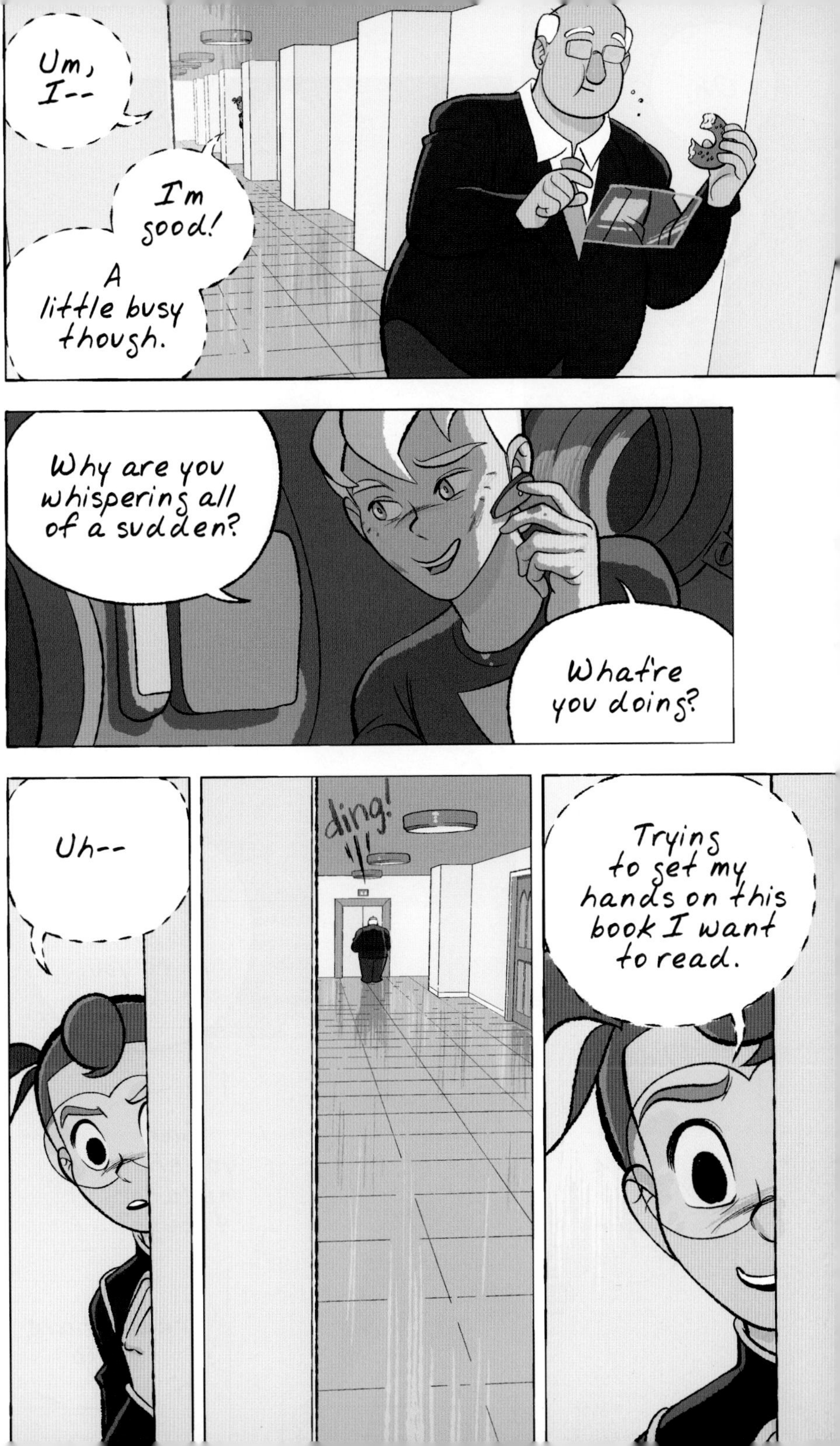
Um, I--
I'm good!
A little busy though.
Why are you whispering all of a sudden?
Whatre you doing?
Uh--
ding!
Trying to get my hands on this book I want to read.

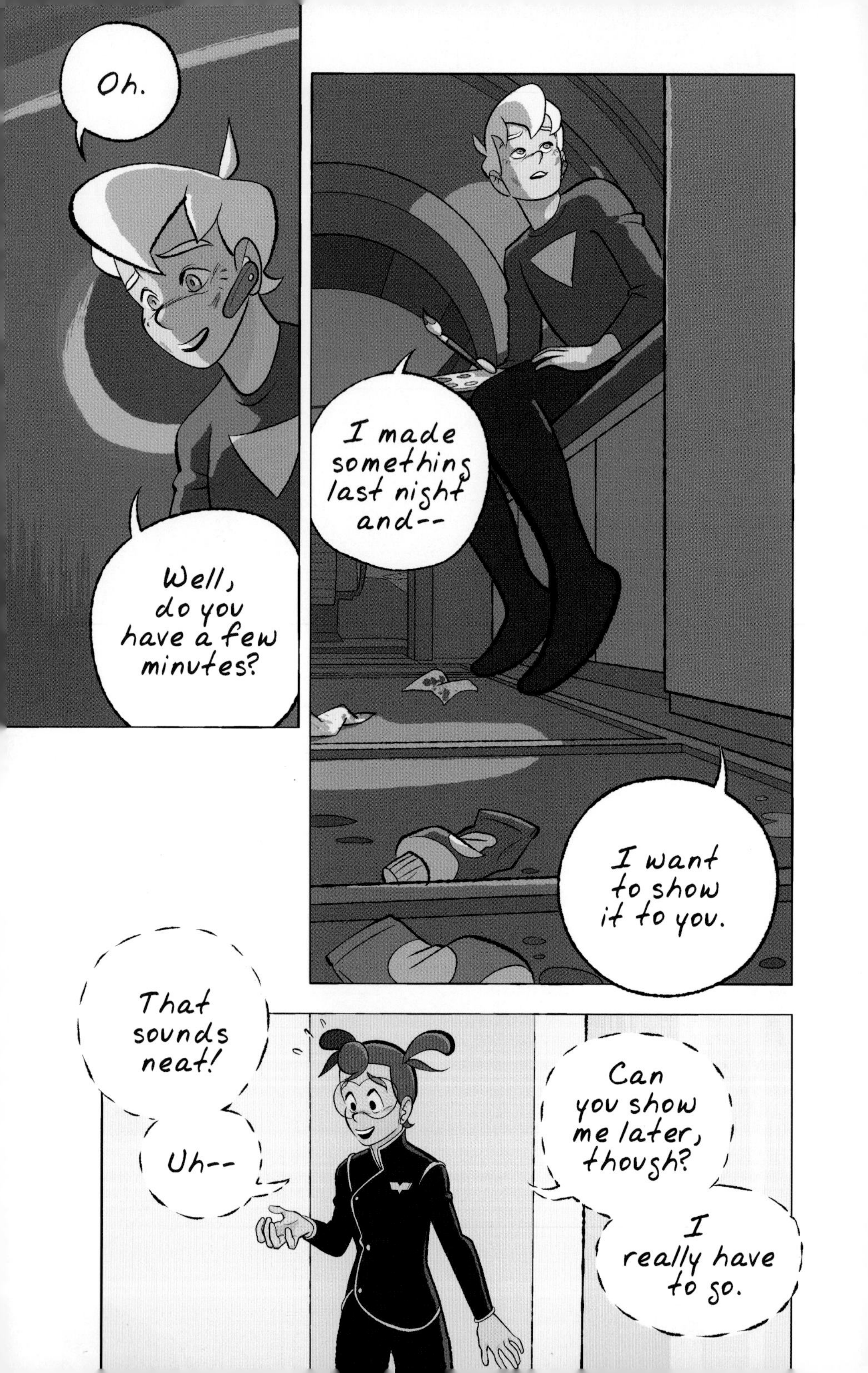
Oh.
Well, do you have a few minutes?
I made somethins last night and--
I want to show it to you.
That sounds neat!
Uh--
Can you show me later, though?
I really have to go.

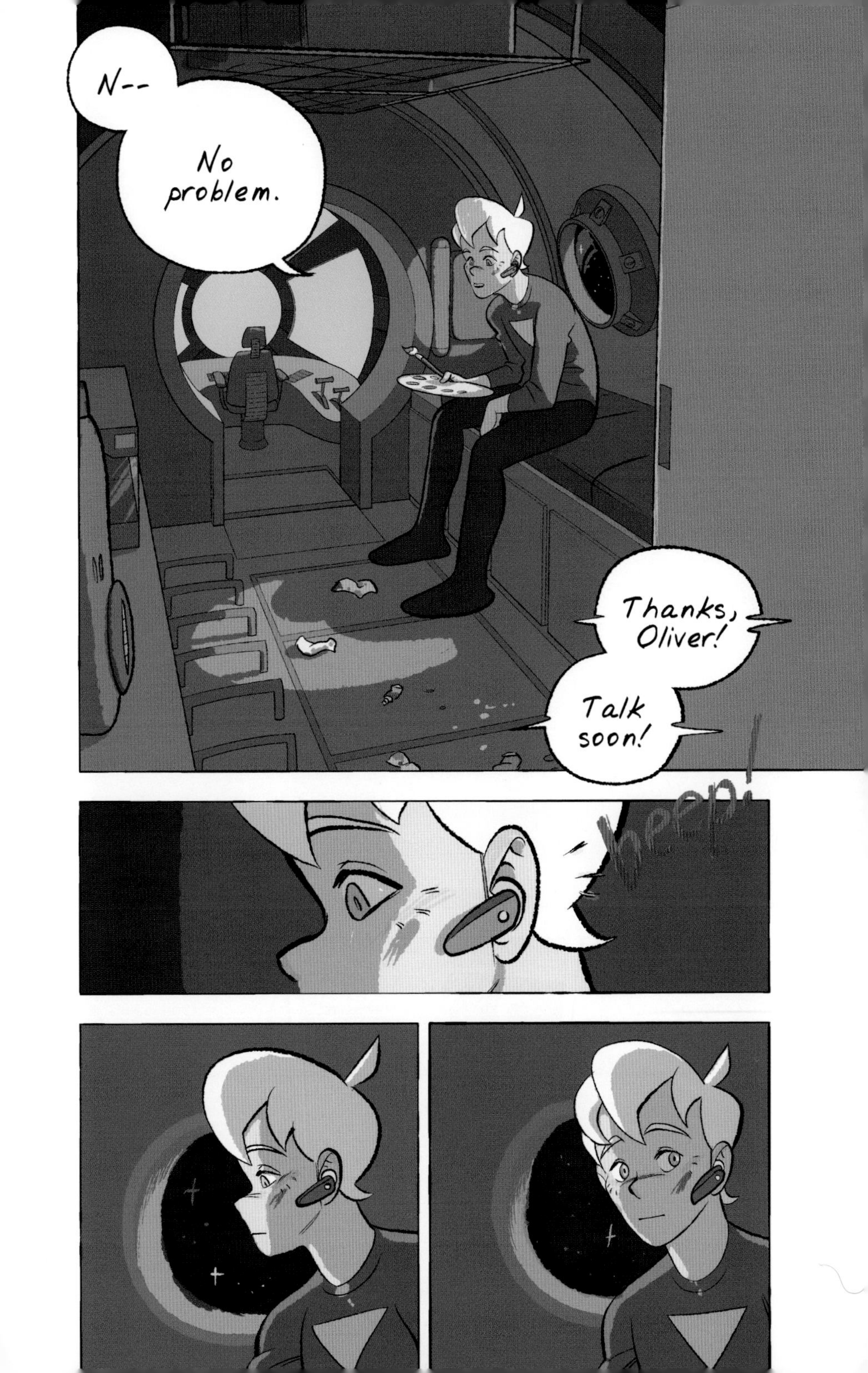
N--
No problem.
Thanks, Oliver!
Talk soon!
beep!

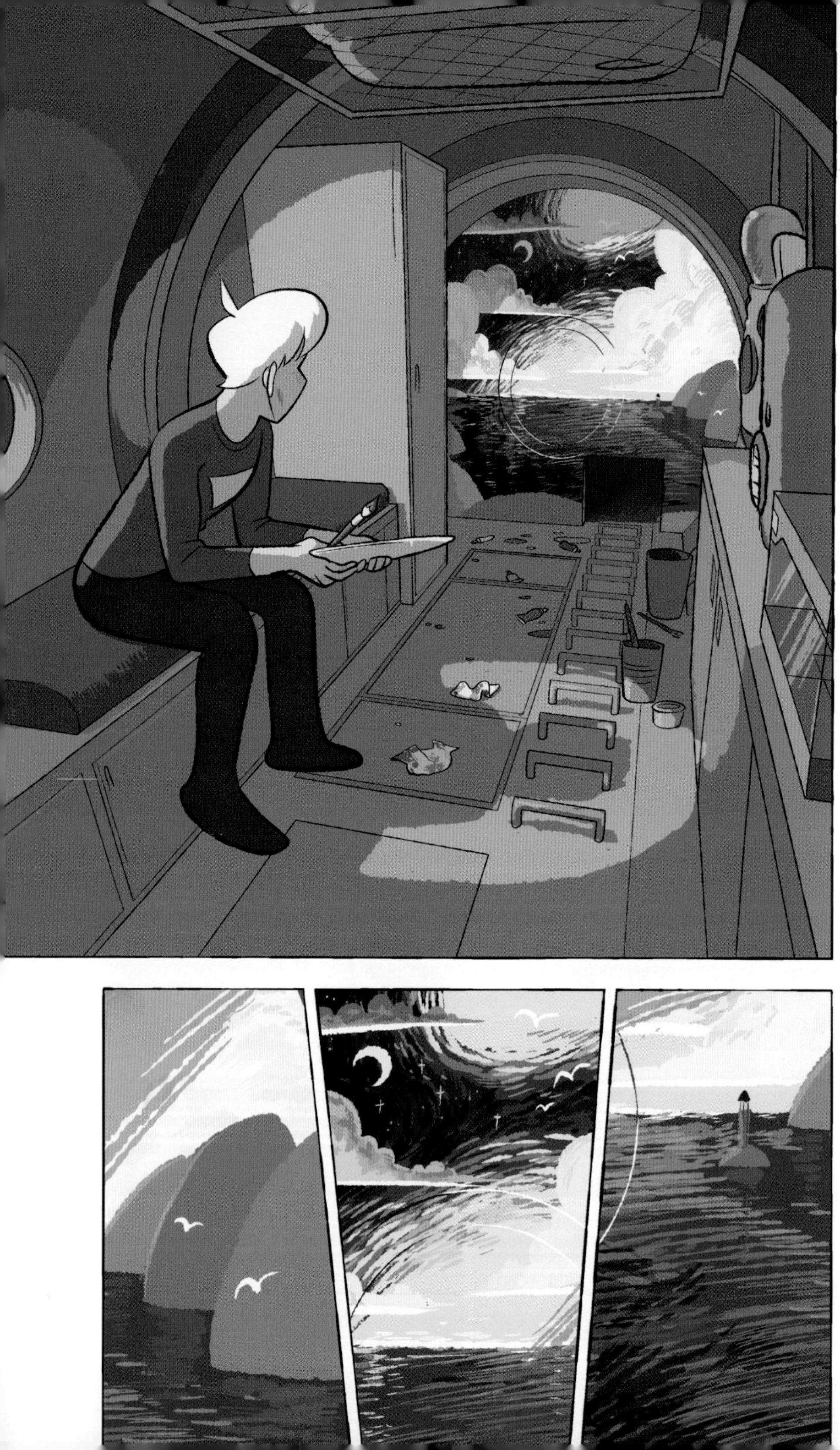

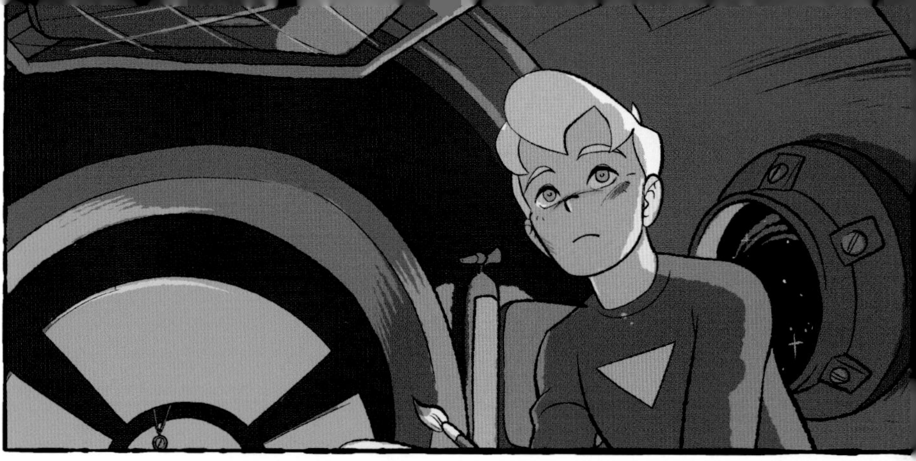

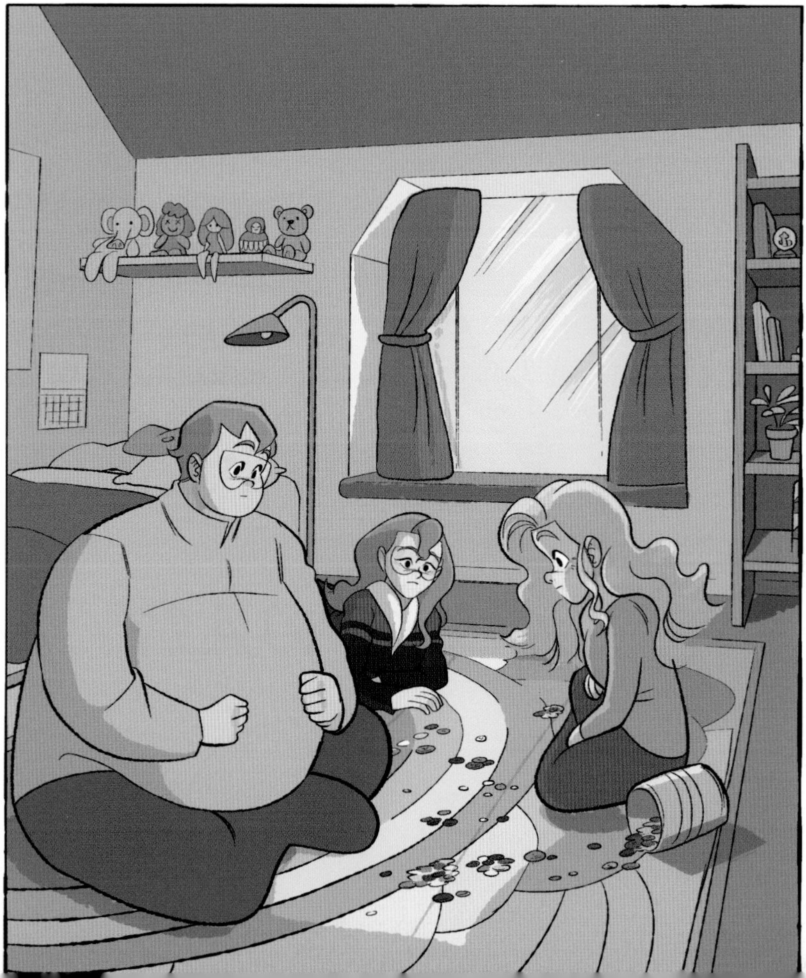

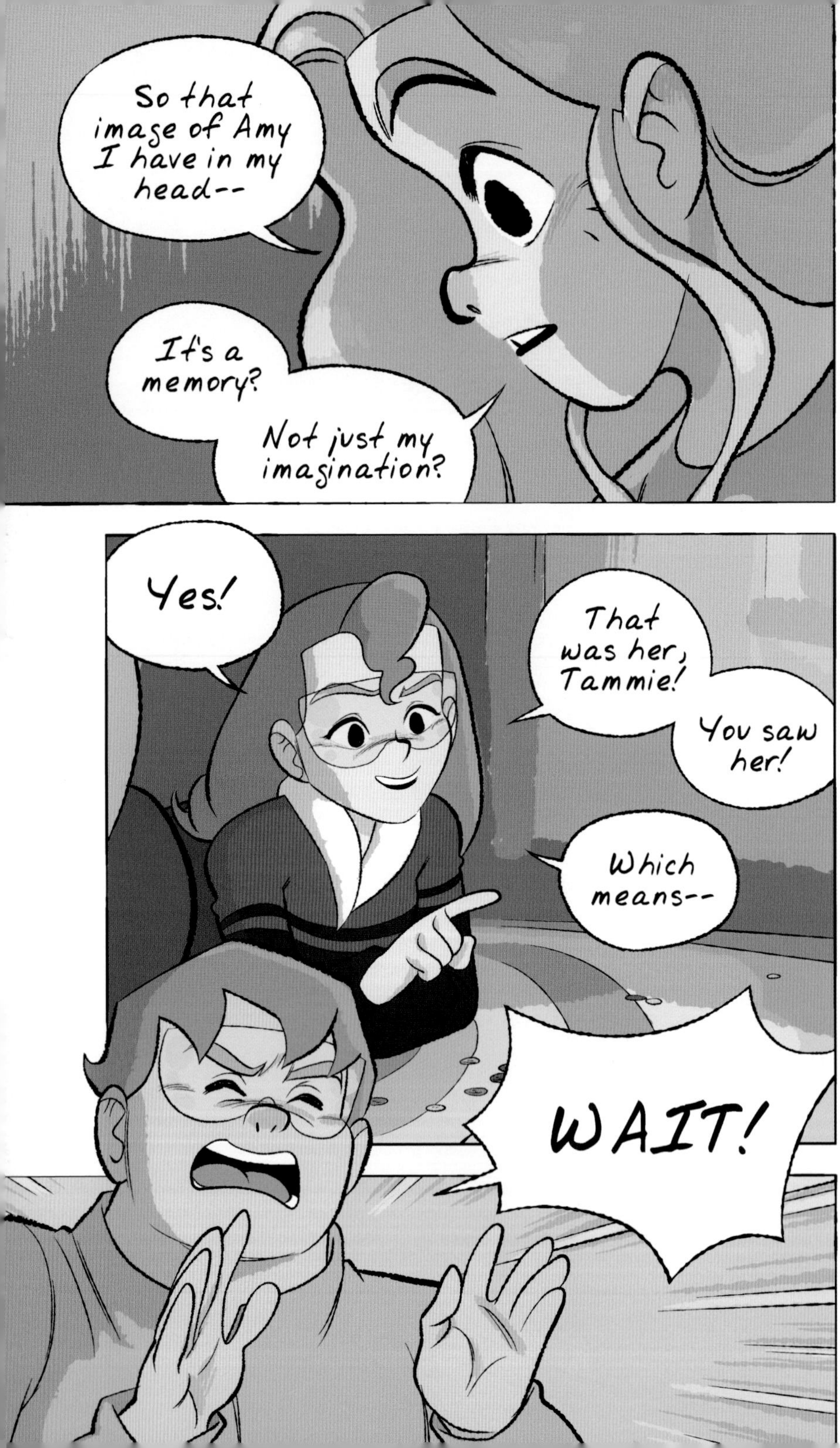
So that image of Amy I have in my head--
It's a memory?
Not just my imagination?
Yes!
That was her, Tammie!
You saw her!
Which means--
WAIT!

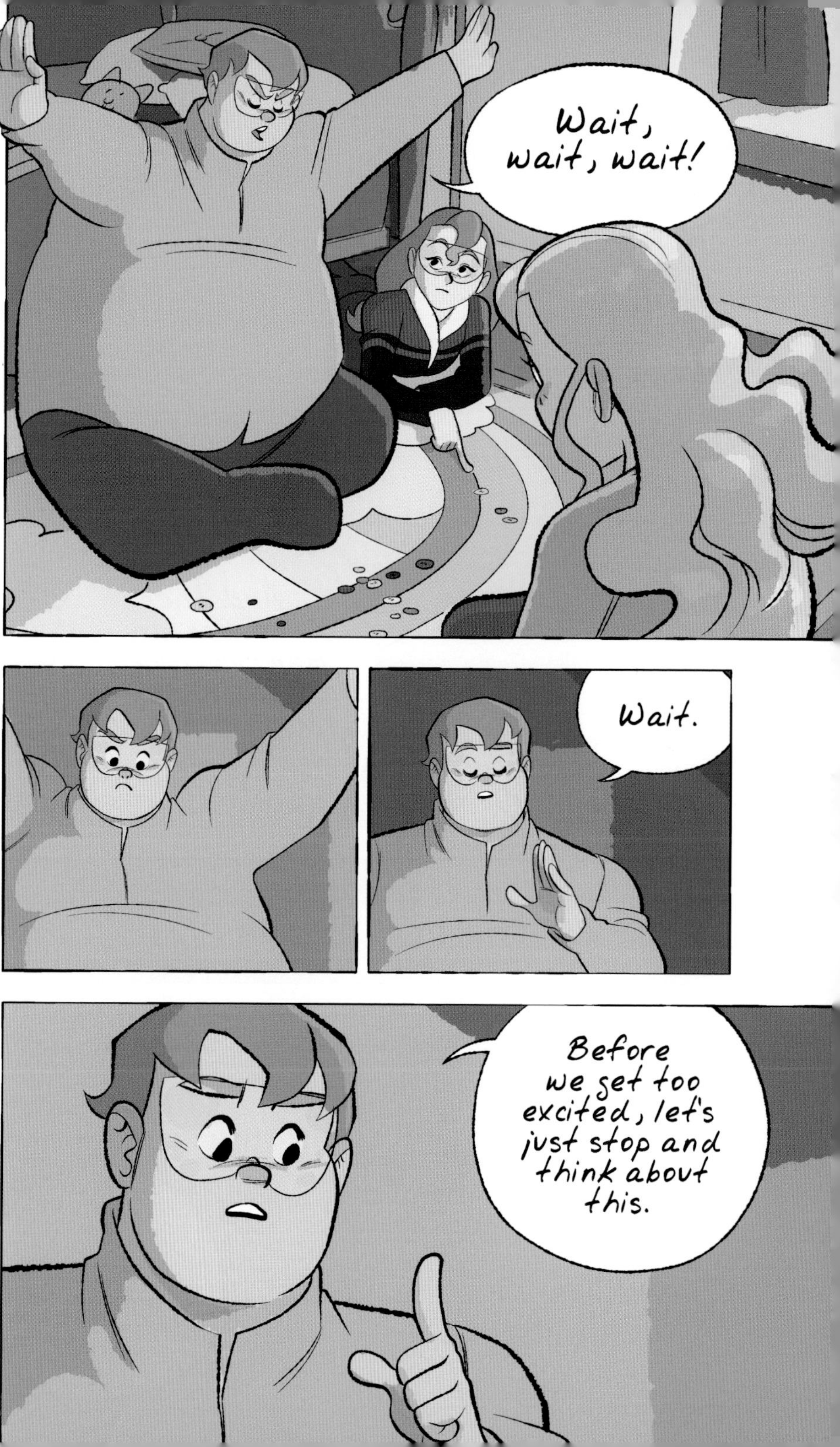
Wait, wait, wait!
Wait.
Before we get too excited, let's just stop and think about this.

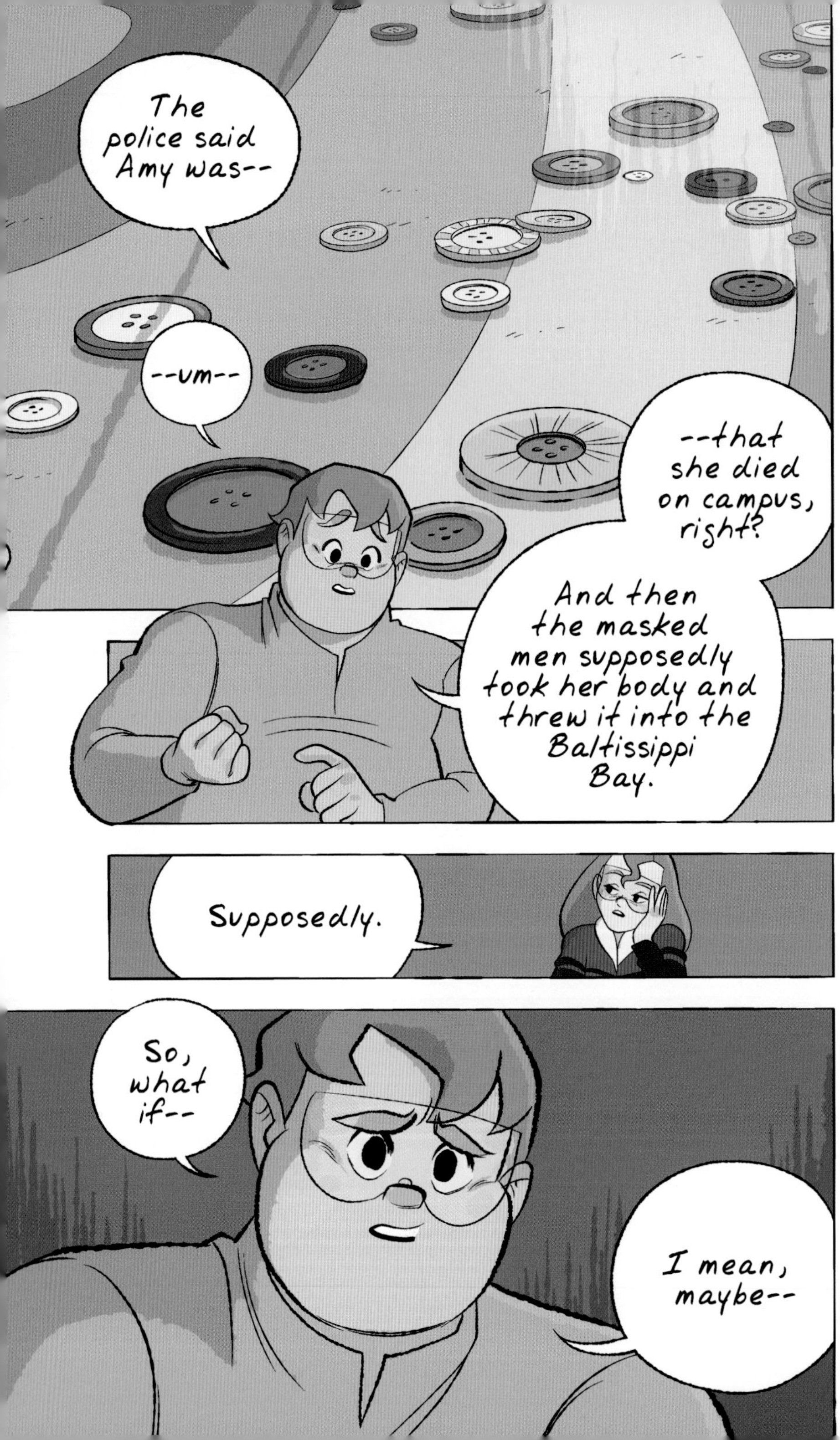

The police said Amy was--
--um--
--that she died on campus, right?
And then the masked men supposedly took her body and threw it into the Baltissippi Bay.
Supposedly.
So, what if--
I mean, maybe--

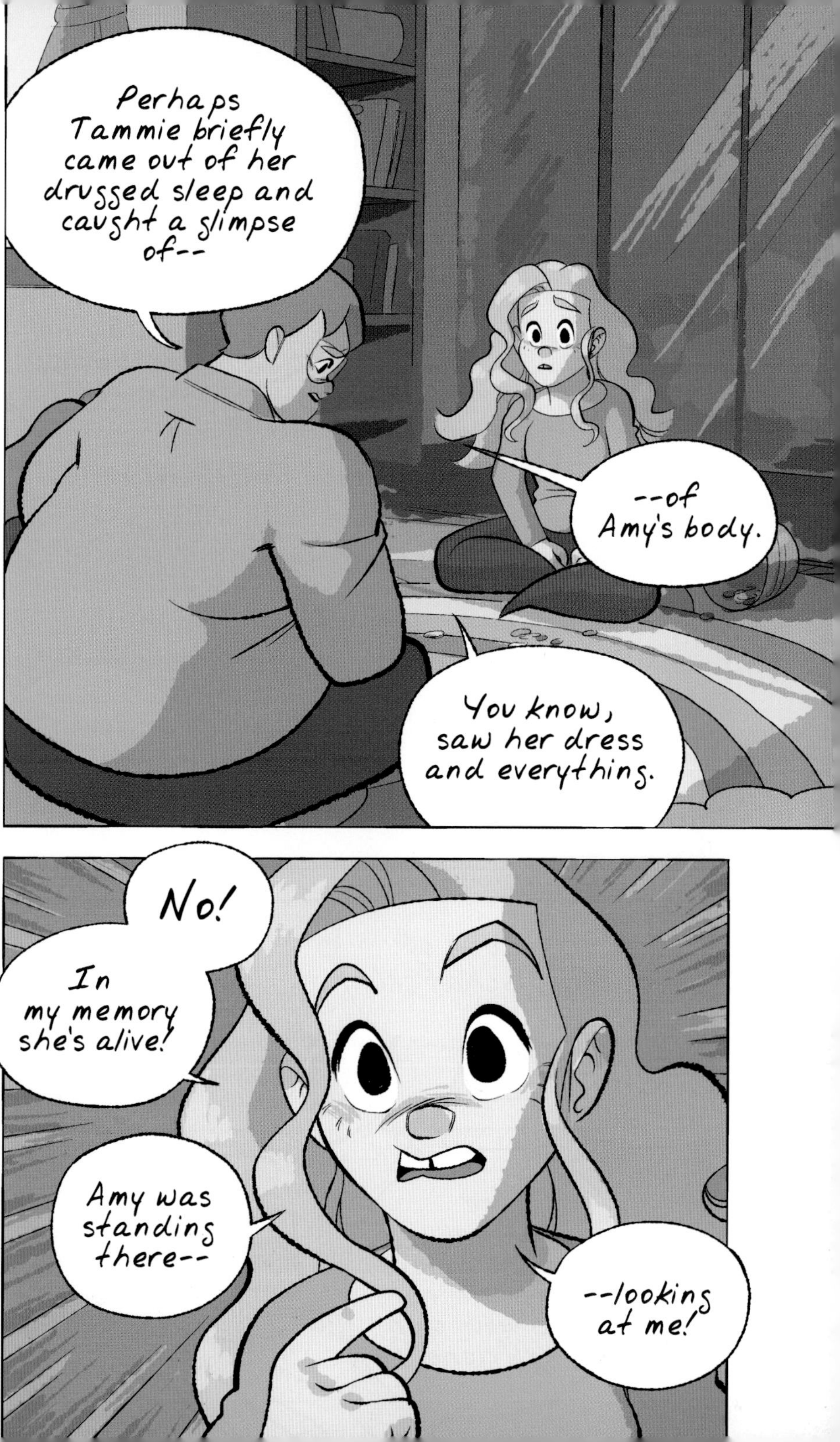
Perhaps Tammie briefly came out of her drugged sleep and caught a glimpse of--
--of Amy's body.
You know, saw her dress and everything.
No!
In my memory she's alive!
Amy was standing there--
--looking at me!

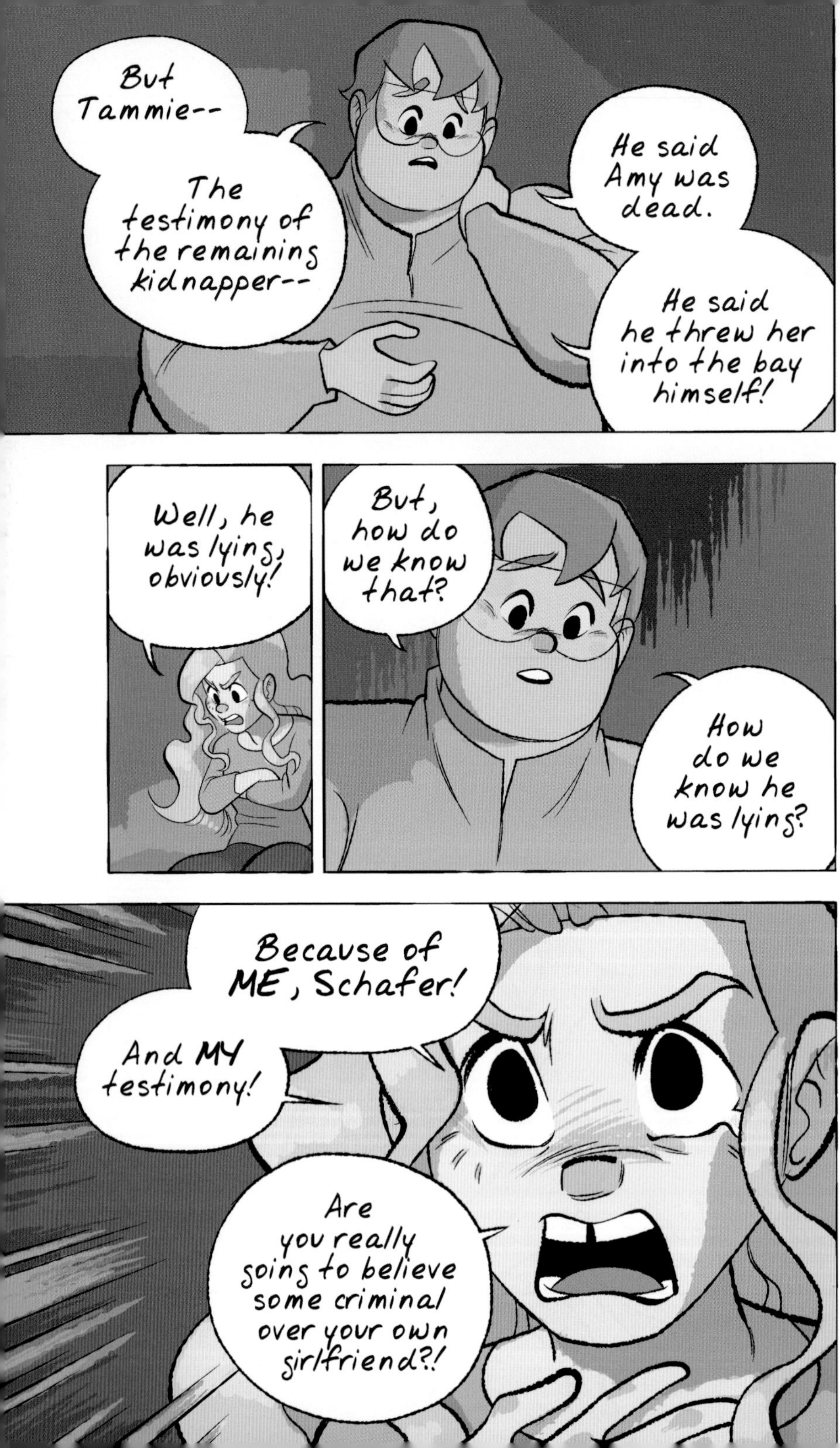
But Tammie--
The testimony of the remaining kidnapper--
He said Amy was dead.
He said he threw her into the bay himself!
Well, he was lying, obviously!
But, how do we know that?
How do we know he was lying?
Because of ME, Schafer!
And MY testimony!
Are you really going to believe some criminal over your own girlfriend?!

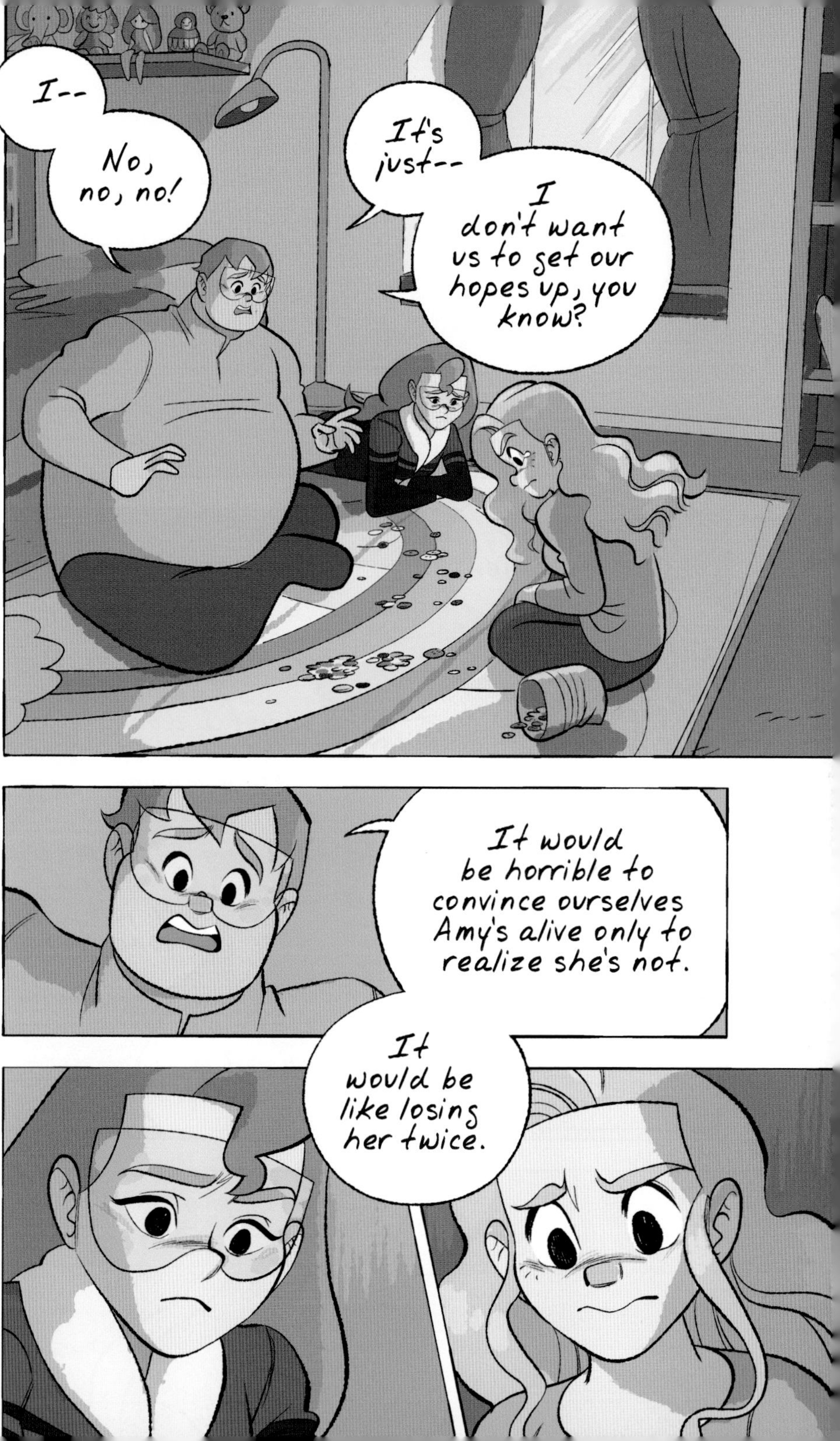
I--
No, no, no!
It's just--
I don't want us to get our hopes up, you know?
It would be horrible to convince ourselves Amy's alive only to realize she's not.
It would be like losing her twice.

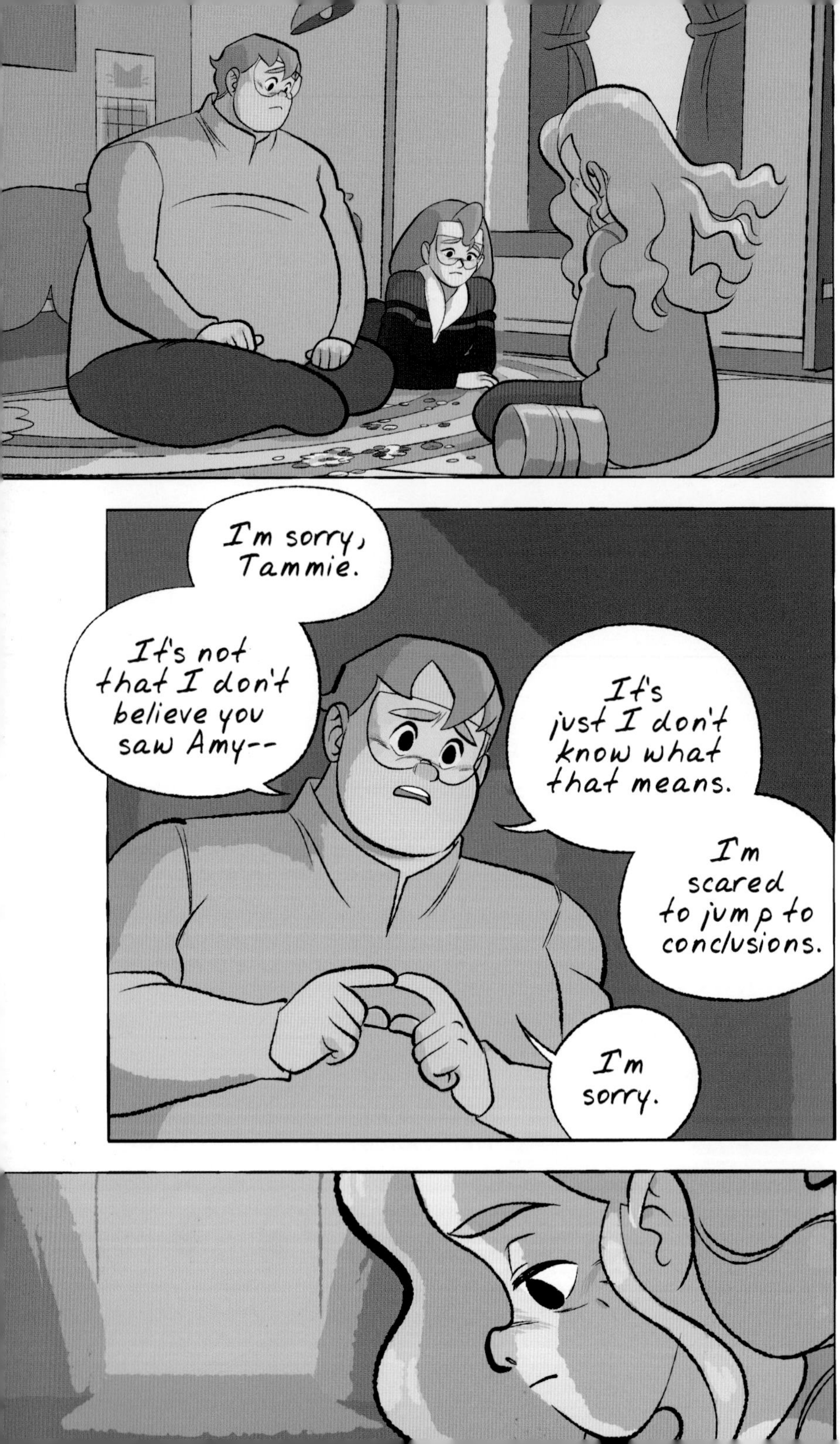
I'm sorry, Tammie.
It's not that I don't believe you saw Amy--
It's just I don't know what that means.
I'm scared to jump to conclusions.
I'm sorry.

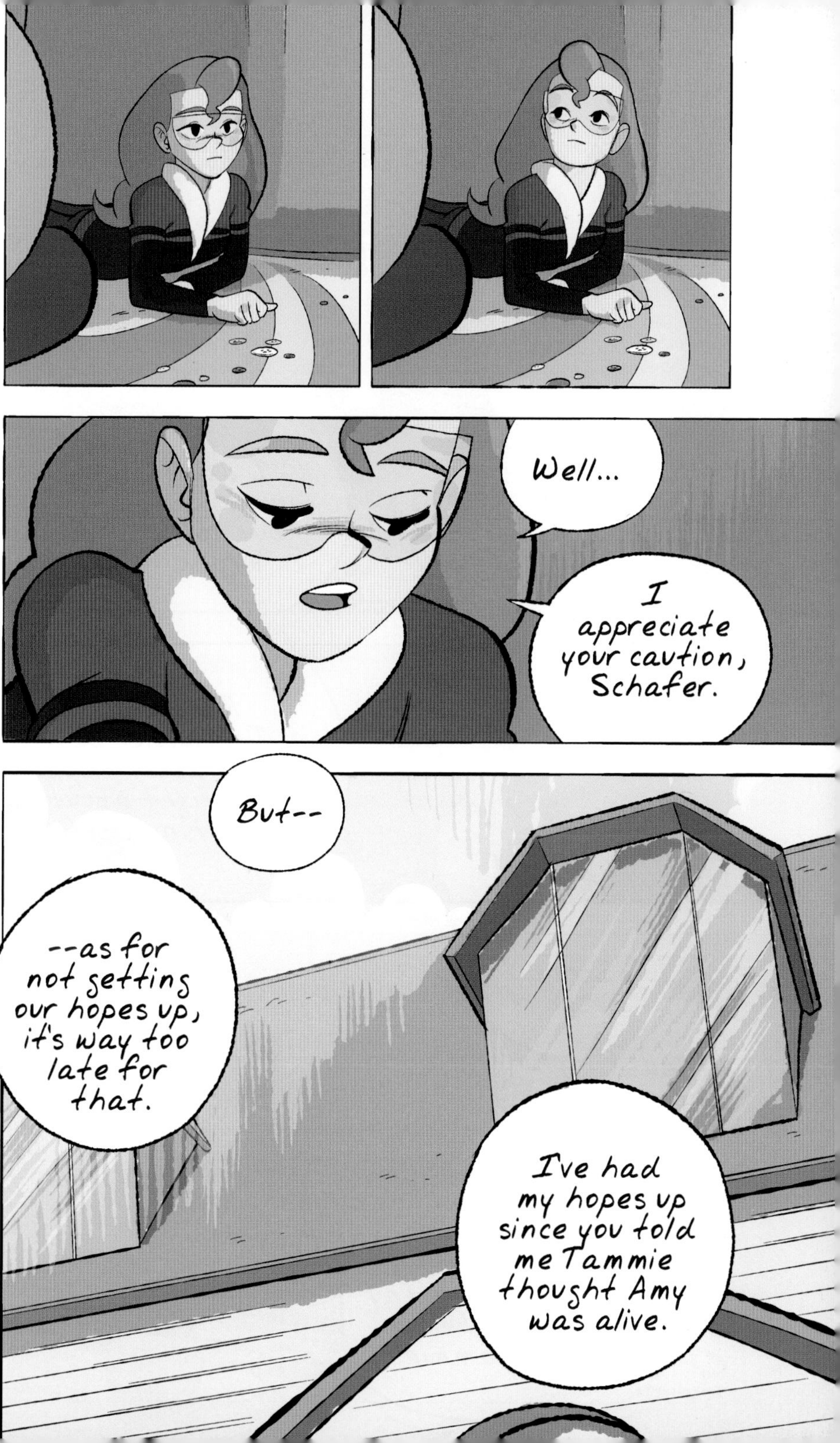
Well...
I appreciate your caution, Schafer.
But--
--as for not getting our hopes up, it's way too late for that.
I've had my hopes up since you told me Tammie thought Amy was alive.

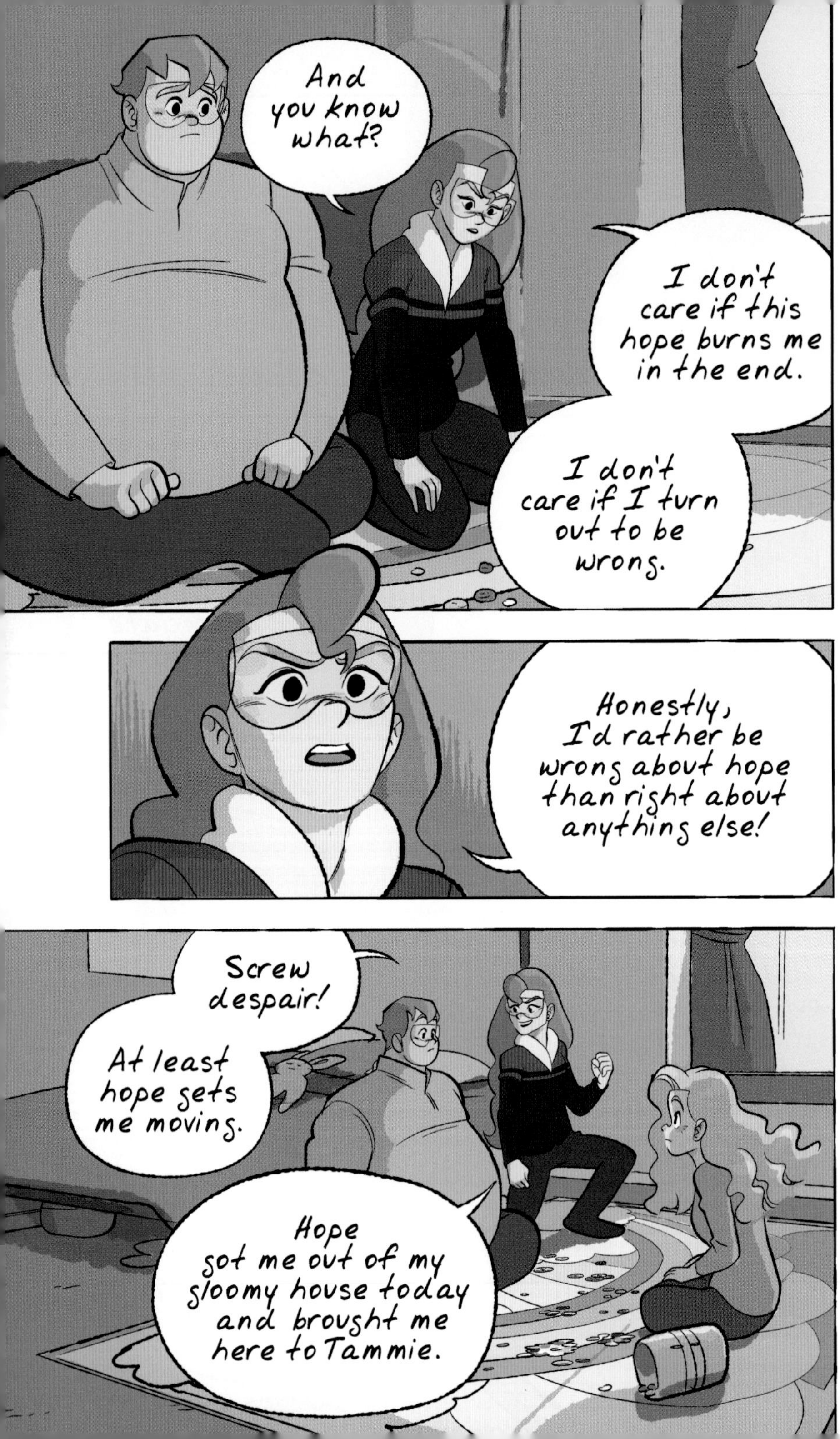
And you know what?
I don't care if this hope burns me in the end.
I don't care if I turn out to be wrong.
Honestly, I'd rather be wrong about hope than right about anything else!
Screw despair!
At least hope gets me moving.
Hope got me out of my gloomy house today and brought me here to Tammie.

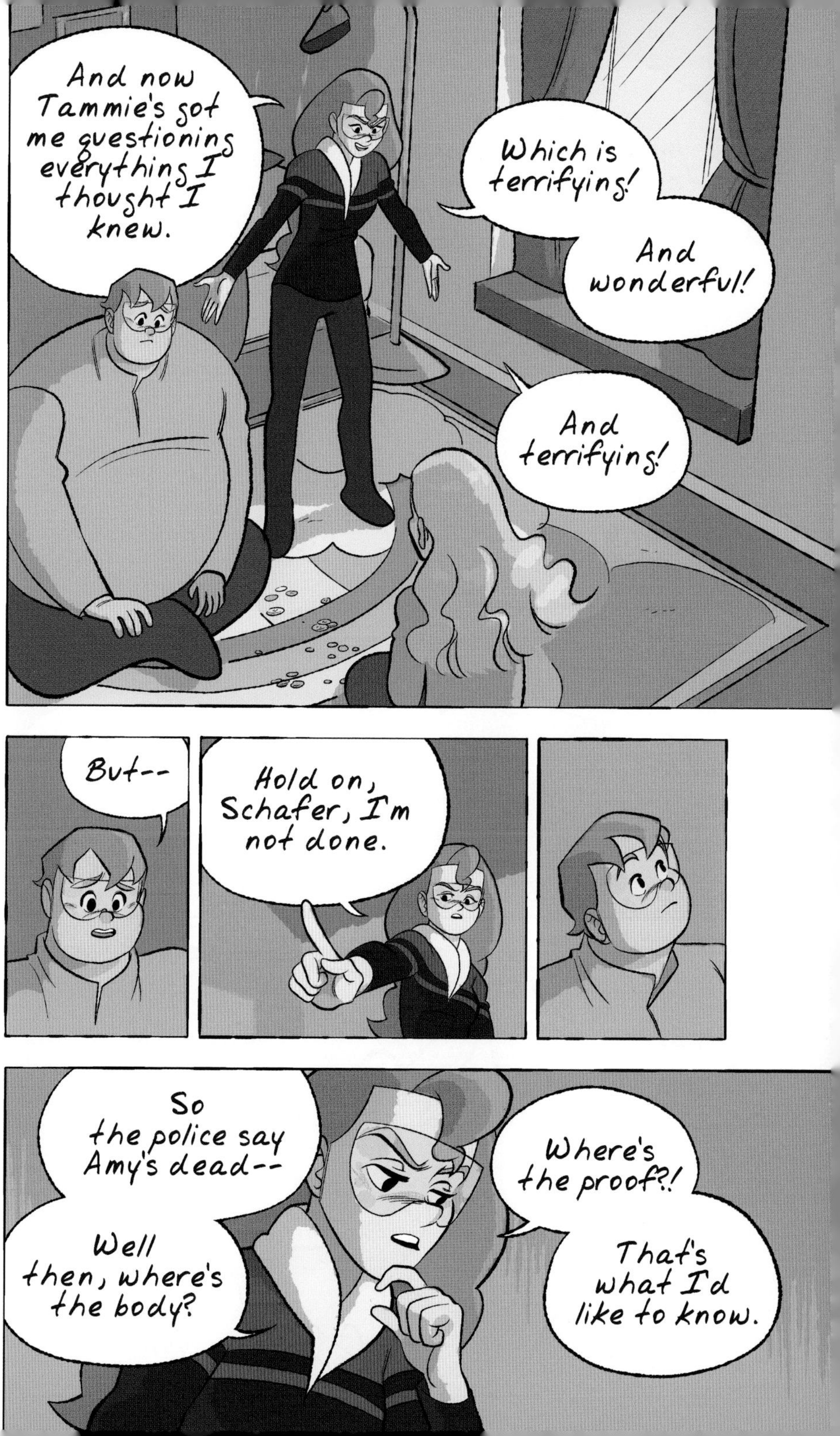
And now Tammie's got me questioning everything I thought I knew.
Which is terrifying!
And wonderful!
And terrifying!
But--
Hold on, Schafer, I'm not done.
So the police say Amy's dead--
Well then, where's the body?
Where's the proof?!
That's what I'd like to know.

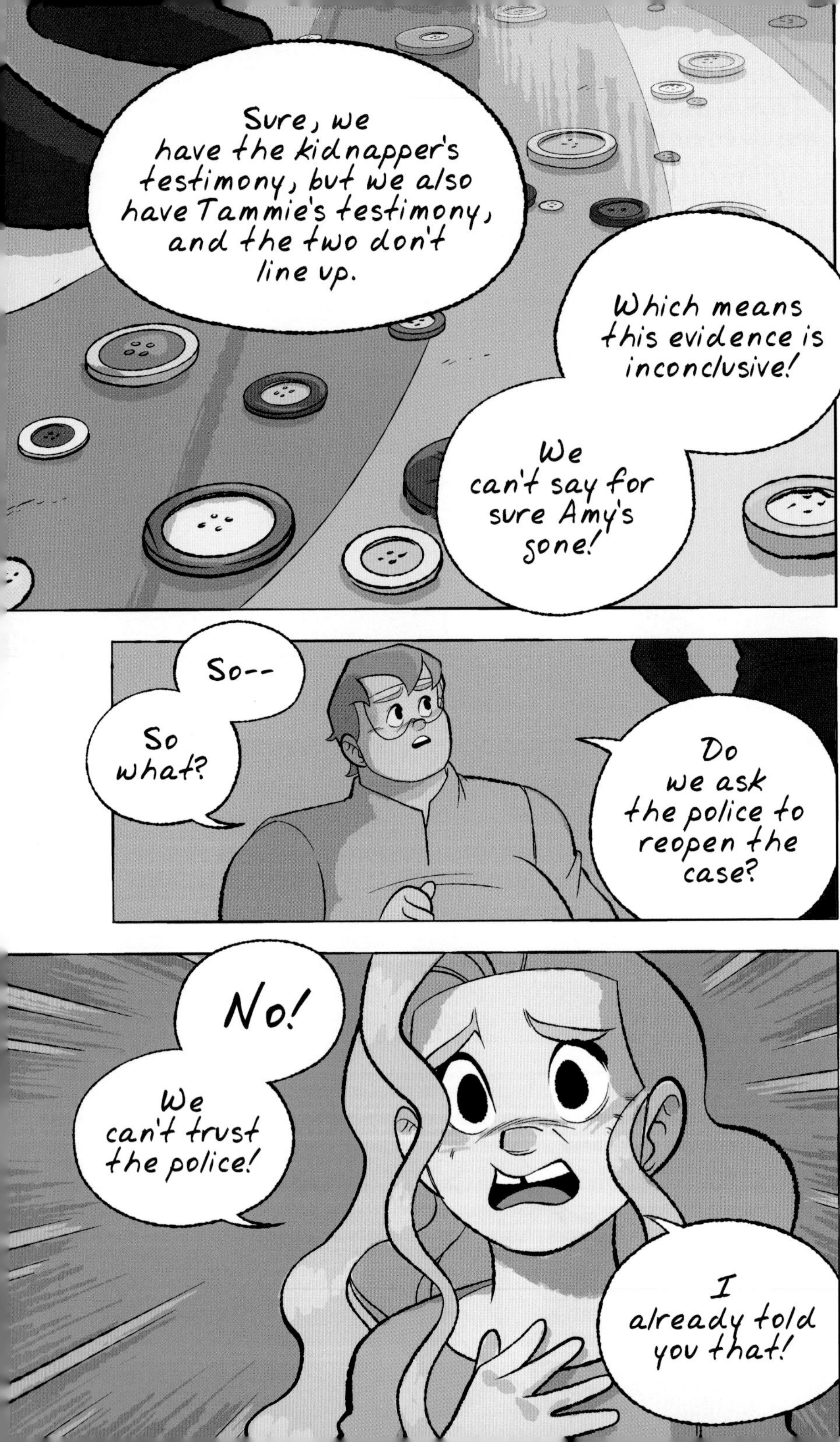
Sure, we have the kidnapper's testimony, but we also have Tammie's testimony, and the two don't line up.
Which means this evidence is inconclusive!
We can't say for sure Amy's gone!
So--
So what?
Do we ask the police to reopen the case?
No!
We can't trust the police!
I already told you that!

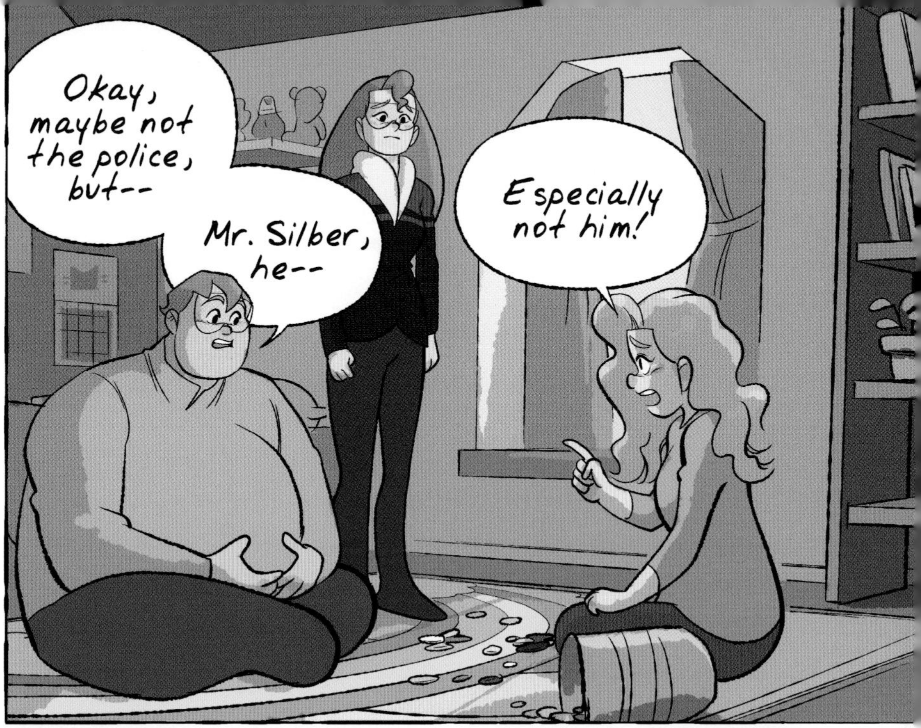
Okay, maybe not the police, but--
Mr. Silber, he--
Especially not him!

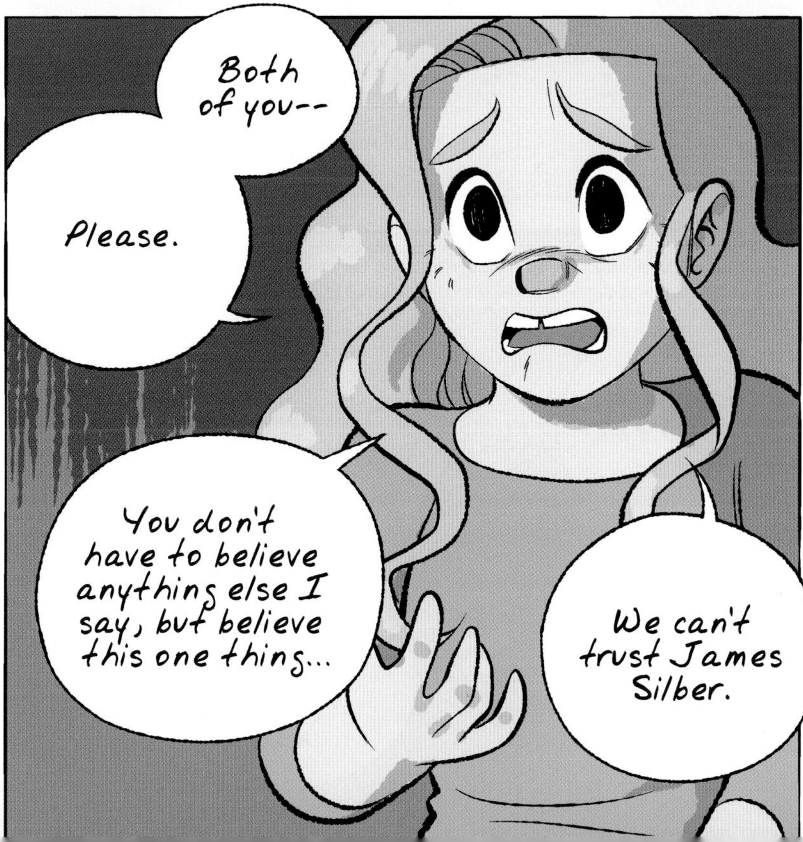
Both of you--
Please.
You don't have to believe anything else I say, but believe this one thing...
We can't trust James Silber.

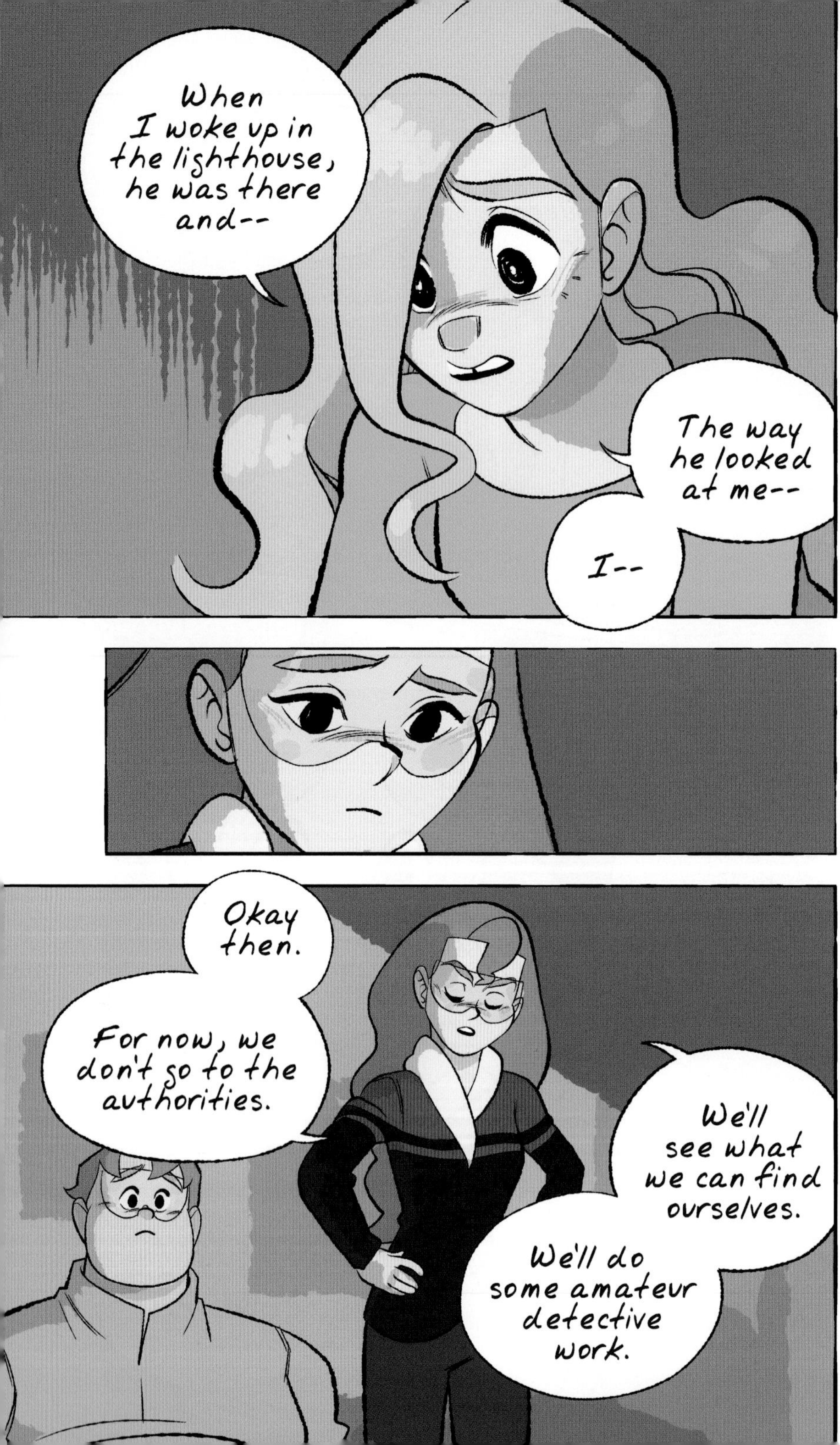
When I woke up in the lighthouse, he was there and--
The way he looked at me--
I--
Okay then.
For now, we don't go to the authorities.
We'll see what we can find ourselves.
We'll do some amateur detective work.

How?

Where do we start?

Heh--

Now that I think about it, I've got the first clue right here in my pocket!

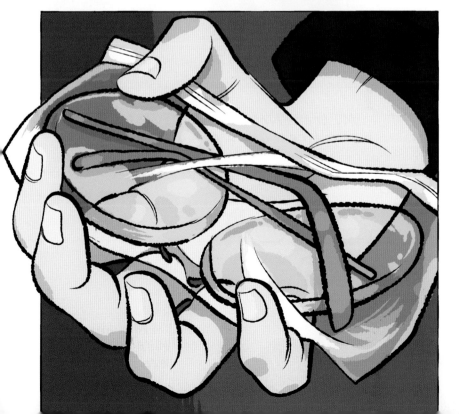

I walk to Langley's door,
my heart pounding.

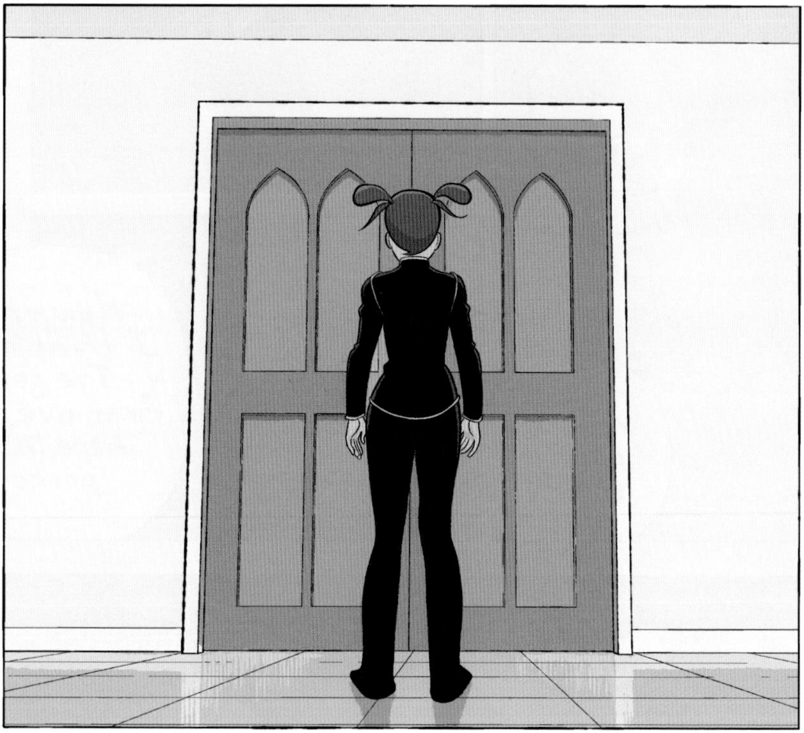

My breathing is heavy, but it
doesn't feel like a panic attack--

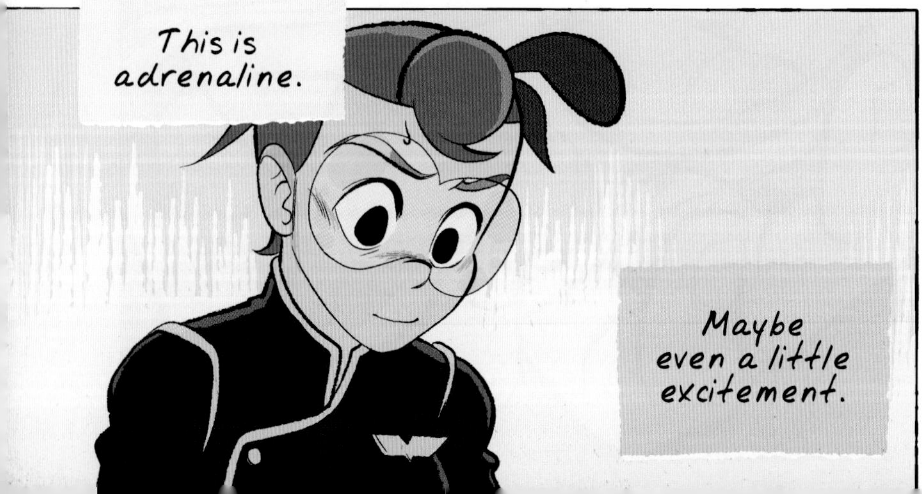
This is adrenaline.
Maybe even a little excitement.

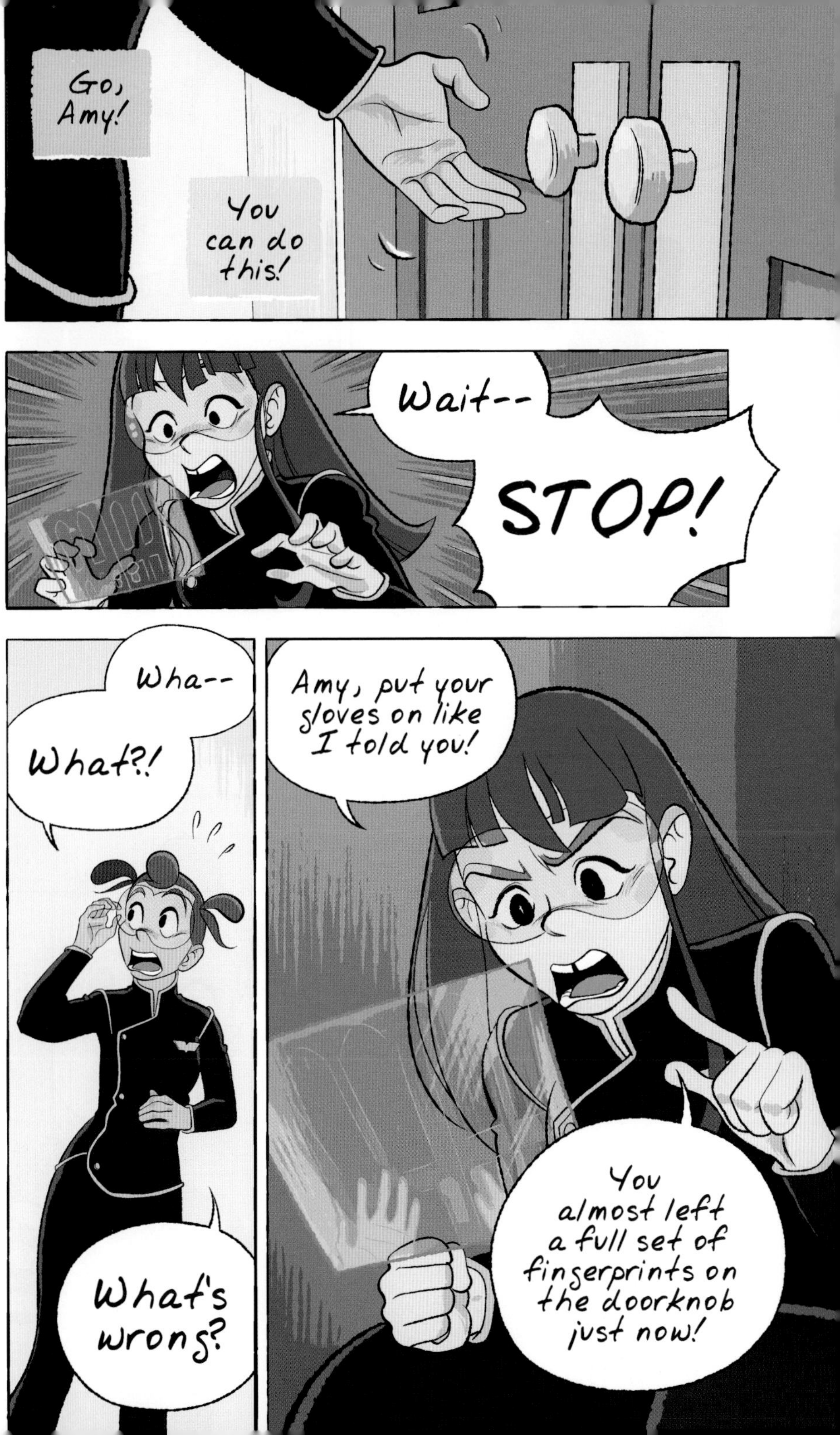
Go, Amy!
You can do this!
Wait--
STOP!
Wha--
What?!
Amy, put your gloves on like I told you!
What's wrong?
You almost left a full set of fingerprints on the doorknob just now!

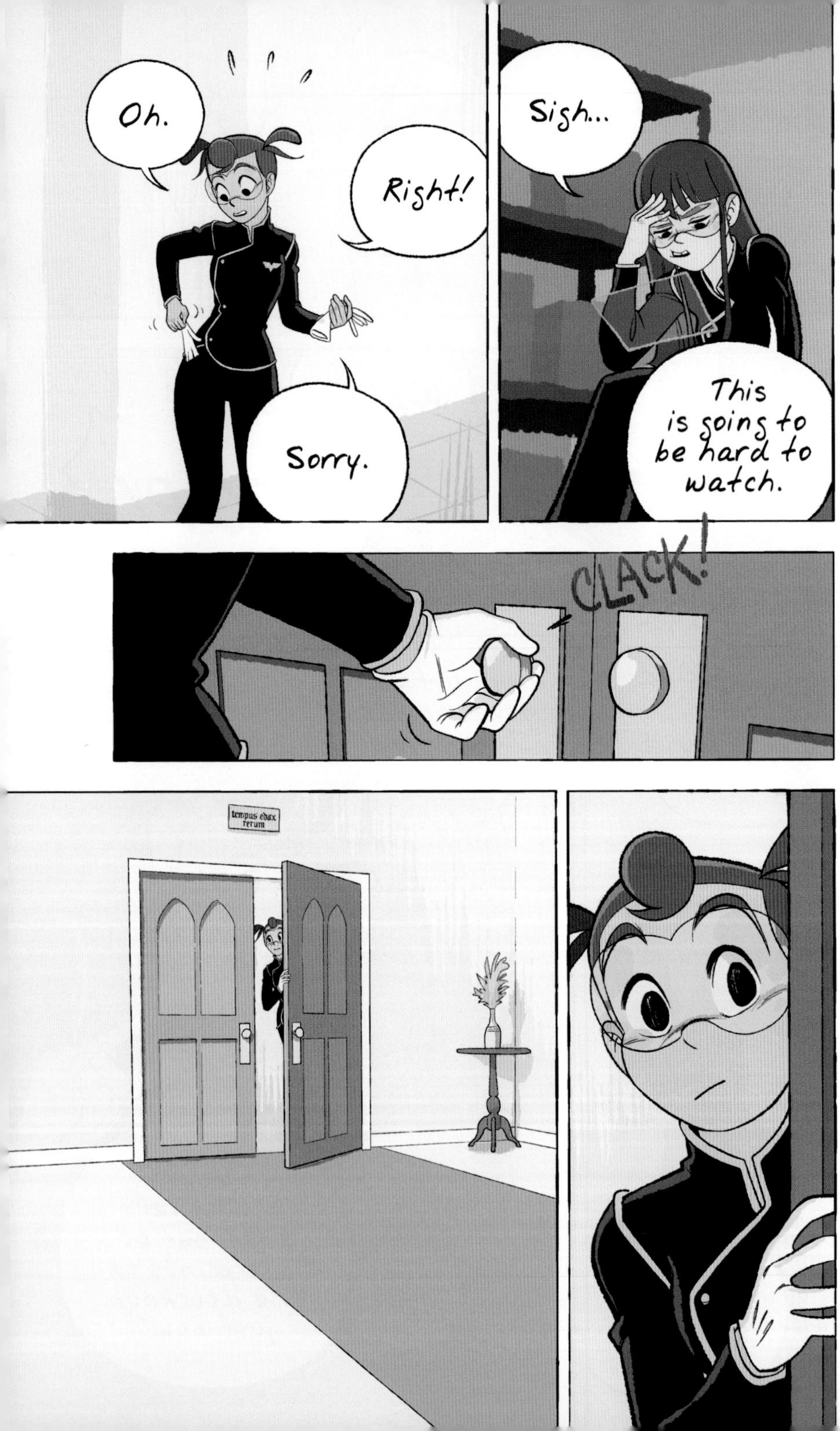
Oh.
Right!
Sorry.
Sigh...
This is going to be hard to watch.
CLACK!
tempus edax rerum

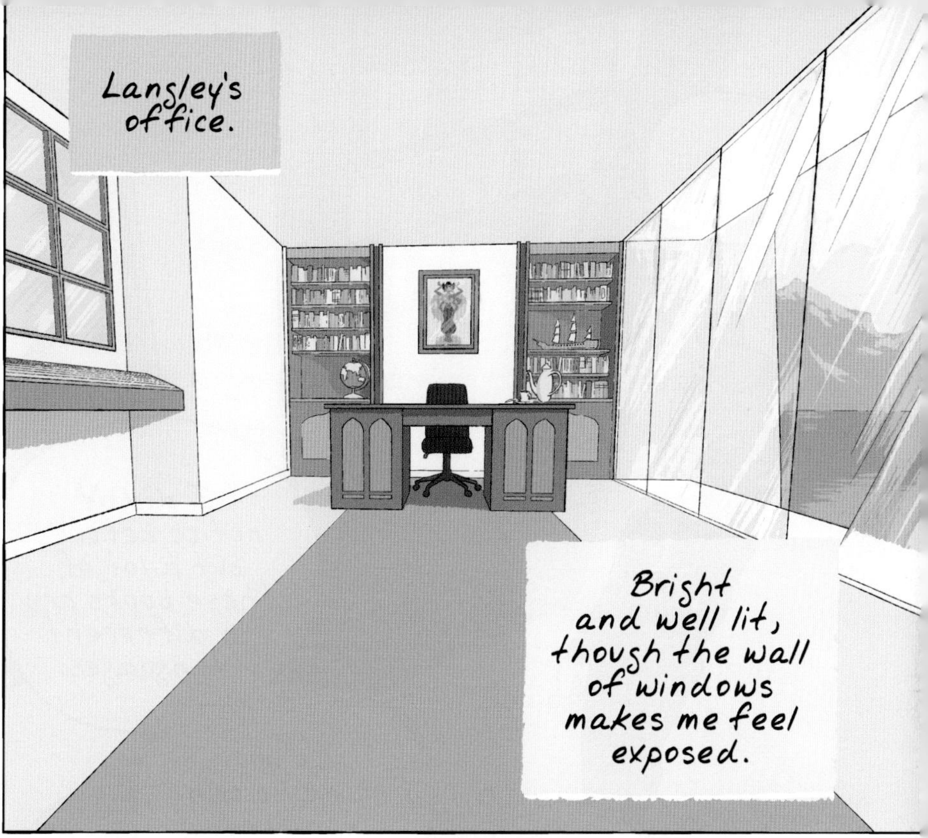
Lansley's office.
Bright and well lit, though the wall of windows makes me feel exposed.

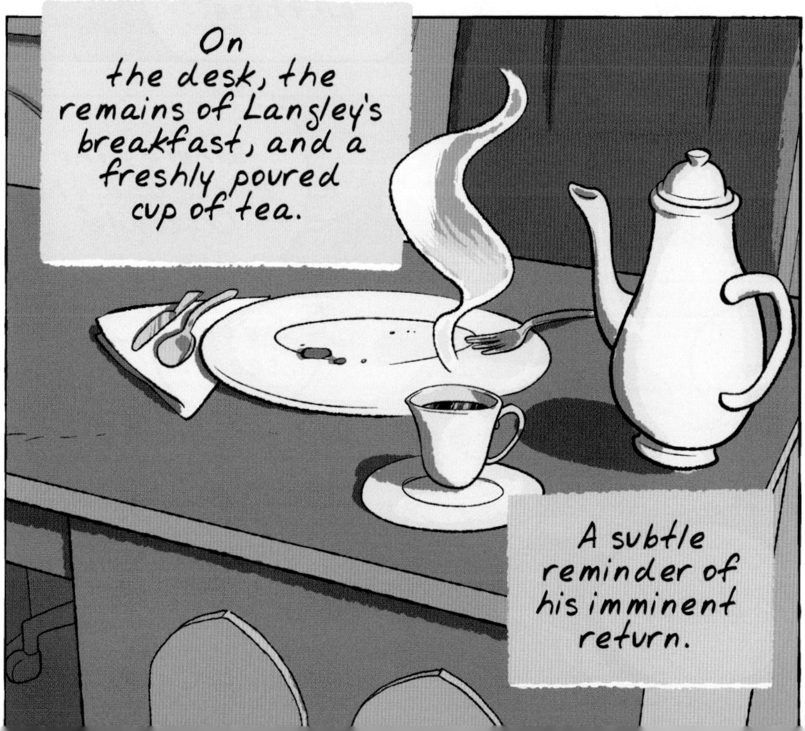
On the desk, the remains of Lansley's breakfast, and a freshly poured cup of tea.
A subtle reminder of his imminent return.

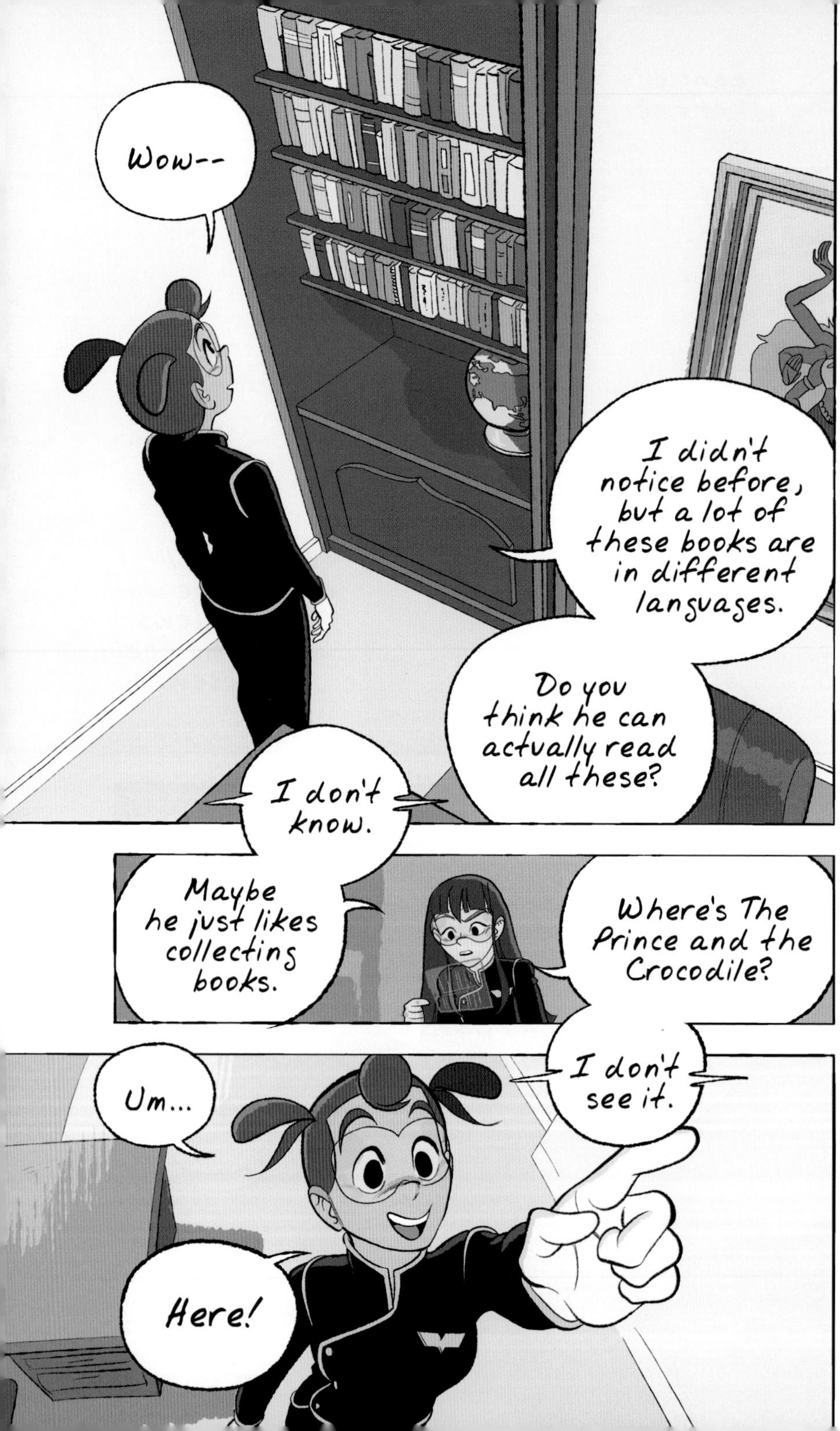
Wow--
I didn't notice before, but a lot of these books are in different languages.
Do you think he can actually read all these?
I don't know.
Maybe he just likes collecting books.
Where's The Prince and the Crocodile?
I don't see it.
Um...
Here!

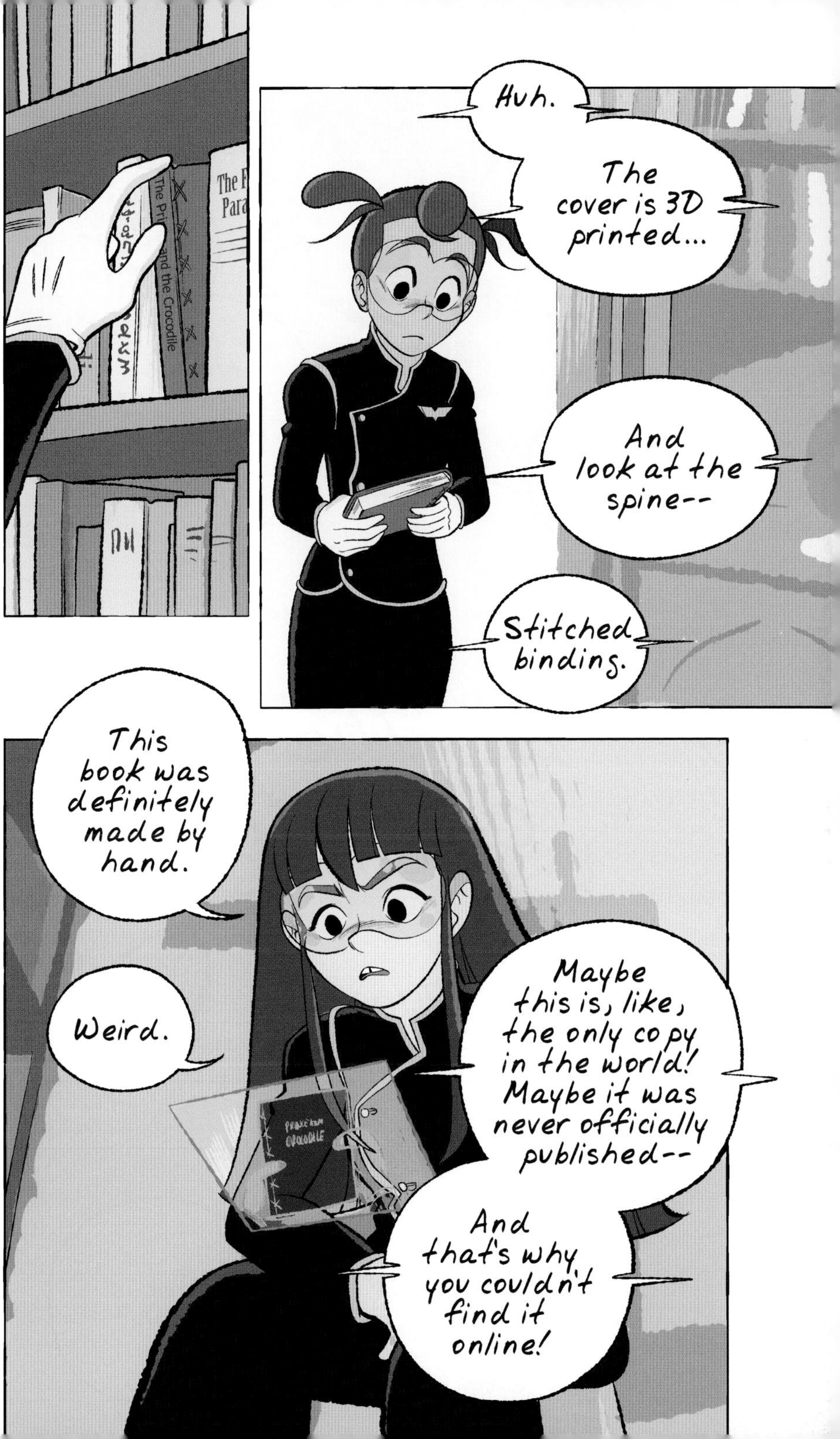
The Prince and the Crocodile
Huh.
The cover is 3D printed...
And look at the spine--
Stitched binding.
This book was definitely made by hand.
Weird.
Maybe this is, like, the only copy in the world! Maybe it was never officially published--
And that's why you couldn't find it online!

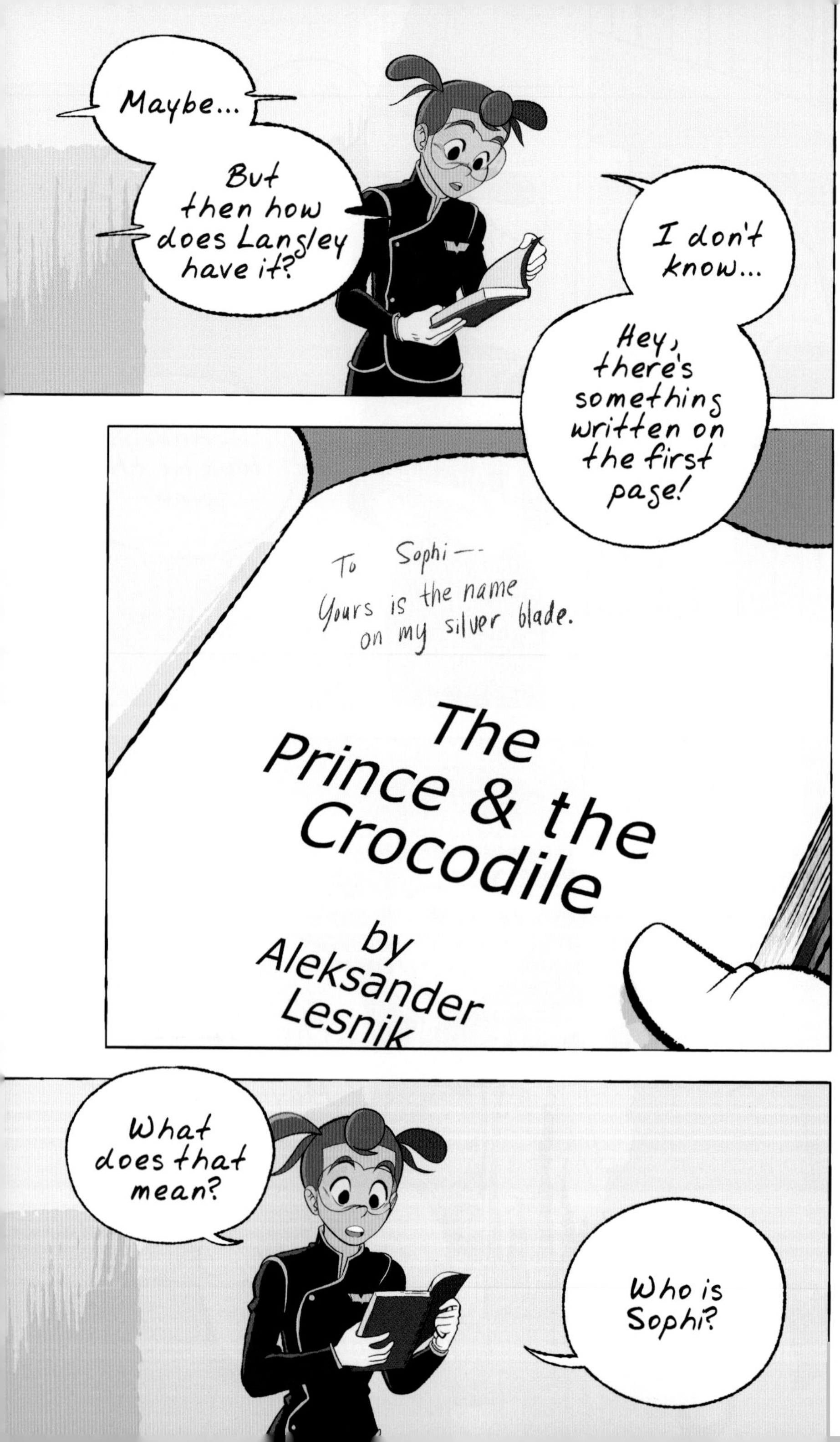
Maybe...
But then how does Langley have it?
I don't know...
Hey, there's something written on the first page!
To Sophi—
Yours is the name on my silver blade.
The Prince & the Crocodile
by Aleksander Lesnik
What does that mean?
Who is Sophi?

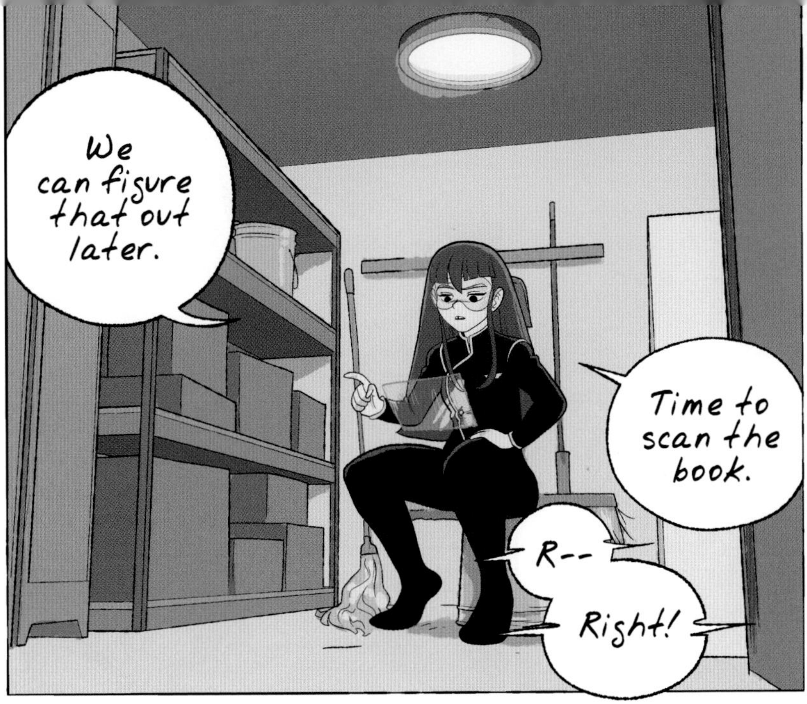
We can figure that out later.
Time to scan the book.
R--
Right!

I lay the book down flat and start flipping through it, page by page, while Qiana records my video stream.

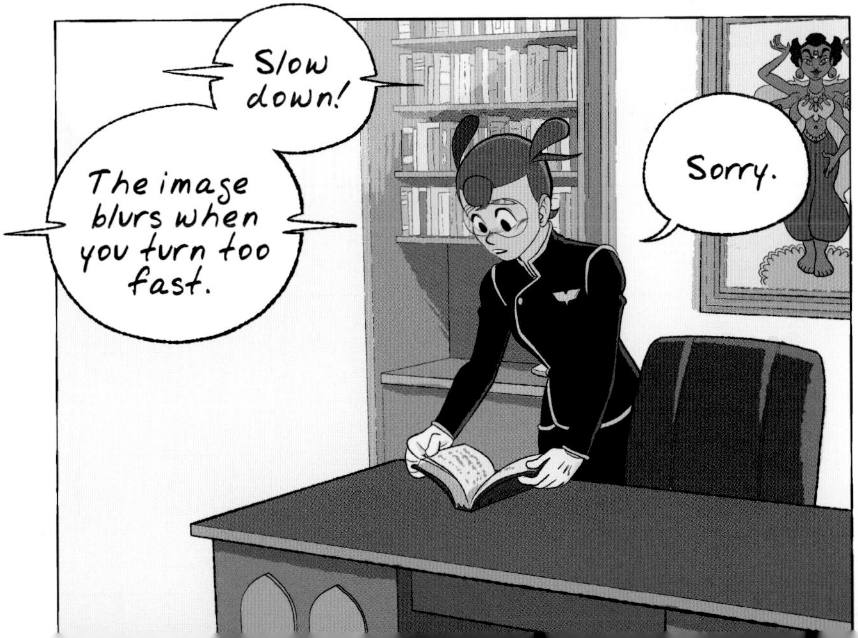
Slow down!
The image blurs when you turn too fast.
Sorry.

Feeling time drawing in like a noose, I take a deep breath, and slow down.

One page.

Then the next.

As the seconds tick by...

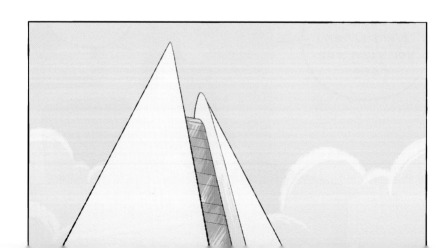

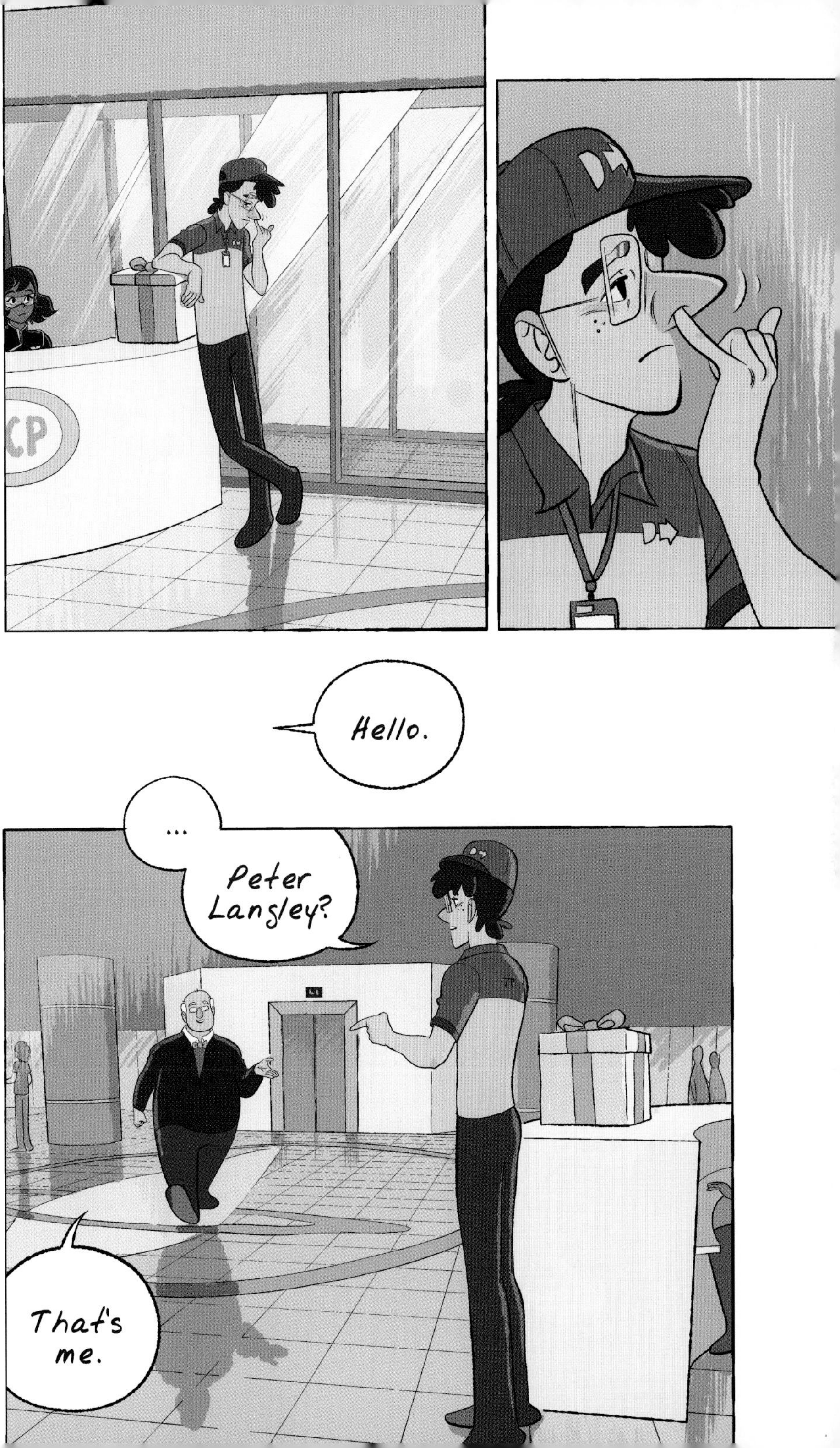
Hello.
...
Peter Langsley?
That's me.

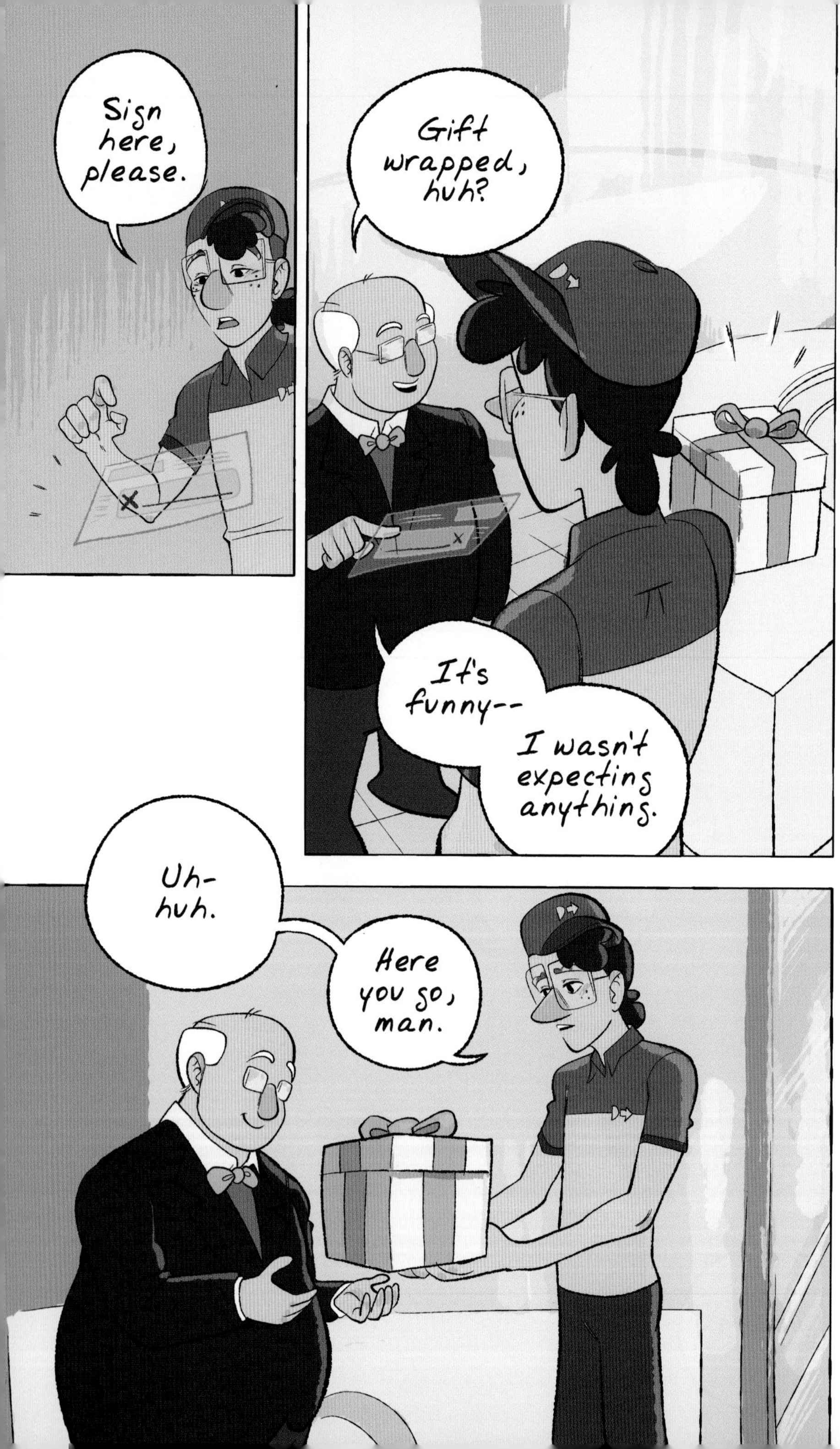
Sign here, please.
Gift wrapped, huh?
It's funny--
I wasn't expecting anything.
Uh-huh.
Here you go, man.

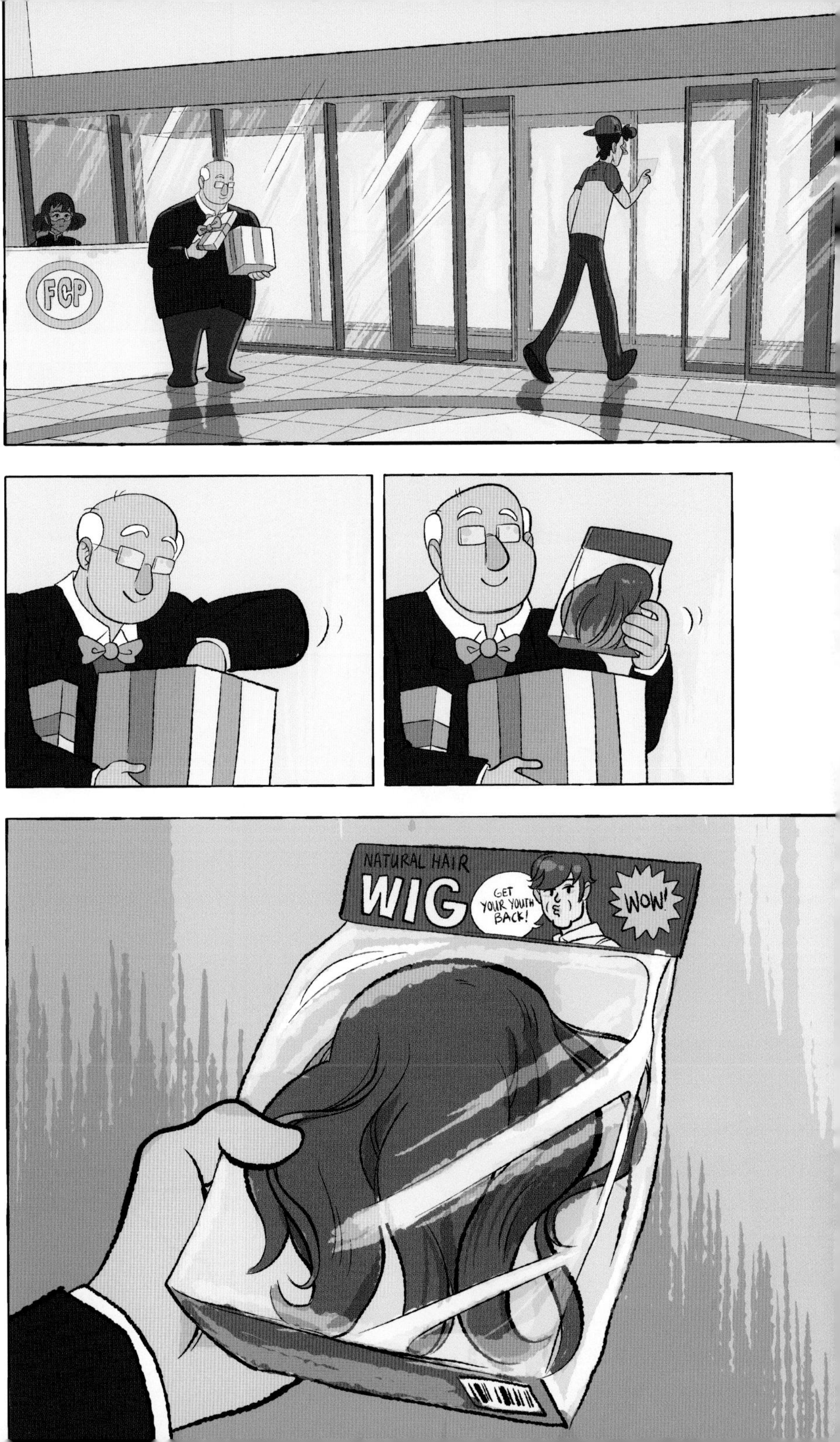
FCP
NATURAL HAIR
WIG
GET YOUR YOUTH BACK!
WOW!

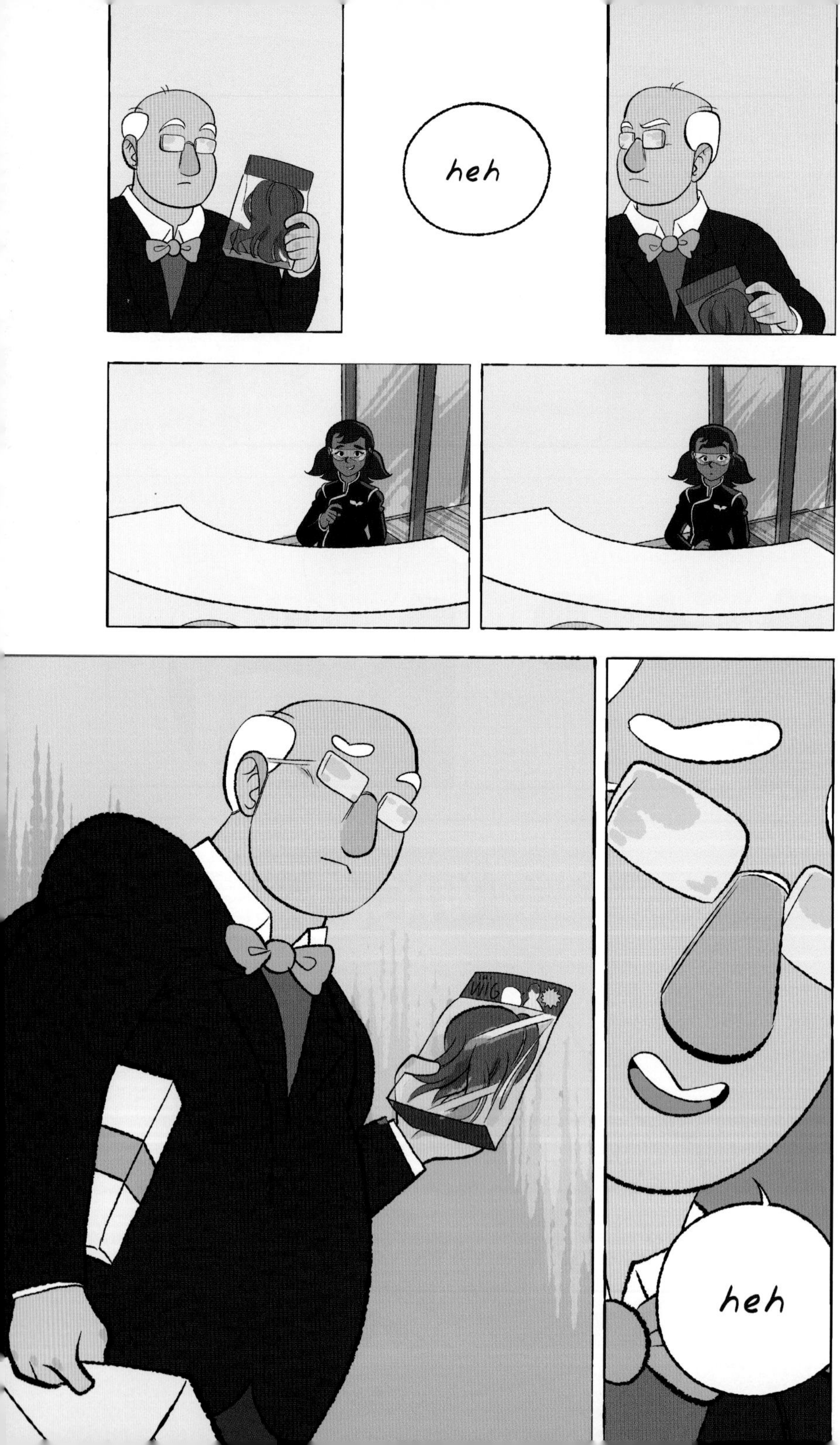
heh
WIG
heh

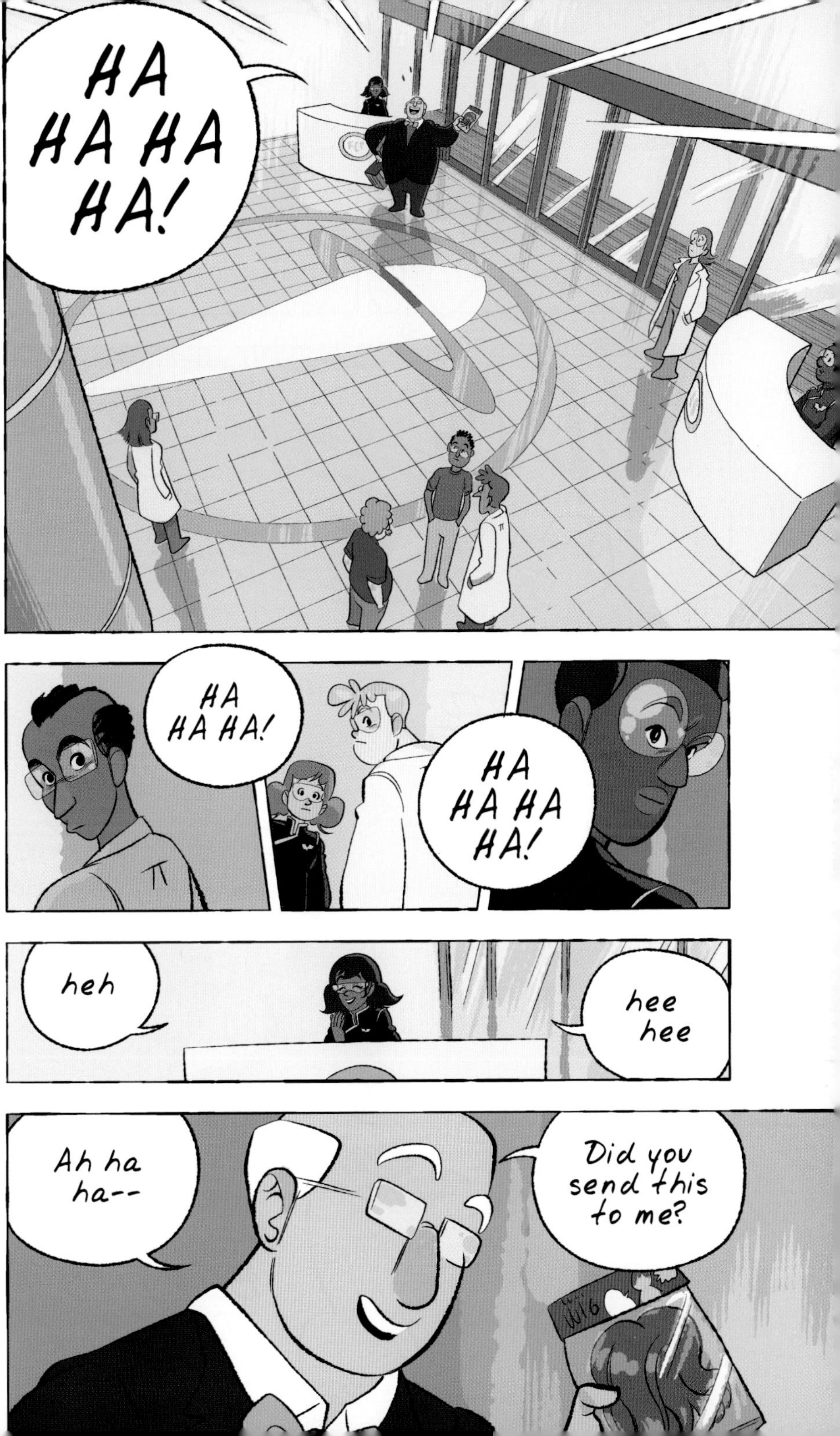
HA HA HA HA HA HA!
HA HA HA!
HA HA HA HA HA!
heh
hee hee
Ah ha ha--
Did you send this to me?
WIG

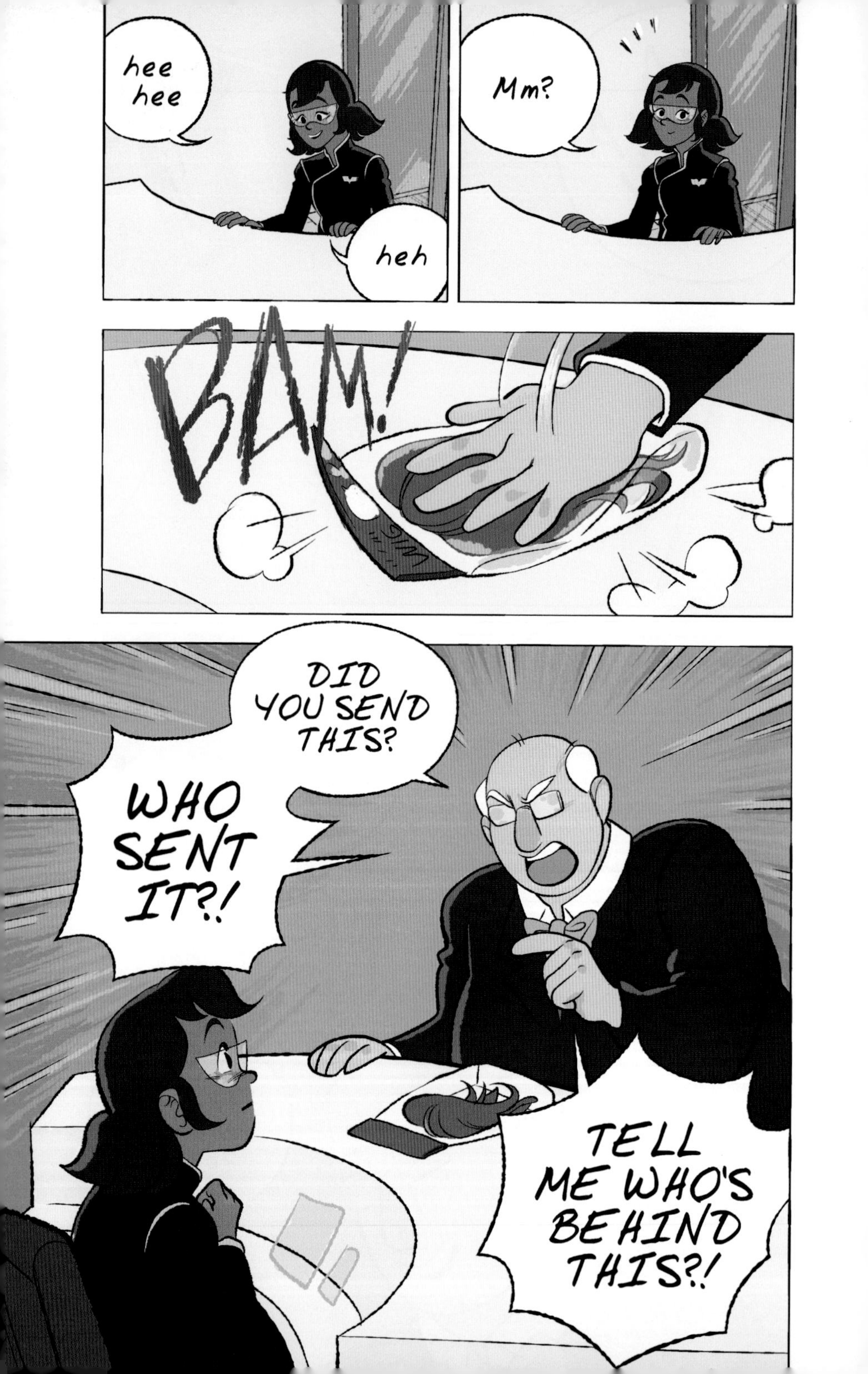
hee hee
heh
Mm?
BAM!
DID YOU SEND THIS?
WHO SENT IT?!
TELL ME WHO'S BEHIND THIS?!

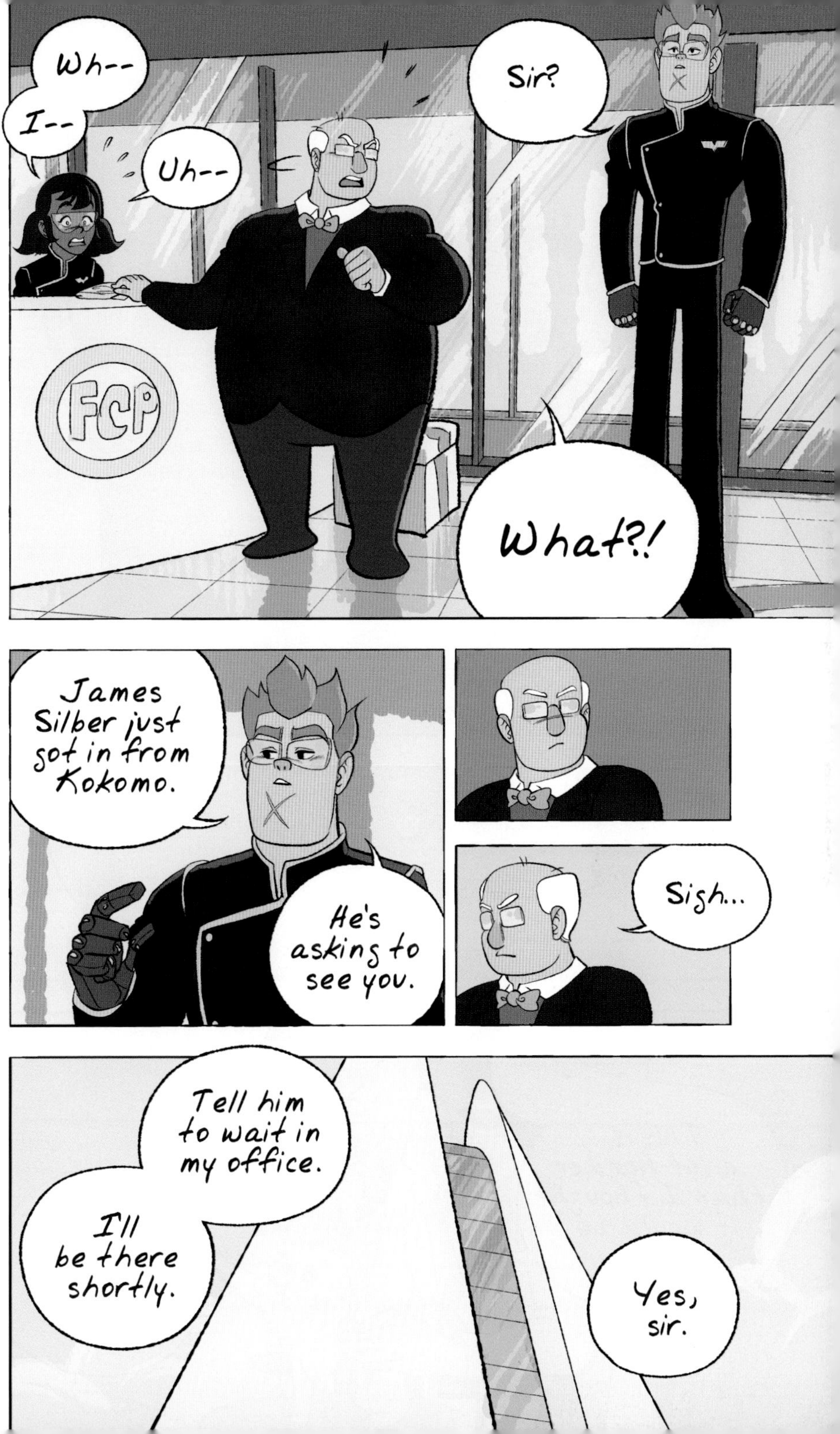
Wh--
I--
Uh--
Sir?
What?!
James Silber just got in from Kokomo.
He's asking to see you.
Sigh...
Tell him to wait in my office.
I'll be there shortly.
Yes, sir.

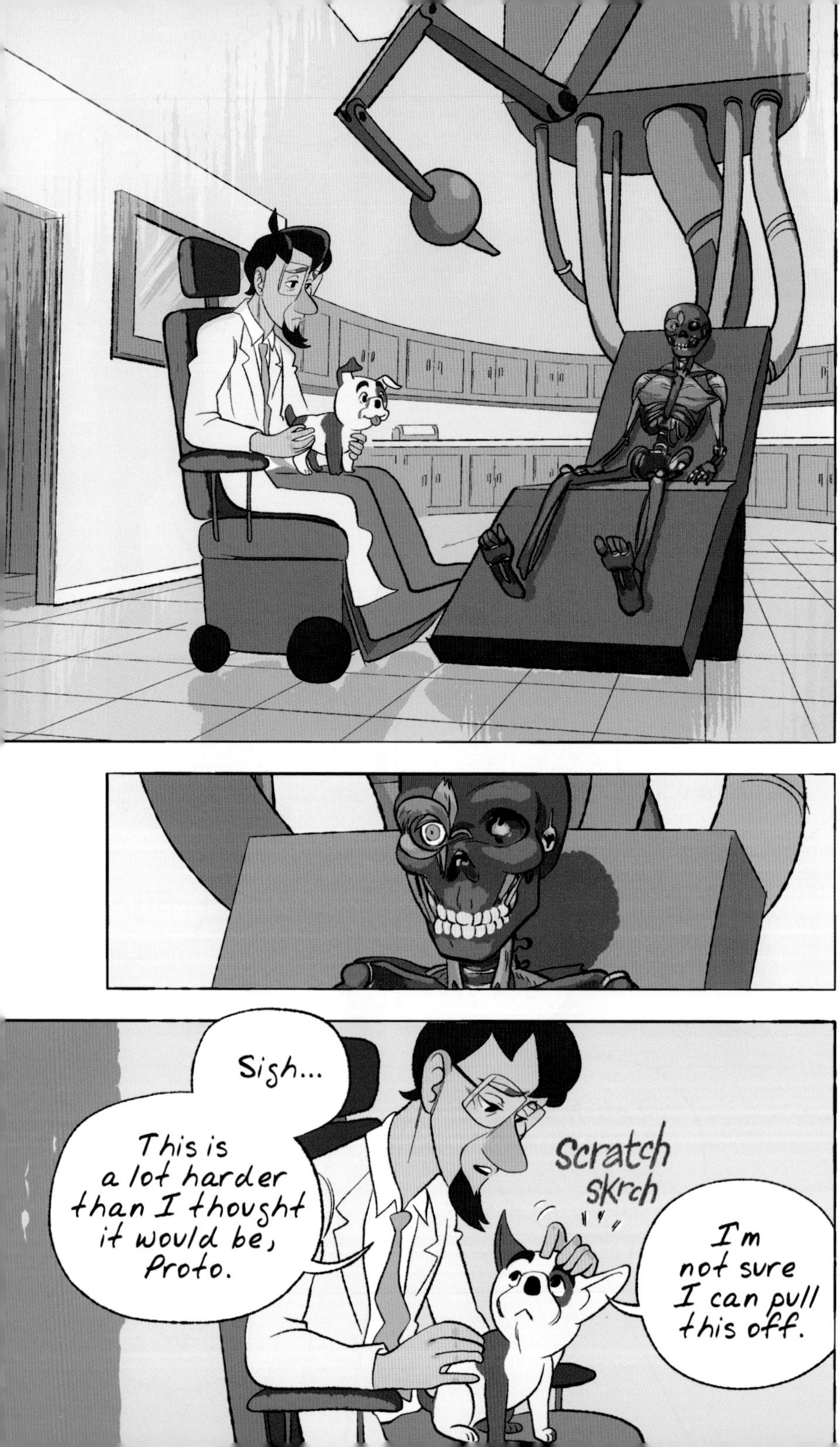
Sigh...
This is a lot harder than I thought it would be, Proto.
Scratch skrch
I'm not sure I can pull this off.

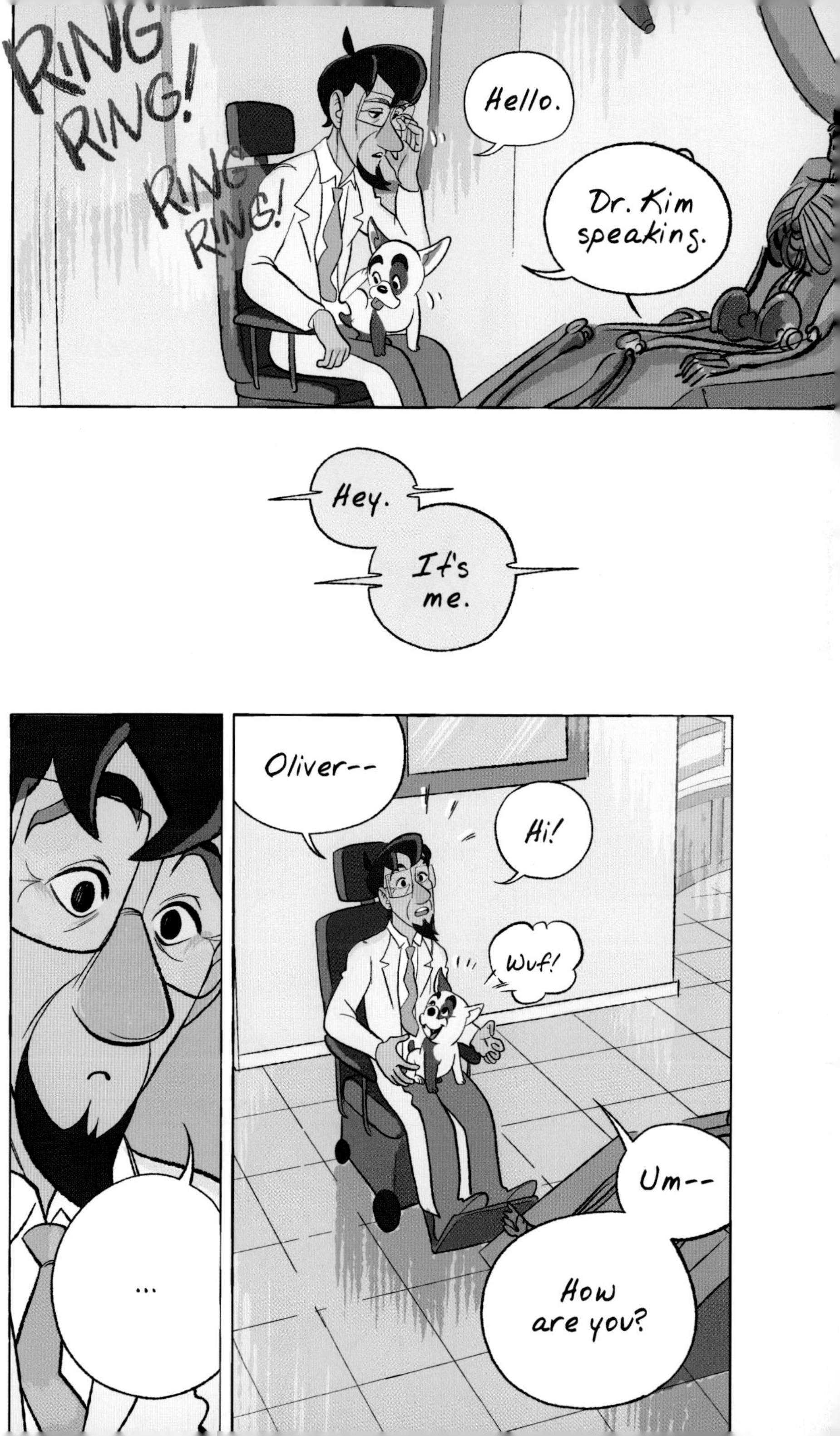
RING RING!
RING RING!
Hello.
Dr. Kim speaking.
Hey.
It's me.
...
Oliver--
Hi!
Wuf!
Um--
How are you?

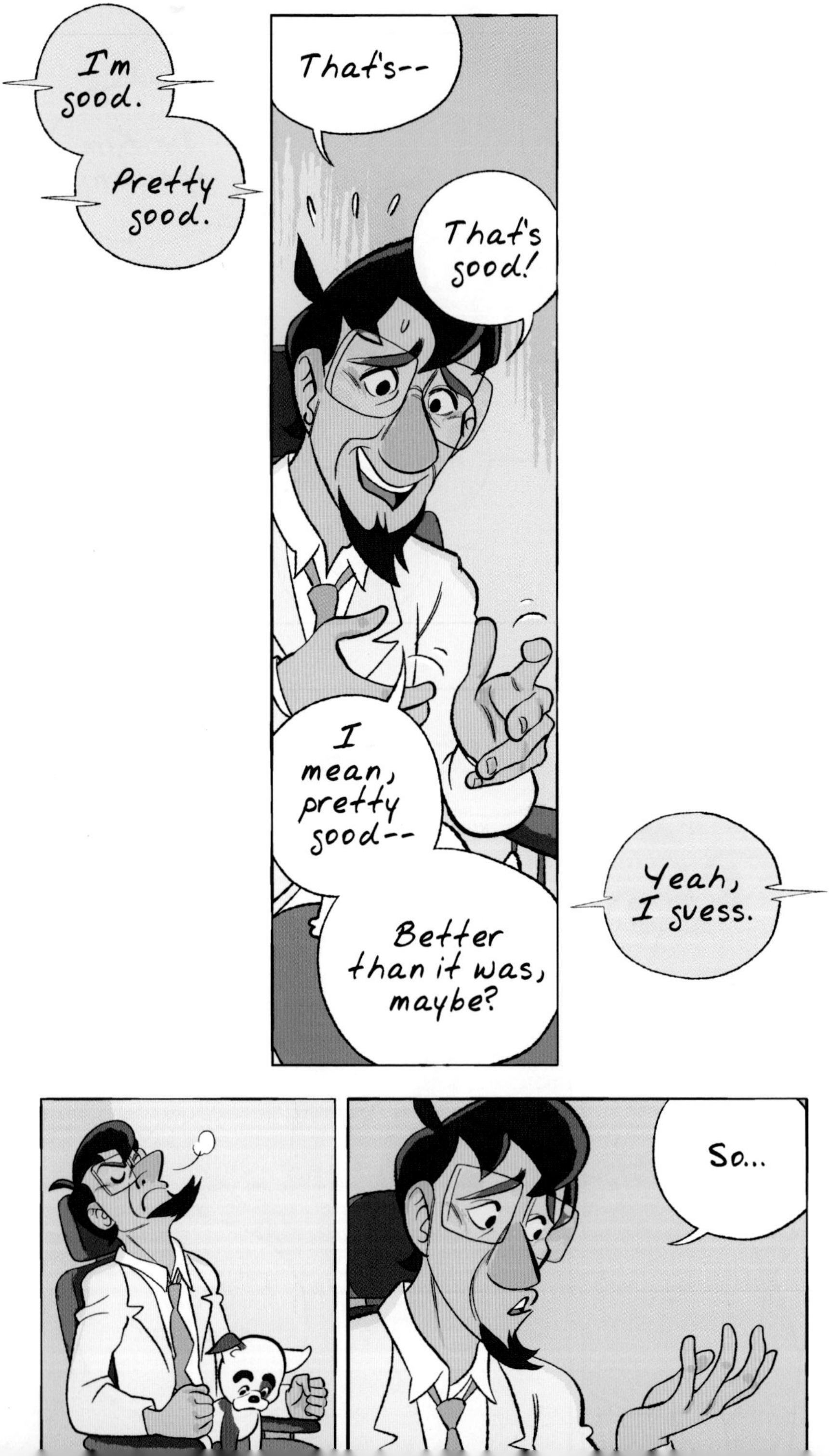

I'm good.
Pretty good.
That's--
That's good!
I mean, pretty good--
Better than it was, maybe?
Yeah, I guess.
So...

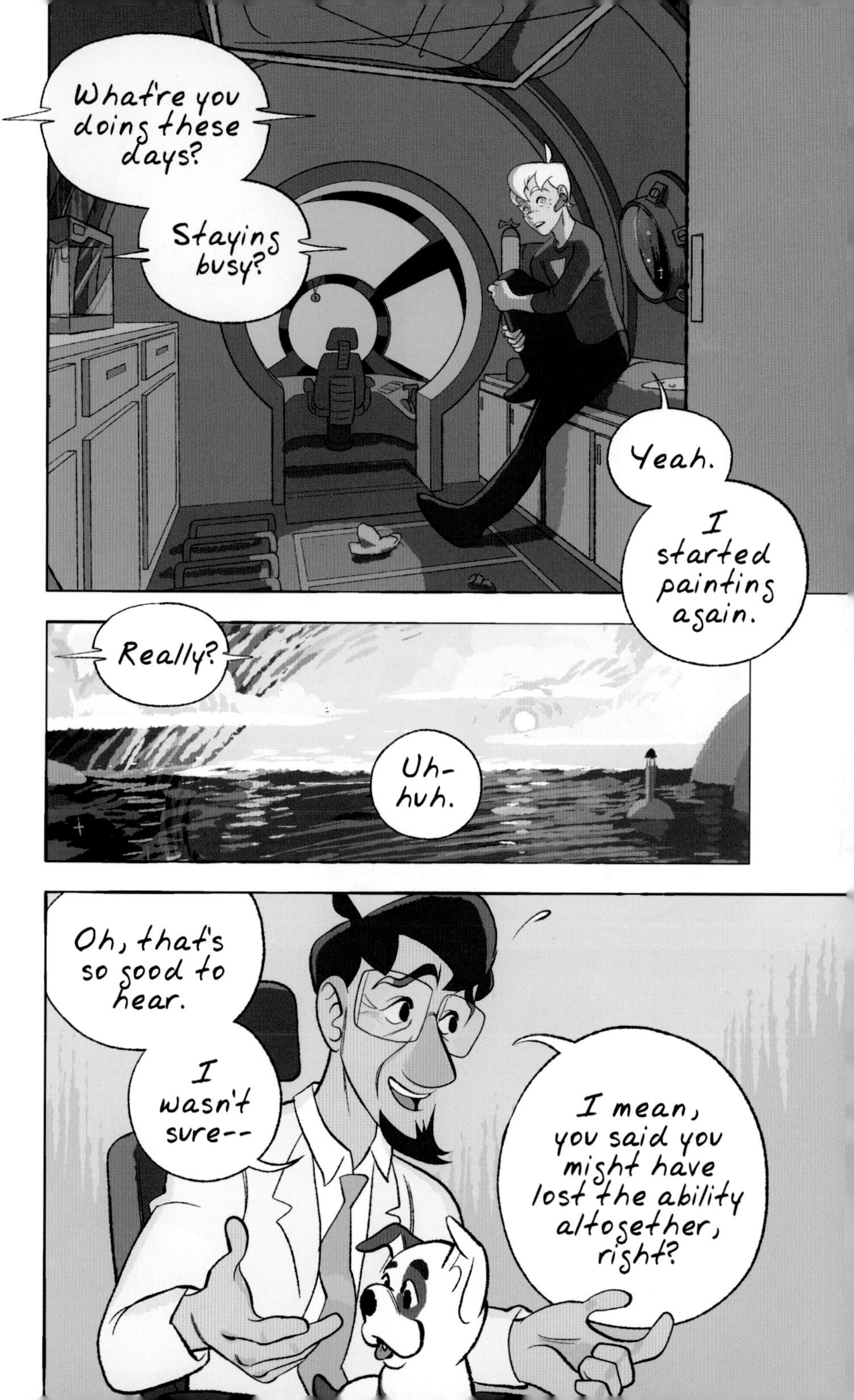
What're you doing these days?
Staying busy?
Yeah.
I started painting again.
Really?
Uh-huh.
Oh, that's so good to hear.
I wasn't sure--
I mean, you said you might have lost the ability altogether, right?

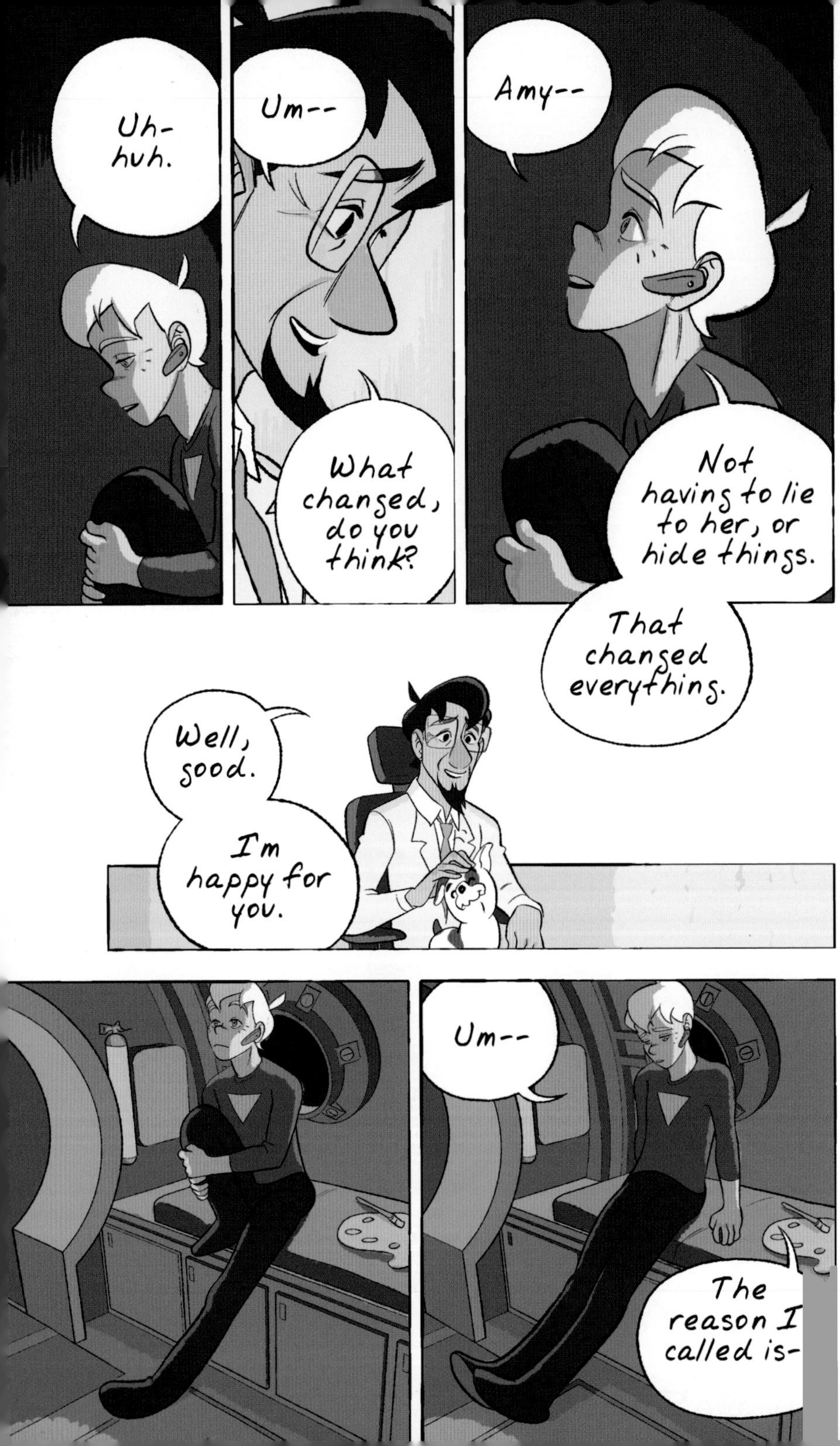
Uh-huh.
Um--
What changed, do you think?
Amy--
Not having to lie to her, or hide things.
That changed everything.
Well, good.
I'm happy for you.
Um--
The reason I called is-

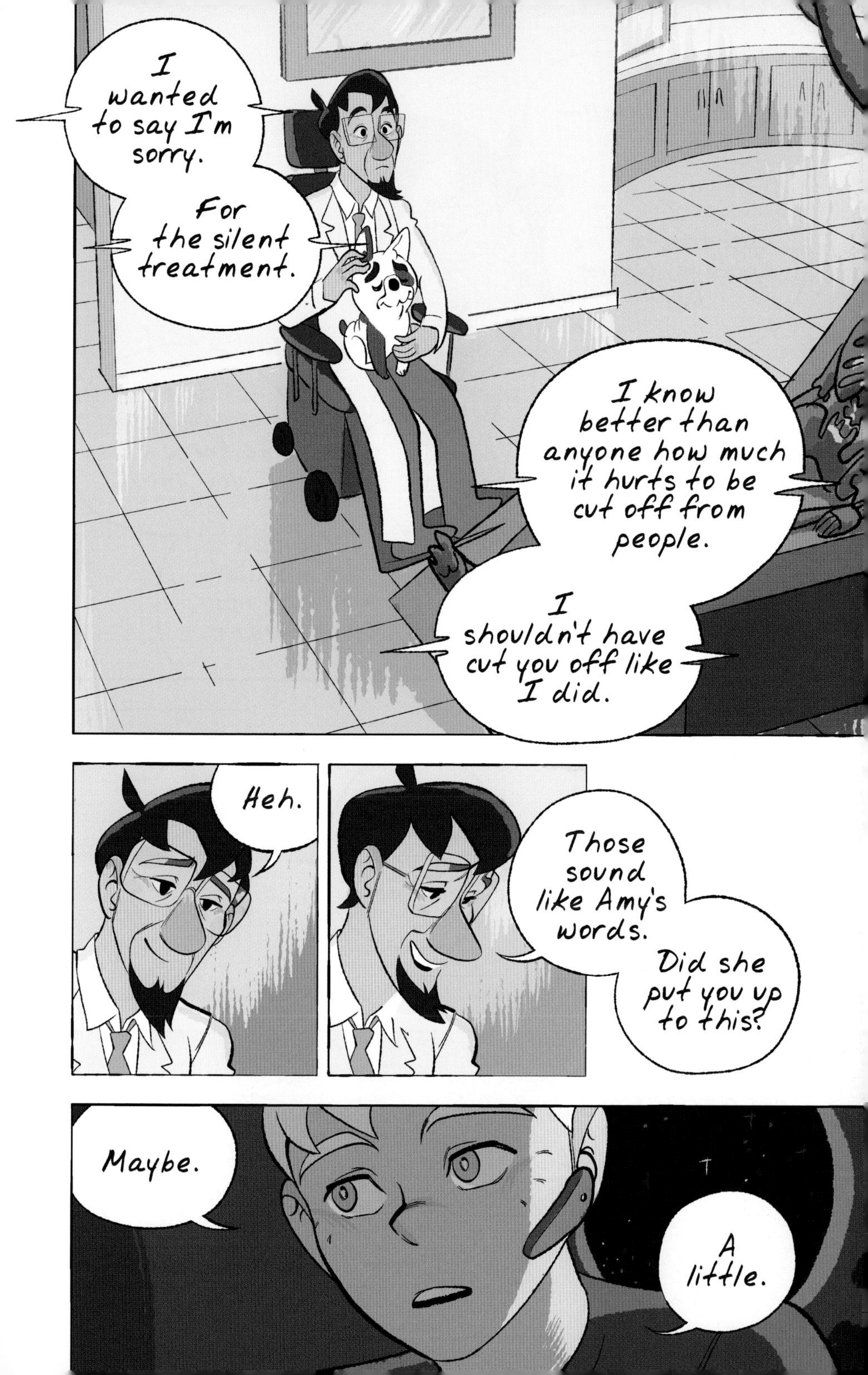
I wanted to say I'm sorry.
For the silent treatment.
I know better than anyone how much it hurts to be cut off from people.
I shouldn't have cut you off like I did.
Heh.
Those sound like Amy's words.
Did she put you up to this?
Maybe.
A little.

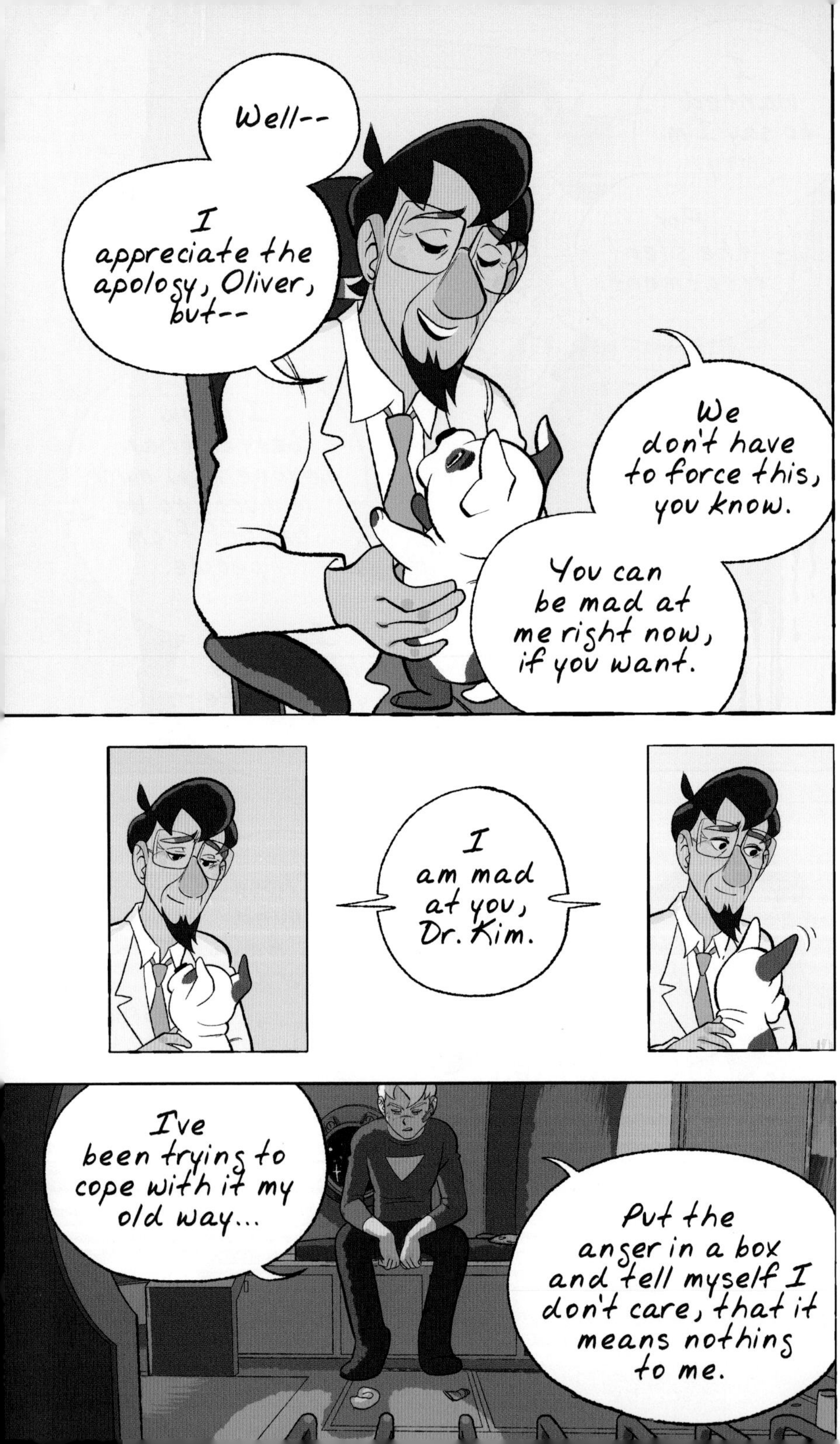
Well--
I appreciate the apology, Oliver, but--
We don't have to force this, you know.
You can be mad at me right now, if you want.
I am mad at you, Dr. Kim.
I've been trying to cope with it my old way...
Put the anger in a box and tell myself I don't care, that it means nothing to me.

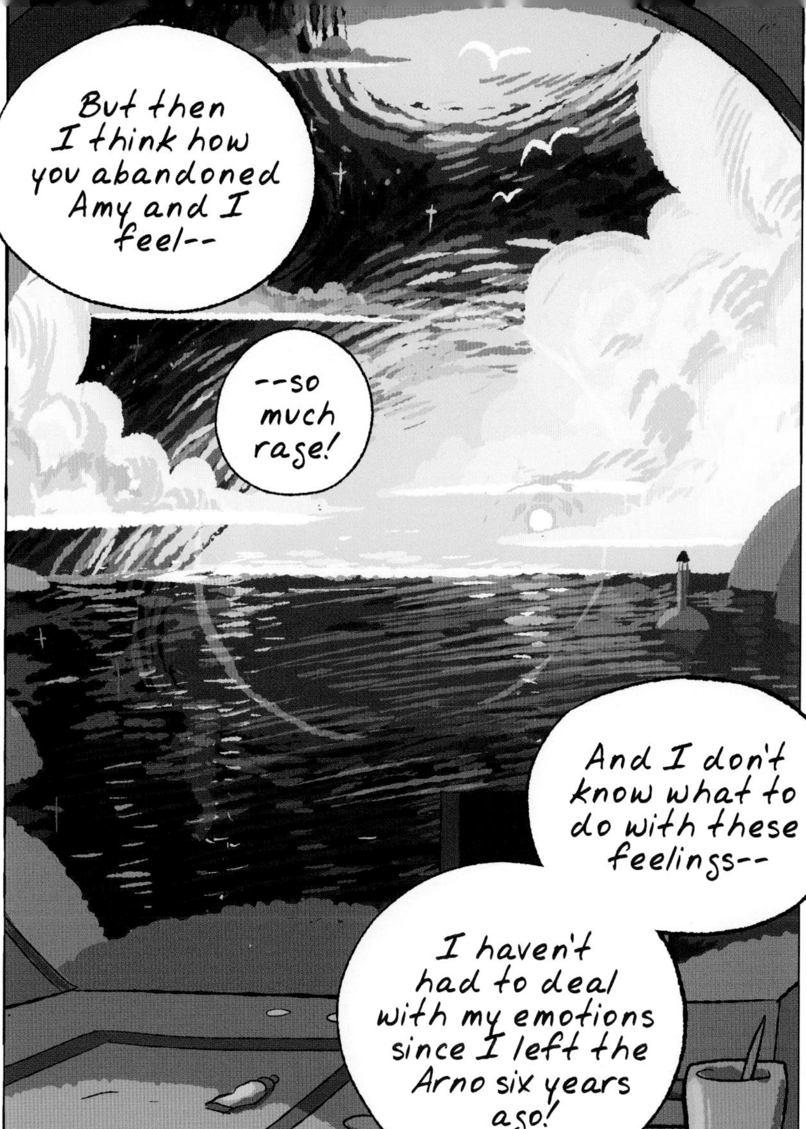
But then I think how you abandoned Amy and I feel--
--so much rage!
And I don't know what to do with these feelings--
I haven't had to deal with my emotions since I left the Arno six years ago!

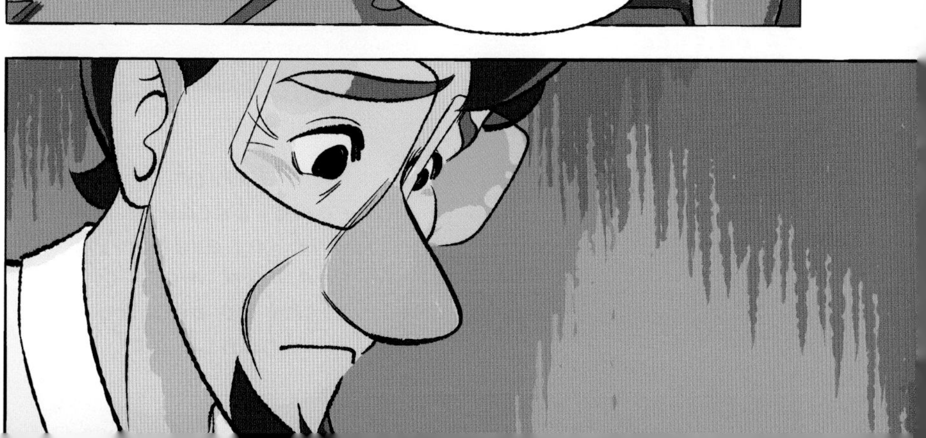

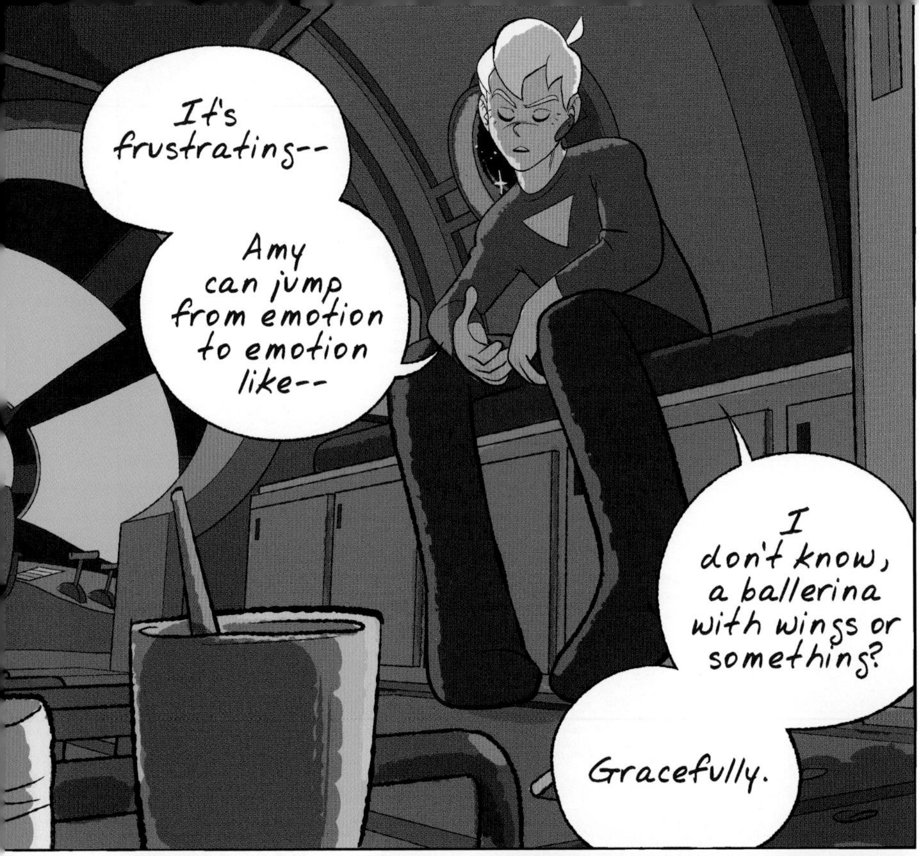
It's frustrating--
Amy can jump from emotion to emotion like--
I don't know, a ballerina with wings or something?
Gracefully.

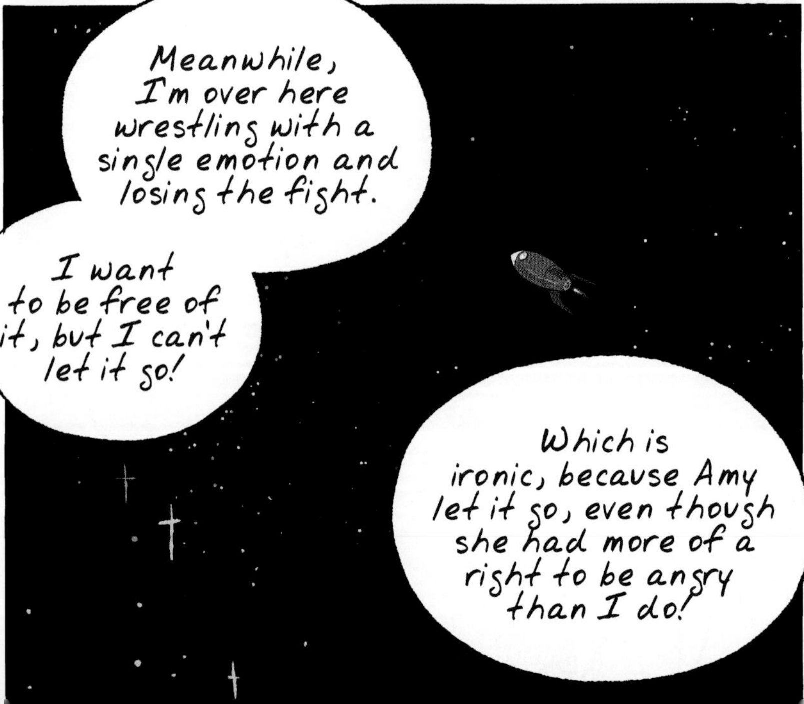
Meanwhile, I'm over here wrestling with a single emotion and losing the fight.
I want to be free of it, but I can't let it so!
Which is ironic, because Amy let it so, even though she had more of a right to be angry than I do!

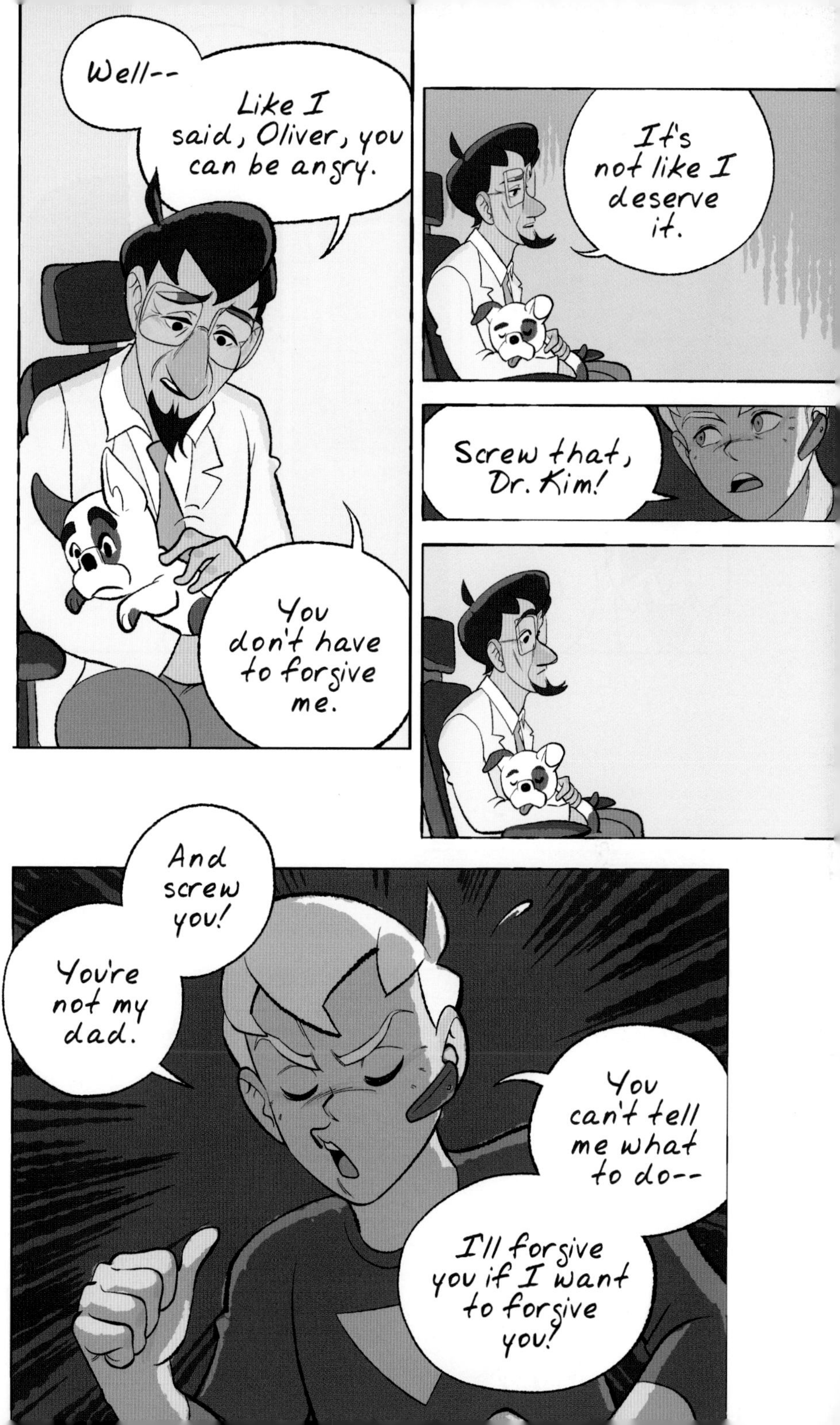
Well--
Like I said, Oliver, you can be angry.
You don't have to forgive me.
It's not like I deserve it.
Screw that, Dr. Kim!
And screw you!
You're not my dad.
You can't tell me what to do--
I'll forgive you if I want to forgive you!

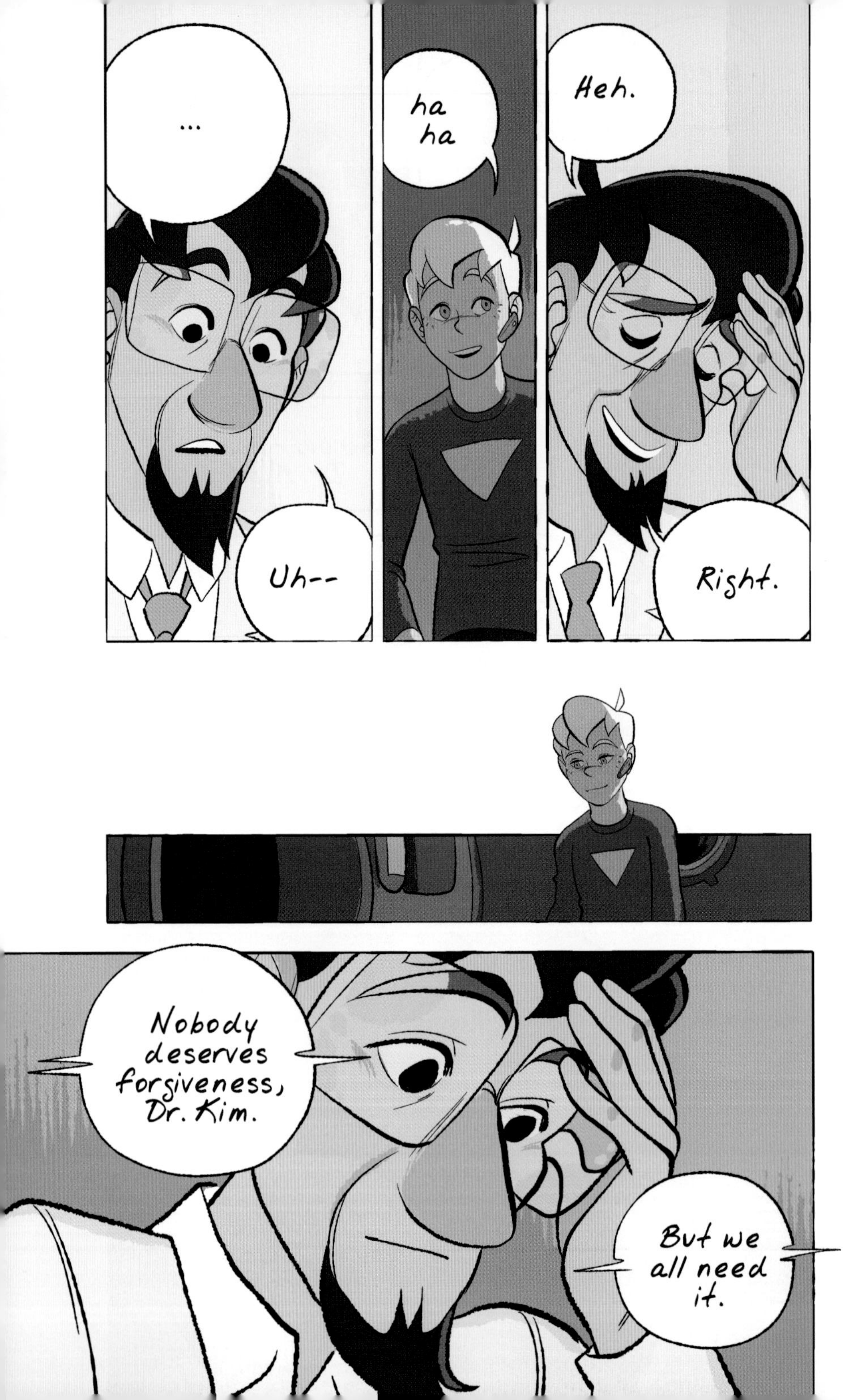
...
Uh--
ha ha
Heh.
Right.
Nobody deserves forgiveness, Dr. Kim.
But we all need it.

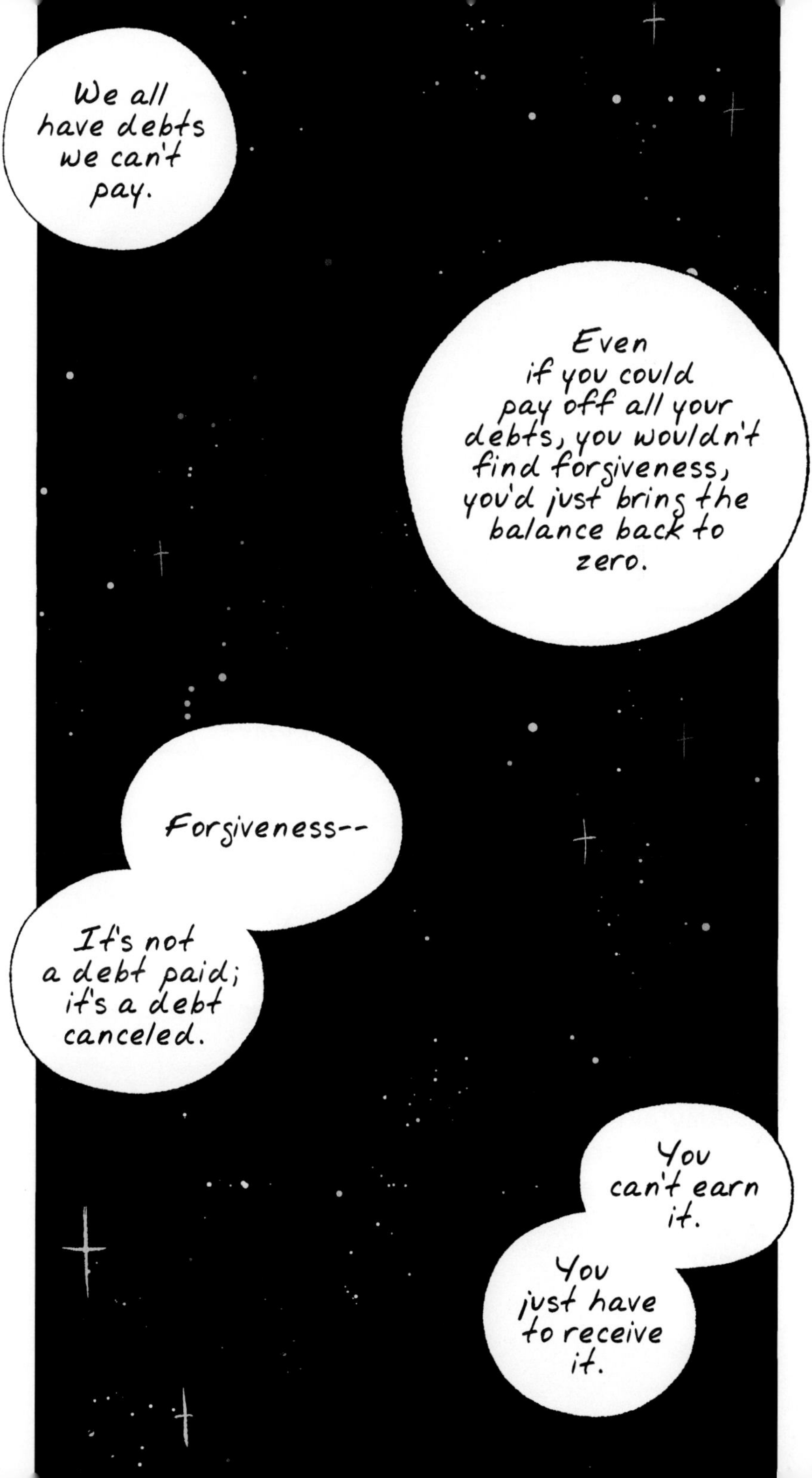
We all have debts we can't pay.
Even if you could pay off all your debts, you wouldn't find forgiveness, you'd just bring the balance back to zero.
Forgiveness--
It's not a debt paid; it's a debt canceled.
You can't earn it.
You just have to receive it.

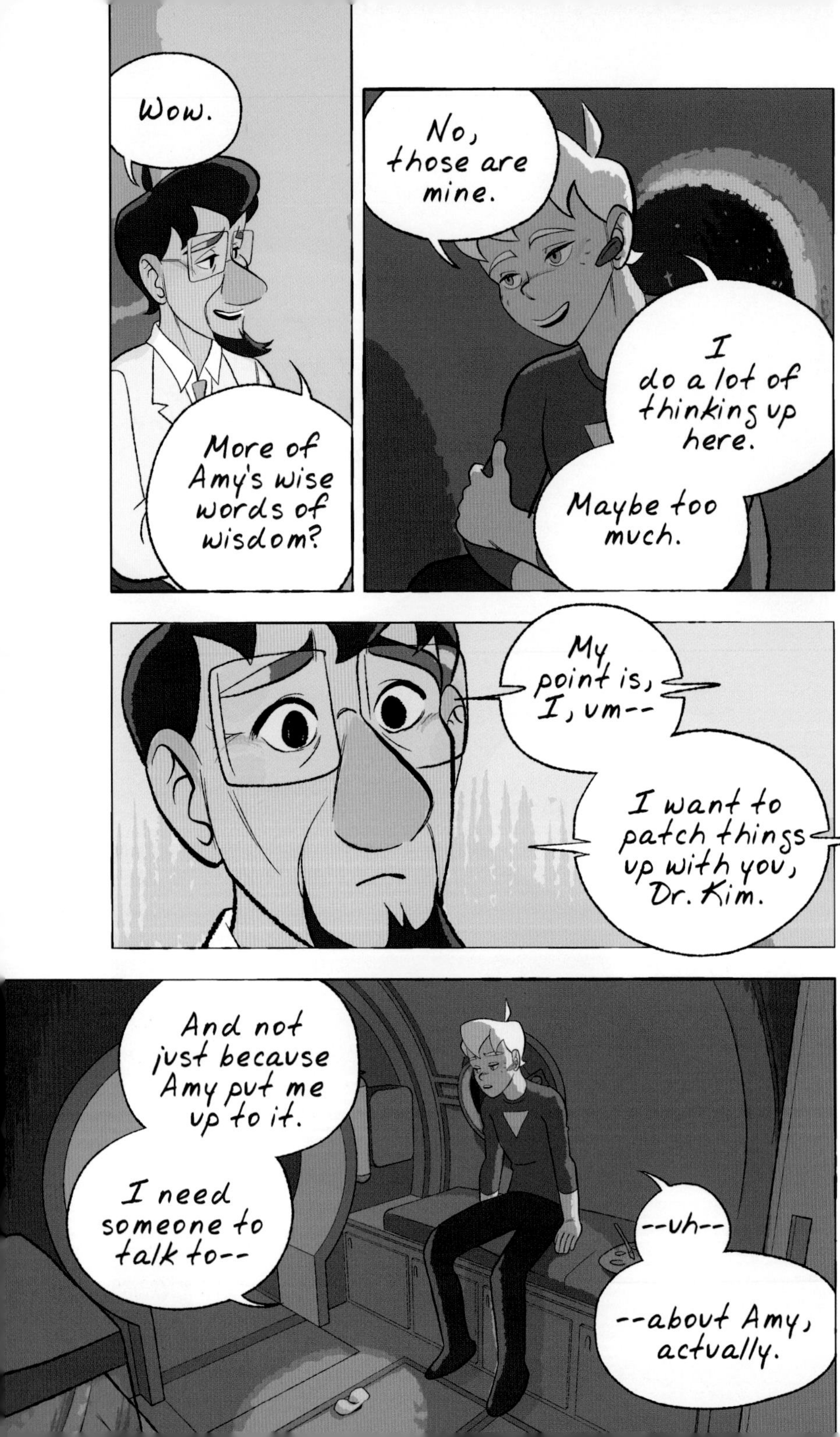
Wow.
No, those are mine.
More of Amy's wise words of wisdom?
I do a lot of thinking up here.
Maybe too much.
My point is, I, um--
I want to patch things up with you, Dr. Kim.
And not just because Amy put me up to it.
I need someone to talk to--
--uh--
--about Amy, actually.

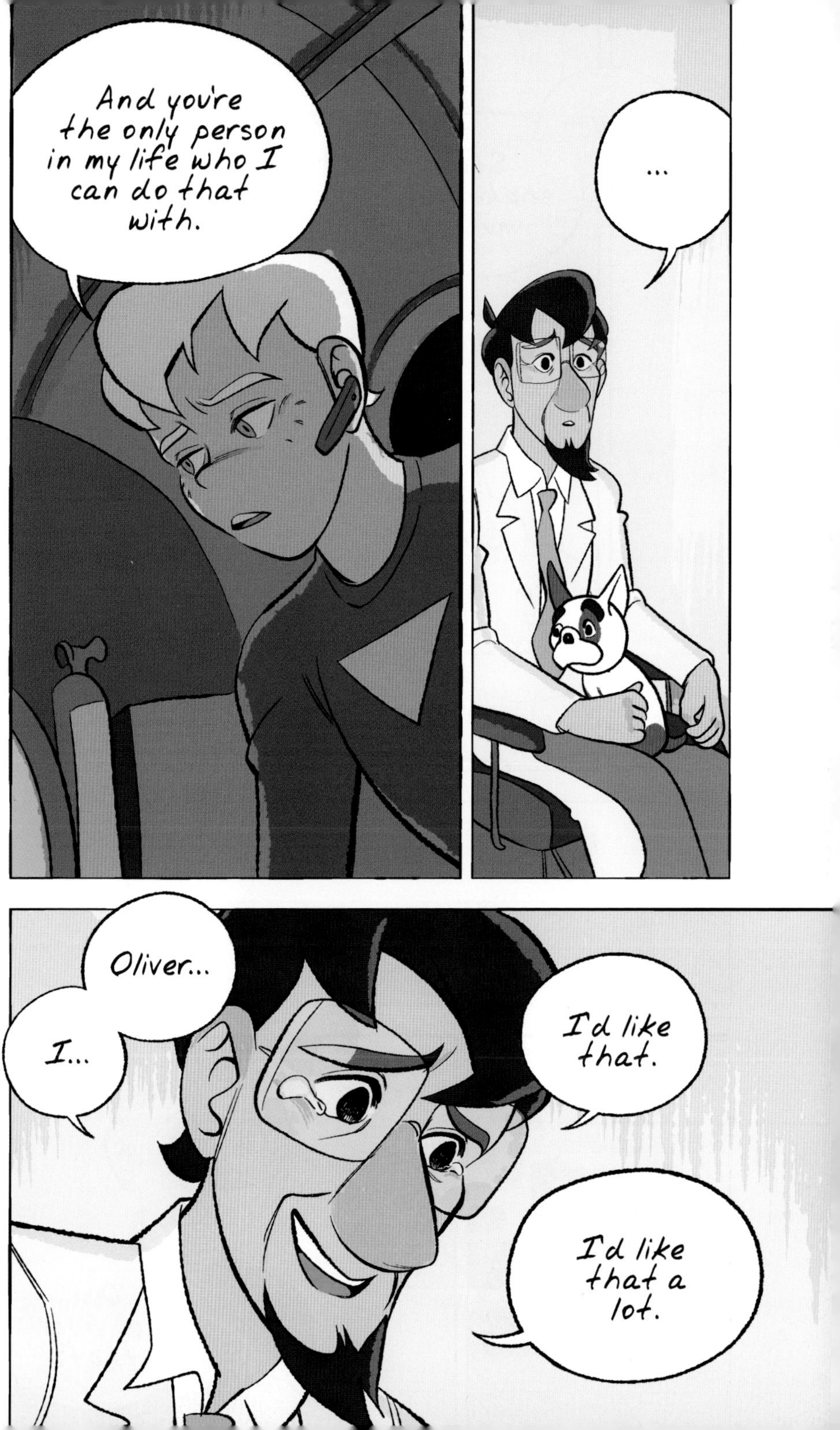
And you're the only person in my life who I can do that with.
...
Oliver...
I...
I'd like that.
I'd like that a lot.

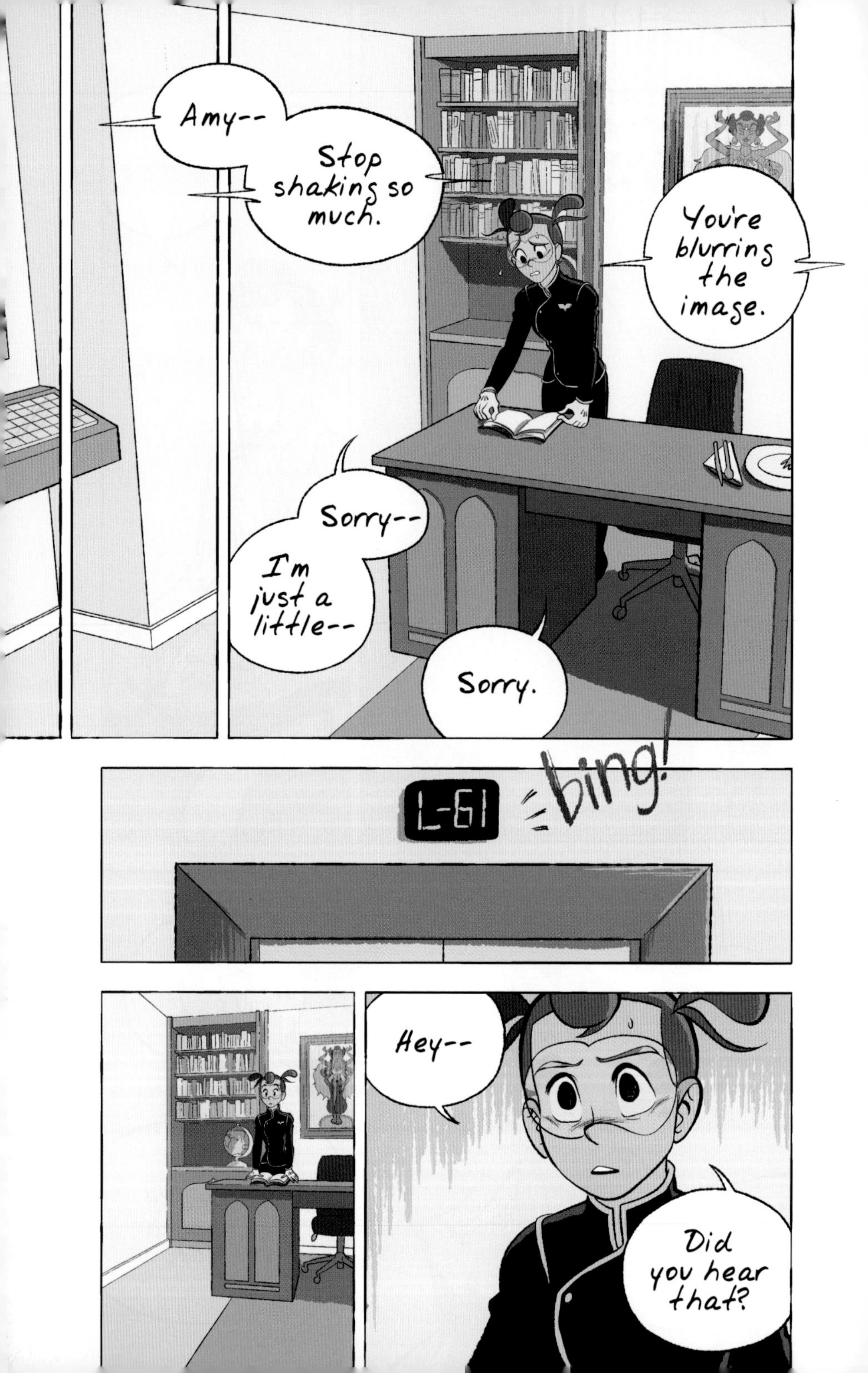
Amy--
Stop shaking so much.
You're blurring the image.
Sorry--
I'm just a little--
Sorry.
L-61
bing!
Hey--
Did you hear that?

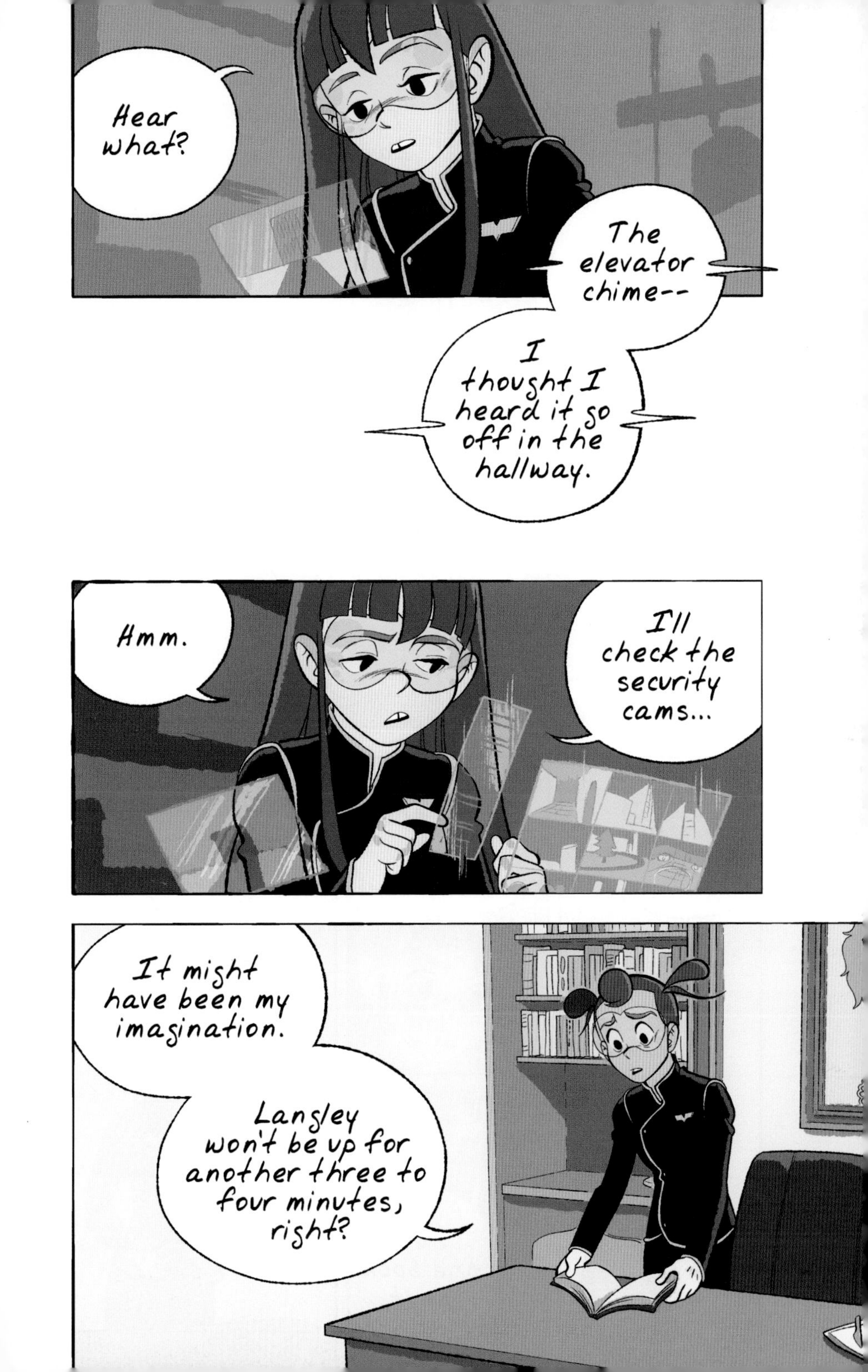
Hear what?
The elevator chime--
I thought I heard it go off in the hallway.
Hmm.
I'll check the security cams...
It might have been my imagination.
Langley won't be up for another three to four minutes, right?

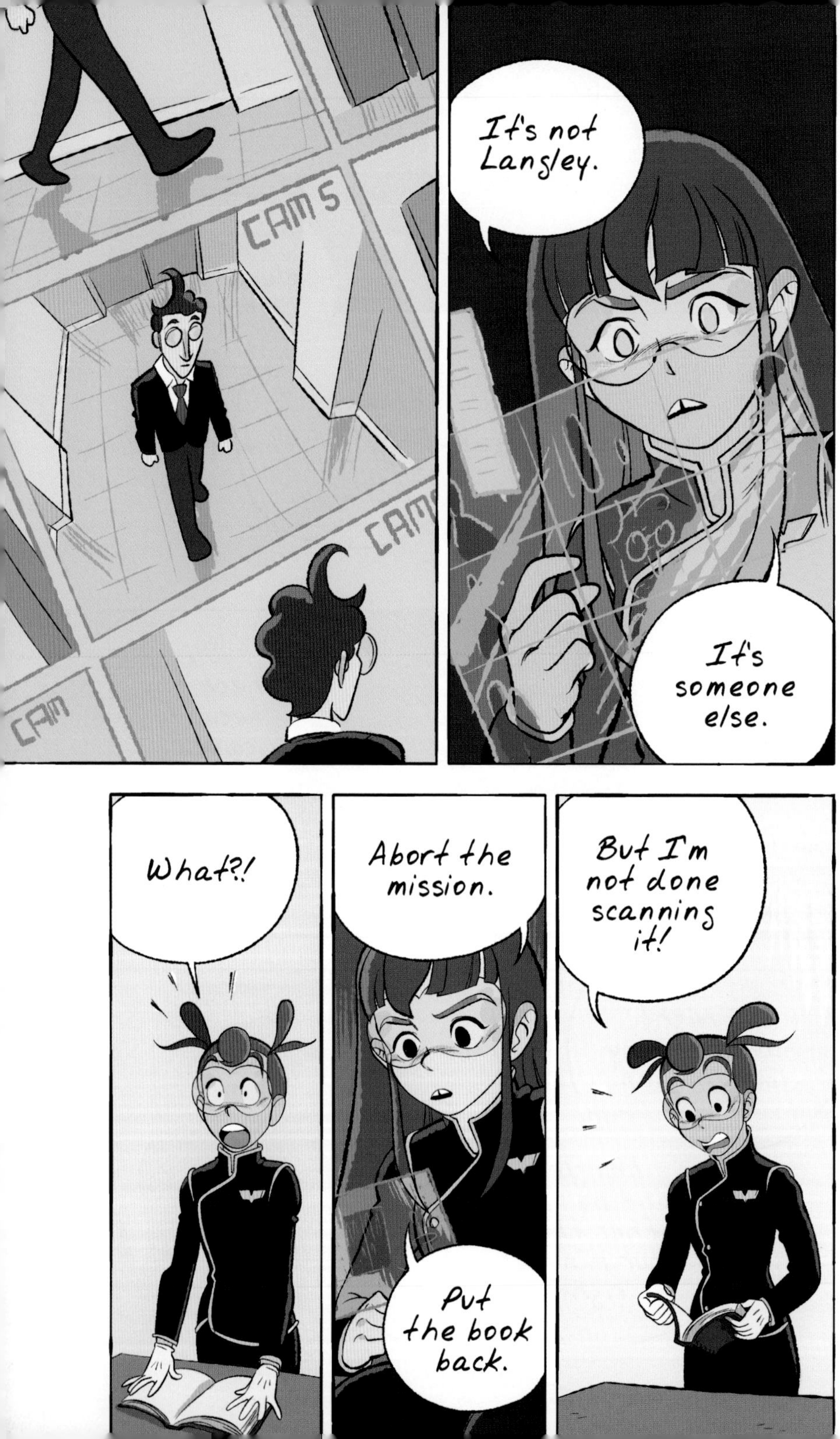
CAM 5
CAM
CAM
It's not Langley.
It's someone else.
What?!
Abort the mission.
Put the book back.
But I'm not done scanning it!

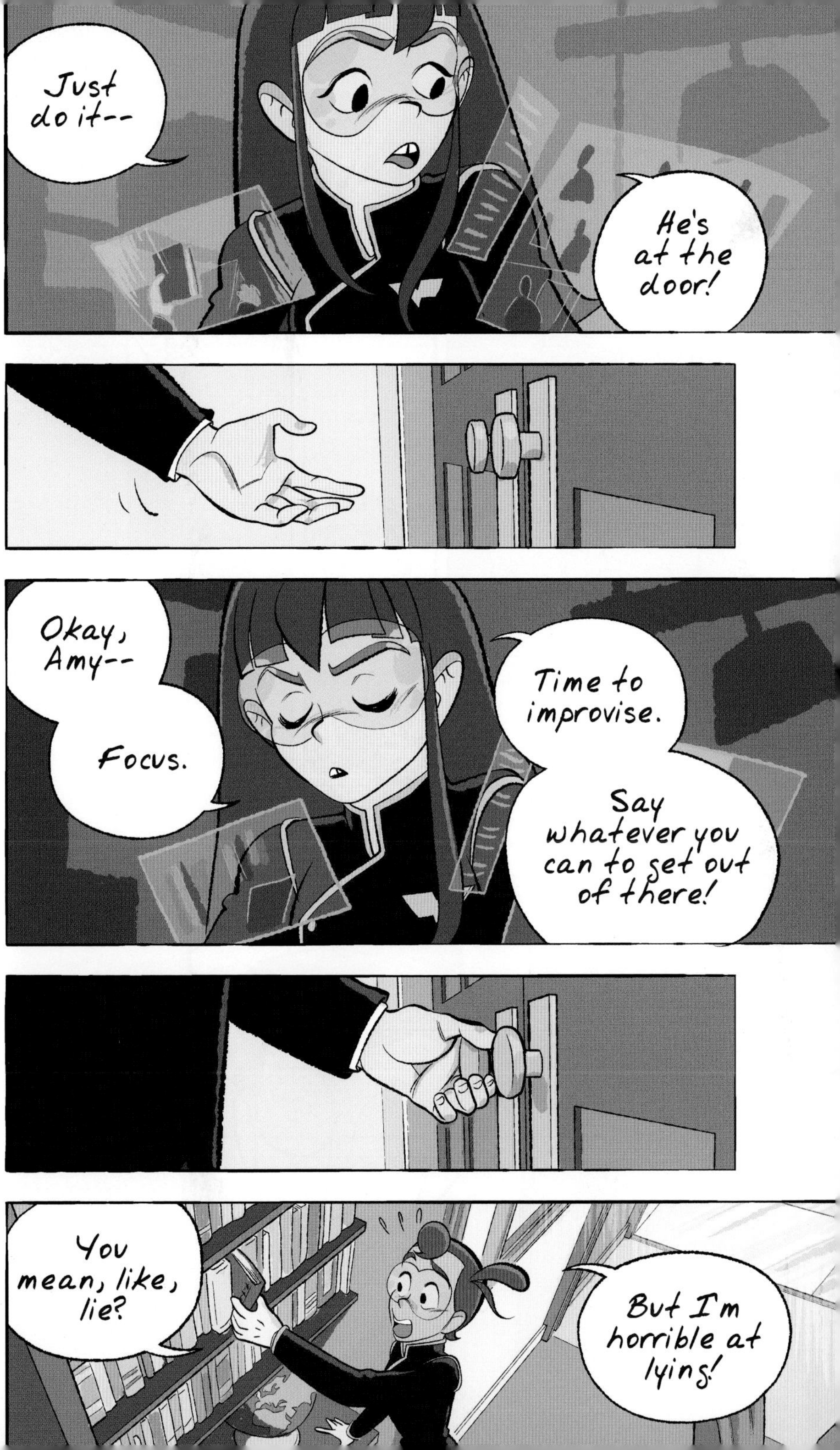
Just do it--
He's at the door!
Okay, Amy--
Focus.
Time to improvise.
Say whatever you can to get out of there!
You mean, like, lie?
But I'm horrible at lying!

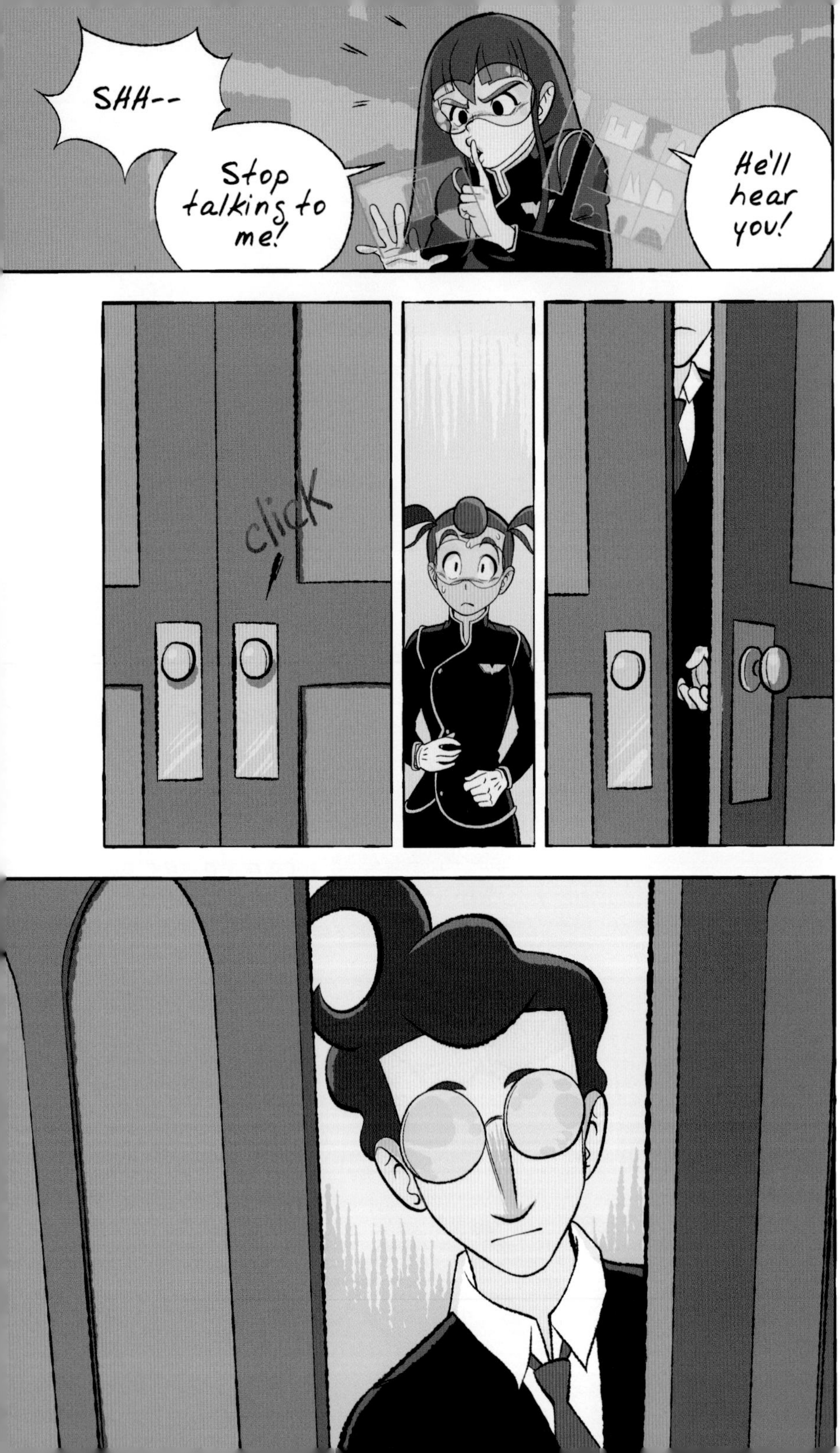
SHH--
Stop talking to me!
He'll hear you!
click

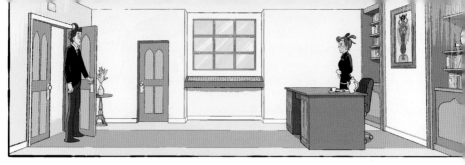

Oh.

Hello.

...

Hi.

The man's aura reads pretty simply: basil leaf and balsamic vinegar.

Black pepper.

Click!

In that medley of flavors, I sense the outline of a keen intellect, a mind more awake than most.

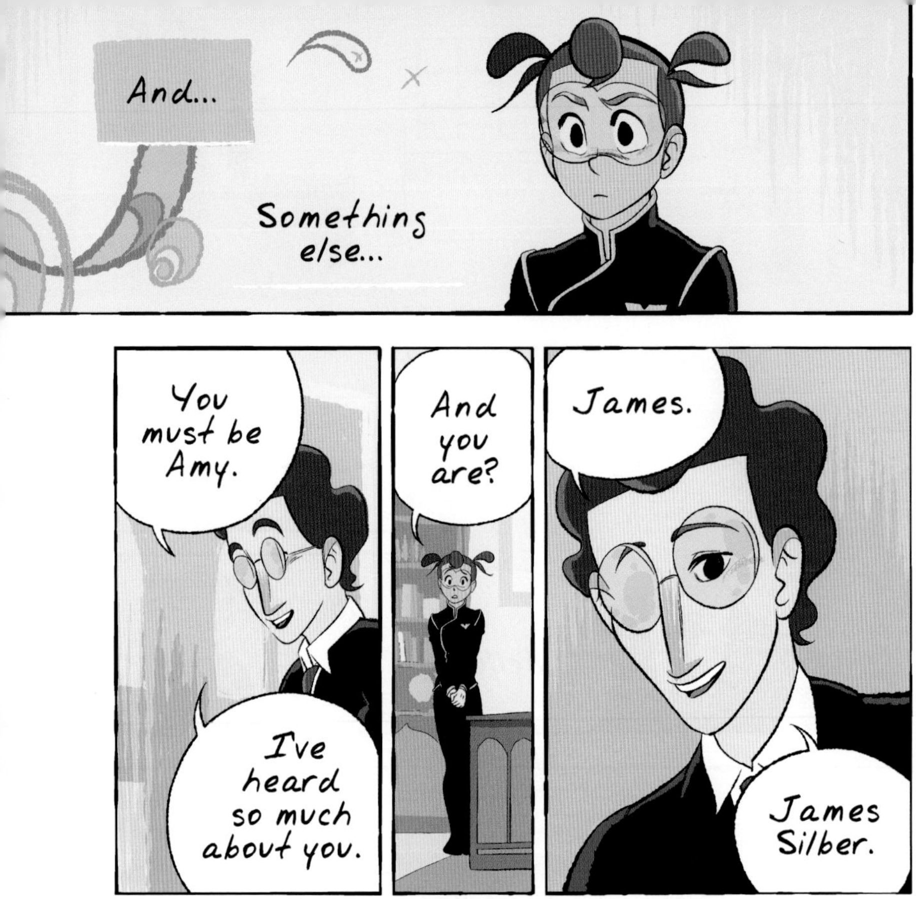

And...
Something else...
You must be Amy.
I've heard so much about you.
And you are?
James.
James Silber.

Our eyes meet, and strangely I feel relief wash over me.

Something about this man's presence puts me at ease.

I feel safe, almost like I'm back home.

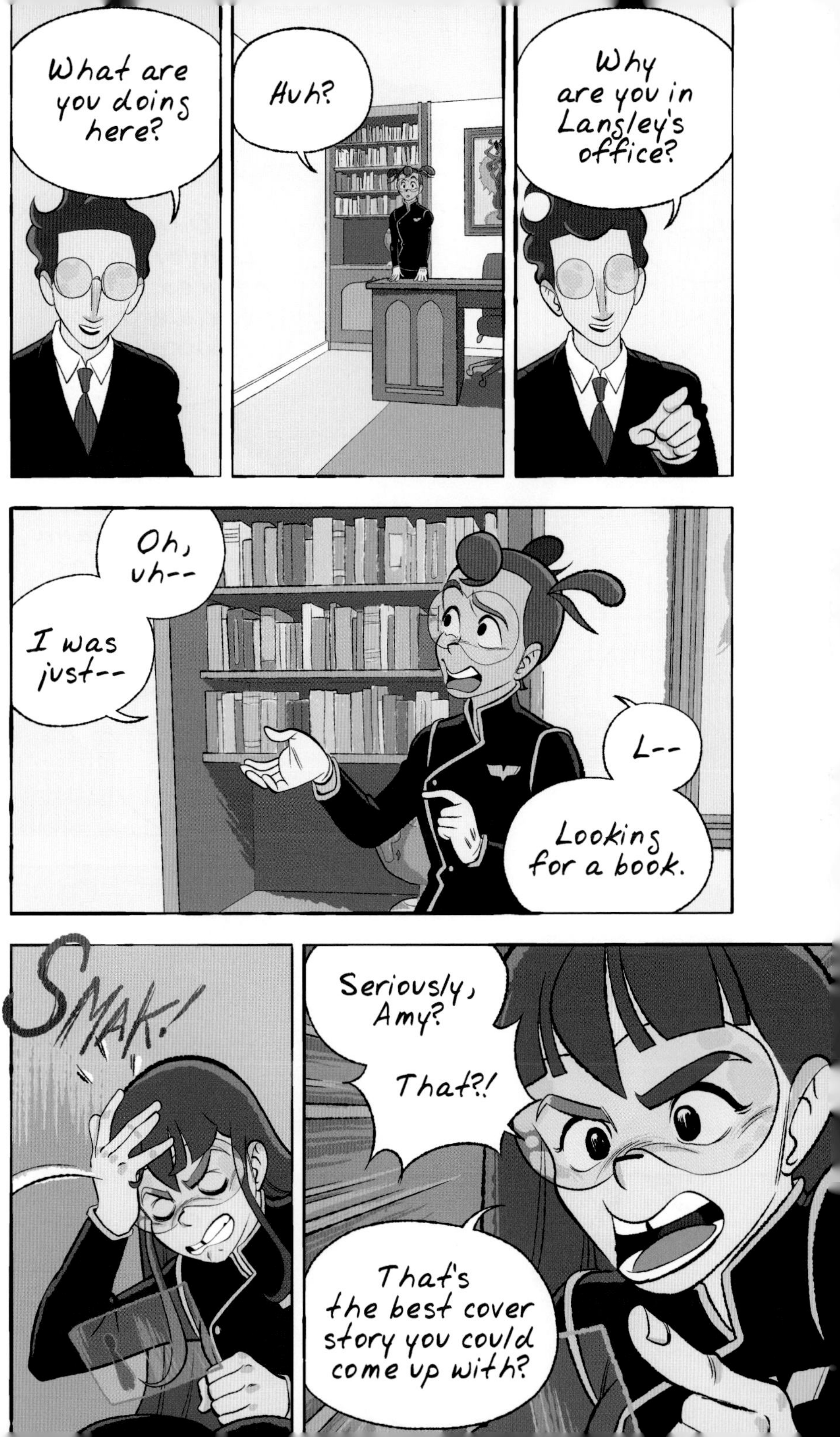
What are you doing here?
Huh?
Why are you in Langley's office?
Oh, uh--
I was just--
L--
Looking for a book.
SMAK!
Seriously, Amy?
That?!
That's the best cover story you could come up with?

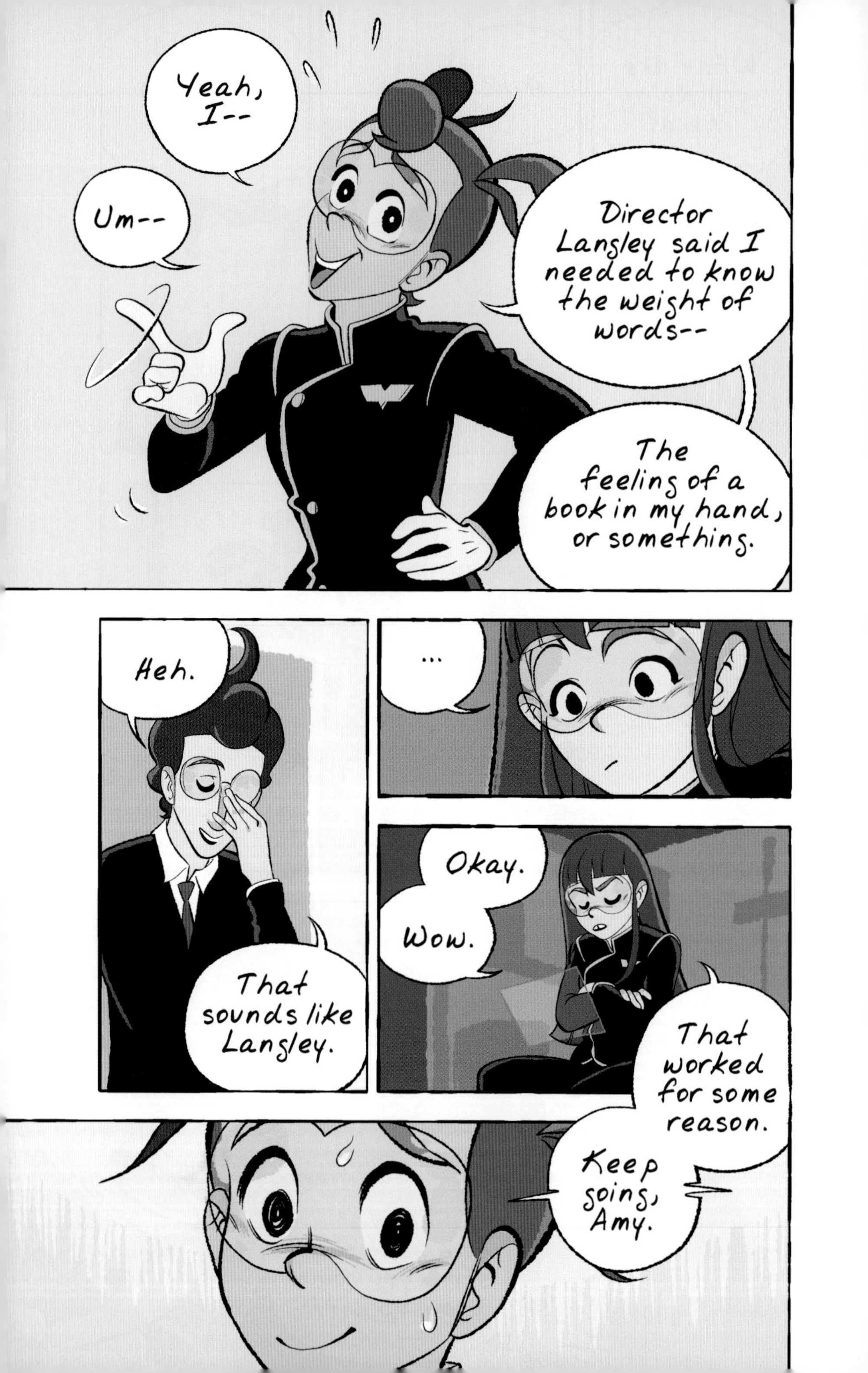
Yeah, I--
Um--
Director Langley said I needed to know the weight of words--
The feelings of a book in my hand, or something.
Heh.
That sounds like Langley.
...
Okay.
Wow.
That worked for some reason.
Keep going, Amy.

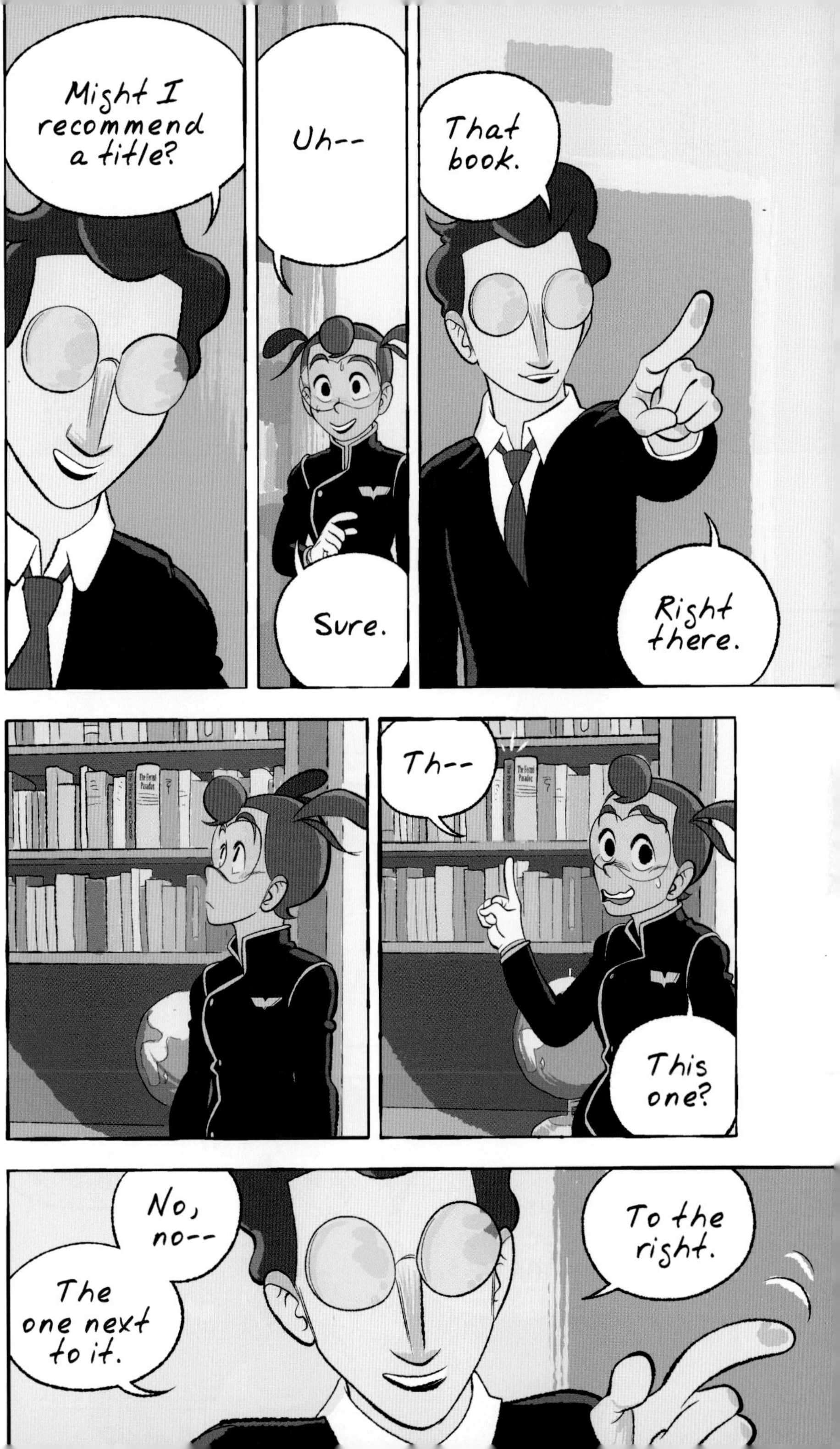
Might I recommend a title?
Uh--
Sure.
That book.
Right there.
Th--
This one?
No, no--
The one next to it.
To the right.

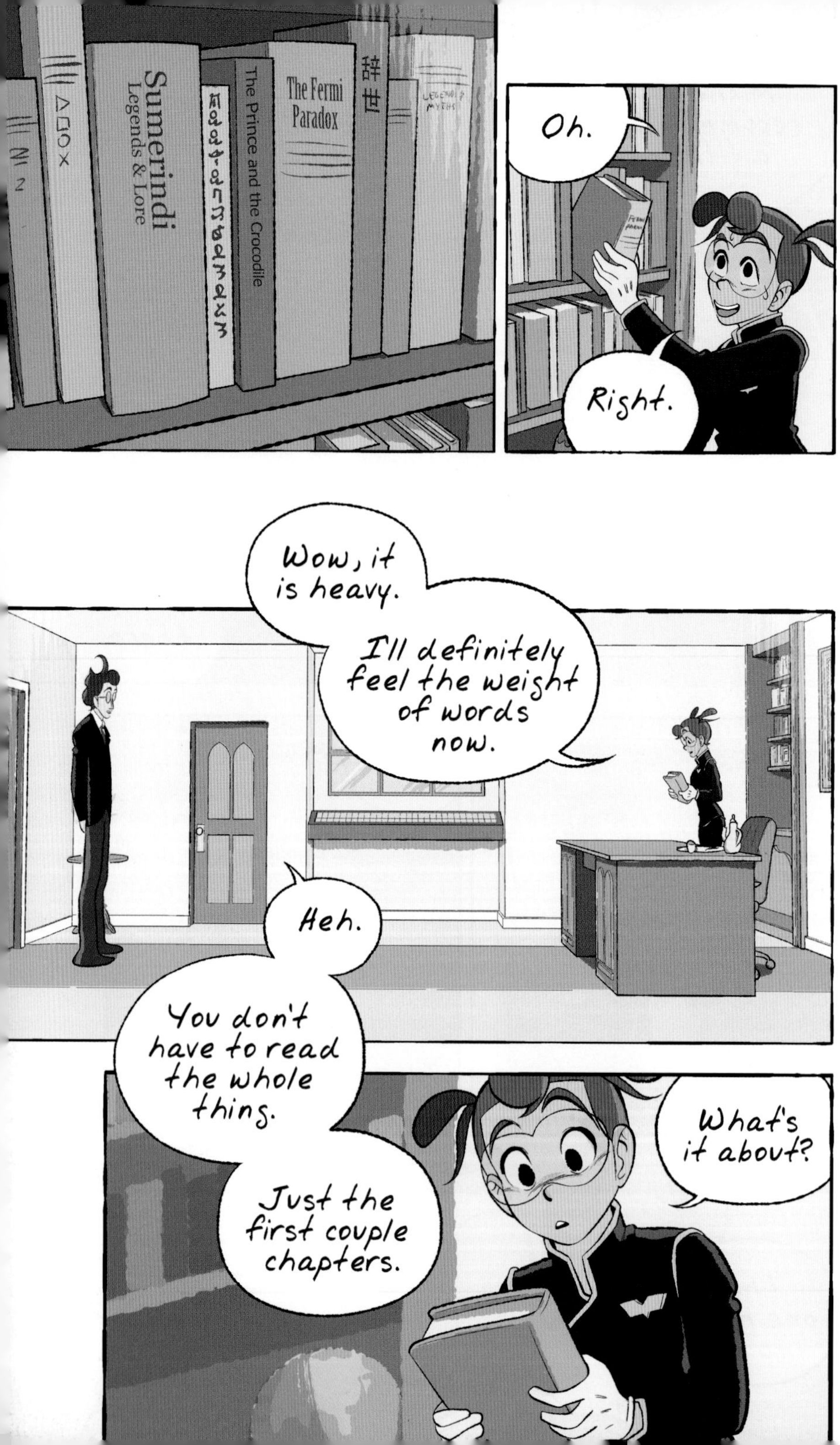

Sumerindi Legends & Lore
The Prince and the Crocodile
The Fermi Paradox
Oh.
Right.
Wow, it is heavy.
I'll definitely feel the weight of words now.
Heh.
You don't have to read the whole thing.
Just the first couple chapters.
What's it about?

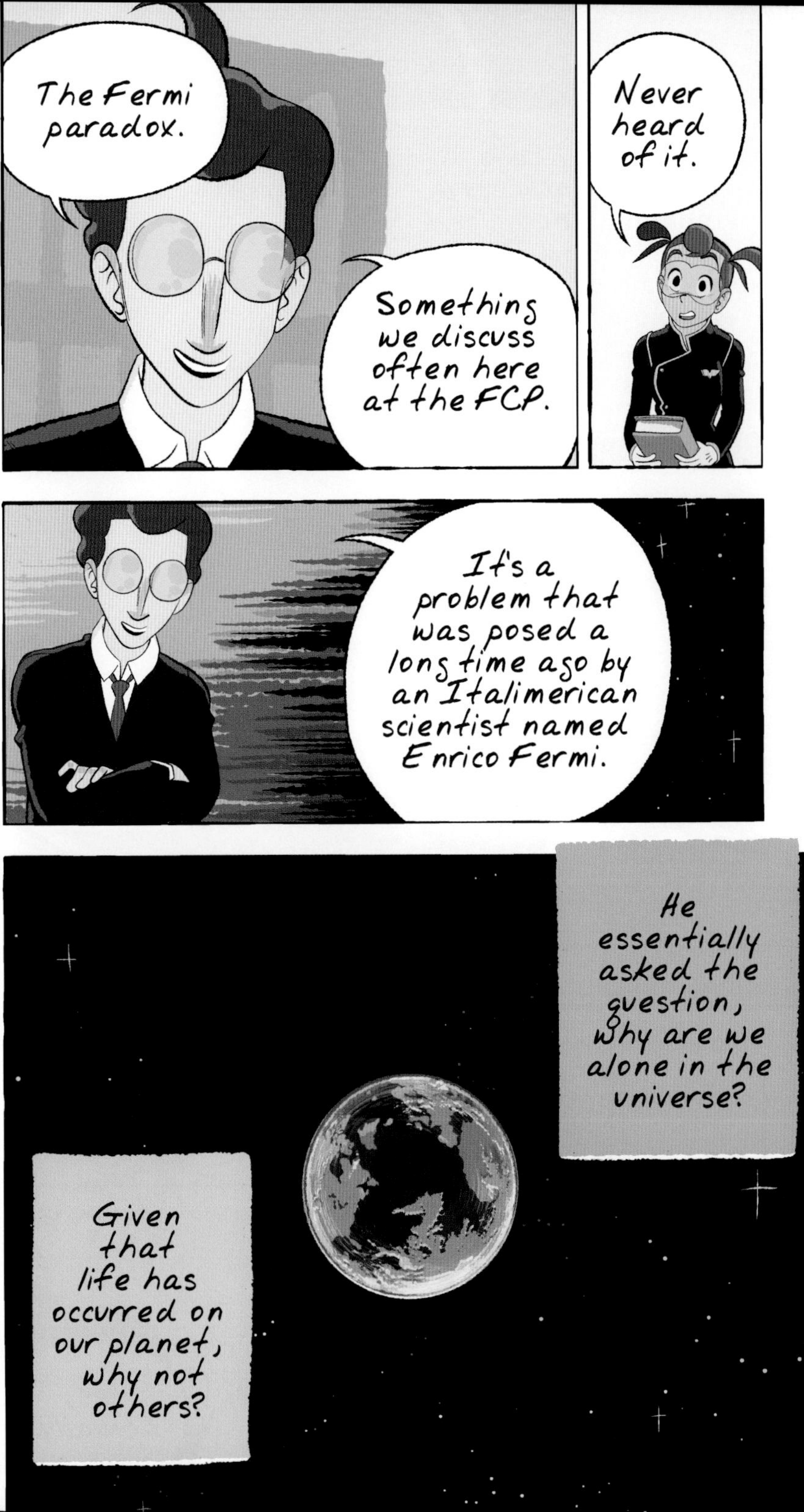
The Fermi paradox.
Never heard of it.
Something we discuss often here at the FCP.
It's a problem that was posed a long time ago by an Italimerican scientist named Enrico Fermi.
He essentially asked the question, why are we alone in the universe?
Given that life has occurred on our planet, why not others?

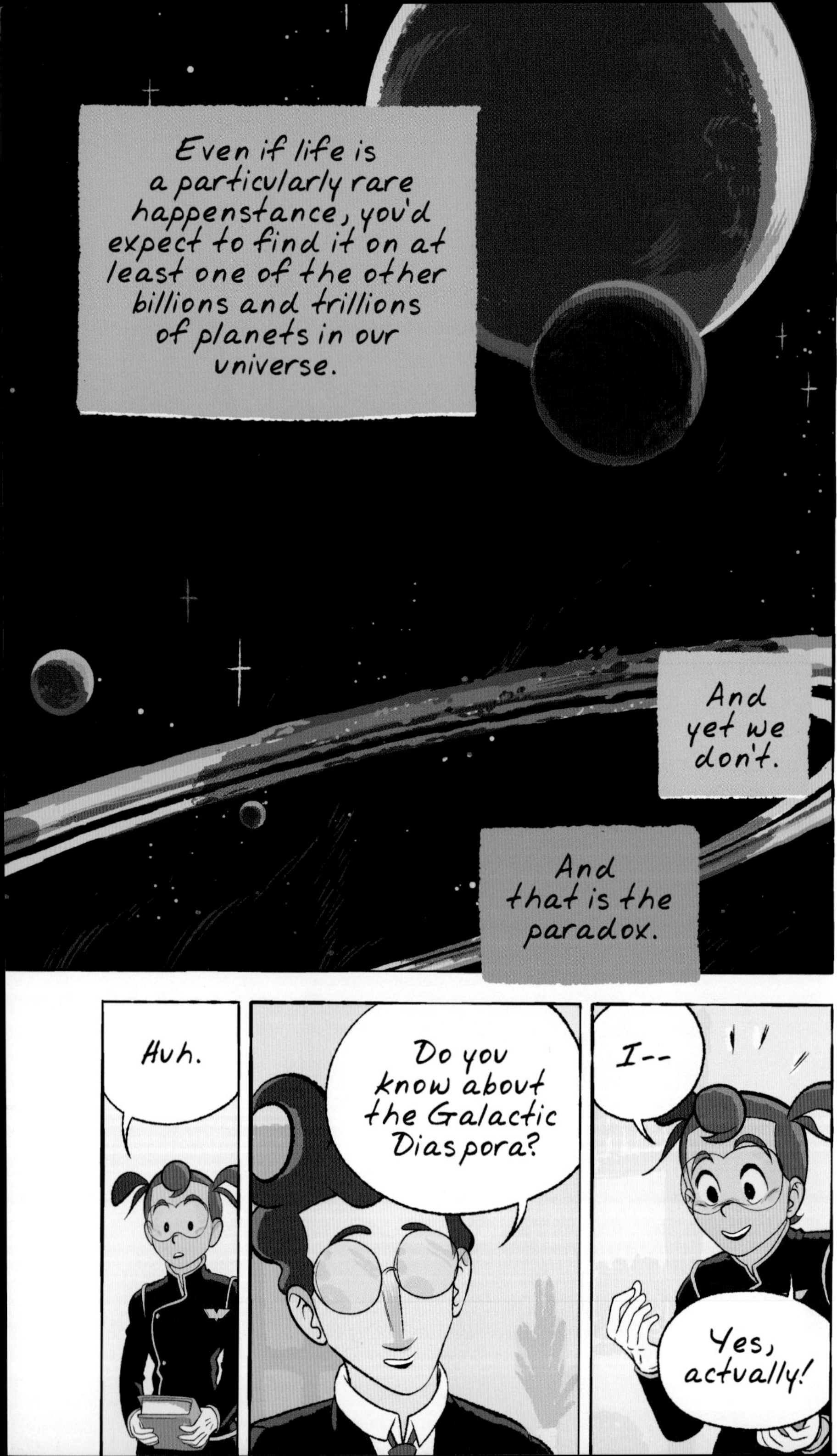
Even if life is a particularly rare happenstance, you'd expect to find it on at least one of the other billions and trillions of planets in our universe.
And yet we don't.
And that is the paradox.
Huh.
Do you know about the Galactic Diaspora?
I--
Yes, actually!

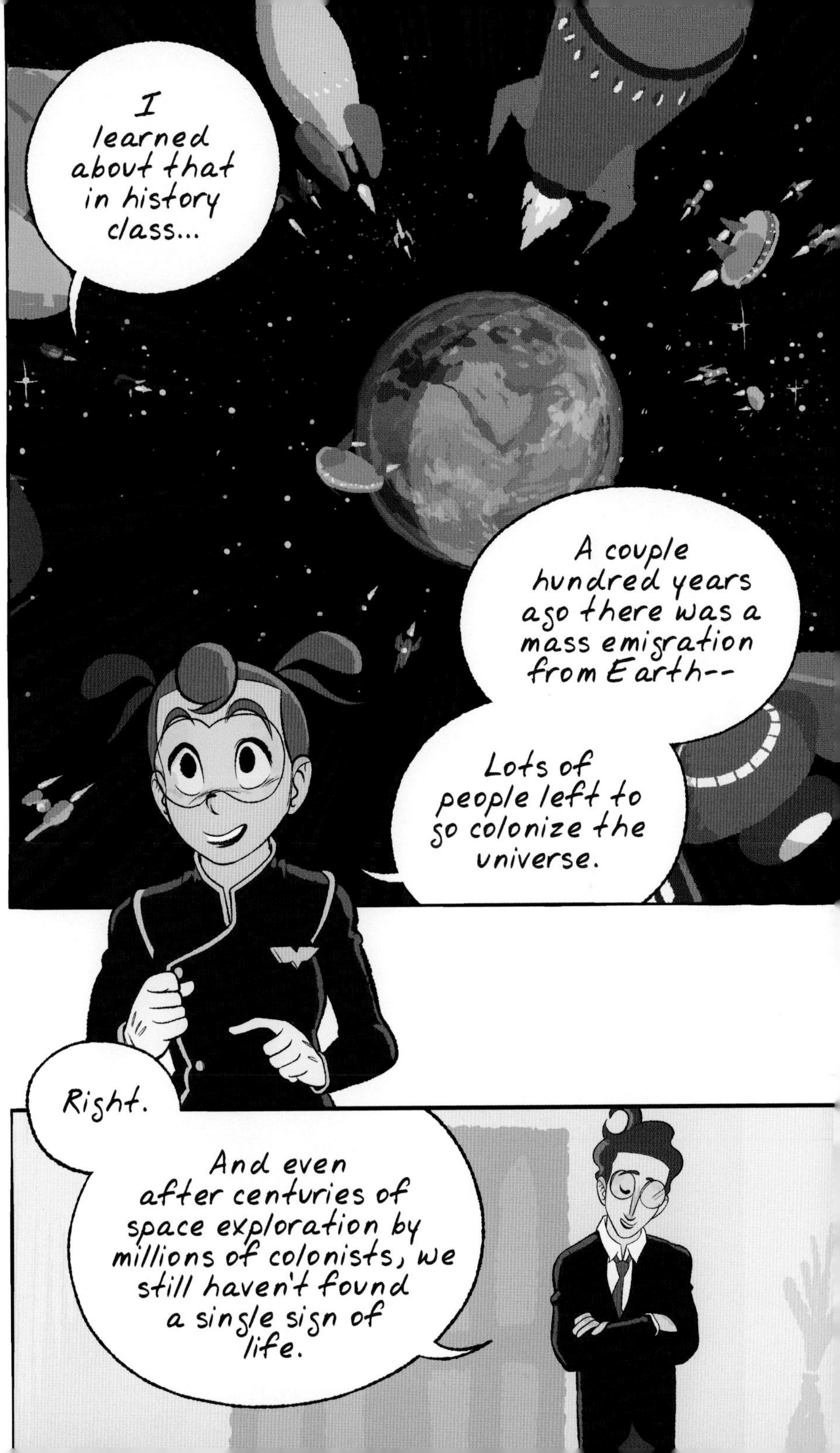
I learned about that in history class...
A couple hundred years ago there was a mass emigration from Earth--
Lots of people left to go colonize the universe.
Right.
And even after centuries of space exploration by millions of colonists, we still haven't found a single sign of life.

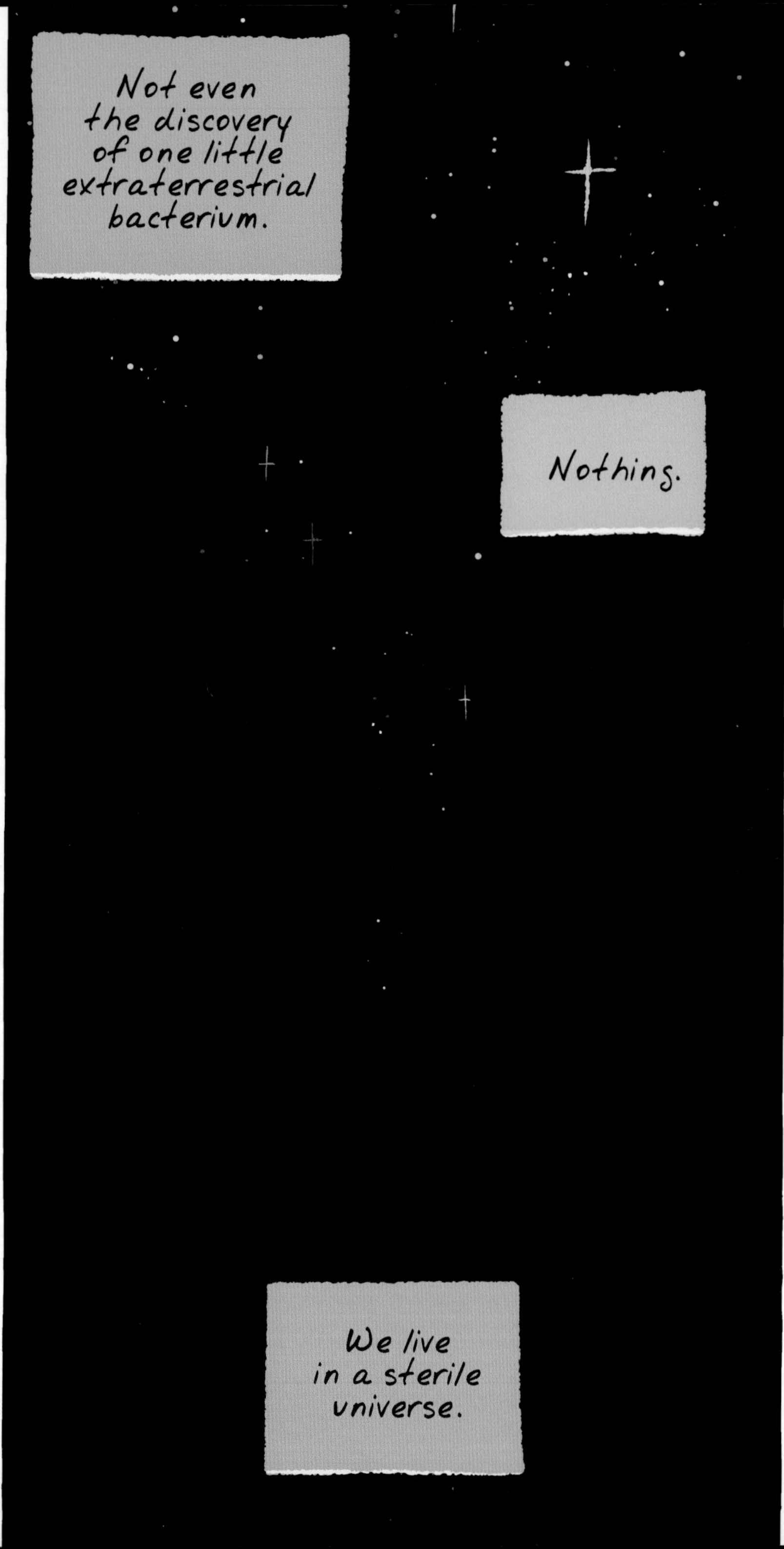
Not even the discovery of one little extraterrestrial bacterium.
Nothing.
We live in a sterile universe.

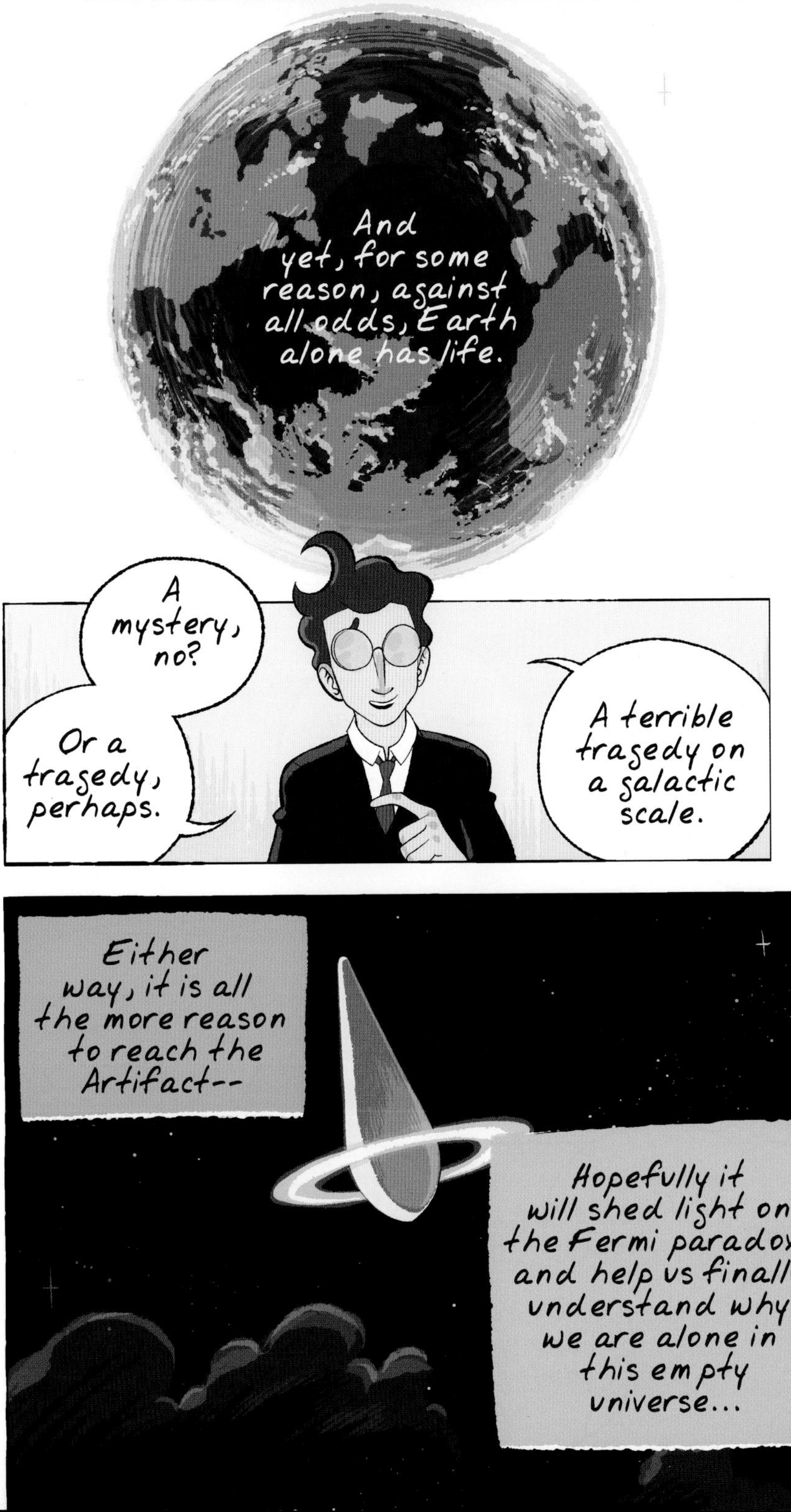
And yet, for some reason, against all odds, Earth alone has life.
A mystery, no?
Or a tragedy, perhaps.
A terrible tragedy on a galactic scale.
Either way, it is all the more reason to reach the Artifact--
Hopefully it will shed light on the Fermi paradox, and help us finally understand why we are alone in this empty universe...

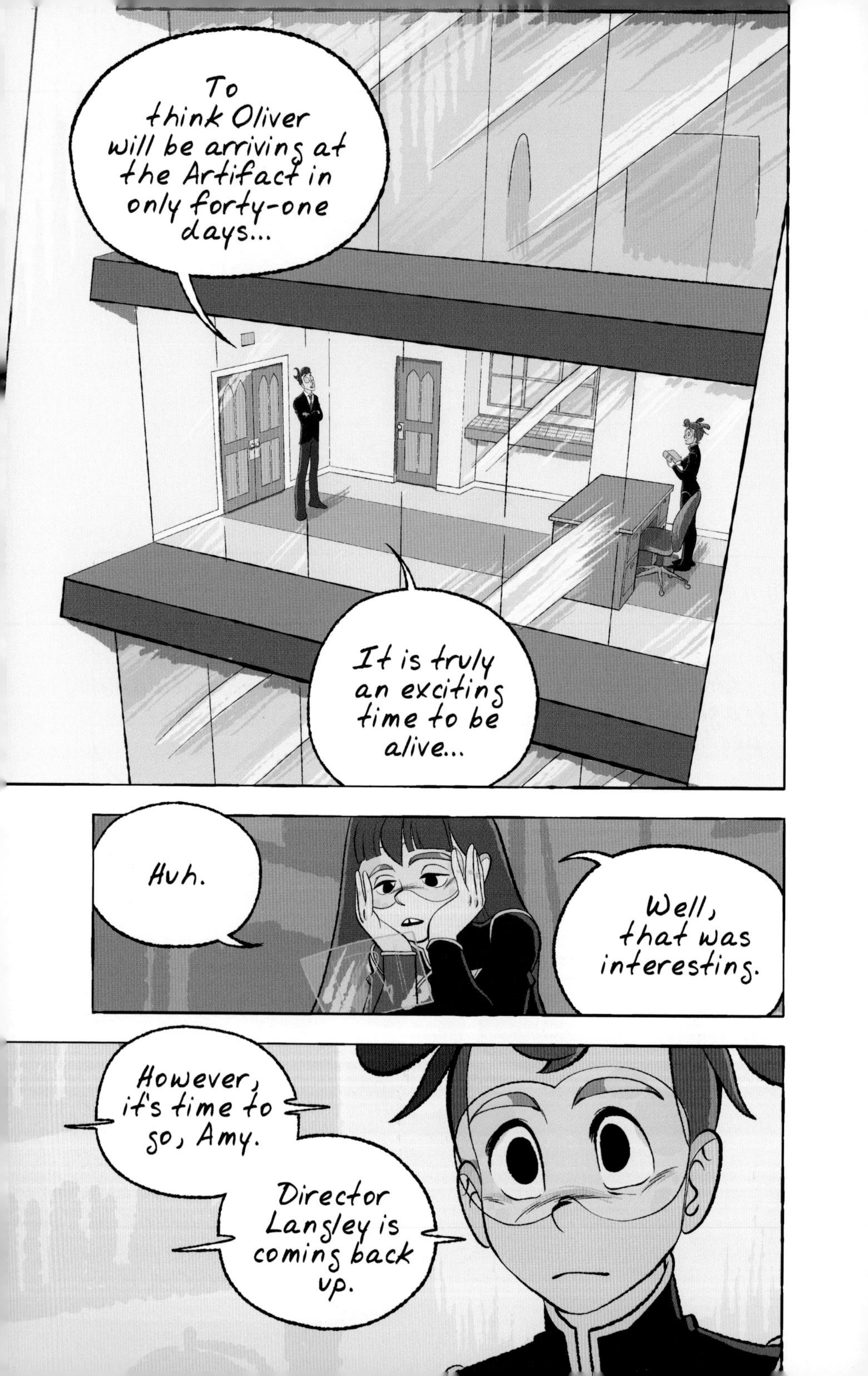
To think Oliver will be arriving at the Artifact in only forty-one days...
It is truly an exciting time to be alive...
Huh.
Well, that was interesting.
However, it's time to go, Amy.
Director Langley is coming back up.

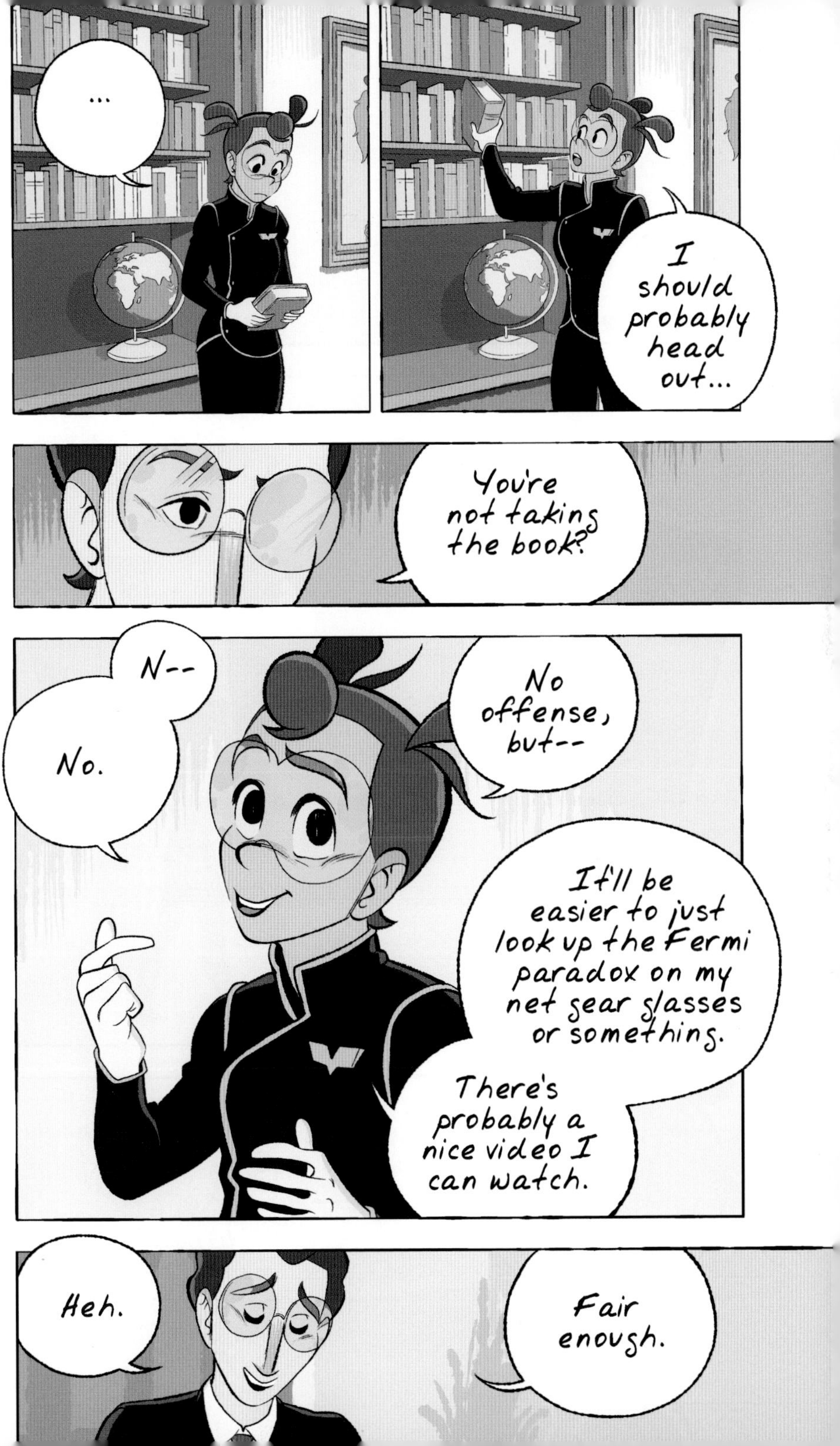
...
I should probably head out...
You're not taking the book?
N--
No.
No offense, but--
It'll be easier to just look up the Fermi paradox on my net gear glasses or something.
There's probably a nice video I can watch.
Heh.
Fair enough.

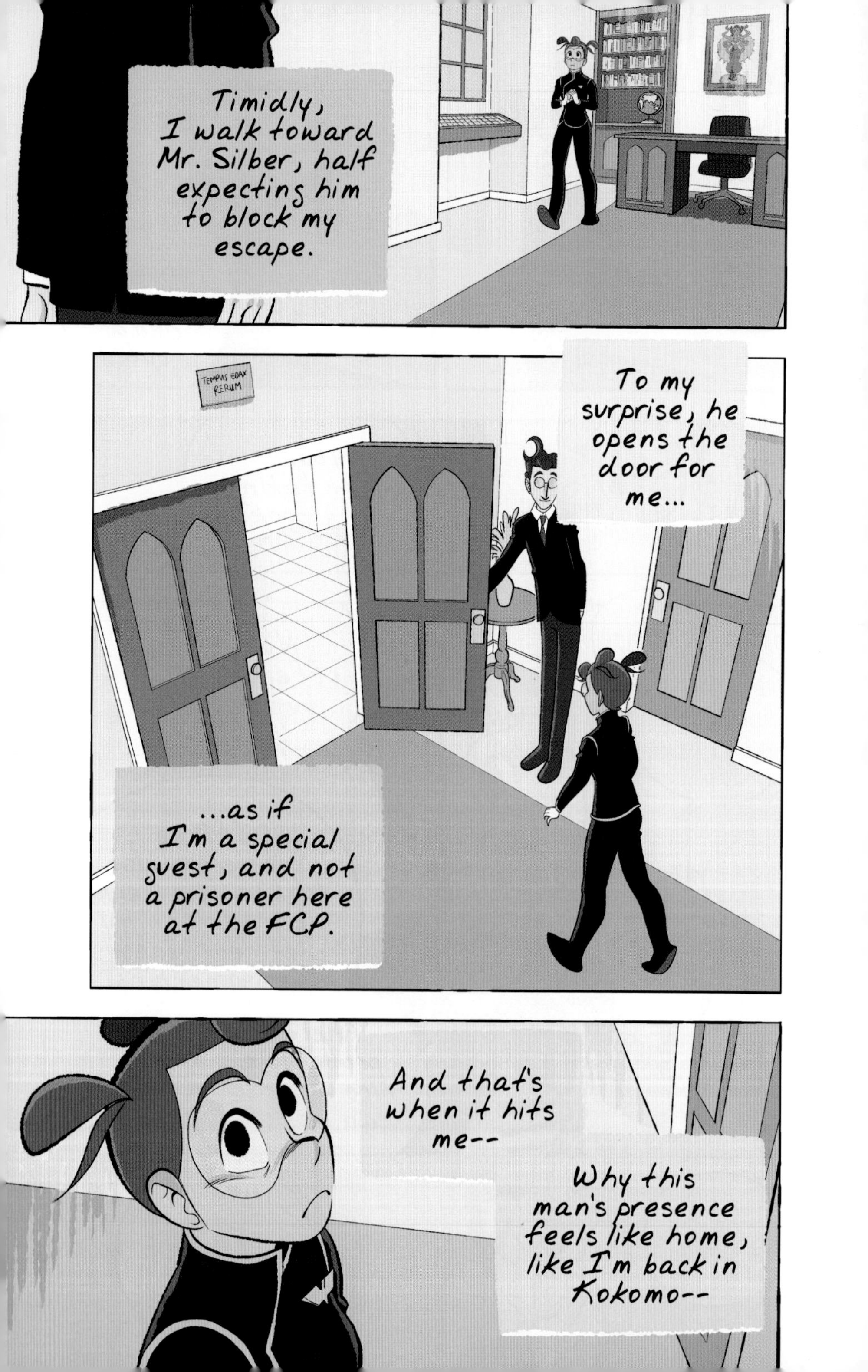
Timidly, I walk toward Mr. Silber, half expecting him to block my escape.
TEMPUS EDAX RERUM
To my surprise, he opens the door for me...
...as if I'm a special guest, and not a prisoner here at the FCP.
And that's when it hits me--
Why this man's presence feels like home, like I'm back in Kokomo--

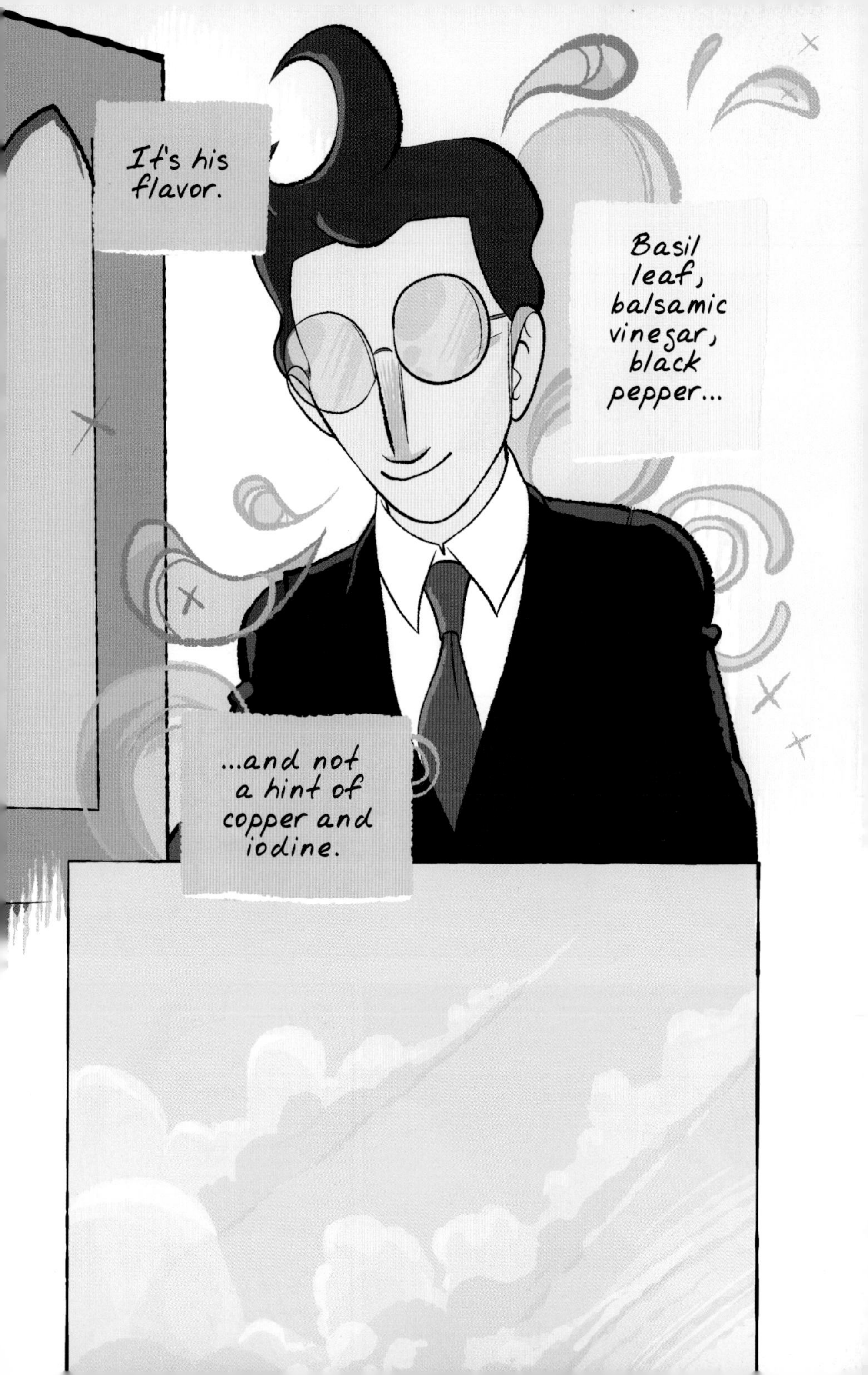
It's his flavor.
Basil leaf, balsamic vinegar, black pepper...
...and not a hint of copper and iodine.

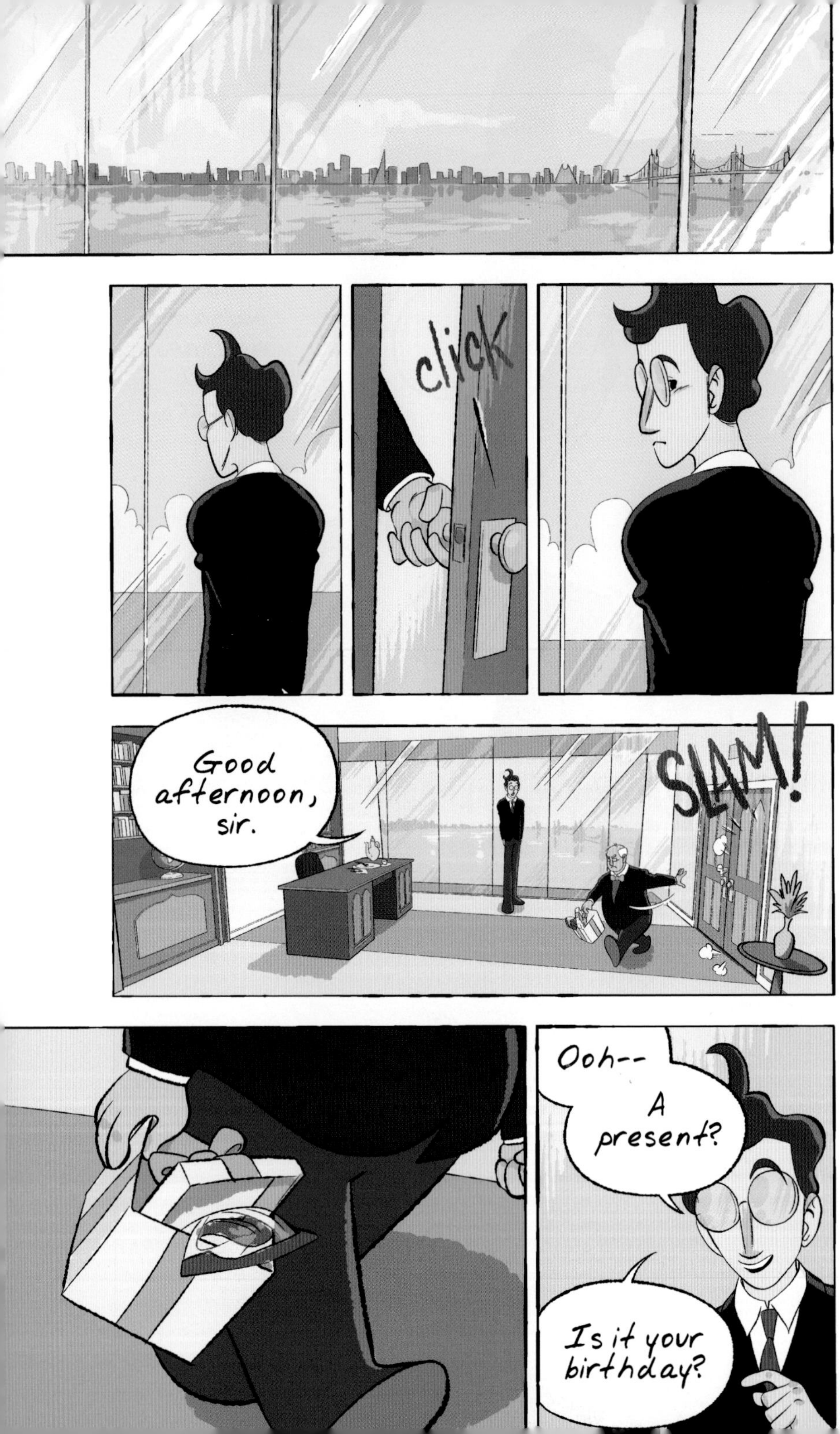
click
Good afternoon, sir.
SLAM!
Ooh--
A present?
Is it your birthday?

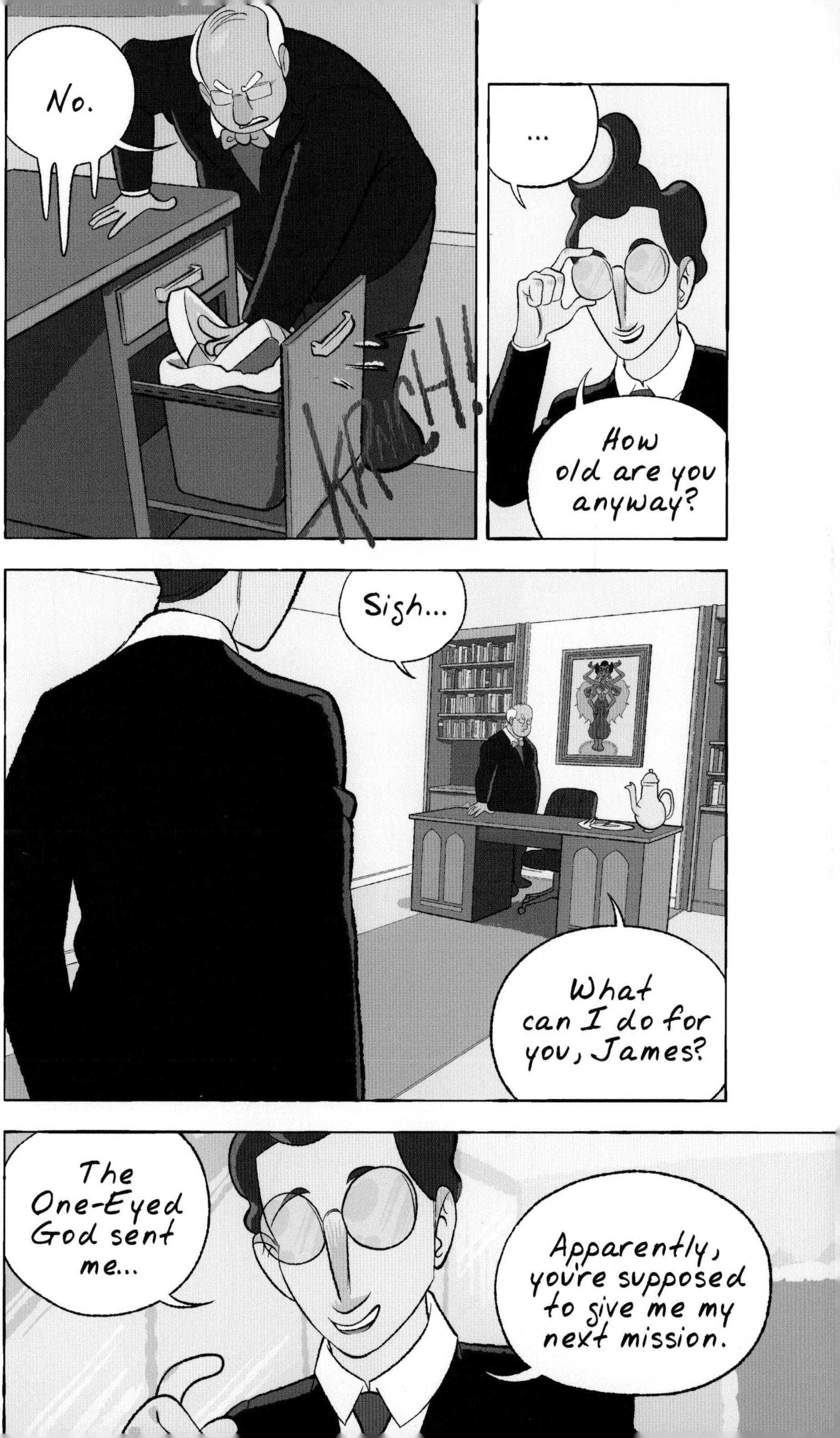
No.
KRUNCH!
...
How old are you anyway?
Sigh...
What can I do for you, James?
The One-Eyed God sent me...
Apparently, you're supposed to give me my next mission.

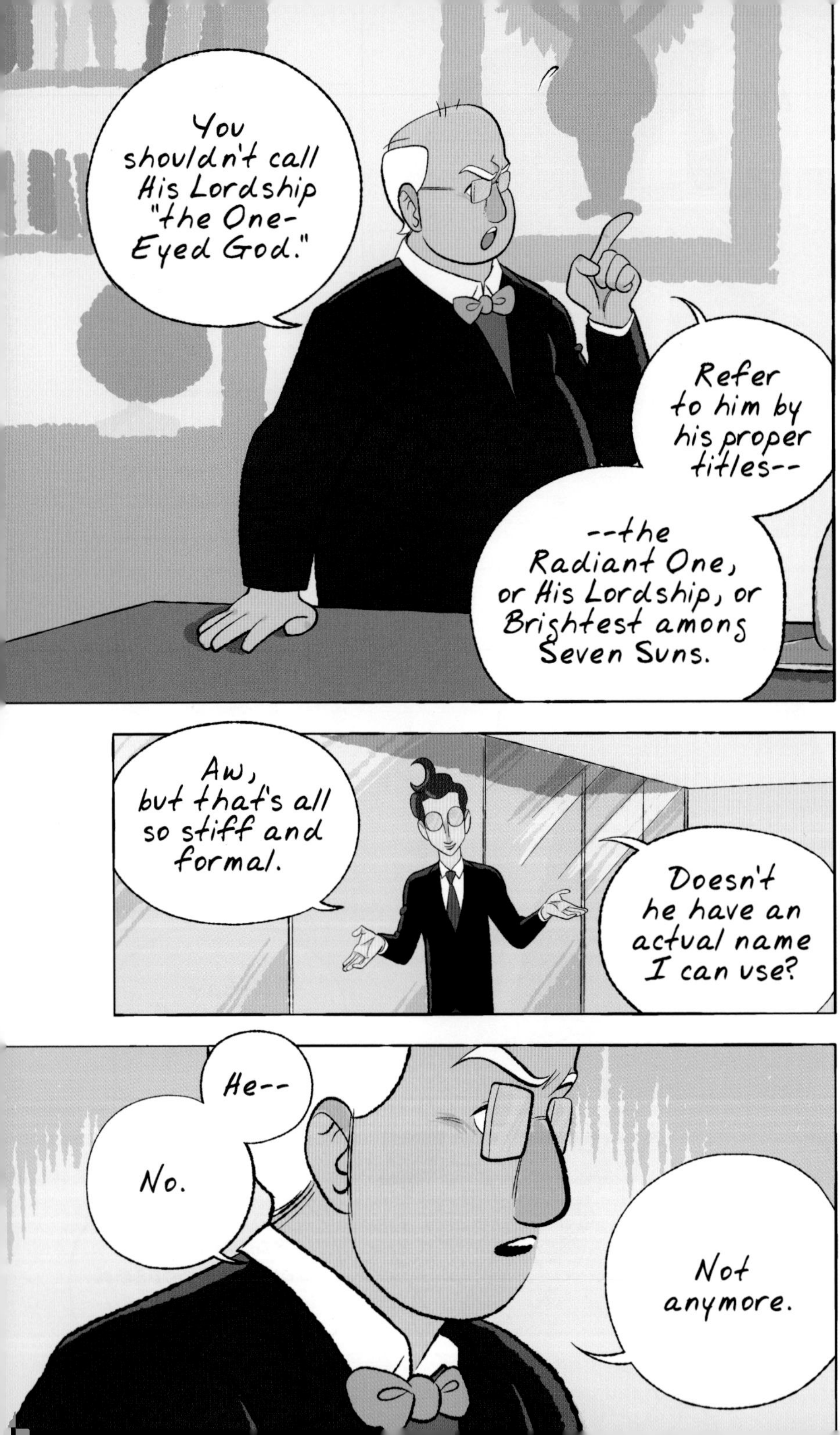
You shouldn't call His Lordship "the One-Eyed God."
Refer to him by his proper titles--
--the Radiant One, or His Lordship, or Brightest among Seven Suns.
Aw, but that's all so stiff and formal.
Doesn't he have an actual name I can use?
He--
No.
Not anymore.

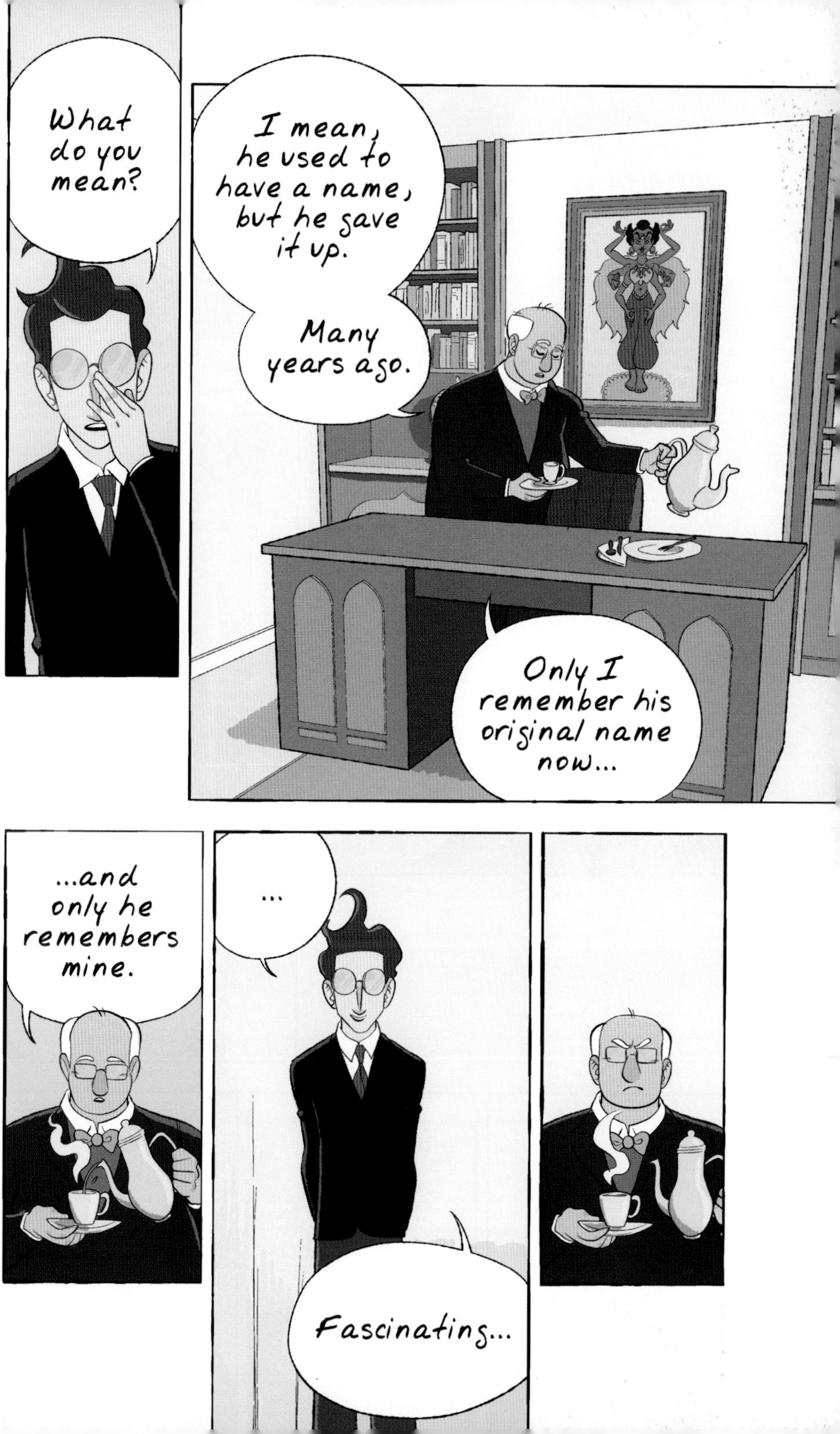
What do you mean?
I mean, he used to have a name, but he gave it up.
Many years ago.
Only I remember his original name now...
...and only he remembers mine.
...
Fascinating...

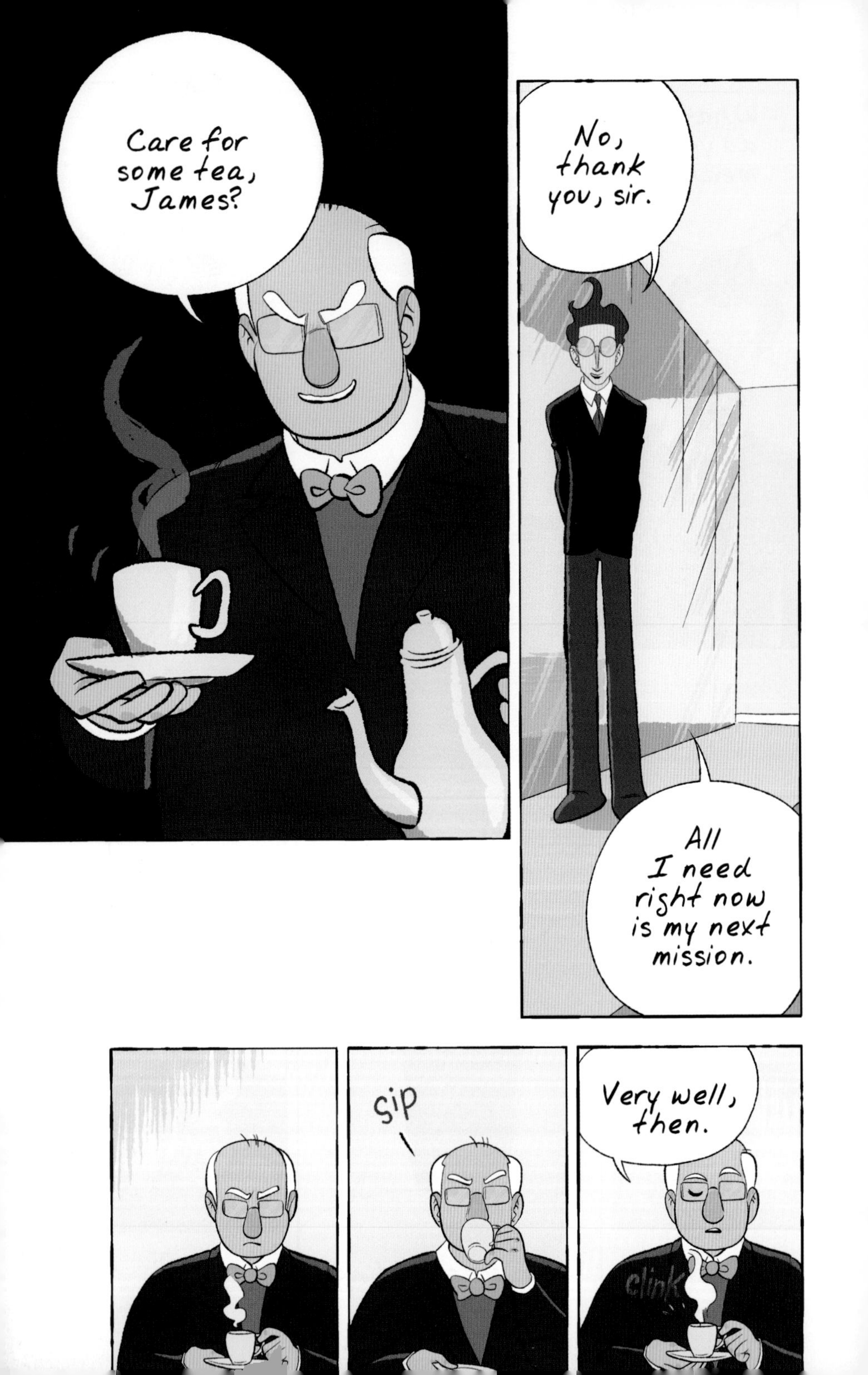
Care for some tea, James?
No, thank you, sir.
All I need right now is my next mission.
sip
Very well, then.
clink

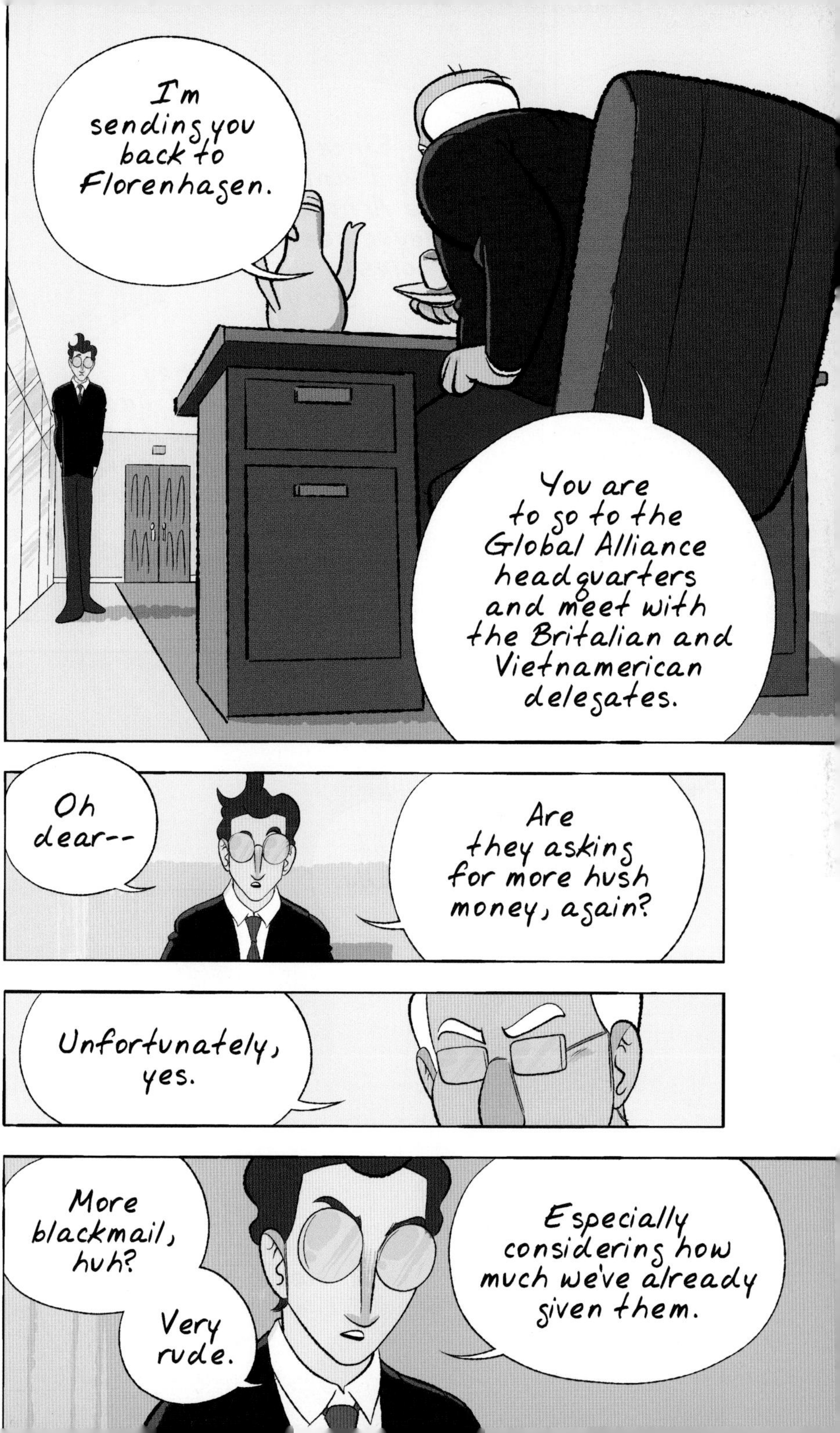
I'm sending you back to Florenhagen.
You are to go to the Global Alliance headquarters and meet with the Britalian and Vietnamerican delegates.
Oh dear--
Are they asking for more hush money, again?
Unfortunately, yes.
More blackmail, huh?
Very rude.
Especially considering how much we've already given them.

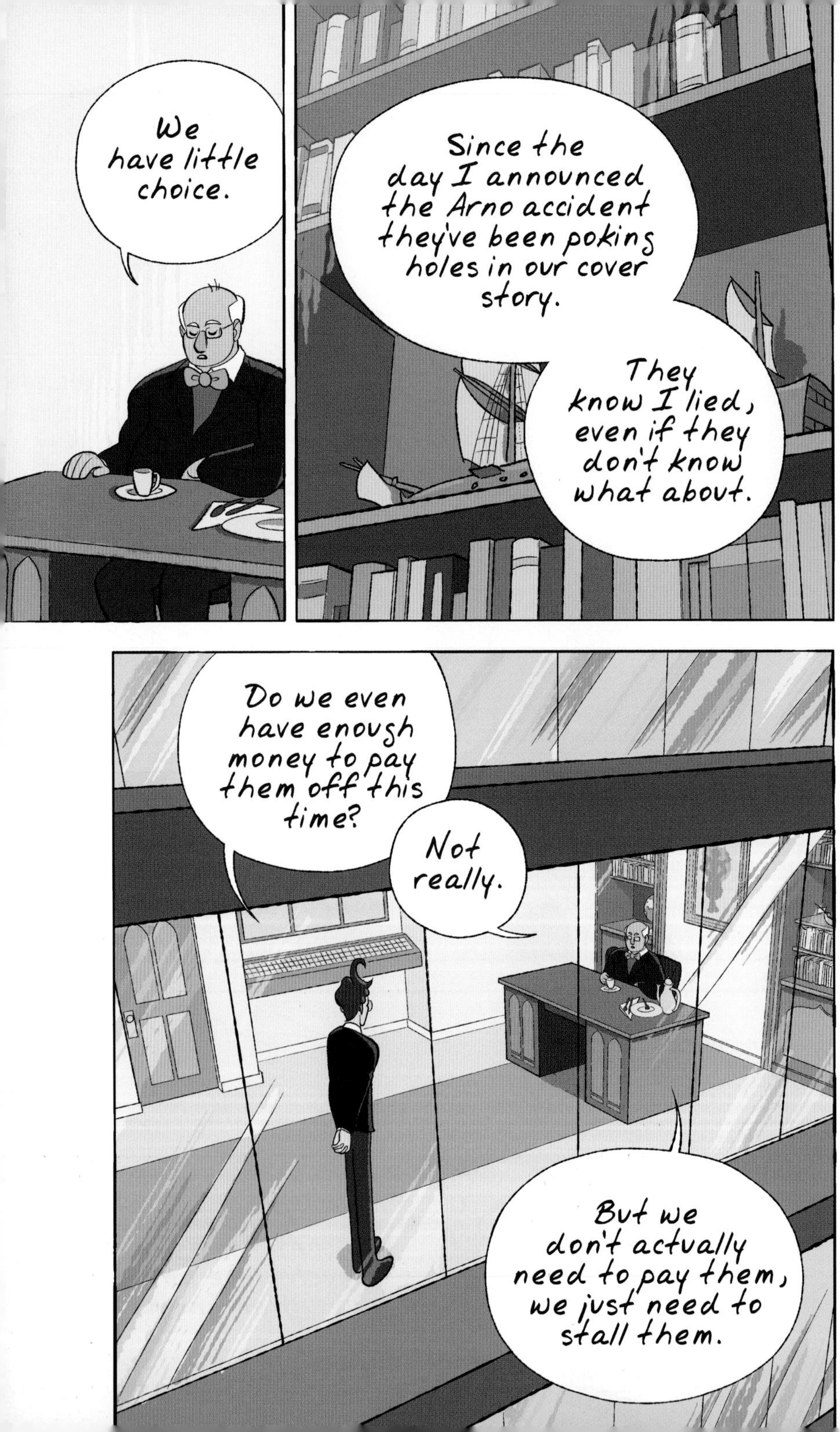
We have little choice.
Since the day I announced the Arno accident they've been poking holes in our cover story.
They know I lied, even if they don't know what about.
Do we even have enough money to pay them off this time?
Not really.
But we don't actually need to pay them, we just need to stall them.

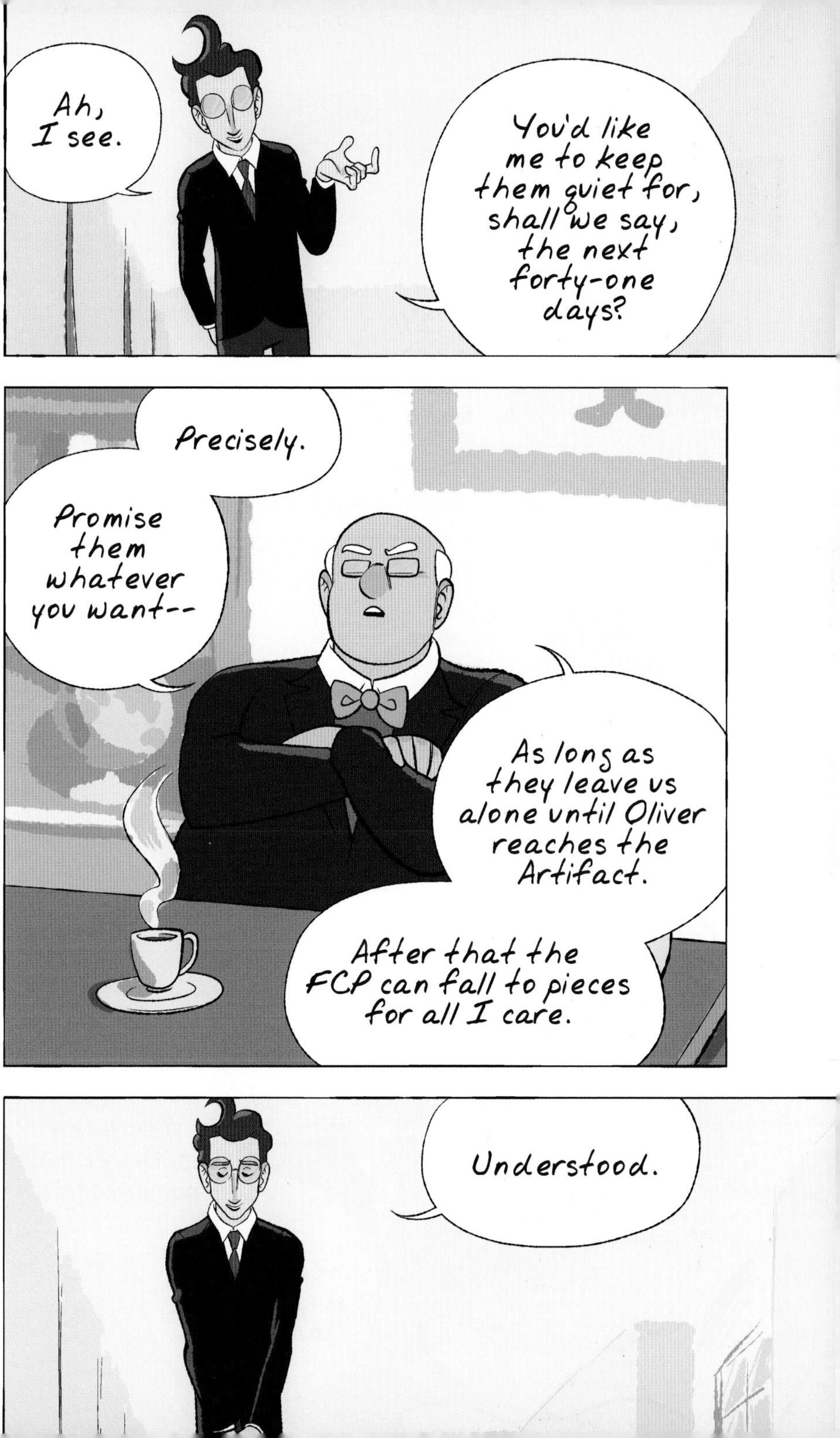
Ah, I see.
You'd like me to keep them quiet for, shall we say, the next forty-one days?
Precisely.
Promise them whatever you want--
As long as they leave us alone until Oliver reaches the Artifact.
After that the FCP can fall to pieces for all I care.
Understood.

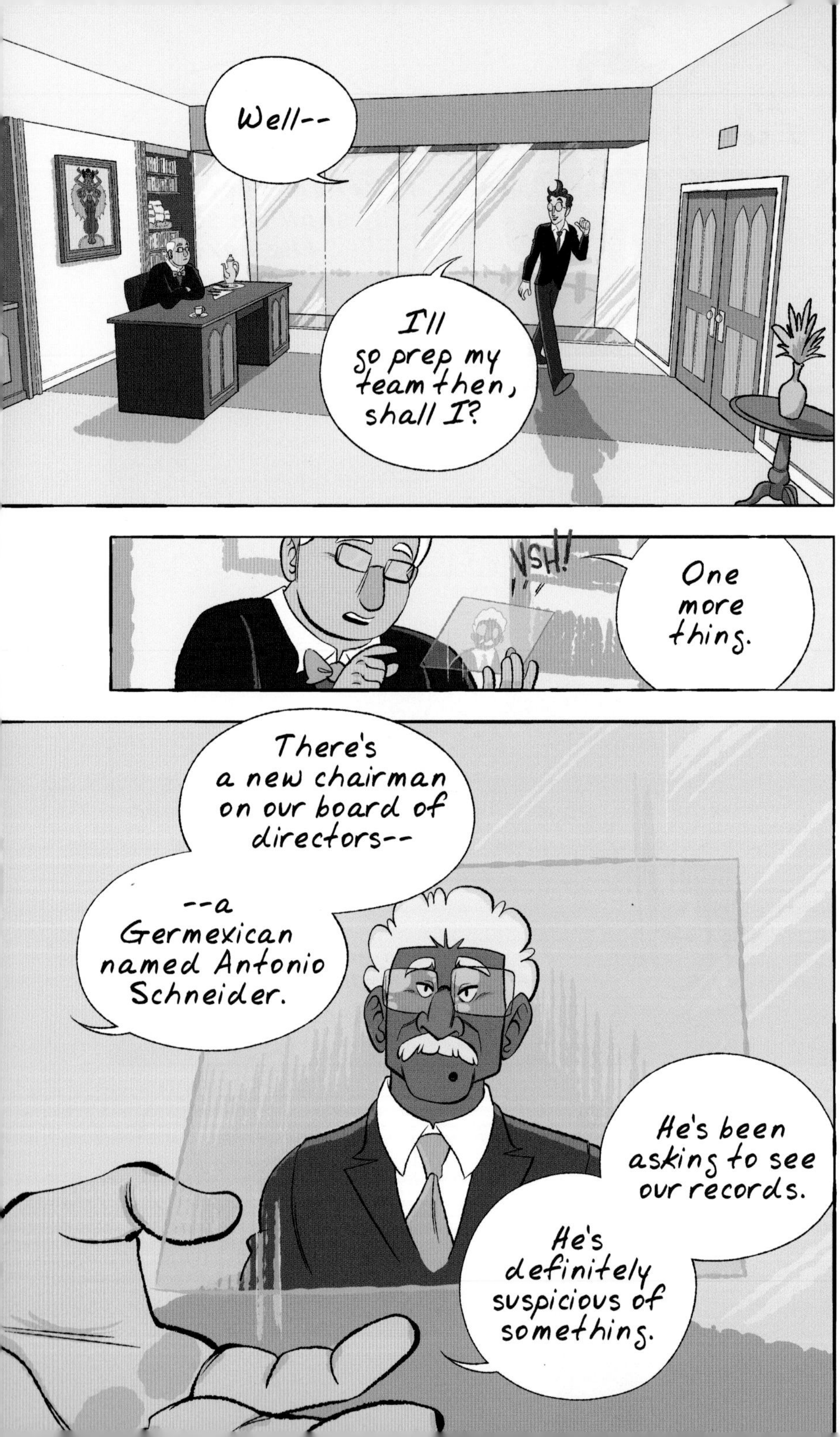
Well--
I'll go prep my team then, shall I?
VSH!
One more thing.
There's a new chairman on our board of directors--
--a Germexican named Antonio Schneider.
He's been asking to see our records.
He's definitely suspicious of something.

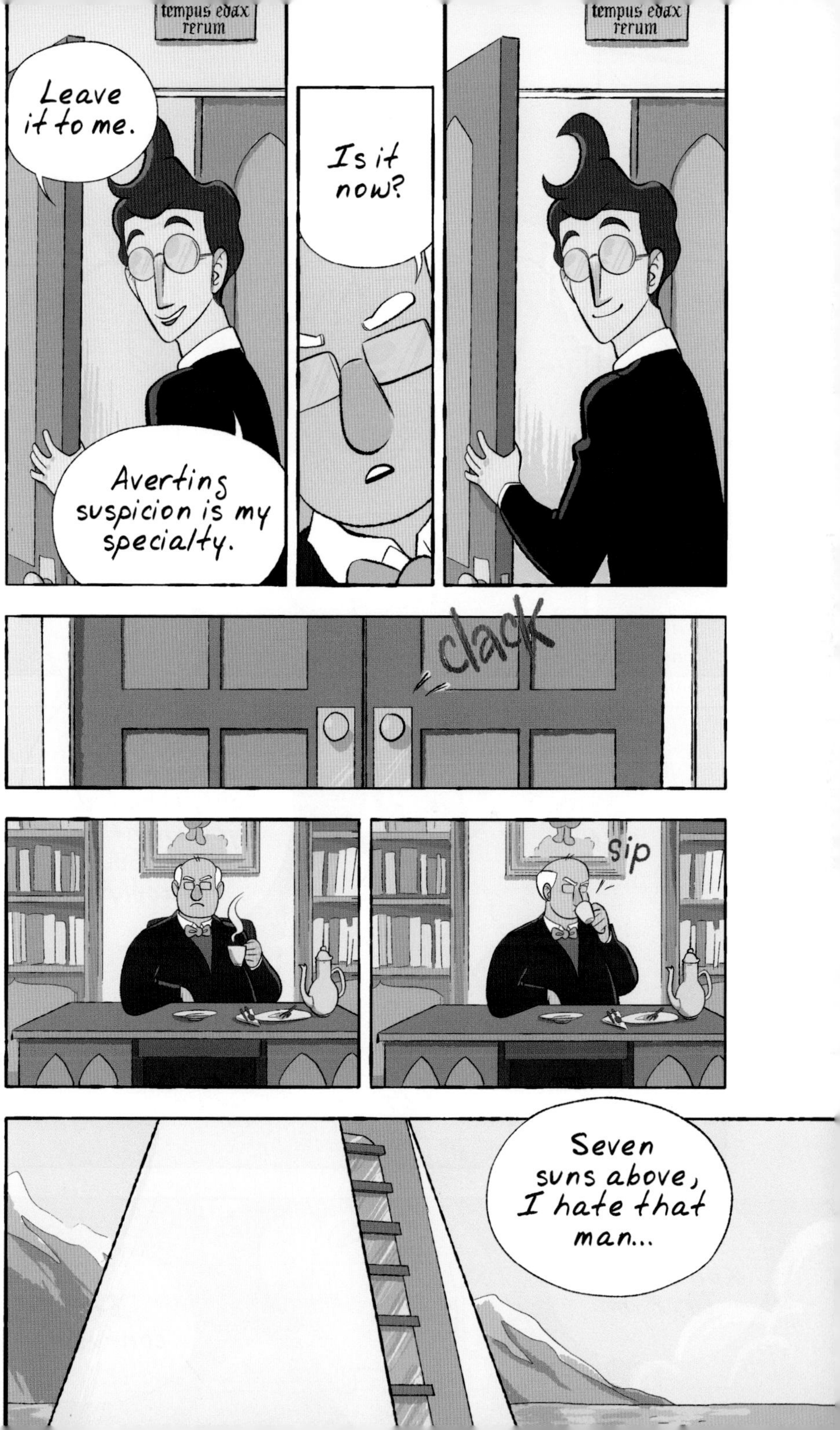
tempus edax rerum
Leave it to me.
Avertins suspicion is my specialty.
Is it now?
tempus edax rerum
clack
sip
Seven suns above, I hate that man...

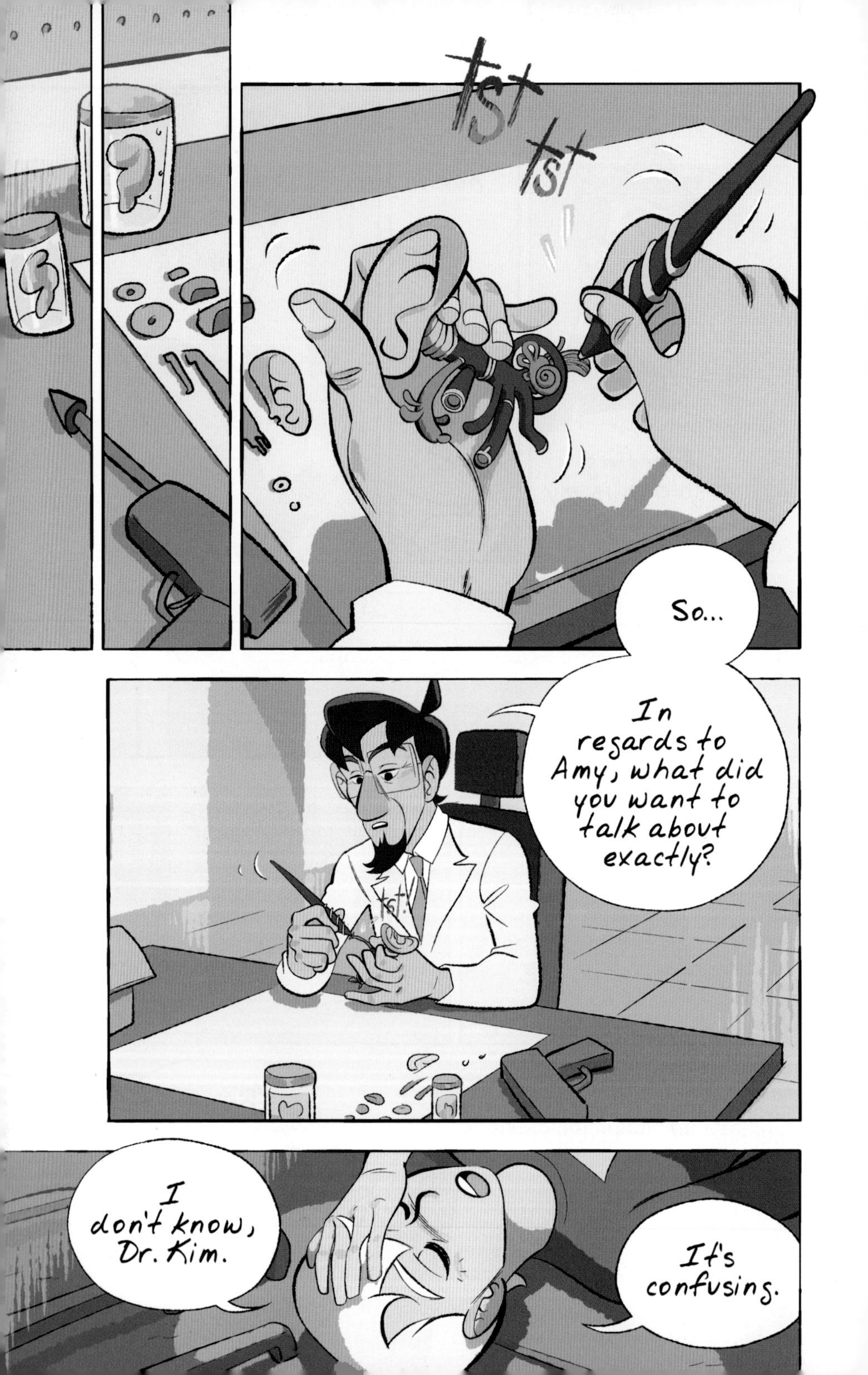
tst tst
So...
In regards to Amy, what did you want to talk about exactly?
tst
I don't know, Dr. Kim.
It's confusing.

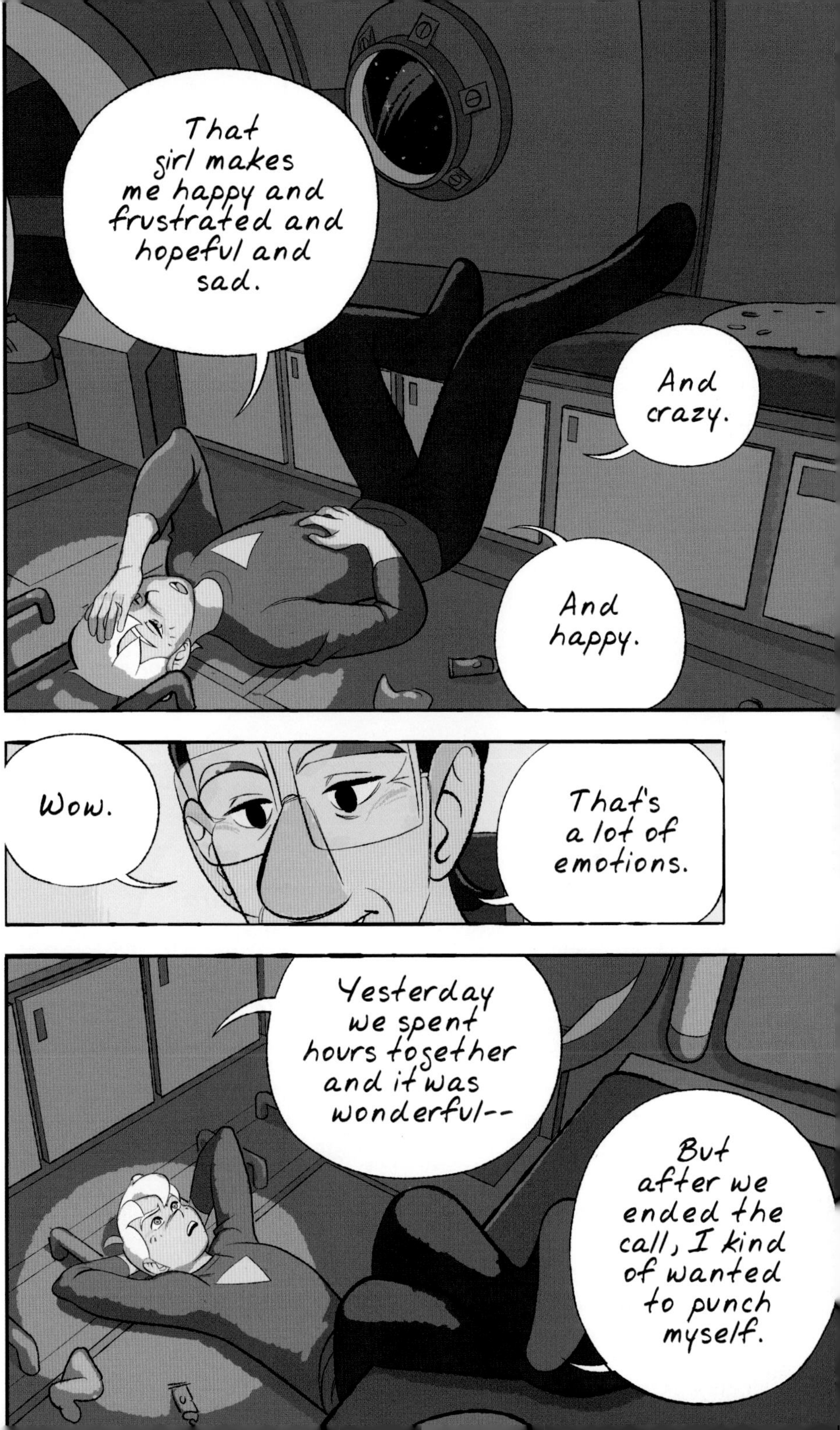

That girl makes me happy and frustrated and hopeful and sad.
And crazy.
And happy.
Wow.
That's a lot of emotions.
Yesterday we spent hours together and it was wonderful--
But after we ended the call, I kind of wanted to punch myself.

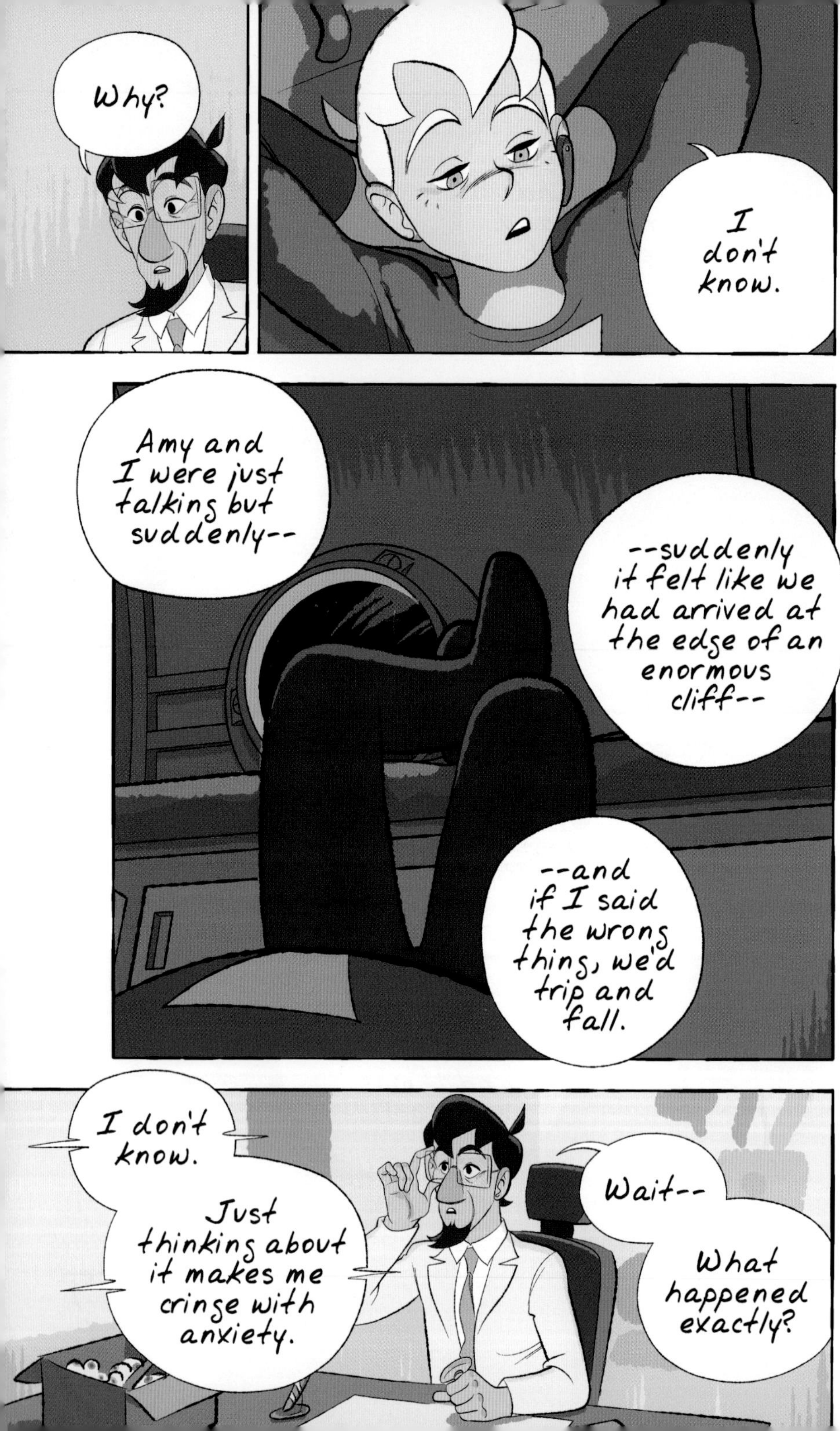
Why?
I don't know.
Amy and I were just talking but suddenly--
--suddenly it felt like we had arrived at the edge of an enormous cliff--
--and if I said the wrong thing, we'd trip and fall.
I don't know.
Just thinking about it makes me cringe with anxiety.
Wait--
What happened exactly?

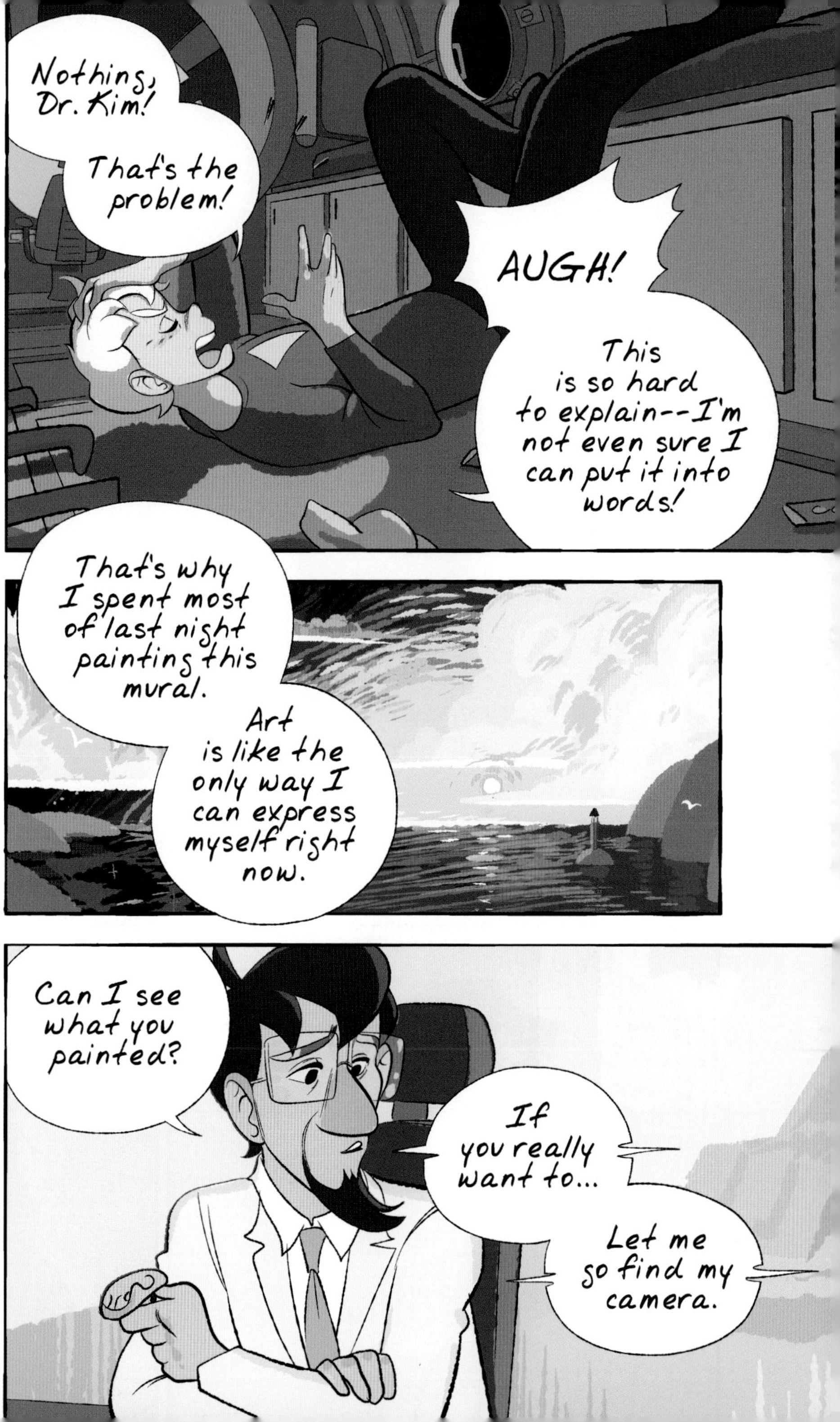
Nothing, Dr. Kim!
That's the problem!
AUGH!
This is so hard to explain--I'm not even sure I can put it into words!
That's why I spent most of last night painting this mural.
Art is like the only way I can express myself right now.
Can I see what you painted?
If you really want to...
Let me go find my camera.

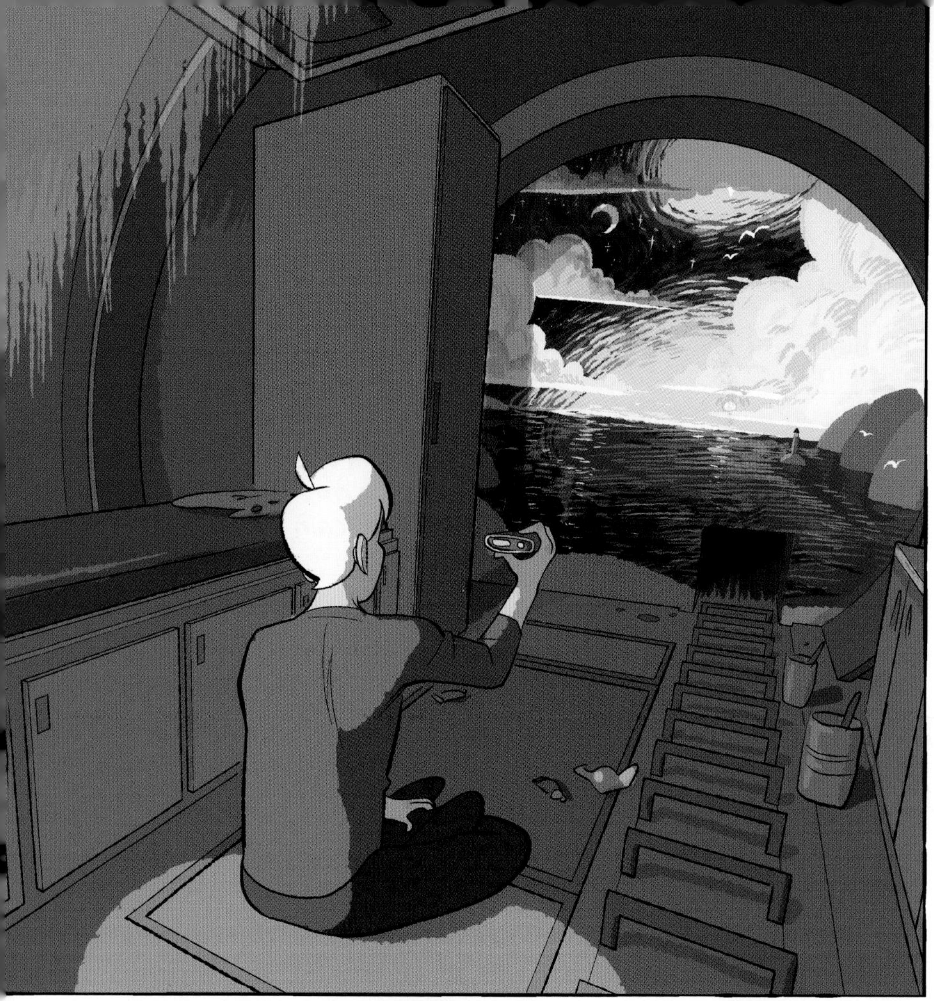

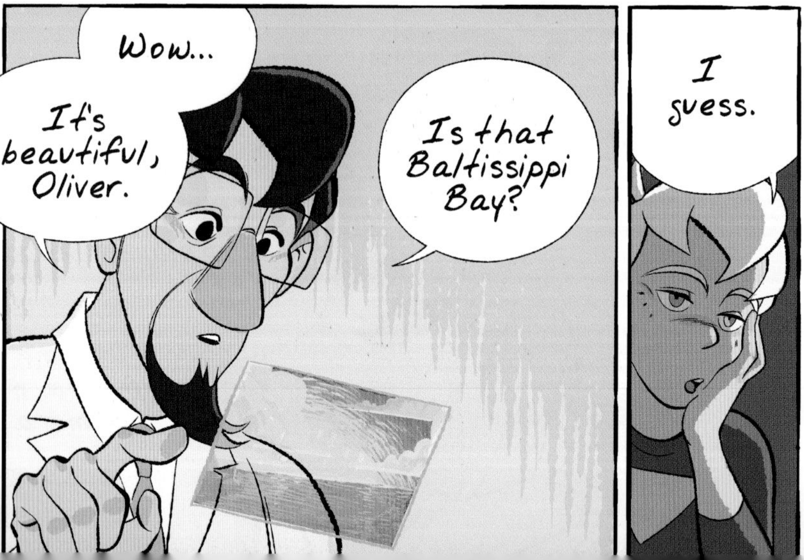

Wow...
It's beautiful, Oliver.
Is that Baltissippi Bay?
I guess.

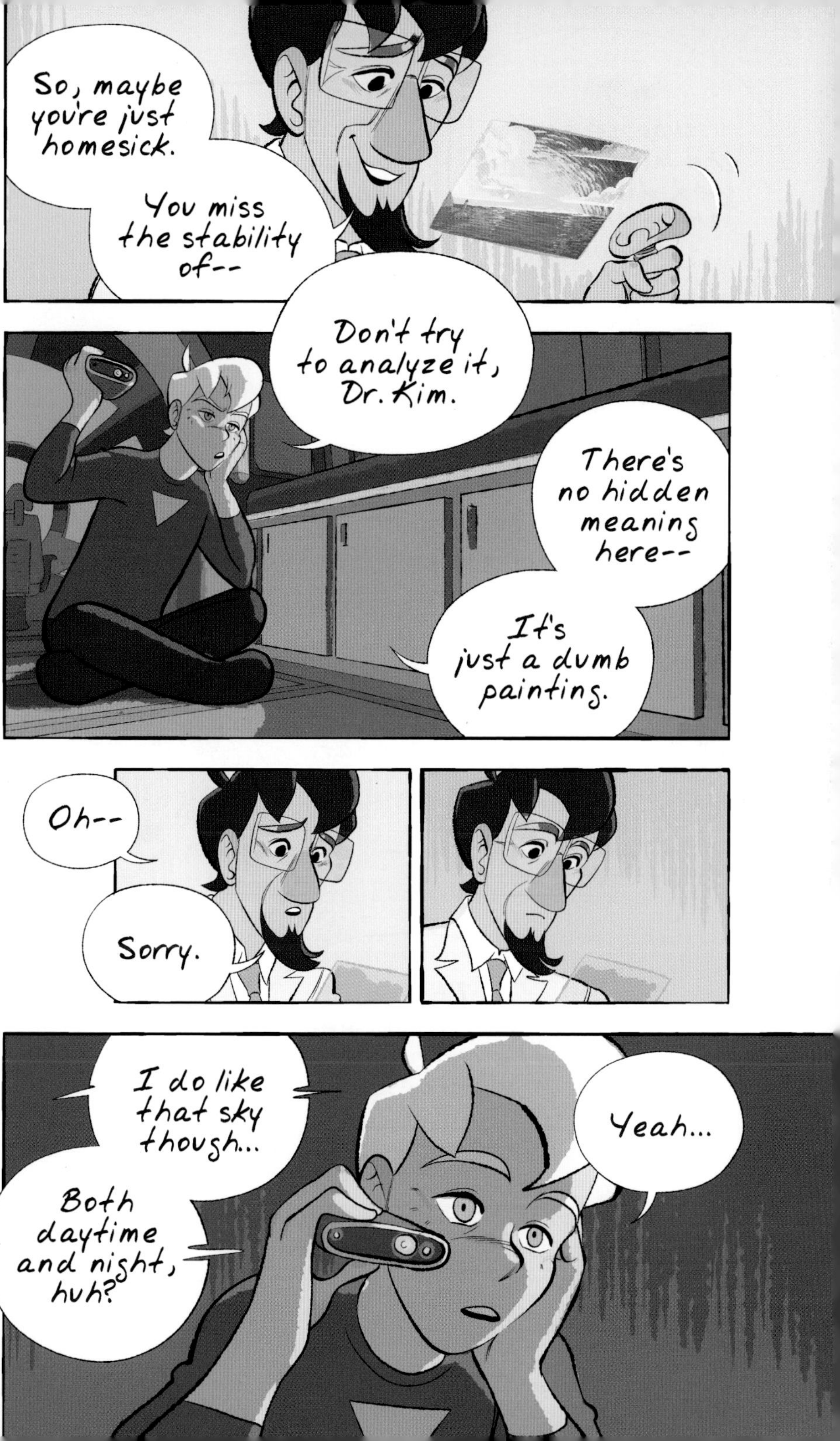
So, maybe you're just homesick.
You miss the stability of--
Don't try to analyze it, Dr. Kim.
There's no hidden meaning here--
It's just a dumb painting.
Oh--
Sorry.
I do like that sky though...
Both daytime and night, huh?
Yeah...

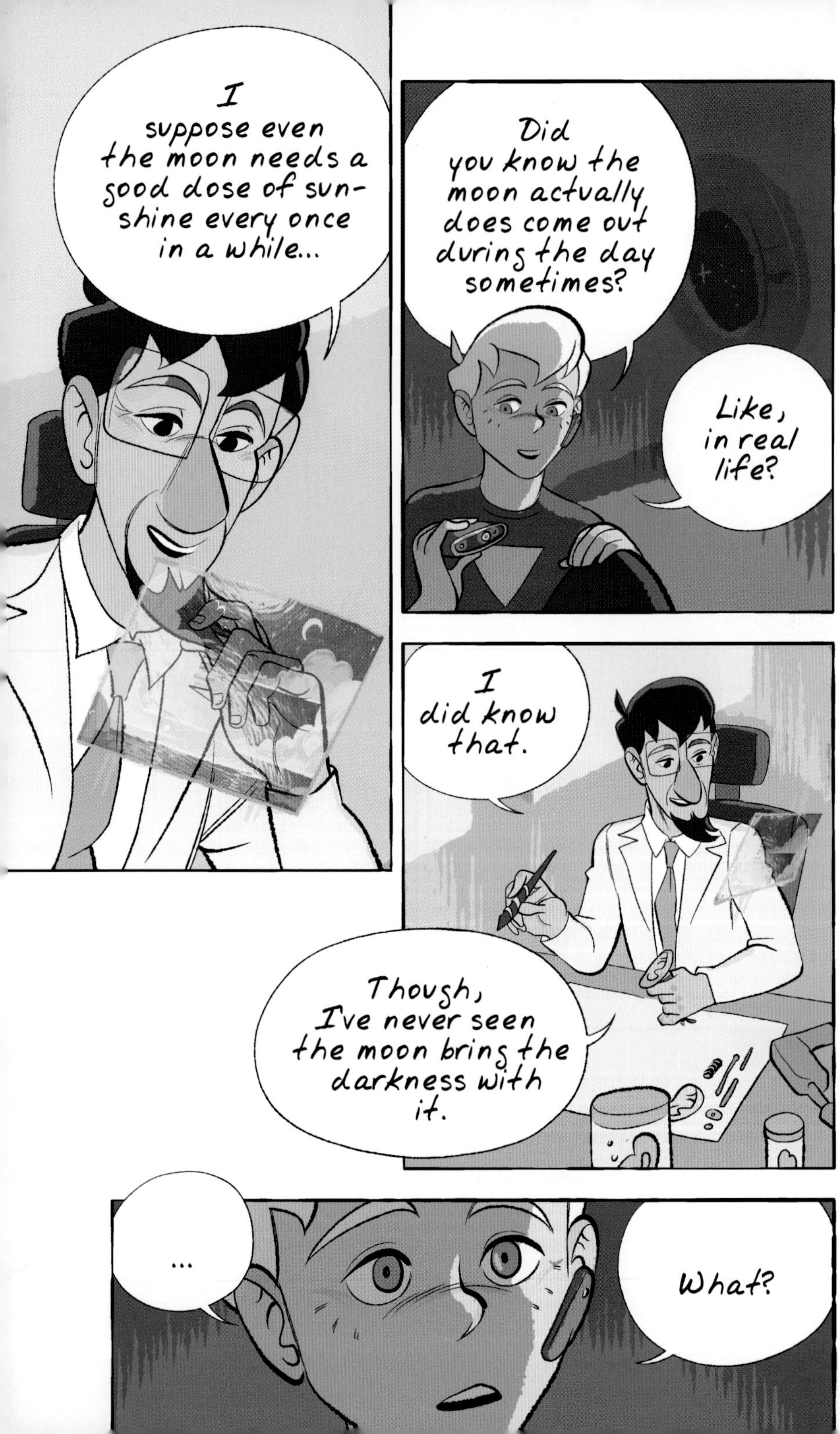
I suppose even the moon needs a good dose of sun-shine every once in a while...
Did you know the moon actually does come out during the day sometimes?
Like, in real life?
I did know that.
Though, I've never seen the moon bring the darkness with it.
...
What?

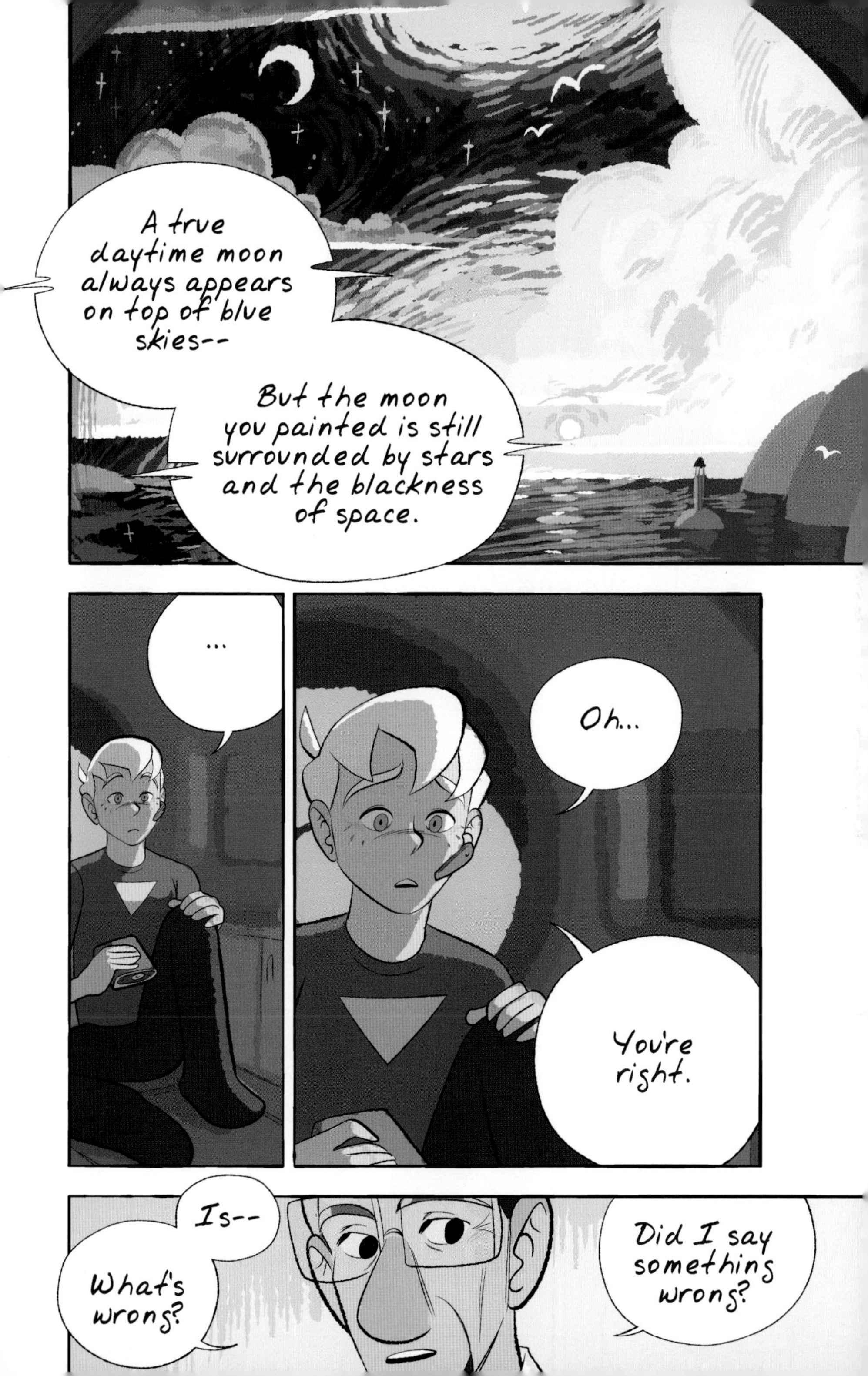

A true daytime moon always appears on top of blue skies--
But the moon you painted is still surrounded by stars and the blackness of space.
...
Oh...
You're right.
Is--
What's wrong?
Did I say something wrong?

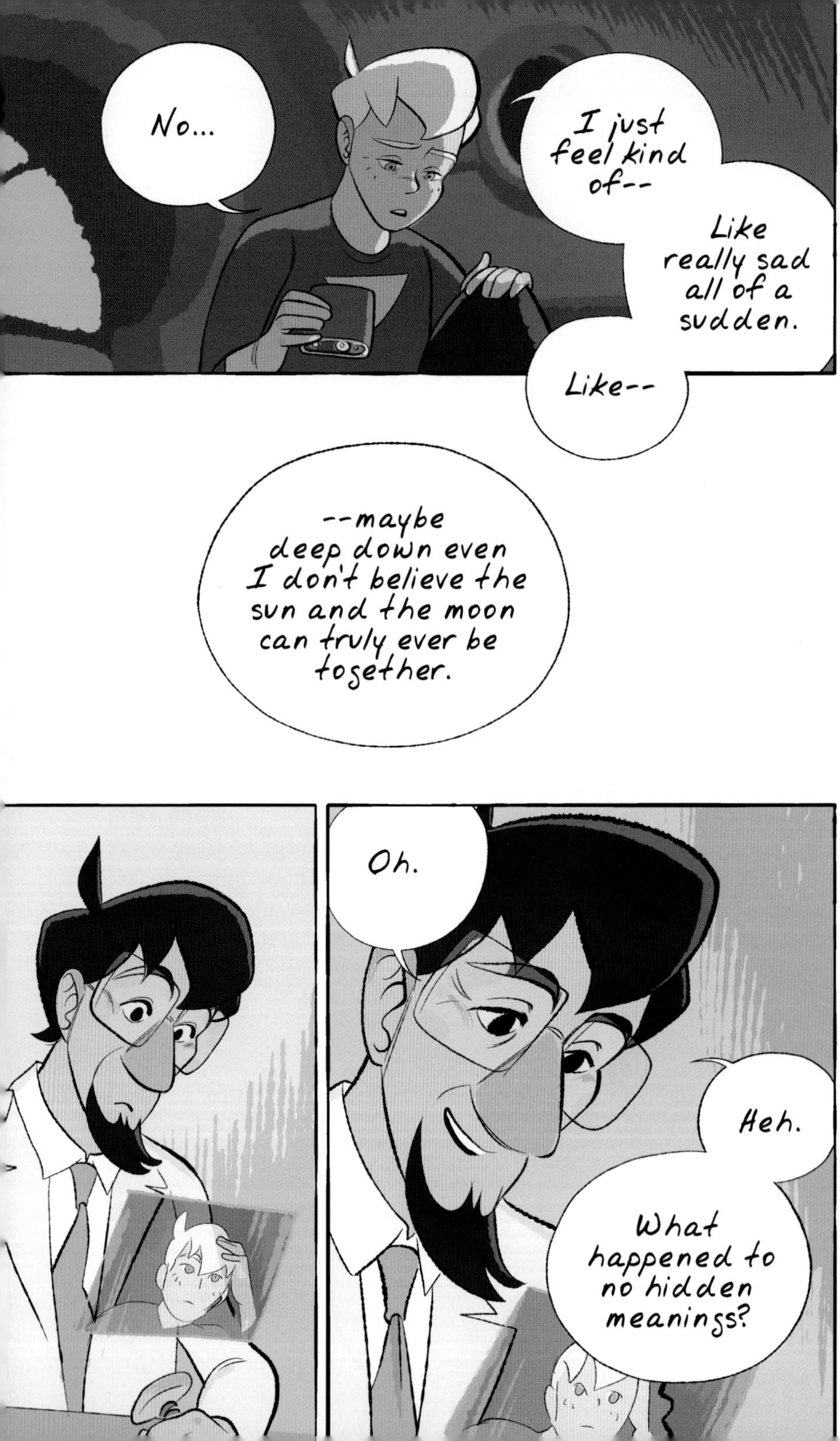
No...
I just feel kind of--
Like really sad all of a sudden.
Like--
--maybe deep down even I don't believe the sun and the moon can truly ever be together.
Oh.
Heh.
What happened to no hidden meanings?

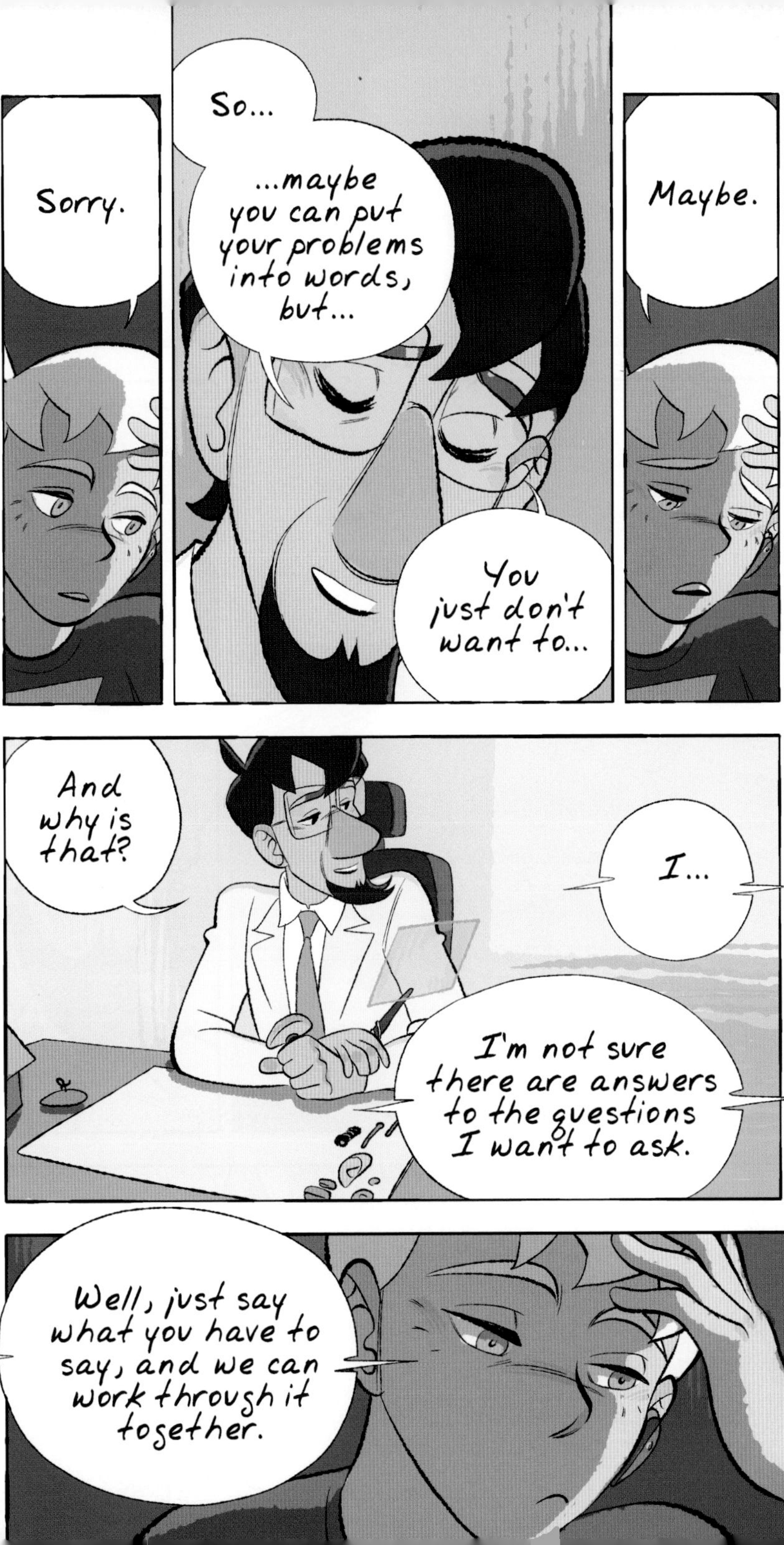
Sorry.
So...
...maybe you can put your problems into words, but...
You just don't want to...
Maybe.
And why is that?
I...
I'm not sure there are answers to the questions I want to ask.
Well, just say what you have to say, and we can work through it together.

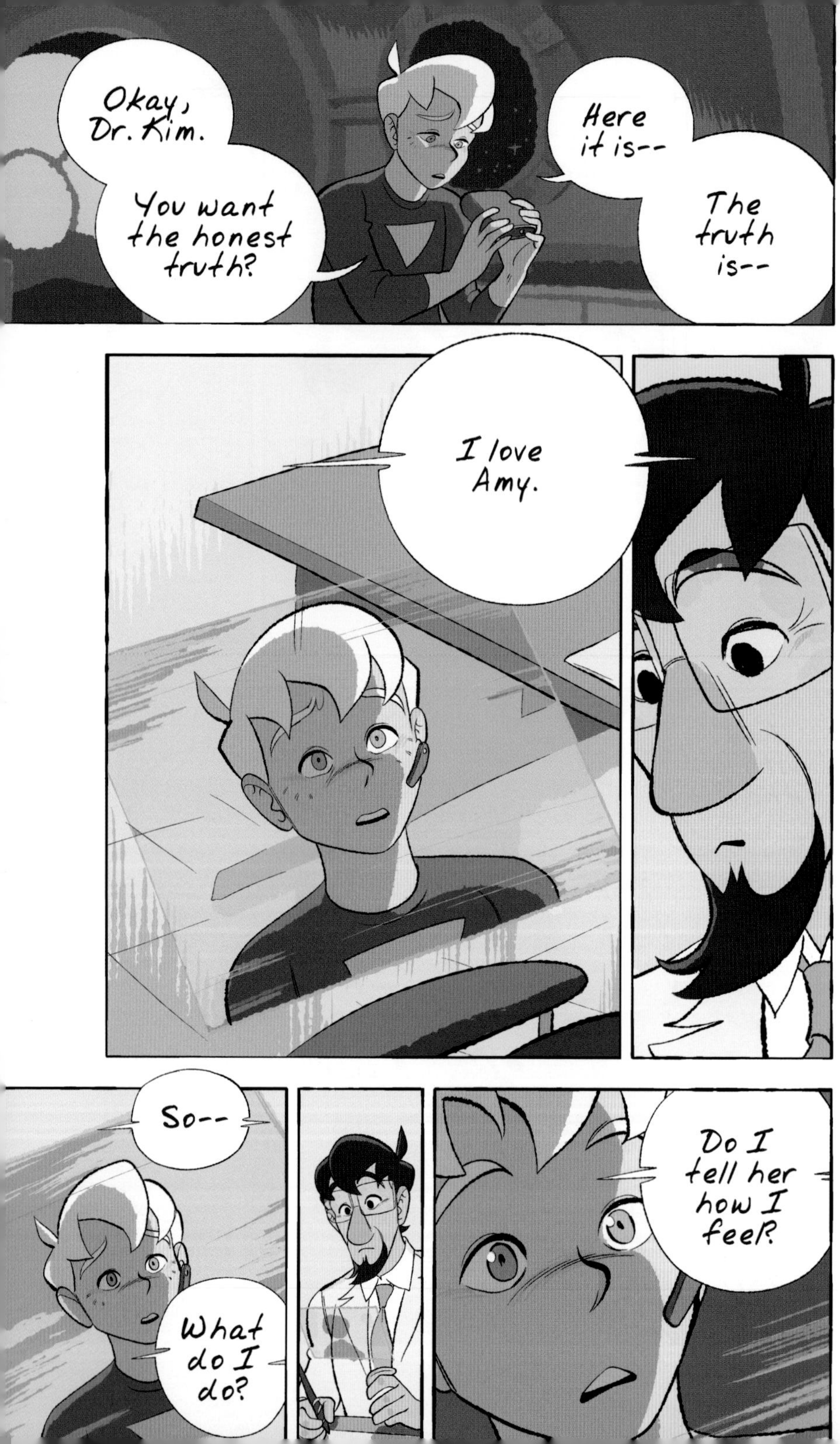
Okay, Dr. Kim.
You want the honest truth?
Here it is--
The truth is--
I love Amy.
So--
What do I do?
Do I tell her how I feel?

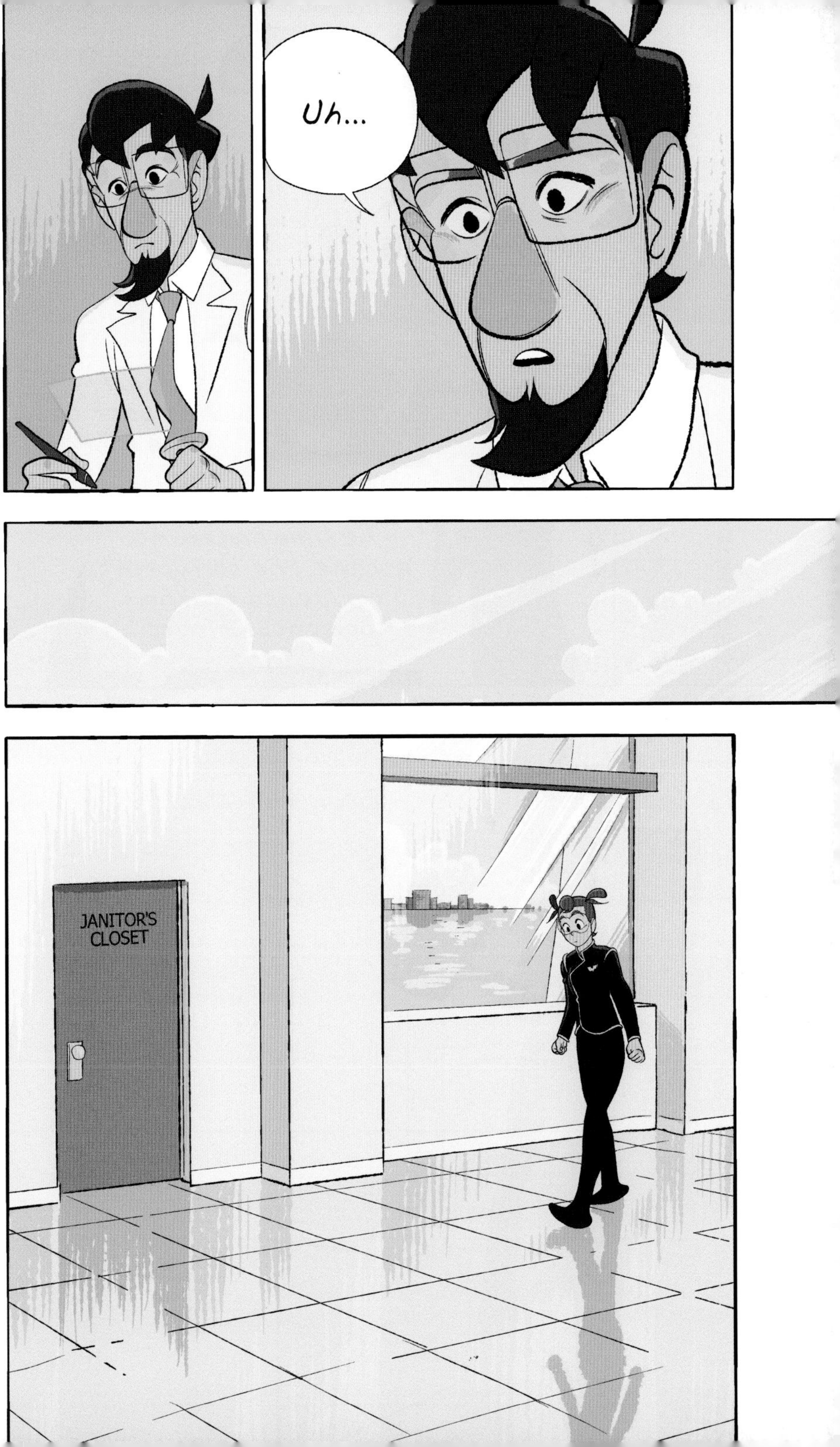
Uh...
JANITOR'S CLOSET

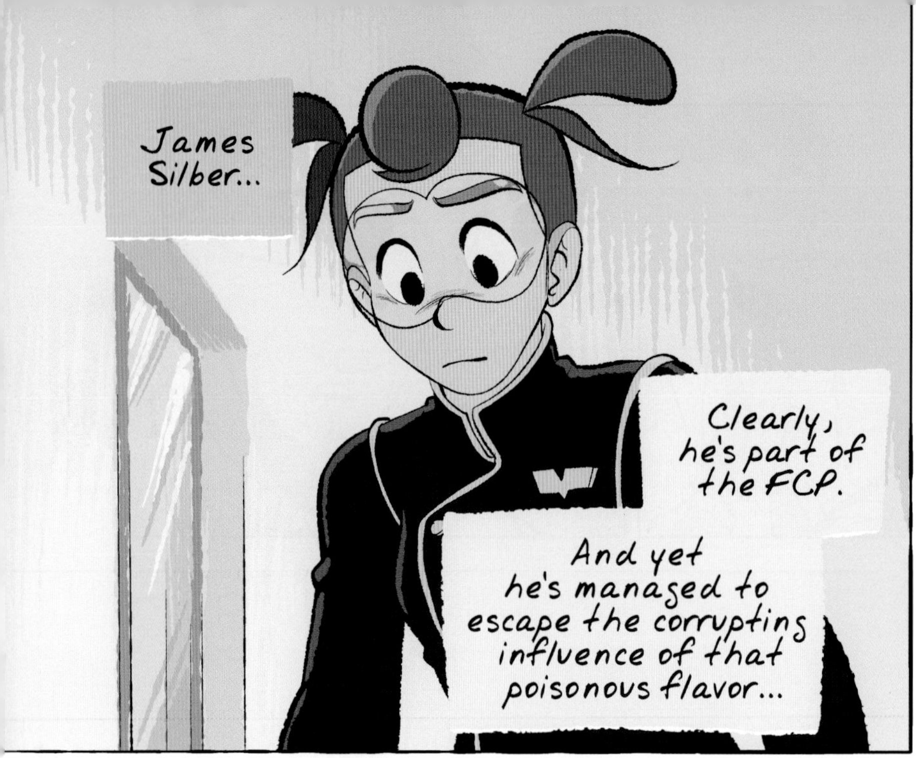
James Silber...
Clearly, he's part of the FCP.
And yet he's managed to escape the corrupting influence of that poisonous flavor...

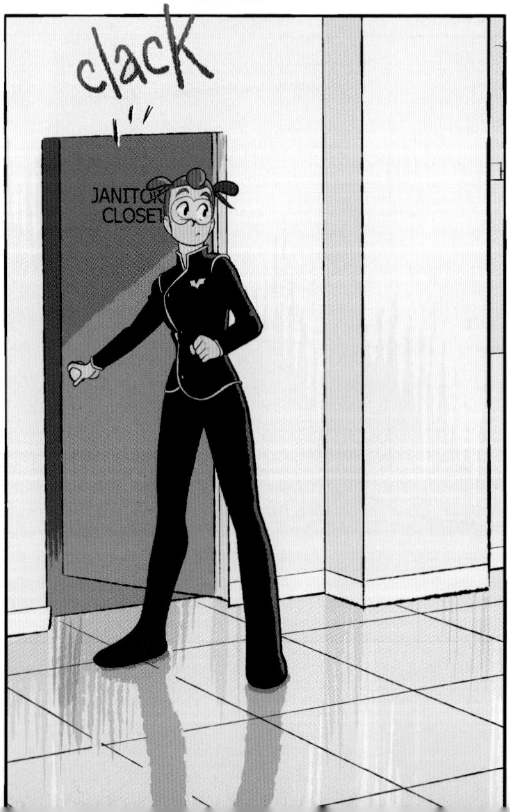
clack
JANITOR'S CLOSET

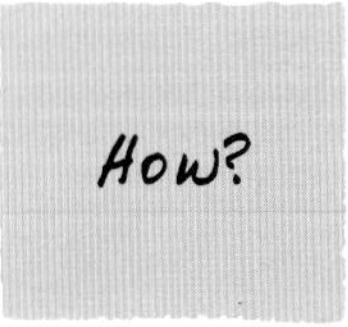
How?

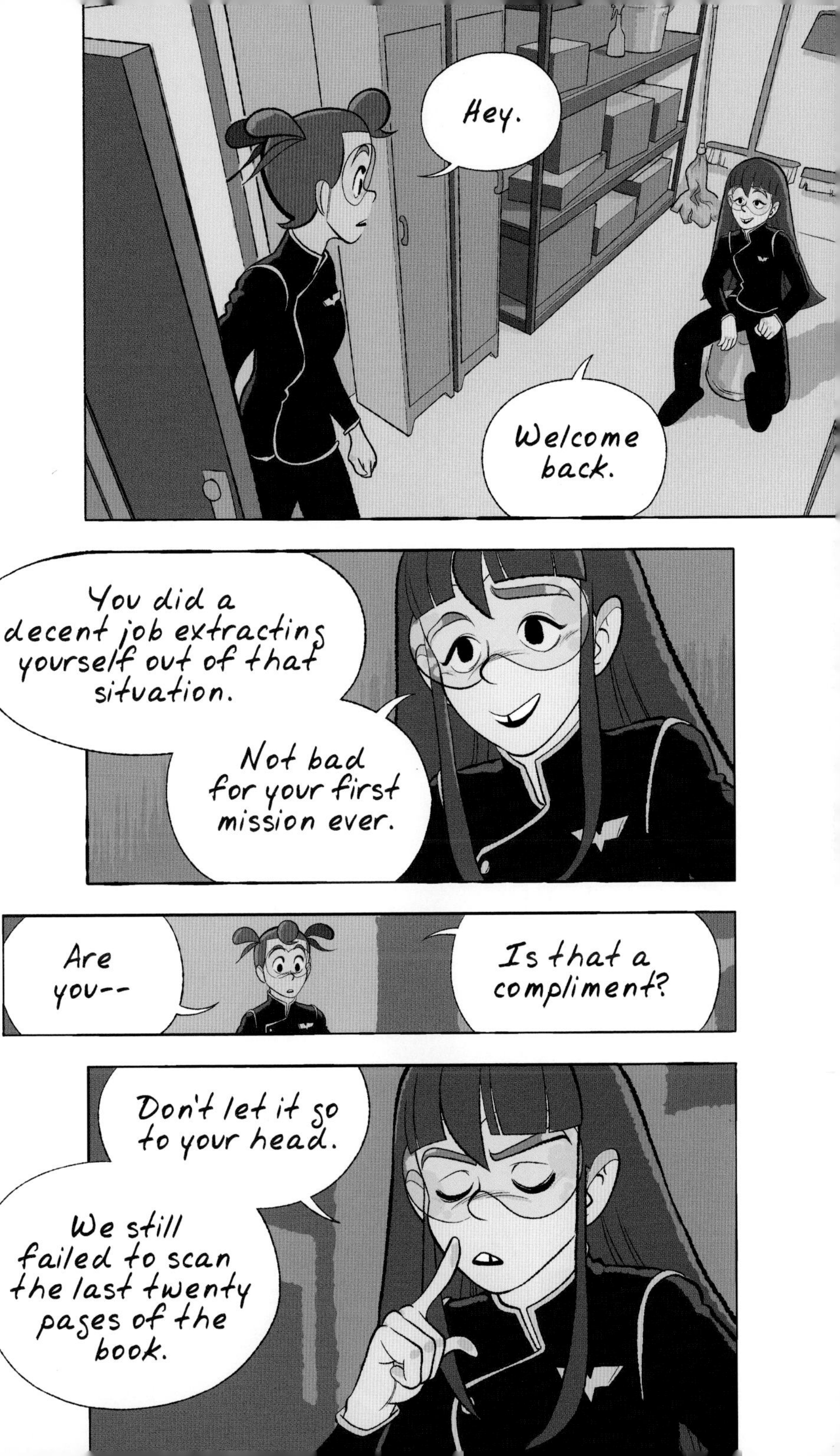
Hey.
Welcome back.
You did a decent job extracting yourself out of that situation.
Not bad for your first mission ever.
Are you--
Is that a compliment?
Don't let it go to your head.
We still failed to scan the last twenty pages of the book.

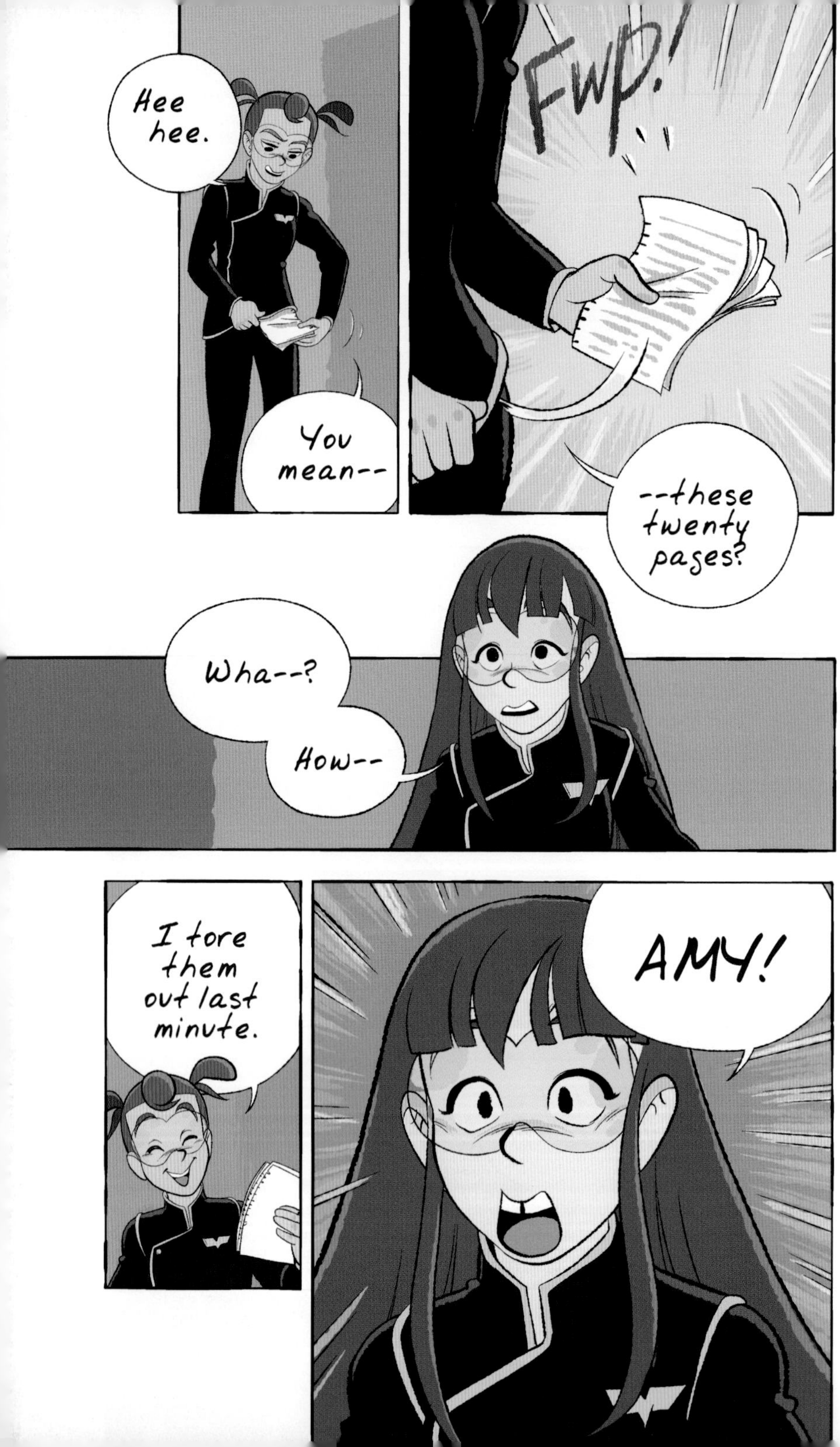
Hee hee.
You mean--
FWP!
--these twenty pages?
Wha--?
How--
I tore them out last minute.
AMY!

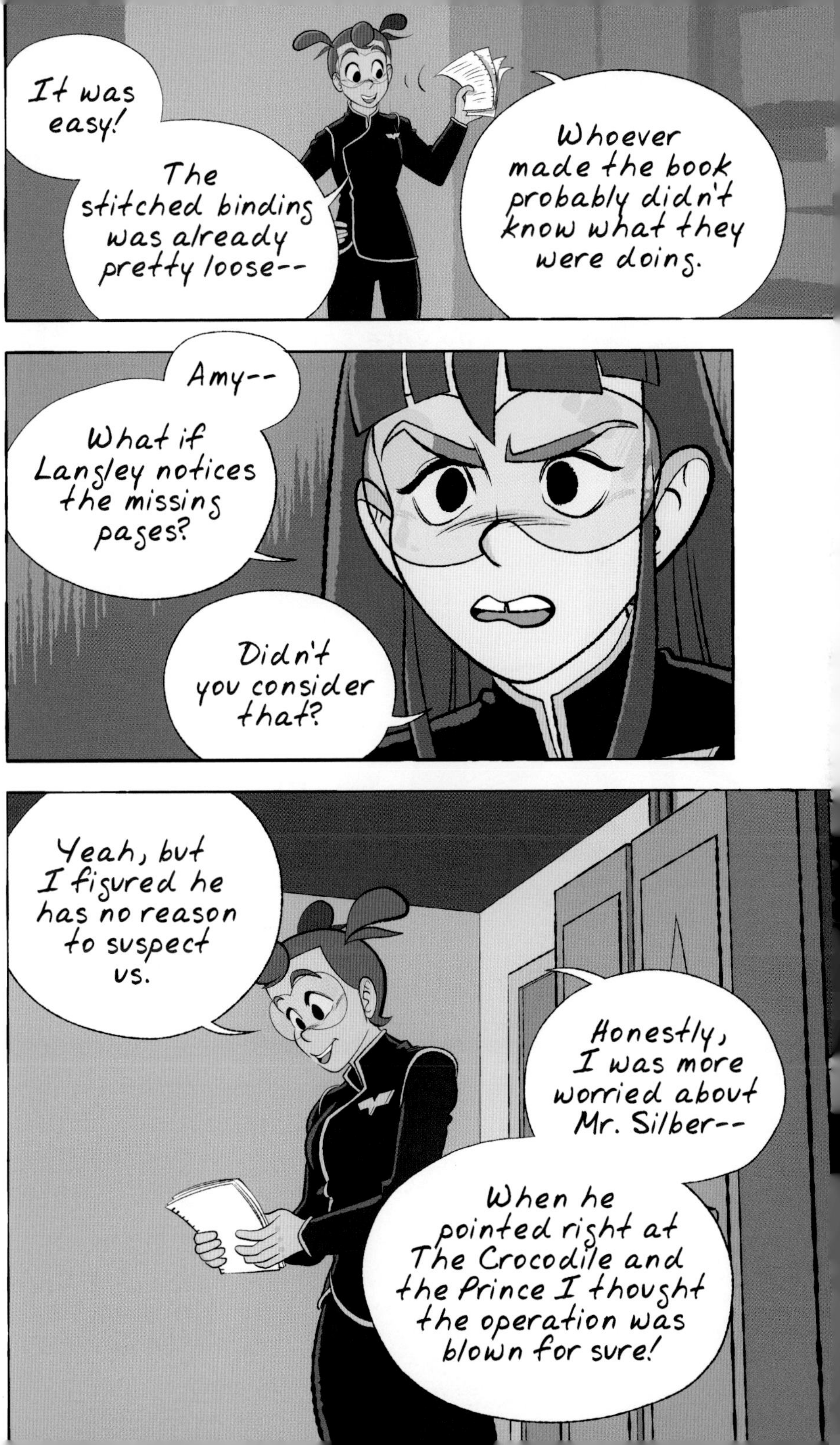
It was easy!
The stitched binding was already pretty loose--
Whoever made the book probably didn't know what they were doing.
Amy--
What if Langley notices the missing pages?
Didn't you consider that?
Yeah, but I figured he has no reason to suspect us.
Honestly, I was more worried about Mr. Silber--
When he pointed right at The Crocodile and the Prince I thought the operation was blown for sure!

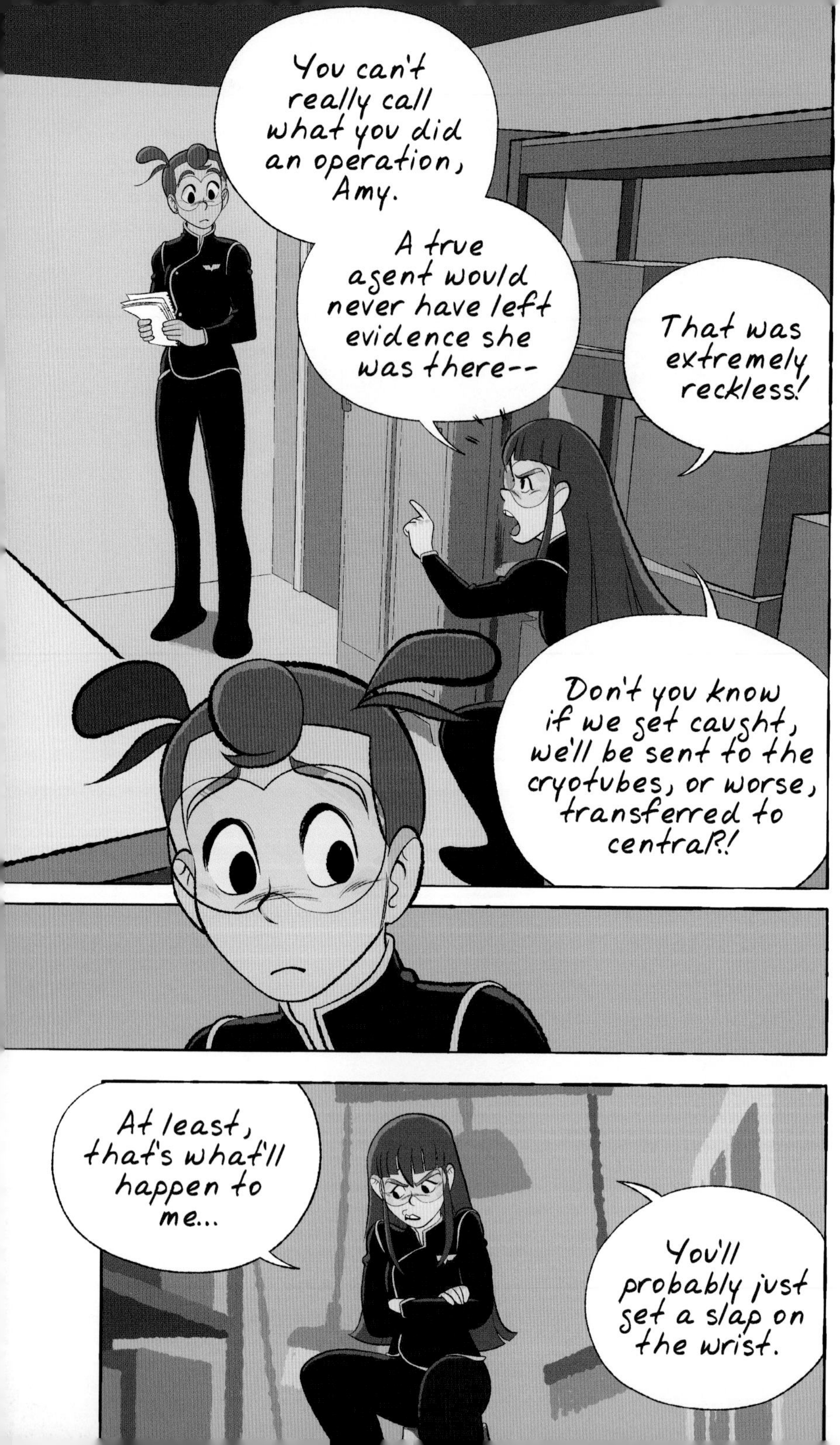
You can't really call what you did an operation, Amy.
A true agent would never have left evidence she was there--
That was extremely reckless!
Don't you know if we get caught, we'll be sent to the cryotubes, or worse, transferred to central?!
At least, that's what'll happen to me...
You'll probably just get a slap on the wrist.

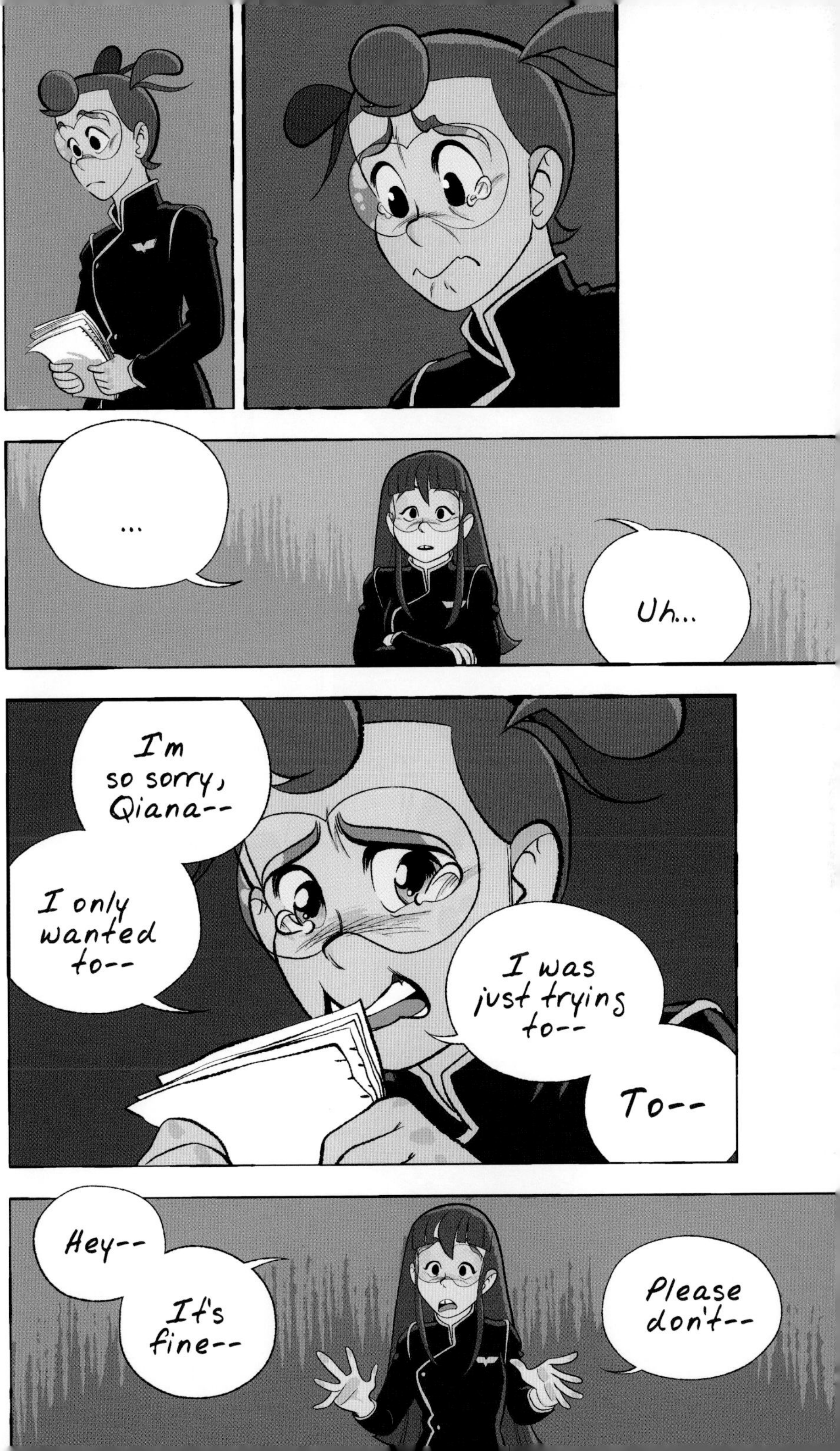
...
Uh...
I'm so sorry, Qiana--
I only wanted to--
I was just trying to--
To--
Hey--
It's fine--
Please don't--

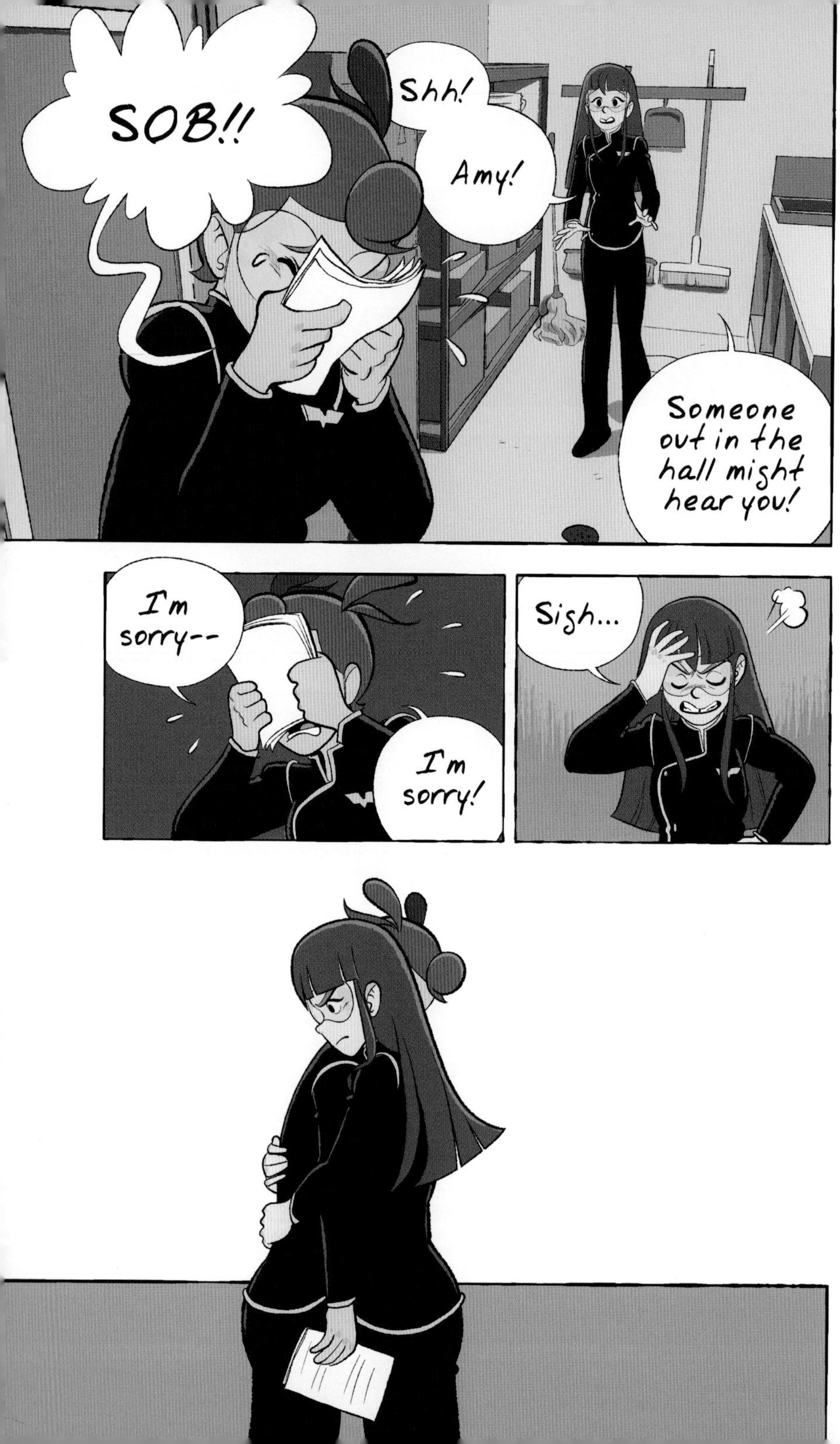
SOB!!
Shh!
Amy!
Someone out in the hall might hear you!
I'm sorry--
I'm sorry!
Sigh...

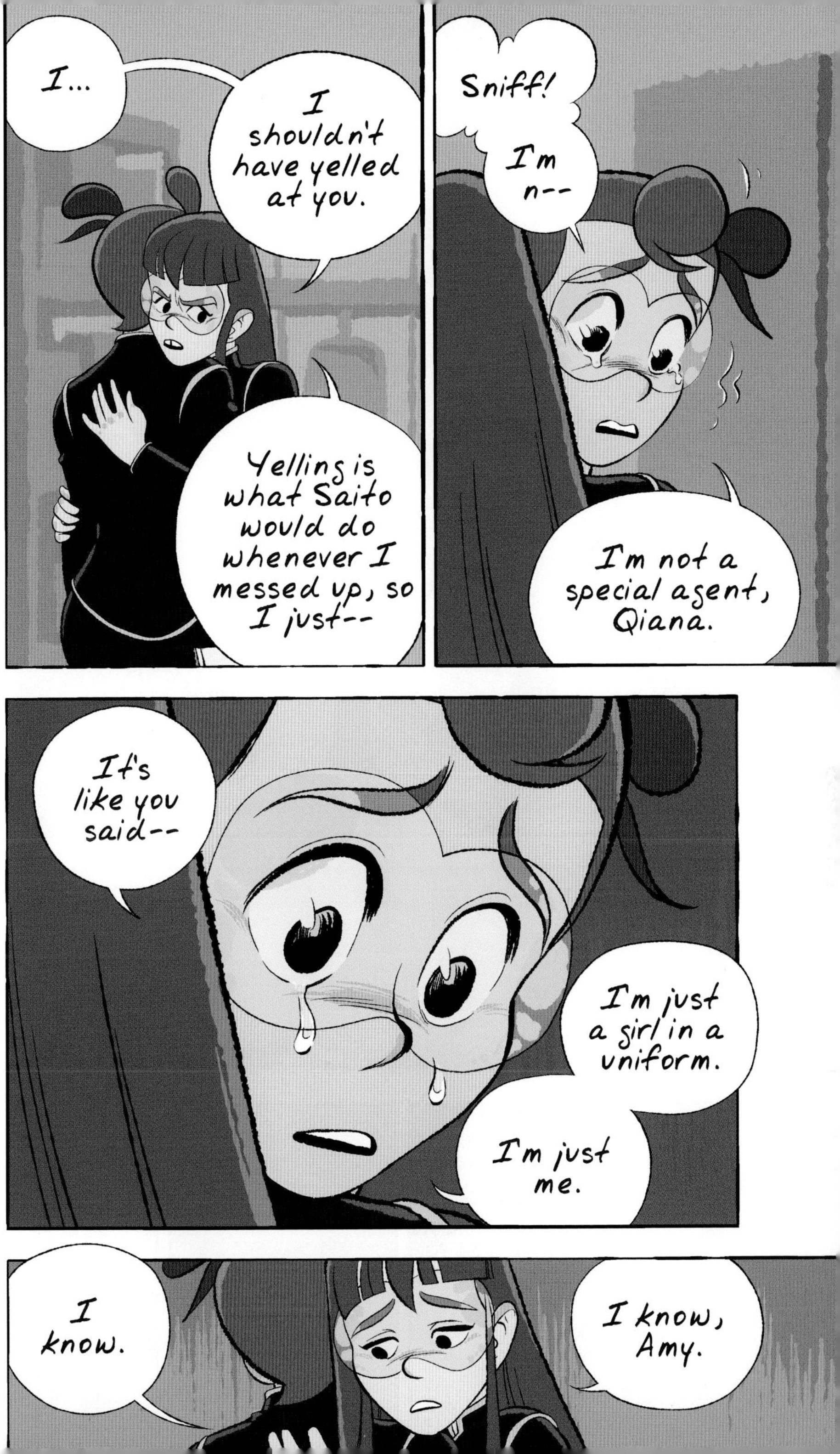
I...
I shouldn't have yelled at you.
Yellings is what Saito would do whenever I messed up, so I just--
Sniff!
I'm n--
I'm not a special agent, Qiana.
It's like you said--
I'm just a girl in a uniform.
I'm just me.
I know.
I know, Amy.

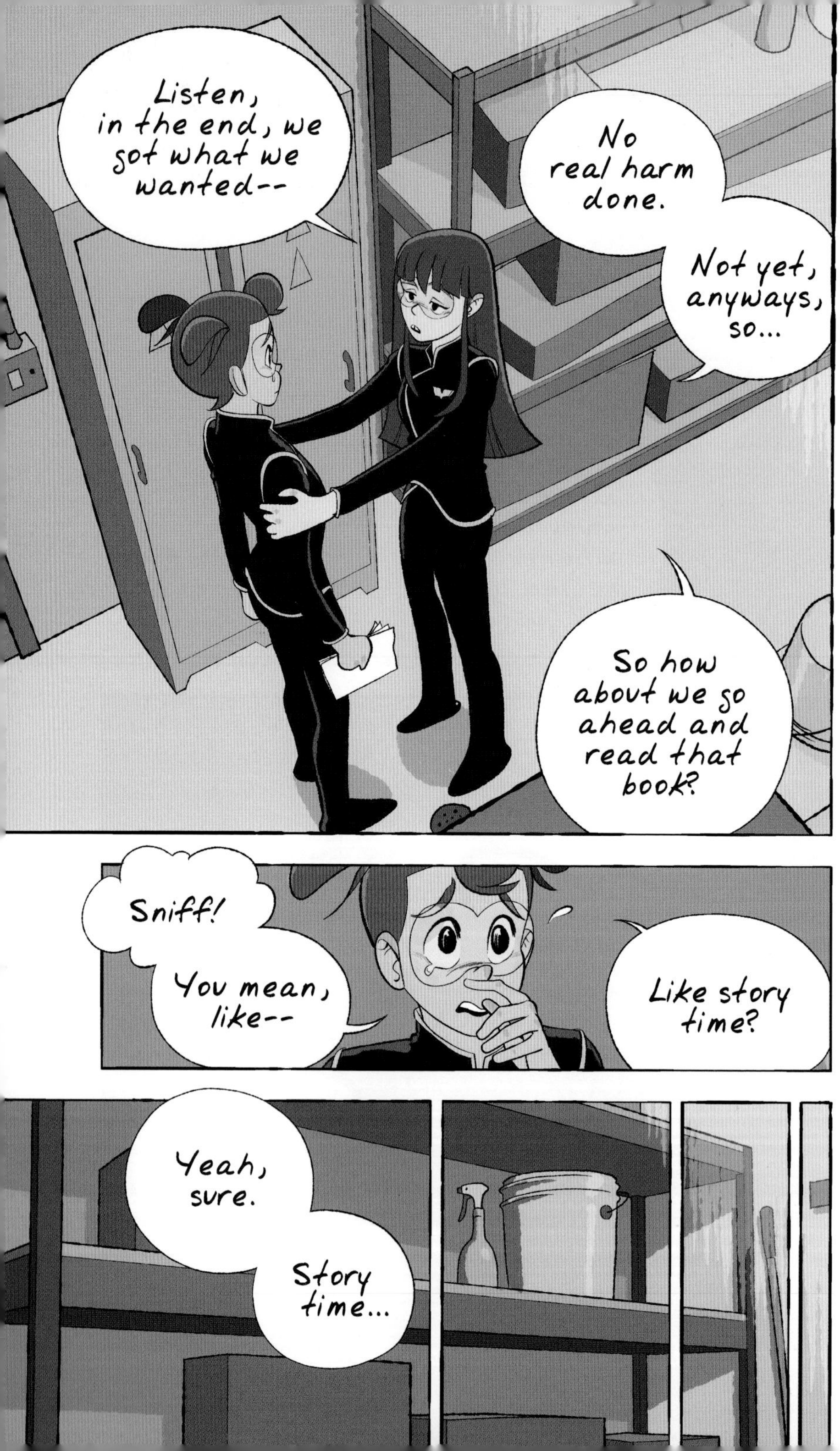
Listen, in the end, we got what we wanted--
No real harm done.
Not yet, anyways, so...
So how about we go ahead and read that book?
Sniff!
You mean, like--
Like story time?
Yeah, sure.
Story time...

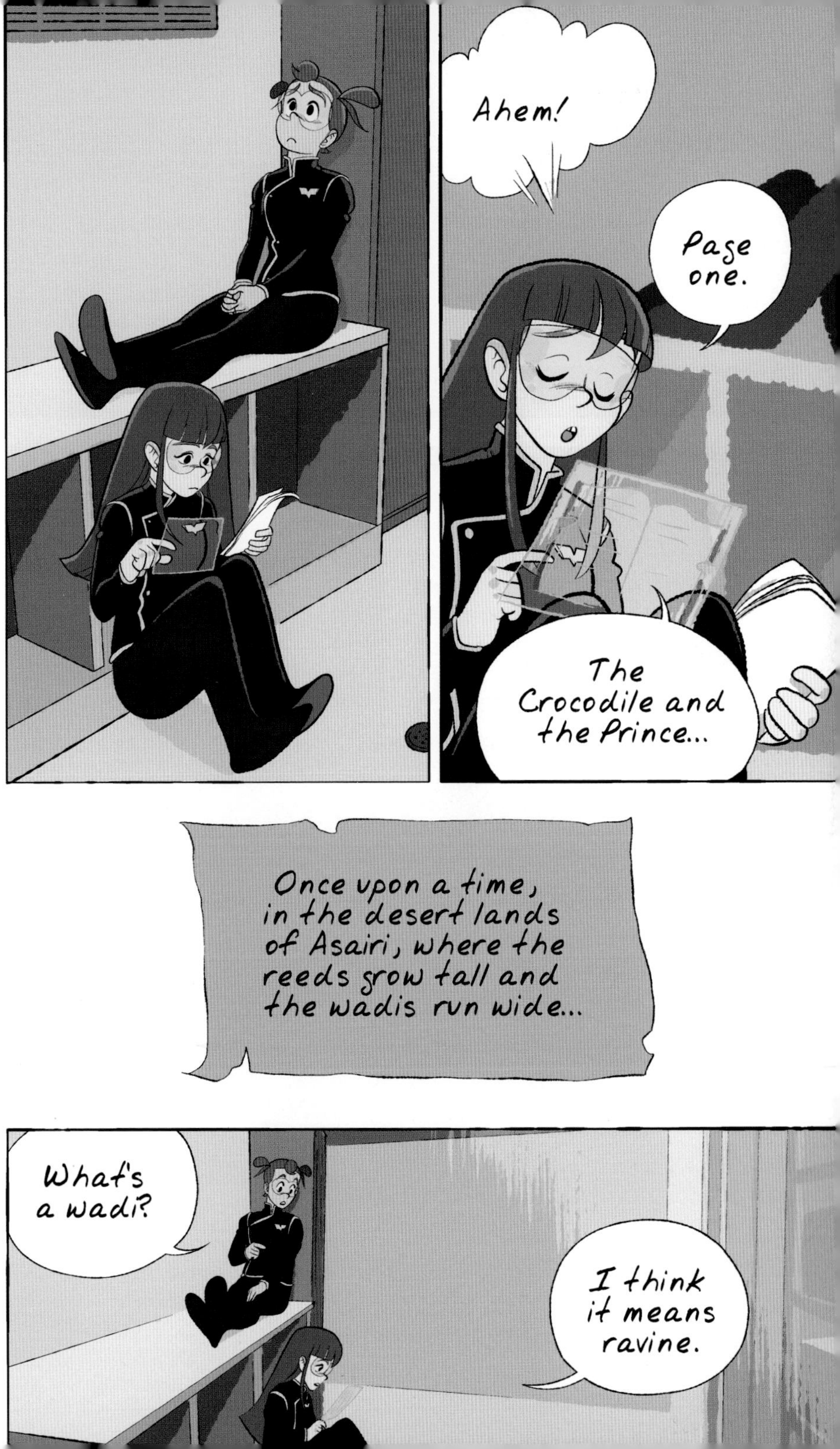
Ahem!
Page one.
The Crocodile and the Prince...
Once upon a time, in the desert lands of Asairi, where the reeds grow tall and the wadis run wide...
What's a wadi?
I think it means ravine.

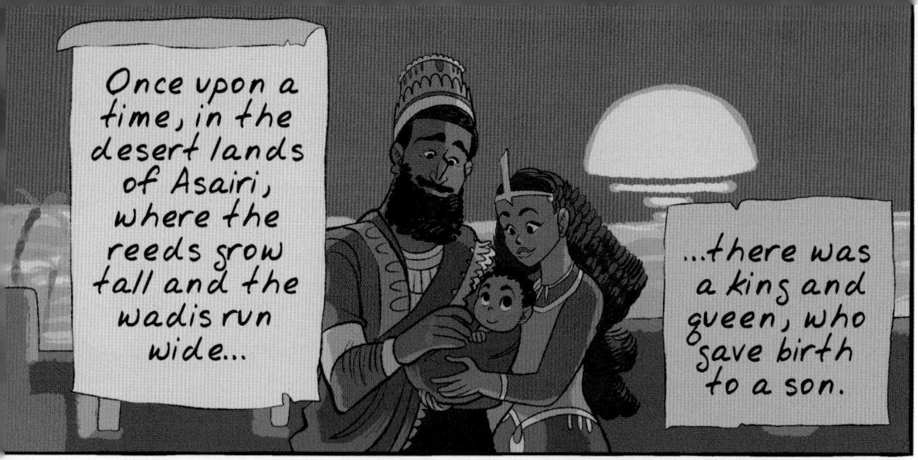
Once upon a time, in the desert lands of Asairi, where the reeds grow tall and the wadis run wide...
...there was a king and queen, who gave birth to a son.

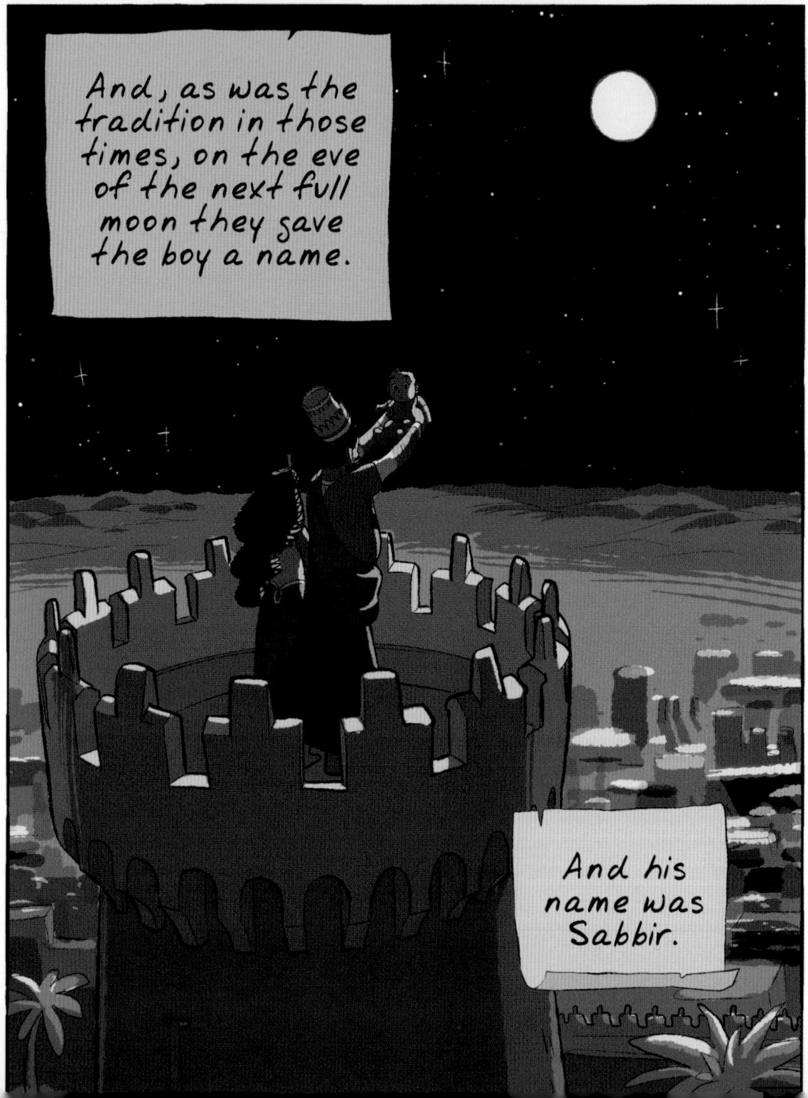
And, as was the tradition in those times, on the eve of the next full moon they gave the boy a name.
And his name was Sabbir.

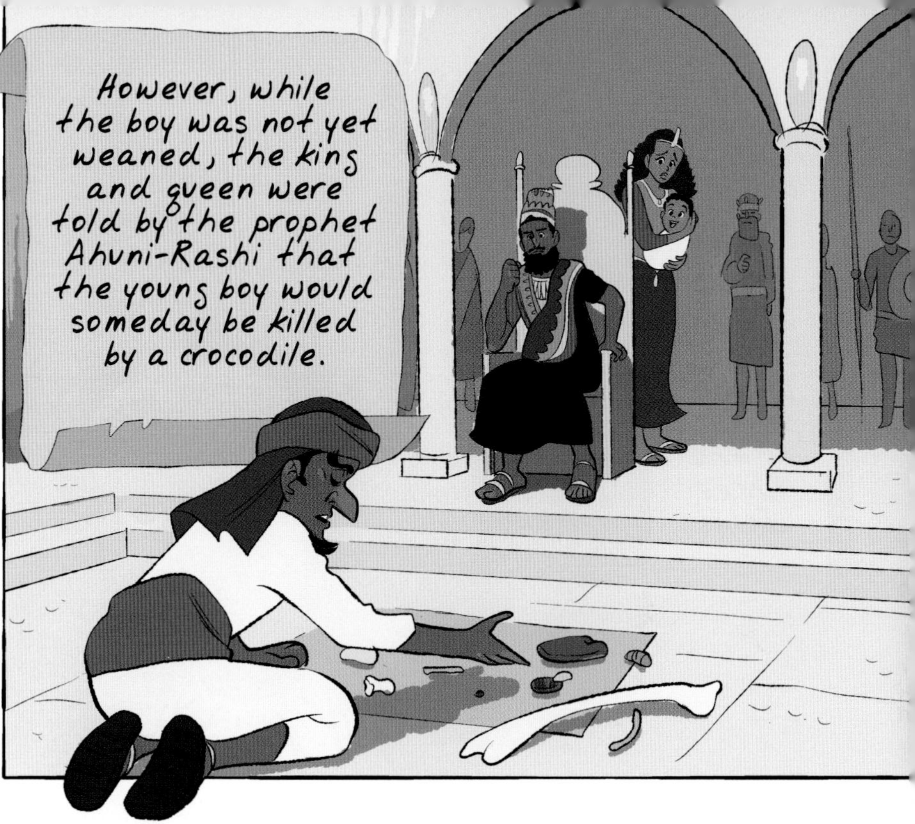
However, while the boy was not yet weaned, the king and queen were told by the prophet Ahuni-Rashi that the young boy would someday be killed by a crocodile.

And so that very day the king of Asairi issued a decree that every crocodile in the land, from the Olibsu River to the Nahid Mountains, be hunted and killed.

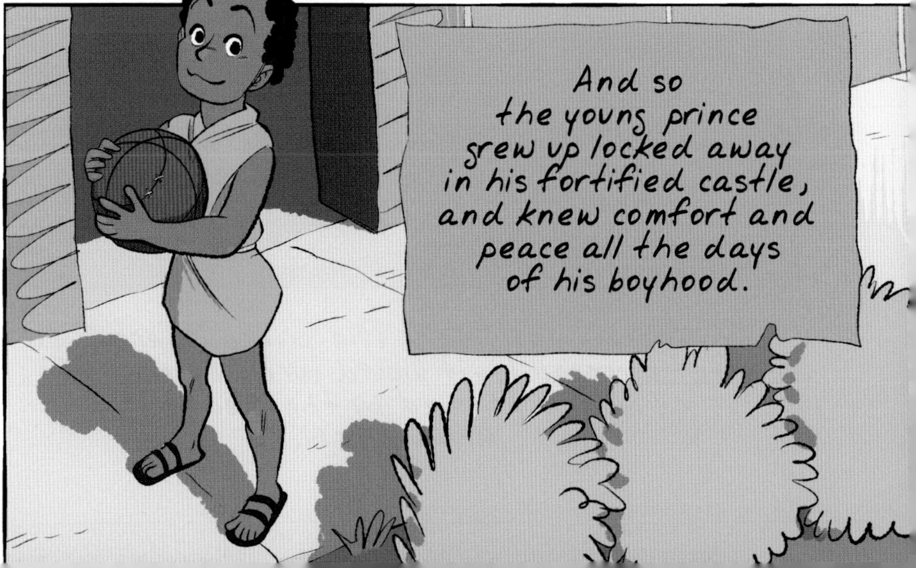
And so the young prince grew up locked away in his fortified castle, and knew comfort and peace all the days of his boyhood.

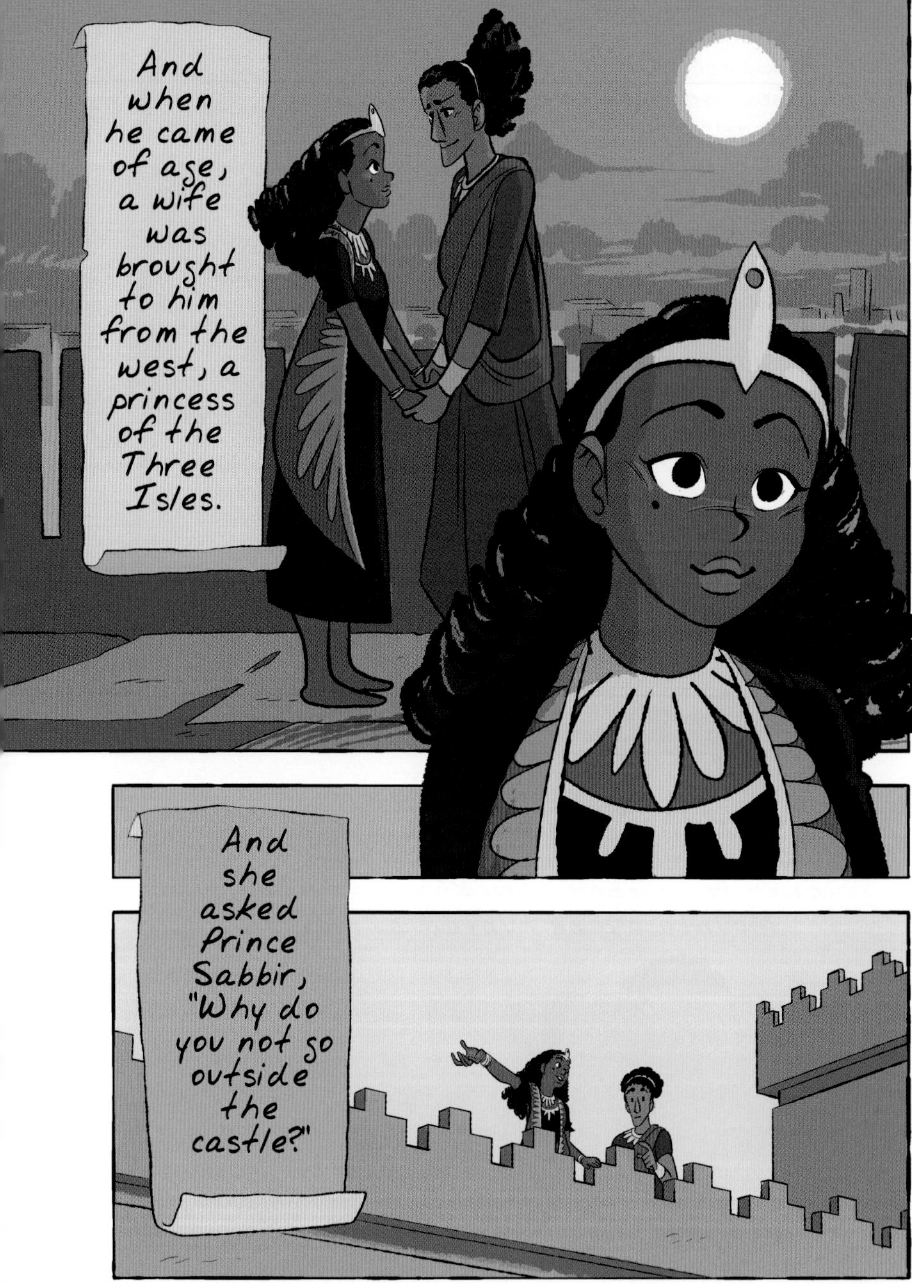
And when he came of age, a wife was brought to him from the west, a princess of the Three Isles.
And she asked Prince Sabbir, "Why do you not go outside the castle?"

"It is forbidden," said the prince. "Were I to meet a crocodile, it would surely be my end, as was prophesied by the great seer Ahuni-Rashi."

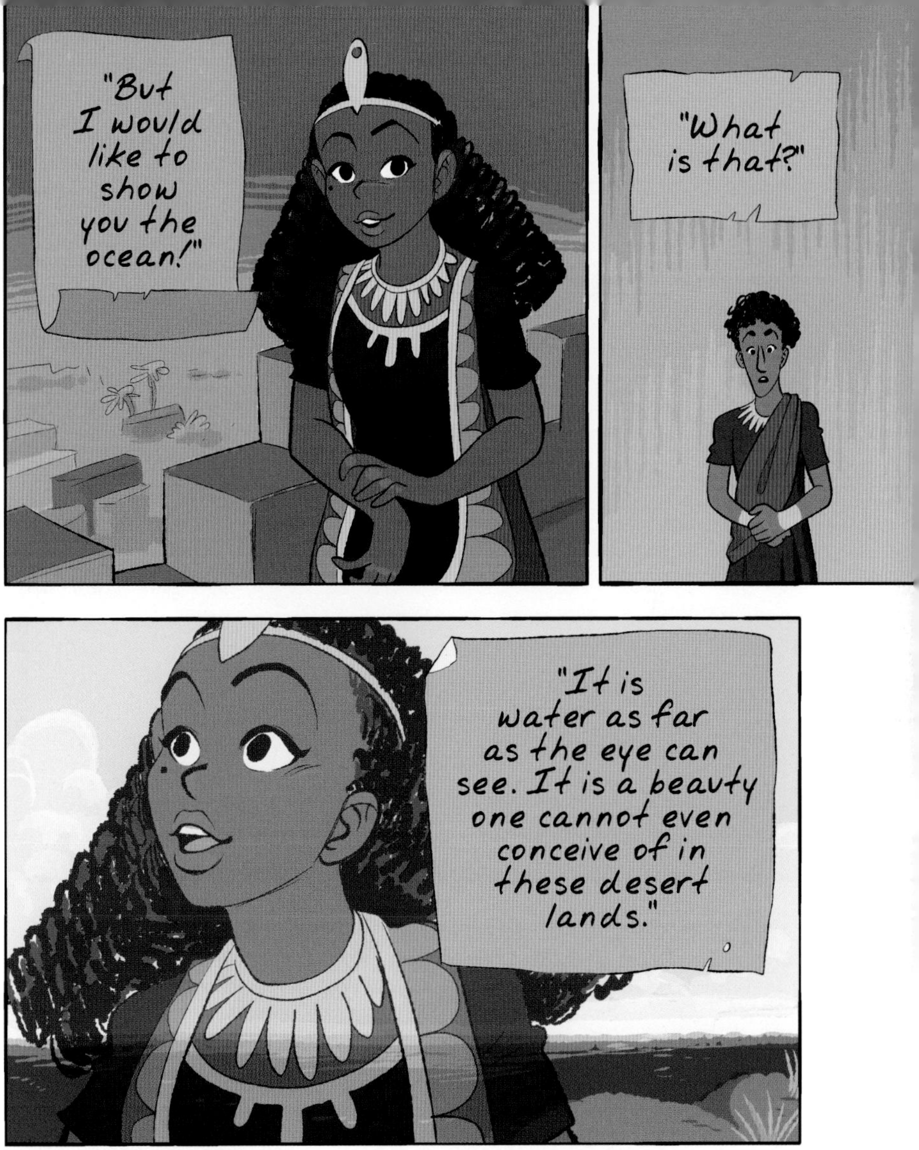
"But I would like to show you the ocean!"
"What is that?"
"It is water as far as the eye can see. It is a beauty one cannot even conceive of in these desert lands."

Tempted by his wife's passionate descriptions of the ocean, Prince Sabbir decided to leave his palace for the first time in his life.

And his wife was his guide.

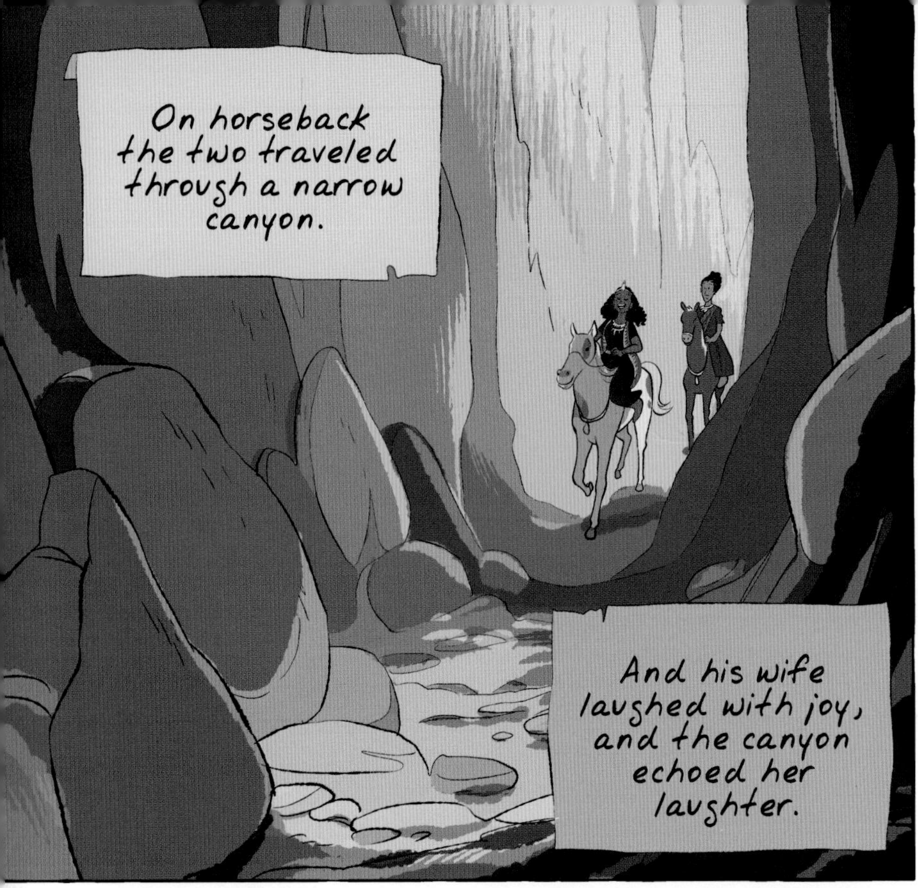
On horseback the two traveled through a narrow canyon.
And his wife laughed with joy, and the canyon echoed her laughter.

But when the prince shouted up at the rocky cliffs that he might hear his own echo, instead a terrible voice shouted back, saying:

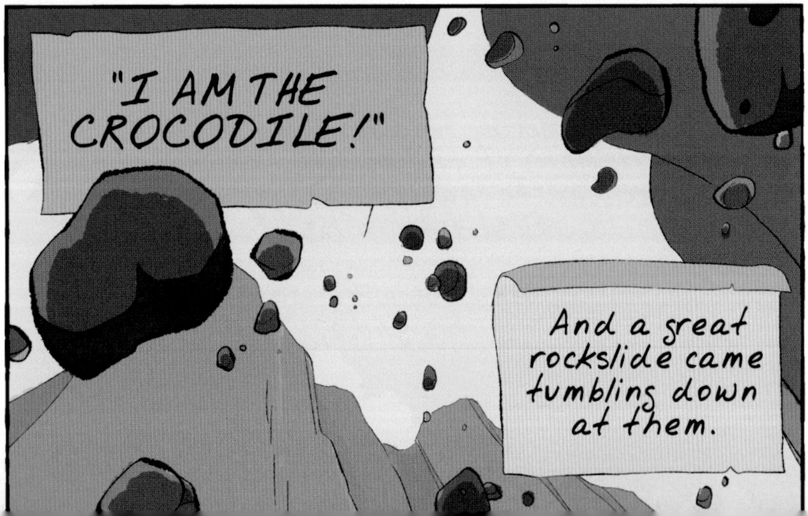
"I AM THE CROCODILE!"
And a great rockslide came tumbling down at them.

But the princess only laughed and whipped their horses forward to safety.

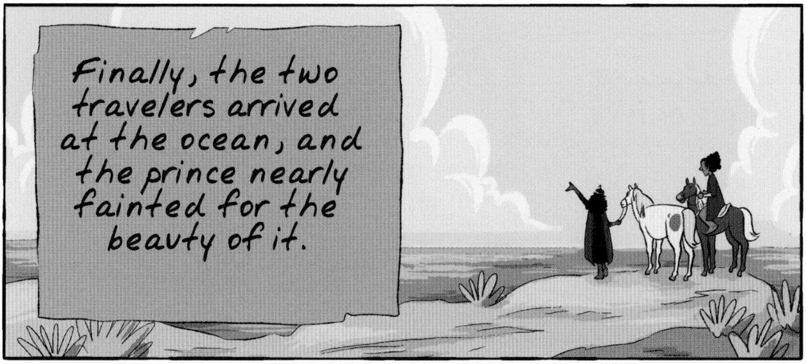
Finally, the two travelers arrived at the ocean, and the prince nearly fainted for the beauty of it.

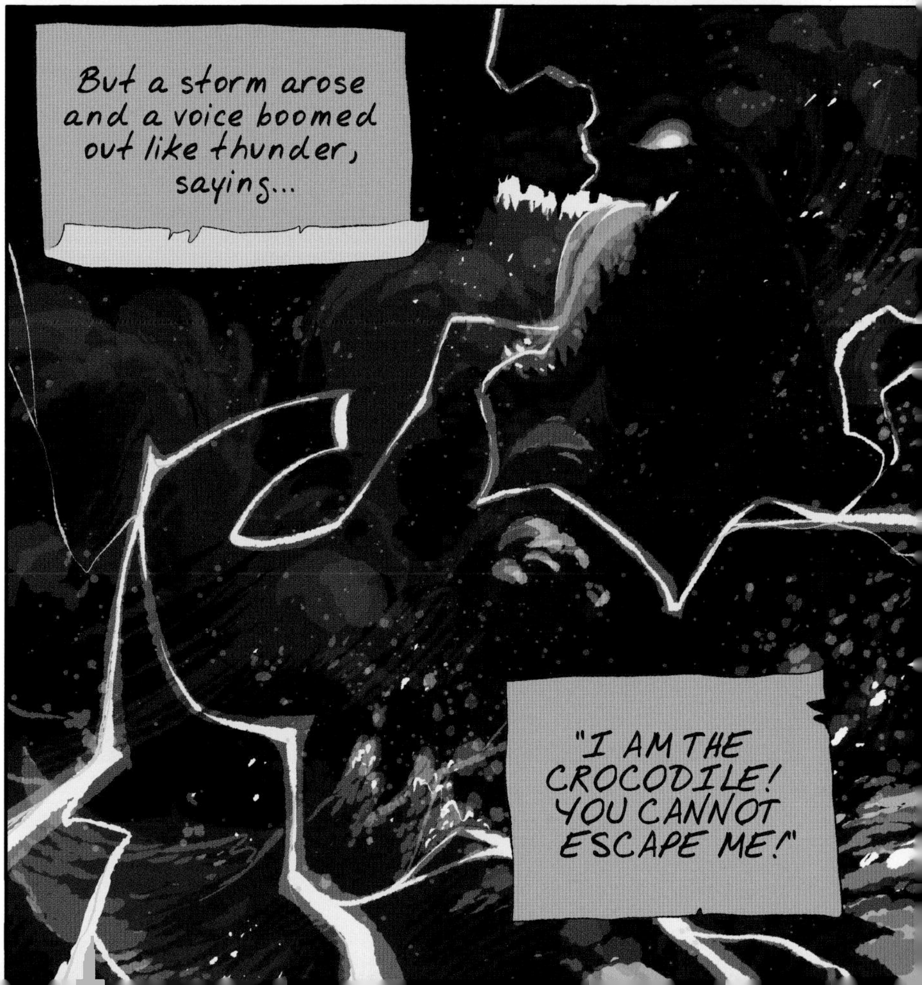
But a storm arose and a voice boomed out like thunder, saying...
"I AM THE CROCODILE! YOU CANNOT ESCAPE ME!"

And the princess laughed and danced in the rain, but the prince had had enough.

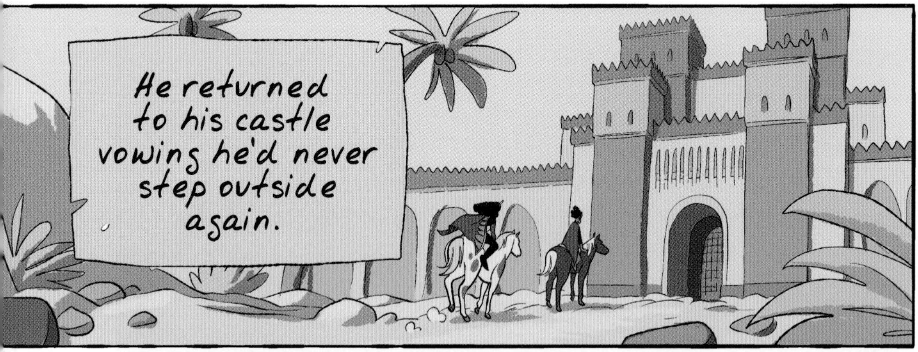
He returned to his castle vowing he'd never step outside again.

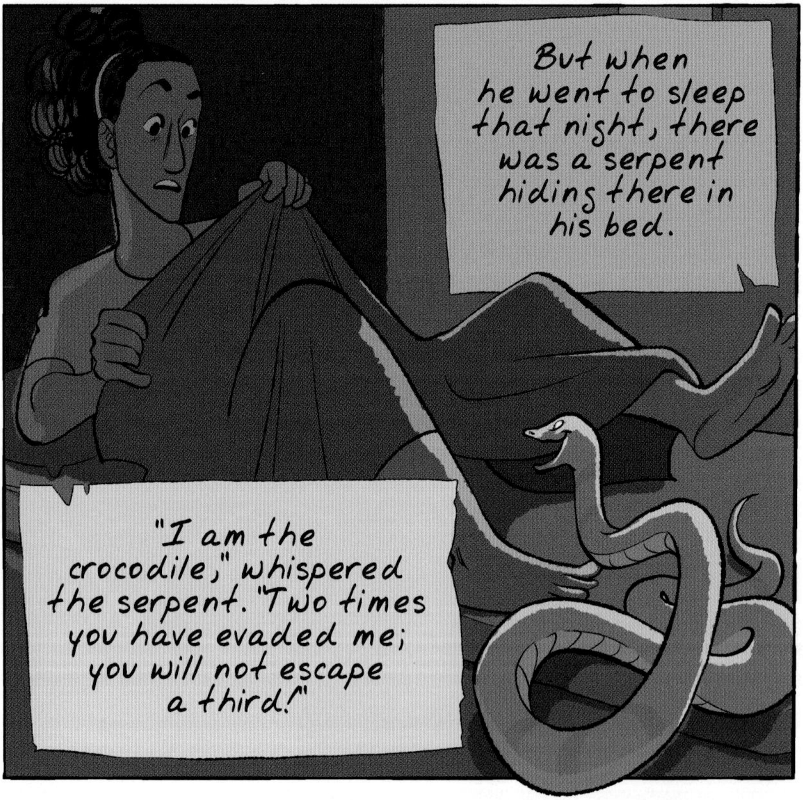
But when he went to sleep that night, there was a serpent hiding there in his bed.
"I am the crocodile," whispered the serpent. "Two times you have evaded me; you will not escape a third!"

And the snake bit him on the ankle.

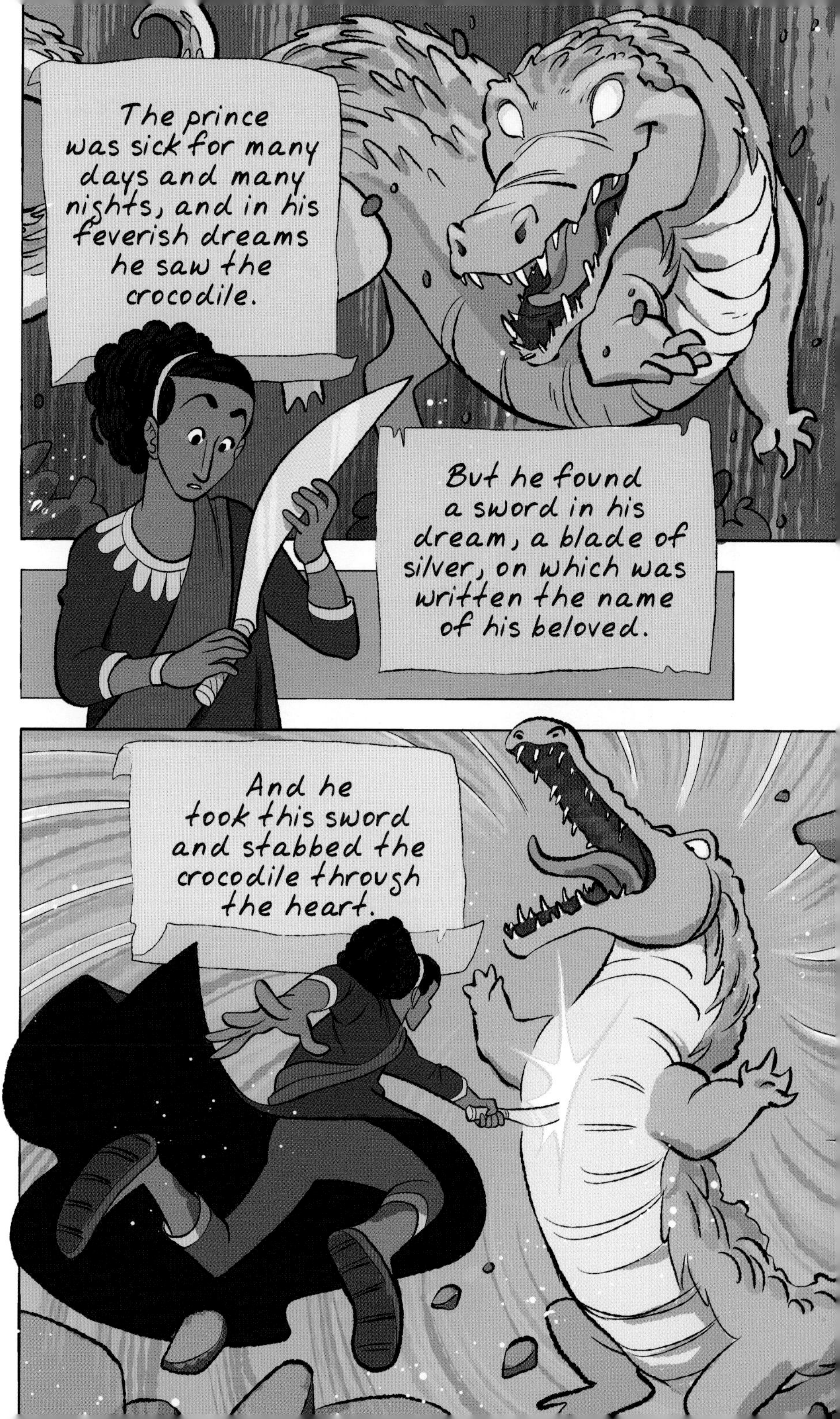
The prince was sick for many days and many nights, and in his feverish dreams he saw the crocodile.
But he found a sword in his dream, a blade of silver, on which was written the name of his beloved.
And he took this sword and stabbed the crocodile through the heart.

And when he woke up, he had recovered from the snake's venom.

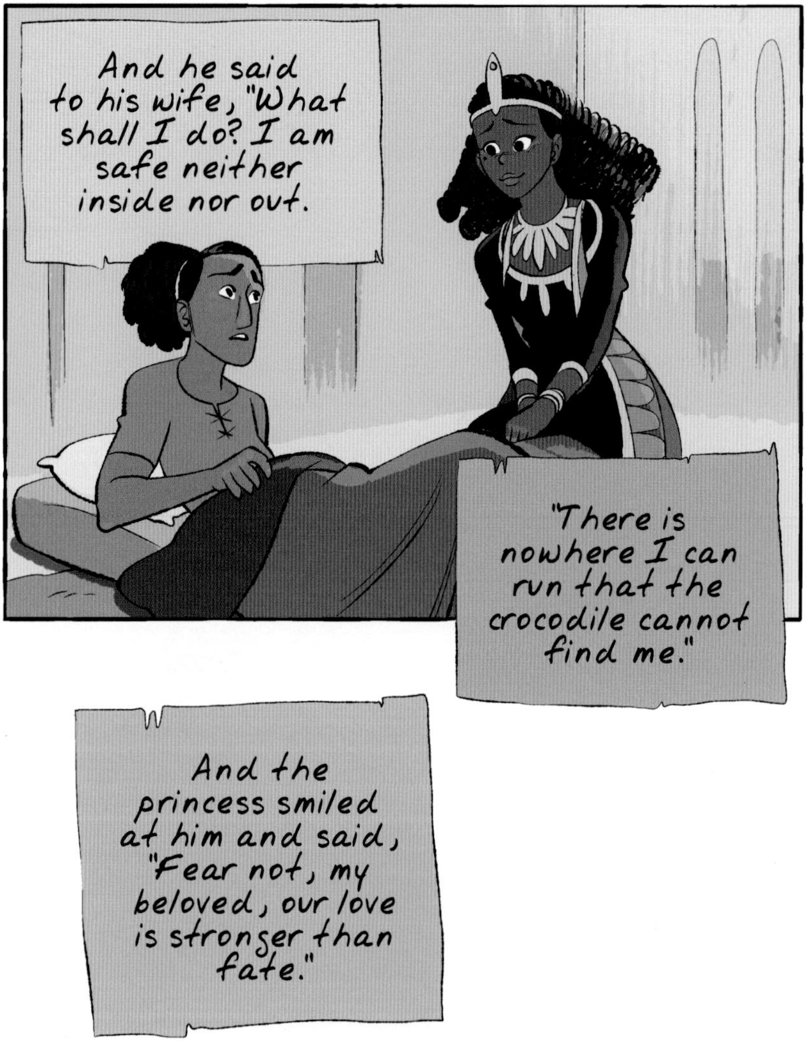
And he said to his wife, "What shall I do? I am safe neither inside nor out.
"There is nowhere I can run that the crocodile cannot find me."

And the princess smiled at him and said, "Fear not, my beloved, our love is stronger than fate."

And the two lived happily ever after.

COMING SOON . . .

Stephen McCranie's
SPACE BOY
16

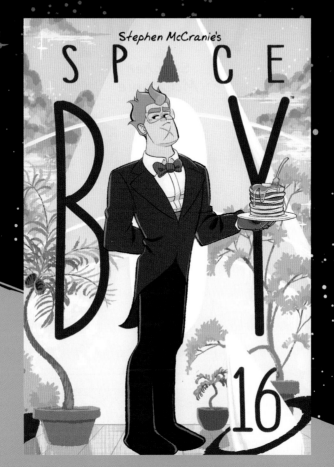

WHERE IS AMY?

The students of South Pines Academy search desperately for clues, trying to unravel the mystery of what happened on homecoming night.

Stuck at the First Contact Project facility, Amy and Qiana begin to pull at the threads of a conspiracy that goes all the way to the top of the FCP.

Meanwhile, deep in space, Oliver must come to terms with his new feelings for Amy and what that may mean for the two of them—and the entirety of the project he's devoted his life to.

Available July 2023!

YOU CAN ALSO READ MORE *SPACE BOY* COMICS ON WEBTOONS.COM!

Li'l Amy

by
Stephen McCranie

Dad?
Yes, sweet pea?
How are babies made?
...
Uh...
Well, it's like--
So, when a bee loves a bird very much--
There's a--
You know, a stork that, um--
Ask your mother.

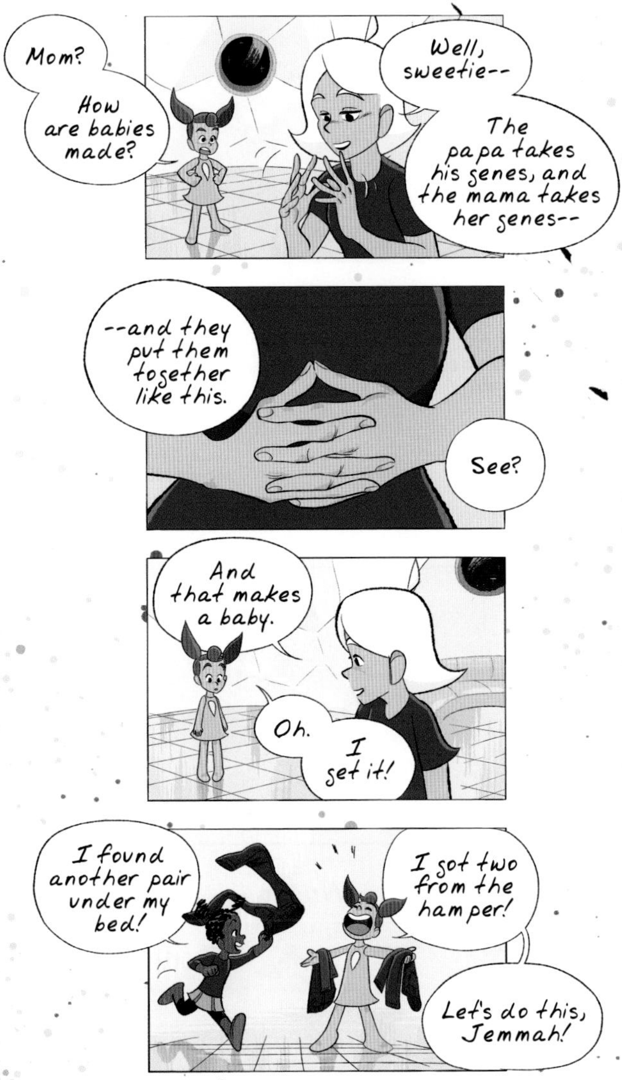
Mom?
How are babies made?
Well, sweetie--
The papa takes his genes, and the mama takes her genes--
--and they put them together like this.
See?
And that makes a baby.
Oh.
I get it!
I found another pair under my bed!
I got two from the hamper!
Let's do this, Jemmah!

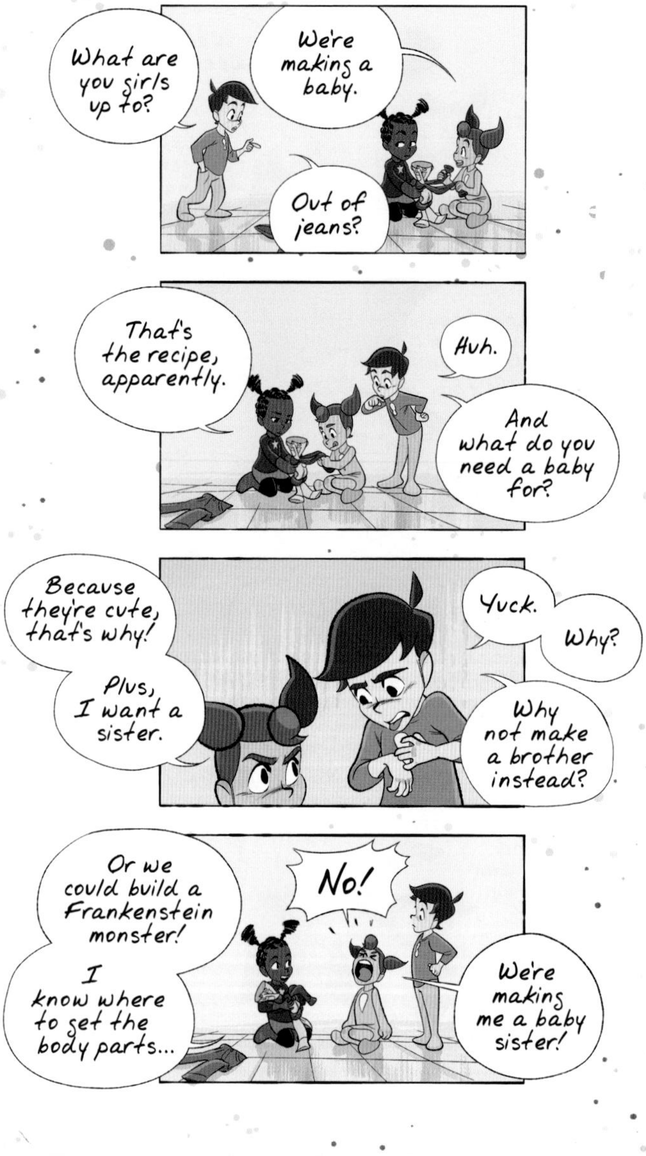
What are you girls up to?
We're making a baby.
Out of jeans?
That's the recipe, apparently.
Huh.
And what do you need a baby for?
Because they're cute, that's why!
Plus, I want a sister.
Yuck.
Why?
Why not make a brother instead?
Or we could build a Frankenstein monster!
I know where to get the body parts...
No!
We're making me a baby sister!

Doesn't look like it's working, does it?
I don't understand...
We put the jeans together.
Where's the baby?
Hmm...
You know, before my sister was born, my mom always said she had a "bun in the oven."
So--
What?
Are we supposed to bake this or something?
Couldn't hurt!

To Be Continued

HAVE YOU READ THEM ALL?

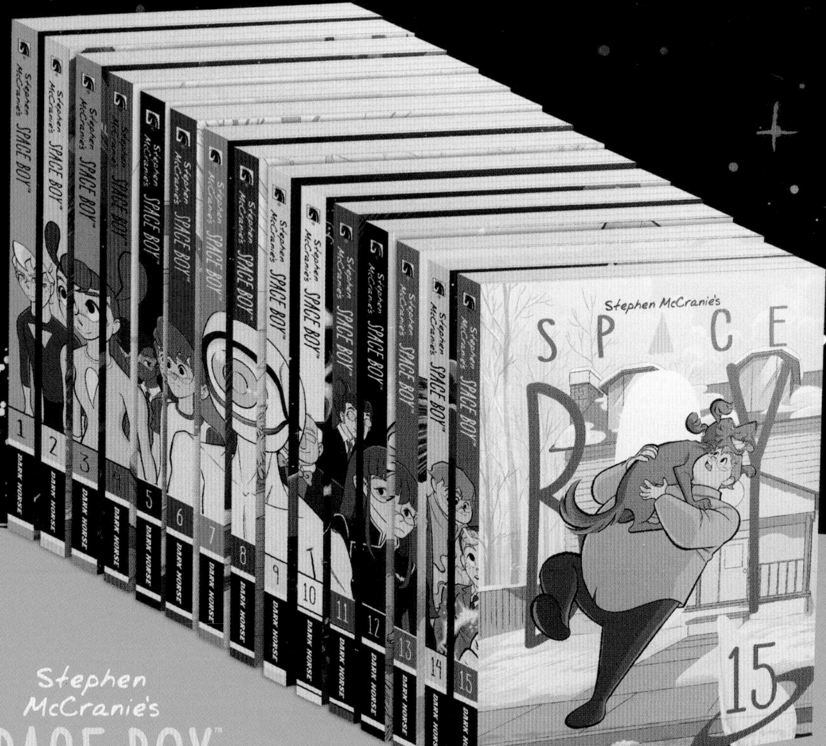
Stephen McCranie's
SPACE BOY
15
DARK HORSE

Stephen McCranie's

SPACE BOY™

VOLUME 1
$12.99 • ISBN 978-1-50670-648-1

VOLUME 2
$12.99 • ISBN 978-1-50670-680-1

VOLUME 3
$12.99 • ISBN 978-1-50670-842-3

VOLUME 4
$12.99 • ISBN 978-1-50670-843-0

VOLUME 5
$12.99 • ISBN 978-1-50671-399-1

VOLUME 6
$12.99 • ISBN 978-1-50671-400-4

VOLUME 7
$12.99 • ISBN 978-1-50671-401-1

VOLUME 8
$12.99 • ISBN 978-1-50671-402-8

VOLUME 9
$12.99 • ISBN 978-1-50671-883-5

VOLUME 10
$10.99 • ISBN 978-1-50671-884-2

VOLUME 11
$10.99 • ISBN 978-1-50671-885-9

VOLUME 12
$10.99 • ISBN 978-1-50672-577-2

VOLUME 13
$10.99 • ISBN 978-1-50672-876-6

VOLUME 14
$12.99 • ISBN 978-1-50672-877-3

VOLUME 15
$12.99 • ISBN 978-1-50672-878-0

"ONE OF THE BEST PIECES OF SEQUENTIAL ART TO COME OUT IN THIS OR ANY OTHER FORMAT IN THE PAST DECADE."

–ENTERTAINMENT MONTHLY

DARK HORSE BOOKS

AVAILABLE AT YOUR LOCAL COMICS SHOP OR BOOKSTORE. TO FIND A COMICS SHOP IN YOUR AREA, VISIT COMICSHOPLOCATOR.COM. FOR MORE INFORMATION OR TO ORDER DIRECT, VISIT DARKHORSE.COM.